One Calamitous Spring

One Calamitous Spring

A NOVEL OF SANTA FE

Edward F. Mendez

Casa de Snapdragon LLC   New Mexico

Previously Printed by Reinas Viejas Amargas under ISBN 978-0-9893004-0-7

Library of Congress Cataloging-in-Publication Data
Mendez, Edward F.
  One Calamitous Spring : a novel of Santa Fe / Edward F. Mendez.
    pages cm
  ISBN 978-1-937240-35-6 (pbk.)
  1. Family secrets--Fiction. 2. New Mexico--Fiction. I. Title.

PS3613.E48228O54 2014
813'.6--dc23

2013040585

20131116
Casa de Snapdragon LLC
12901 Bryce Avenue, NE
Albuquerque, NM 87112
http://www.casadesnapdragon.com
Printed in the United States of America

I would like to thank Dr. Stacy N. Broun, whose gifts have allowed me to be able to see myself more clearly. Without a less obstructed view, few of the good events in my life would have been possible after 2003. Dr. Broun also introduced me to Dr. Laurel Hallman who made me weep when she showed me how to believe again. To Dr. Angela Merkert, thank you for "Building Your Own Theology" and teaching me how to express my beliefs. I also thank Rose Watson, MA, who worked tirelessly on my grammar, punctuation, and personal excesses. Rose's down-to-earth counsel prevented this novel from flying off the turntable in my head. To Dr. Linda Wilber-Whittenberg, thank you for your counsel and suggestions. Your warmth and generous ideas helped this novel a great deal. To JB Bryan, thank you for an insightful read and equally insightful suggestions that made the book better. Finally, thanks to Raymond J. McQueen, my spouse, patient first reader, and one-man cheering section. Without you, Ray, nothing is probable.

For
Raymond James McQueen, Jr.
My spouse,
My inspiration,
My soulmate.

Character is destiny.

Heraclitus

Well-behaved women seldom make history.

Laurel Thatcher Ulrich

CHAPTER ONE

Theodora Mercedes Silverton Vigil

Until that day, Theodora Mercedes Silverton Vigil was a proud, serious, well in-control woman. Theodora (never, never "Teddi"), could trace her ancestry in Santa Fe for fourteen generations. The family tree, of which she was just the latest sturdy limb, counted Conquistadors, a governor to a few drunks, and strong women.

Theodora was born in the house in which she still dwelt. Her great-grandfather had built it in 1887 in what was then the highest of styles. Theodore Chase Silverton demanded a house to match his accomplished life; he chose the highest style from the east, Victorian. The house was two stories, with a full attic, sat on a foundation that would outlast the Second Coming, and towered in regal splendor on one and one-half acres in the toniest part of town. Its large windows, pencil tower, and solid brick facing shouted to Santa Fe, "I am here!"

Theodore had made money at every opportunity. Not that he was an opportunist, but Theodore could just do no wrong when it came to making money. Theodore had escaped the Civil War with neither a hair out of place nor a missed morning shave, despite being at the last battle between Generals Grant and Lee. Before the war, he was poor; after the peace, well, that was a new beginning. Theodore resold lumber, collected and sold metal, bought shares in the Little Pittsburg Mine of the Colorado Silver Boom. In fact, he knew Horace Tabor before he was a United States senator. Theodore also bought land from distressed owners in the former Confederacy, and then sold it to carpetbaggers at inflated prices. It really was not so much that Theodore Chase was an opportunist; just he saw opportunities everywhere. Then, Theodore Chase met Gertrudis Innocenta.

Gertrudis Innocenta McIver de Baca had been sent east to see The America of the Founding Fathers: New York, Boston, Washington, D.C., and Philadelphia. She thought Easterners beyond presumptuous in this travesty of geographical reference. Surely, the "East Coast" was sufficient to define the space. Santa Fe, her hometown and the oldest capital in the United States, had been founded in 1610 and that was seventy years before the Pueblo Revolt. While she was impressed by crowded New York, Boston's harbor and "old town," the national capital, and Independence Hall, Gertrudis Innocenta felt that it all looked just too new to represent The America of the Founding Fathers. 1776, indeed! Moreover, from where she hailed, "Founding Fathers" had a richer meaning. The fine restaurants, hotels, and transportation systems (to say nothing of paved streets) had favorably impressed her, in her reserved way, but not sufficiently to tip her favor eastward. Gertrudis Innocenta could hardly wait to get home to old Santa Fe. Then, she met Theodore Chase.

Two days before starting back, Gertrudis Innocenta was asking for her mail at the front desk of Washington's Grand Hotel. The skinny, officious desk clerk handed it to her and turned away as quickly as he could. Did he see a trace of Indian blood in her face? In fact, she was a tiny fraction Native American. Gertrudis Innocenta never noticed. She was used to diffidence from the serving class. Gertrudis Innocenta turned to leave and found herself powdered cheek to impeccably shaved cleft chin. Theodore Chase was just as startled and looked down to discover a new continent in this Spanish-American princess. In his mind, he shattered the commandments on the spot. But, being a gentleman, his countenance never revealed such base thoughts.

Gertrudis Innocenta, she looked up from the impeccably shaved cleft chin to see a perfect Greek nose surmounted by eyes even bluer than hers. In her mind, Gertrudis Innocenta imagined travel for two, and then shattered the commandments on the spot. But, Gertrudis Innocenta was a lady and all searching on Theodore's part could find not a scintilla of her thoughts, merely her physical perfection. Neither believed in love at first sight, but neither could they each explain their instant, mutual passion. Each was momentarily wordless.

Gertrudis Innocenta and Theodore Chase were married by the justice of the peace on their way to the train station. Gertrudis Innocenta was preparing her announcements to her, no doubt, shocked, family. After all, one merely sends a daughter out to see a little of the world and she returns a wife. Would they be happy? Would they be sad? Would outrage be the modus of the day? Good Lord, was Theodore Chase Silverton even a Catholic?

Theodore Chase had liquidated all his assets in one long eighteen hour day. He didn't care whether he got top dollar, Theodore Chase was in love. His wealth was more than adequate in cash and bliss.

In the carriage, Gertrudis Innocenta chose her words and carefully and clearly asked, "Theodore Chase, are you a Catholic?"

Theodore Chase was more surprised at her since their first mutual sighting, but smiled, lied, and said, "Yes, my dear, I am. I was baptized at St. Patrick's Cathedral in New York."

This was the only Catholic Church he could think of on the spot. And what a spot! He was as unchurched as many from educated families from the east who no longer cared to put up a Christian front. His father was generally ambivalent, he was after all, an accountant, and his mother was an unremitting atheist.

"We were regular church goers if not particularly devout," Theodore Chase added, extending his lie.

"Oh, that doesn't matter, Theodore Chase, you just made my Santa Fe announcements much easier than I had imagined. You are Catholic; how perfect!"

They boarded their train without further incident.

Theodore Chase continued to make money easily in Santa Fe. Gertrudis Innocenta, whose family had lots of old money and lands, never noticed. Instead, Gertrudis Innocenta proceeded to have nine children: one still-born, one dying in infancy, and the remaining seven—seven, what a perfect number, not even and not too odd—the remaining seven growing quite nicely. It was Theodore Chase who insisted that the Victorian style was what his illustrious family required despite Gertrudis Innocenta's expectations that they would always live with her family in their two hundred-year-old adobe. Instinctively, Theodore Chase knew that such living arrangements offered "complications" that were not attractive to a man accustomed to his manly manifest destiny. The house was built. Gertrudis Innocenta was truly surprised at how exciting the construction, anticipation, and potential grandeur captured her enthusiasm. She even held off her family's objections, pleadings, and emotional blackmail to continue following ancient traditions. No, Gertrudis Innocenta had made up her mind.

Theodore and Gertrudis Silverton's third daughter, Perpetua Angelica, eloped with Alfonso Parral Immaculata Sepulveda. The Sepulveda's daughter, Immaculata Mercedes, married Pedro Pico Smyth after a courtship that Immaculata had orchestrated. Evidently, Pedro thought theirs would be a casual acquaintance. Nevertheless, Pedro and Immaculata had a very happy, productive marriage with five children reaching adulthood.

The Smyth's third daughter, born in the house her great-grandparents built, was Theodora Mercedes who, at eighteen, went to live with Angel Silverton Vigil, her second cousin. They never married, but Theodora took his name under pressure from her family. Even her strength could not resist the crashing waves of conformity that swept across her attention at every opportunity. Thereafter, only pitiful ripples washed ashore and only from the disapproving looks of the priests and the bishop. After all, her family was a cornerstone of Santa Fe society and Catholicism and certain standards were expected—no, demanded. Theodora Mercedes was unmoved. They could all parade during Santa Fe Fiesta in their Knights of Columbus finery all they wanted but their white plumes would wither under Theodora Mercedes' gaze, if she ever bothered to look.

In 1954, Theodora Mercedes discovered the Social Liberal Church of Santa Fe. It was perfect—neither Catholic or full of idiotic creeds nor priests that chapped her intelligence and independence. No one needed to tell Theodora Mercedes to think or what to think. The new arrangement suited her immediate family except for the usual suspects: her parents, Catholic society, and of course, the church. So, all was perfect. Theodora Mercedes found something she liked; and that it made a statement was a bonus.

Theodora Mercedes was now in her late prime, sixty-seven years old. She lived again in the big house her great grandparents had built and she and the house were both as solid and intense as the New Mexico sun; prolonged exposure to either could cause blindness at best or madness at worst.

Theodora Mercedes' house was well-populated. Her youngest son, Barrington Wilson Silverton Vigil, had barely finished high school. Barrington's hidden unhappiness had compelled him to experiment with alcohol and marijuana. Evidently, he was smart enough to avoid meth, though he certainly had schoolmates who did not. When Theodora Mercedes realized that Barrington was failing his sophomore year and had detached himself from reality, she intervened. His mother was determined to help him and enrolled him in college. He had excelled when he attended a small state college in Guanajuato, Mexico. Barrington (never,

never "Barry"), had fully flowered and lost his drives to self-destruction in Guanajuato. He acted in Cervantes' plays during the annual festival, wrote sonnets, danced with locals and tourists at the clubs, delighted in learning new and fascinating ideas about his world. Barrington discovered happiness, contentment, the joy of serious study (he was a forensic linguist), and fell in love (two semesters). He returned to Santa Fe and his mother's house a different person, indeed, almost a man. Barrington landed a suitable, challenging position at the North American Language Institute but still preferred to live at home. He was nearly a full-fledged adult, but for one dark secret. Barrington was gay. He lived in the same fear as a small mouse in a room full of surly cats that his mother would find him out. Barrington had never underestimated anything or anyone as he had Theodora Mercedes.

For her part, Theodora Mercedes had surmised her son's orientation when Barrington was about four years old; she was a keen observer. It was not just that Barrington liked to dress-up. When he was only a toddler playing by himself in the yard, Theodora Mercedes noted that Acmon Blue butterflies lighted on him as if he were a buddleia shrub. Blue flocks of piñon jays would gather to him in loud, talkative conversation as if secretly called. They would hover over him and drop seeds into his tiny hands as he sat quietly. When the jays moved on Barrington would scatter the seeds from where he, a tiny Buddha, sat. The next morning, exotic and obscenely colored flowers and vines would be blooming with the cerulean sunrise and little Barrington sat in his same spot, one with the flowers. By evening and the freezing temperatures, the flowers would all wilt and the next day the unspoken magic would begin anew. There was something special, mysterious about Barrington that Theodora Mercedes and nature acknowledged freely. To Theodora Mercedes, having a gay son was like having the aspen grove up on Tesuque Peak. It was there. It was natural. It was beautiful. It was not hers to change even if she wished it (which she did not). But Theodora Mercedes went along with her son's charade to keep him comfortable. Strangely, Theodora Mercedes called out anyone else's lapses unreservedly, but deferred to her son's secret. Barrington would tell her when he was ready.

Barrington would sneak out late at night to visit with his secret clan, was fashion conscious as a scarlet macaw (even his most casual clothes were studies in layering), although not effeminate, and occasionally would sneak a lover into his bedroom. At his age, Barrington's sexual adventures were boisterous despite his precautions. Between shushings, Theodora Mercedes could often hear him and his partner in the throes of wild ecstasies as they rutted like crazed young lions. Consuelo, the housekeeper, would occasionally complain about stains on the sheets and used condoms lost under his bed, but was wary of taking this conversation further. The first time Consuelo found copious semen stains on the sheets, more than just one boy abusing himself, she promptly brought this to Doña Theodora's attention and demanded that she call in the priest. Somehow, Consuelo managed to keep her position and, frankly, her life, but learned that more than a mere mention was tantamount to playing with molten glass.

One morning, Consuelo found a black condom. She said nothing. Then, she began finding black condoms exclusively. Well, this was too much—probably well beyond the unnatural that was already commonplace. Consuelo decided to act. She collected black condoms until they filled an empty tissue box and presented it to Doña Theodora. Doña Theodora's laser-like eyes would have cut Consuelo in two if only Doña Theodora had not been caught off guard. Doña Theodora rose to her full height, five foot, five inches, and looked Consuelo straight in her eyes, an upward angle of about twenty-three degrees. The force of this look pushed Consuelo backwards until she landed in a chair. Doña Theodora was in mid-vituper, Consuelo shrinking smaller every moment, when Barrington innocently walked in. Momentary three-way shock stopped all sound and action. Barrington, unknowing of what he walked in on, stopped—the short-hairs on his neck standing at attention. He retreated as he came. Consuelo saw her escape, grabbed the tissue box, and ducked out in the opposite direction to wash the dishes.

Theodora Mercedes' other household members included her middle daughter, Innocenta Perpetua Vigil Silert, and her three children. Two of Innocenta's children were unremarkable. Her youngest, a son named Raul Theodore Vigil Silert, was remarkable. He had a normal infancy until about age two. Then he developed a faraway look, quit conversing, and developed astounding talents with mathematics, numbers, statistics, and sometimes soccer skills.

Innocenta's husband, George Alfonso Silverton Silert (another second cousin), had neither understanding nor tolerance for his unusual son and walked out. Innocenta never saw or heard from him again. There was a rumor that George worked in the molybdenum mines in Northern New Mexico and had been killed in an industrial accident. The truth was, George had arrived to work one fine Monday morning drunk as three Irishmen and had walked in front of a sixty-ton hauler. When they had dug George out of the enormous tire treads, coiled him into an empty oil drum, and called Innocenta (no one knows how they found her), she declined to claim his body and George's short chapter in her life came to a close. Innocenta never learned that Theodora Mercedes had contacted the sheriff's office and paid for George's burial in a non-denominational cemetery near Questa. While she had no respect for the man, he had been the father of her grandchildren and for that she was beholden to George.

Theodora Mercedes was very close and protective of her grandchild, Raul Theodore. If there was trouble at school, she moved Innocenta out of her path and handled the issue herself. Theodora Mercedes' fierceness earned her the nickname, "Hurricane Theo," but no one, no—no one—at the school was careless enough to ever say this within earshot of Doña Theodora. One could say that Doña Theodora was so effective at handling the school's "inefficiencies" regarding Raul Theodore that only extraordinary circumstances resulted in her being called. The calls became as rare as wild giraffes wearing sneakers in Santa Fe.

One week before that day in which Theodora Mercedes' strengths would be tried, her sister, Angelica Gertrudis, called to invite Theodora Mercedes to visit her in Albuquerque. Angelica Gertrudis had gone to college at the University of New Mexico, majoring in art. While there, she had an infamous and very satisfying affair with an assistant life-drawing instructor, Reigh de Sousa Hoffmann. Reigh was of very mixed blood. He had Native American, Portuguese, French-Canadian, and Sephardic Jewish blood. Raised in the Conservative sect of Jewry, he fell out with the sect and his family when he questioned why he should follow a set of written, unwritten, and archaic traditions stemming from a minor barbaric tribe wandering the desert five thousand years ago. In fact, he referred to the god of the Torah as "that trumpeting juvenile delinquent," or, "the fat drum-roll," or "the Evil Santa Claus in the Sky." While he raised good points, the idea of speaking them aloud was clearly out of bounds and he was assessed multiple penalties by everyone surrounding him. This happened spectacularly the day before his Bar Mitzvah and an earthly vision of hell breaking loose ensued. Reigh would not back down. The rabbi would not make him a man of the community. Reigh's family went into crisis mode—things were thrown, tears were shed, screaming could be heard; all to no avail. Reigh was sent to Albuquerque to live with an equally outcast Bohemian aunt, Esther Lamont. Reigh finished high school third in his class and attended New York's Parsons School of Design, an irony not lost on Reigh or his aunt, before returning to Albuquerque.

Angelica Gertrudis had married Reigh de Sousa Hoffman, and was now a Social Liberal Church of Albuquerque member, an idea she picked up from Theodora Mercedes. In fact, she and Reigh were deacons in their tiny church. Angelica Gertrudis had only one child by Reigh, Alfonso Pedro Silverton Hoffmann. Fonzo, as he was called, was studious, meticulous, majored in accounting, lived at home in his parent's small house, and was stupifyingly boring. Theodora Mercedes could not decide which she abhorred more, his nickname, demeaning to their ancestors, Fonzo's meticulous ways, or his empty personality. Theodora Mercedes loved her sister and avoided her sister's son. She was, however, very fond of Reigh.

The first time Alfonso (Theodora Mercedes refused to call him by his nickname) visited his aunt and cousins on his own, Theodora Mercedes was afraid that she would lose her tolerance within the first hour. She felt as if she held her huge cutting knife, made from a pared-down machete, and that she would slash Alfonso and dispatch him like an unworthy chicken. But the knife was in her mind only and the only thing in real danger was her equable bearing. Exactly one hour after Alfonso's arrival, Theodora Mercedes had Consuelo set the table for lunch. Raul Theodore always put out the utensils and always in the same way. When Alfonso rearranged his flatware to his accustomed manner, Raul Theodore let out an ear-piercing howl of protest. A physical tug-of-war ensued with Alfonso being the bigger and stronger, thereby making Raul Theodore all the more fierce. Blood was shed. Innocenta had to lift Raul Theodore and carry him off to calm him, but this task was akin to calming an ant mound when the tarantula was already within the colony's grasp. Alfonso ate his lunch alone with his utensils in exactly the positions that suited his custom and sensibilities. Innocenta and Raul Theodore retreated to Innocenta's bedroom, Theodora Mercedes spent the afternoon in the kitchen berating Consuelo, who had done nothing to merit such treatment, and Barrington remained in his room with a guest who had failed to leave before daylight. This single incident solidified in Theodora Mercedes' mind everything she had intuited about her nephew and she vowed to all the Gods of the Americas that she would avoid him. No cost would be too great. If Alfonso were a bear trap, Theodora Mercedes would sever his jaws at the hinges to escape his company. She said nothing to her sister whom she loved dearly.

Three years prior to her sister Angelica Gertrudis' invitation to visit her in Albuquerque, Theodora Mercedes had restored the family home. Floors were resanded and finished in rich honey-colored tones. Holes in the walls were repaired and colors of sophistication and charm were brushed onto the ancient walls. The kitchen was now Chinese red. Theodora Mercedes' bedroom was a rich bronze color. New insulation made the house cozier in bleak weather and fresher in warm. The banisters were stripped and re-finished. The roof was state-of-the-art standing seam, Teflon coated metal. Theodora Mercedes had the huge attic finished out with a guest room and bath as well as a new room and bath for Barrington across the new third floor hallway. The wiring was brought up to code (not a small feat). The plumbing sported new fixtures. Theodora Mercedes added a water softener downstairs for the first two floors and a new water heater and water softener on the third floor.

Theodora Mercedes' final project was a gift to herself, a solid brass plaque mounted by the front door. It read,

Silverton-de Baca House
 Built in 1887
Still in the family and will remain so.
Now please leave the premises.

It was understood that Theodora Mercedes nearly always spoke her mind but never, or at least rarely, at the cost of good manners, which she held in high regard.

Now Theodora Mercedes was almost prepared to travel to her sister, Angelica Gertrudis,' house. But there were complications. Angelica Gertrudis' house was small. Theodora Mercedes must stay in Alfonso's room which meant that Alfonso had to visit his cousins at Silverton-de Baca House. Theodora Mercedes searched the brilliant skies for any signs that she would actually encounter Alfonso on her way out or on her way into Angelica Gertrudis' house. The skies were clear as mountain waters with no introduced species to spoil the tranquility, so Theodora Mercedes knew that she would not suffer this calamity. She was welcomed as warmly as a pinon log fire when she arrived for her one-week stay.

Alfonso arrived about an hour following Theodora Mercedes' departure. He ascended the front stairs so quietly that no one took notice. He knocked on the door with such delicacy that even the mice under the porch were unawakened. Alfonso decided to sit on the expansive, cushioned wicker chair to wait and promptly fell asleep. It was not until dinner time, when his cousins were beginning to worry for his safety, that it occurred to Raul Theodore to walk out the front door. When he spied Alfonso, snoring in his now-wrinkled suit, he blasted forth a piercing scream of recognition and the household was alerted to Alfonso's presence. The two were quickly separated and Alfonso was rushed to the third floor guest room and bath. By the gods, dinner was uneventful, but no one could imagine why. Both Raul Theodore and Alfonso were dutifully chewing each bite ten times before swallowing—a rule they only had to be told once. Raul Theodore was busy calculating the square root of seventeen, the number of utensils and serving pieces on the table. This took a few minutes and he startled everyone by proclaiming in his proud outside voice, "4.12 31056256176605498214098559741!"

The prolonged data blast caused Barrington to knock over his wine. The two unremarkable children fell off their chairs. Alfonso stood up with such celerity that his chair was launched backwards. Consuelo was heard to drop a platter in the kitchen followed by muffled cursing in Spanish. Only Innocenta remained expressionless, for a moment, until a subtle smile of great pride colonized itself on her face. As everything was newly uprighted or repositioned in their respective chairs, Innocenta distracted Raul Theodore by asking him, "What would be the disambiguation of any conic section of any size only one whole number short at the fourteenth decimal place of pi?"

The exercise kept Raul Theodore from noticing that Alfonso was slowly, secretly rearranging his utensils and the rest of the dinnertime went quietly. Quietly, for more than one reason; the dull Alfonso had nothing to say so his cousins had equal responses. It was physics in action and a positioning of souls that met in an empty, perfect center. The meal was so exhausting that everyone retired immediately following the flan, Consuelo's specialty, and headed straight for bed. Raul Theodore was still working the problem as Innocenta put him to bed with her. She wanted no chance encounters between Raul Theodore and Alfonso as she was ready to drop with fatigue. The night was peaceful while the Milky Way made its noisy mechanical locomotion across the firmament unobserved in every way.

Morning broke at five for Innocenta.

Raul Theodore was shaking her and repeating, "The sum of the squares of the lengths of the longest and shortest axes of the conic section divided by its circumference plus one!"

Innocenta, in a just-awakened stupor, felt overwhelmed by motherhood and her special needs child. She had woven her question of a warp and weft of spontaneity and imagination—she was a very bright woman but certainly no mathematician. Her child had produced a complex solution she had no chance of understanding from a question she intuited with no basis for its construction. Innocenta was flummoxed.

Ever still the devoted mother, she replied, "That's correct, Raul Theodore! How did you calculate this?"

But Raul Theodore was running off to tell everyone in the household. No one who had been at the dinner table would be spared this infusion of solution.

Consuelo had not slept well. The square root of seventeen had reverberated into her bones and she tossed around in bed all night. She had Saturday breakfast to prepare and was hard at work when little Raul Theodore bounced into the kitchen and made his astonishing announcement. Raul Theodore bounced right back out to continue edifying the household and Consuelo continued with her tasks. The rest of the family was greeted as they descended the stairs. Each knew to smile and to praise the boy but quickly moved away, making room for the next poorly informed descendent.

Breakfast was set out for five and Raul Theodore put out the utensils in his precise, usual manner. Neither Consuelo nor anyone at the table remembered that they had an unmemorable guest who was not at breakfast. The weekend proceeded uneventfully for the six: Innocenta, Barrington (no guest), Raul Theodore, the two Unremarkables, and Consuelo.

On Saturday morning Alfonso began by doing what he had delayed the night before. That was to lay out his clothing, hang every item carefully, place his socks and undergarments tidily in their drawers, and position his toiletries on the dresser and the vanity with precision and artful juxtapositioning. An hour passed. It was time for Alfonso's daily shower, taken always, at six a.m. Alfonso shed his pajamas, folded them (neatly, of course), and put them into the dresser drawer. He brushed his teeth for exactly two minutes, flossed between each tooth, shaved with great care, and then evacuated his bowels and bladder. He placed his special, hand-selected shampoo and soap into the shower. The pre-shower ritual was complete. Alfonso stepped into the luxurious hot stream and noticed that the water felt unusually velvety. His shower quickly would deteriorate in quality and enjoyment.

Alfonso could not seem to get the shampoo out of his thinning hair. He kept rinsing and rinsing, scrubbing and scrubbing and his hair felt just as slick. Frustrated, Alfonso tried washing his body, then rinsing, and having the same result. Alfonso scrubbed and scrubbed but his hair and body felt slick and soap covered. He willed himself not to anger or panic and continued to rinse. Fifteen minutes later the hot water ran out and Alfonso began to experience a chill. Alfonso kept rinsing and scrubbing. By Saturday afternoon, he was tired, panicked, freezing and still making an effort at removing the soap from his person. Alfonso entertained his mind by attempting to solve the riddle of the slickness. Did he receive a bad batch of soap? Had his shampoo somehow spoiled in its bottle? Was the plastic bottle to blame? Perhaps Alfonso was hallucinating. Was he merely imagining the effect of slickness? Was it possible he was actually clean but experiencing some magical intervention? The questions were endless and came faster and faster to no avail. Alfonso was still slick.

Across the hall, Barrington was entertaining that Saturday night. He was well occupied with his guest and the black condoms. Very early Sunday morning, Barrington and his guest sneaked out of the house and went straight to the gym to exercise and cleanup.

Innocenta took the children to the Social Liberal Church services where they participated in Children's Religious Education. Innocenta believed that this title was ill-fitted to Social Liberal Church principles and had repeatedly lobbied to change the name to Children's Spiritual Exploration. While the ministers and directors of the congregation appeared to agree with Innocenta, the name was somewhat institutional in the Social Liberal world. Innocenta enjoyed the sermon and hymns. The children always enjoyed RE, even little Raul Theodore. Afterwards, Innocenta took the children to the park to play.

Sunday night, Alfonso was huddled in one corner of the shower shivering but somewhat motionless. He had scrubbed his arms raw. There was no hair left on his legs. His scalp was bleeding.

Monday morning the household took up the weekday routines. Consuelo cooked and began cleaning downstairs. Innocenta walked Raul Theodore and the two Unremarkables to school and then met some girl friends for a little shopping downtown. The Plaza was blessedly empty of tourists between seasons so that Innocenta and the other locals could enjoy their beautiful, historic city. Barrington was at work attempting to reconstruct the San Marcos Pueblo language from fragments preserved by neighboring Pueblos. The San Marcos Pueblo had not existed for three hundred years so the endeavor was slow and required great patience.

Monday night dinner was quite pleasant. The weather was beautiful, Consuelo had fully recovered from the weekend, and the pork roast with kumquat sauce was excellent. Barrington had selected a luscious rosé that met with great approval from Innocenta and Consuelo (who often ate and imbibed in the kitchen).

Tuesday morning, the water meter reader came by. Alfonso was now turning a bleached color and was in a mild hallucinatory state. He was well beyond being cold. The household went about its usual Tuesday routines. Consuelo started cleaning upstairs. Innocenta walked Raul Theodore and the two Unremarkables to school. Barrington was hard at work trying to solve the linguistic puzzles of the San Marcos Pueblo.

On Wednesday morning, Raul Theodore asked Innocenta where that man was who had come to visit. Innocenta realized that no one had seen Alfonso since Friday night. She ran upstairs to ask The Unremarkables if they had seen Alfonso. Their replies were fittingly unremarkable. Barrington was at the Institute. Innocenta called him but was put on hold as Barrington was in a working session with members of the San Idelfonso Pueblo. Innocenta put down the phone and found Consuelo. Consuelo was equally shocked by the news and called the Fire Department.

The local fire station was supervised by a local as dull and slow-moving as a three-toed sloth, Edgar Leopoldo Barrios. Barrios waited until his full crew arrived before taking action. The station cook was making posole that day and Barrios would not sacrifice an excellent posole for a missing person. By six p.m., the posole was ready. The cook ensured that there were plenty of chopped onions, lime wedges, Mexican oregano, and fresh corn tortillas. When the feast was finished, Barrios announced that they would go look for a missing person.

13

The crew arrived at the Silverton-de Baca House at nine p.m.. They immediately questioned Innocenta, the two Unremarkables, and Consuelo. They were advised to stay clear of Raul Theodore. Barrington was nowhere to be found. He was, however, in his room with a now returning guest and was well occupied at the time.

The crew laid out equipment of all sorts while the family watched in awe. Barrios sent a young fireman and an assistant with a very tall ladder to the east side of the house. They propped up the ladder and the young fireman climbed while the other steadied the ladder. When he got to the third floor window he paused and looked in. Barrington and Guest were having amazing sex and the young fireman was transfixed and immoveable. The ladder-steadier was shouting at him but he went unheard. Barrington and Guest heard the shouting filtering through the closed window and stopped to look. There, mesmerized, was the hottest young fireman that either had ever seen. They smiled at him. He smiled back. Barrington and Guest went to the window. Barrington opened the window and they helped the hot young fireman into the room. The shouting continued, so Barrington shut the window again. The ladder was moved away. They helped the fireman out of his gear and the three proceeded to romp together for the rest of the night. Barrington left the drawer of black condoms open.

By ten o'clock, Innocenta decided that she needed to put the children to bed and pushed them through the piles of equipment and firemen into the house. When the children were settled, Innocenta decided that she badly needed a shower. This was not because she felt unclean but because she felt that the soothing soft water would calm her nerves. What a day and evening this had been!

Barrios decided to send a fireman into the house to search for the missing man. Bart searched the downstairs and found nothing. As Bart stepped foot on the second-floor landing, something caught his eye. Innocenta was leaving the bathroom with only a large towel modestly draped around her. Bart looked at her ample, firm bosom that had nourished three children, Innocenta's beautiful face and shapely legs, and forgot why he was there. Innocenta turned to see a handsome fireman about her age, his powder-blue eyes fixed on her. Something snapped in her—Innocenta had not had sex since well before her husband had disappeared. Bart's look turned to lust. Innocenta attempted not to think of sex by thinking about what her dear brother, Barrington, would think of her—but their eyes met.

The force of their thoughts and the attempted denial were deflected outside with cosmic energy and caused the dried-up flowers in the yard to burst into tongues of licking, sensuous flames. The startled firemen, with nothing to do, burst into action while they wondered if the fire had been there all along. Bart and Innocenta disappeared into Innocenta's bedroom and she locked the door. They spent the entire night expending their desires.

In Albuquerque, Theodora Mercedes was uneasy. She did not know why, but she felt—no, knew—that something was not right in Santa Fe. Theodora Mercedes discussed this with Angelica Gertrudis and Reigh but her unease was unremitting. She announced that she would return home that morning.

By eight a.m. Thursday, Alfonso had not been found. The fireman had chopped through the roof only to find three men, including one of their own, having sex on a king-sized bed.

One fireman remarked, "I think I know two of those legs."

His fellow firemen stared at him agape. They quickly moved lower on the roof. They chopped through again and found Bart and Innocenta still making passions unspeakable.

The same fireman remarked, "I know those legs!"

It was unclear to whose legs he referred, but they stared at him again. They decided to abandon the roof. By nine a.m., little Raul Theodore managed to ask Barrios what the firemen were doing. Barrios explained that they were looking for a missing man, Alfonso Pedro Silverton Hoffmann. Raul Theodore calmly took Barrios by the hand, led him up two flights of stairs, and opened the guest room door. Not seeing Alfonso, little Raul Theodore led Barrios to the bathroom door and opened it. There was Alfonso Pedro Silverton Hoffmann still in the shower. He was in a chemically induced coma caused by absorbing too much water and not replacing lost salts or nutrients. His skin was translucent, bleeding, and ghostly looking. Raul Theodore screamed. Alfonso was unreactive but Barrios had a bowel movement caused by extreme shock to the eyes and ears.

By ten-thirty a.m., the MICU had taken Alfonso Pedro Silverton Hoffmann to the hospital. Theodora Mercedes arrived while the firemen, all but two, were cleaning up and putting away equipment. She looked aghast at the holes in her roof, the burned garden, and glanced down at the mail she had already retrieved and unconsciously opened. There by the magic of the digital age was her water bill, $496.24. This was the day I promised you that Theodora Mercedes became less than a proud, serious, well in-control woman. She let out a blood curdling epithet so loud that she aroused, so to speak, the three men, Bart, and Innocenta. By the time she entered the front hallway, all five were downstairs in various states of modestly disheveled dress and looking warily towards the matriarch. Barrios quickly told Theodora Mercedes the story. Theodora Mercedes turned toward Barrington and smiled knowingly. There next to him was a tall, tawny, handsome Native American with broad shoulders, narrow hips, long luxurious hair, and the finest cowboy boots she had ever seen. Her drives flashed an unseemly thought through her subconscious which she dismissed, followed by the slightest blush. Theodora Mercedes was momentarily ashamed then delighted. The young man next to the Native American wasn't too bad looking either.

"Mother, I would like you to meet my boyfriend, James Wheeler Many Ranches of the Butterfly and Pinon Jay Clans. And this is Andy."

"I am pleased to meet you both" Theodora Mercedes replied.

"James is a housing contractor and sculptor. Andy is a, well, a fireman, obviously."

"Mr. Many Ranches, can you do me a quick favor?"

"Yes, Ma'am."

"Can you please inspect the damages to my house and give me a repair estimate within the hour?"

"Yes, Ma'am, I'll get started on it right away."

Andy excused himself and the other two left to inspect the house.

Theodora Mercedes then turned to Innocenta and Bart. Innocenta was panicking—she did not know her lover's name! Theodora Mercedes was waiting.

"Hello, Ma'am, I'm Bart."

Innocenta finally took a breath and smiled at her mother as if she had known Bart's name all along. Theodora Mercedes noted that they both reeked of sex but tried not to show her pleasure at this discovery.

"Will you be seeing or dating my daughter, Bart? By the way, her name is Innocenta."

Innocenta fainted into Bart's strong arms. "Yes, Ma'am, if that's OK with you."

"I think that would be lovely. It appears that my daughter would have

16

no objection either. Can we expect you for dinner tomorrow tonight?"

"Ma'am, I would be honored to share your hospitality."

"Young man, it appears that you already have."

Bart fainted. Theodora Mercedes and Consuelo managed to get the limp bodies of Bart and Innocenta into a plush chair and onto the sofa.

Barrington and James returned and found Theodora Mercedes in the kitchen discussing tomorrow tonight's dinner plans with Consuelo.

"Excuse me Ma'am, I estimate that the repairs will cost $6,045 and take approximately one week to complete."

"Then, Mr. Many Ranches, can you start tomorrow and then join us for dinner?"

"That would be a great honor, Ma'am. What time shall I be here?"

"Six-thirty will be just fine."

"Thank you, Ma'am. I will see you then."

With that, Barrington, with a huge smile on his face, and James walked out to embrace the day.

Innocenta and Bart then appeared in the kitchen smiling sheepishly and holding hands.

"Bart, we will see you at six-thirty tomorrow, yes?"

"Yes, Ma'am."

Bart smiled at Innocenta, gave her hand a squeeze, and departed.

"Innocenta, will you drive me to the hospital?"

"Why, of course, Mother! But I didn't think you liked Alfonso."

"I don't. But that foolish man owes me six-thousand, five-hundred forty-one dollars and twenty-four cents!"

Alfonso Pedro Silverton Hoffmann was still unconscious. Theodora Mercedes, still in peak pique, muttered to herself, "How can they tell?"

She would have to wait, a catastrophe for Alfonso as Theodora Mercedes could now ruminate on her nephew mercilessly. Innocenta left and brought back her book. Theodora Mercedes found she could not read. She kept thinking, "Wake up, damn it!"

At three o'clock, the nurse announced that Alfonso was awake and attentive. Theodora Mercedes marched in like General Patton inspecting sloppy troops. Innocenta tried to keep up but, as always, trailed her mother like a corporal.

"Alfonso, how are you feeling?"

Alfonso, who had raised the blanket over his head at his aunt's approach, dropped the shield low enough to verify that she was not armed. He focused one eye upon her and concentrated on not showing fear. However, the grunt quivered before the general.

"I (pause), I'm OK, I guess."

"You guess. Can you be more definitive, Alfonso?"

"I'm feeling weak but my mind seems all right."

"Ex-cel-lent! You weak-minded idiot wrapped in a moron! Why would you take a five-day shower? What were you doing up there, pretending you were at One Thousand Waves? Who do you think pays for the water used in my house, you little leech!? Wait until I tell your mother about the holes in my roof! Did you know that you were the very first person to enjoy the pleasures of the new guestroom and bath? You think that just because you are (here Theodora Mercedes paused to take a very deep breath)—FAMILY, that your negligence will be overlooked? Well, it will not and you owe me six-thousand, five-hundred forty-one dollars and twenty-four cents! That covers the water bill and estimated damages to my house (another deep and terrifying breath) but not my aggravation, trouble, and torched garden! How and when may I expect payment, you water-logged, empty-headed toad? And by the way, HAVE YOU NEVER HEARD OF SOFT WATER!?"

This final, explosive sentence echoed, to Theodora Mercedes' great satisfaction, down the stark hospital hallways. Four nurses came running and crowded themselves in the doorway.

Innocenta had never heard such a torrent of abuse come from her mother. That even included Theodora Mercedes' encounters with the school principal. Alfonso trembled so badly he was unable to speak except for his eyes—they appeared ready to run off on their own. Theodora Mercedes was shocked enough at his appearance and manner that even she realized that her tirade possessed the force of a chain saw cutting a peeled banana. She felt unforeseen remorse.

Calmly, she continued "I'll tell you what, Alfonso. I will go to my lawyer's office and promptly return with a completed promissory note. All you'll have to do is sign it. Will that be satisfactory? You may pay me when you can."

Alfonso had filled the urine bag during the last thirty seconds and it was spouting on the opposite side of the bed. He could only muster an affirming nod.

"Very well, my dear nephew, I will return shortly. Don't go anywhere."

Forty-five minutes later, Theodora Mercedes and Innocenta returned with said promissory note. Wordlessly, Theodora Mercedes handed the note and a pen to Alfonso. He signed wordlessly.

"Thank you, Alfonso. You have my best wishes for your early recovery. Please give my love and greetings to your parents when you return home."

Theodora Mercedes turned and walked out while Innocenta mouthed "Bye," and kissed Alfonso on the forehead. She walked out trailing her mother as always and marveling at how much could be accomplished in silence.

On Saturday, Theodora Mercedes awoke refreshed and had time to reflect on her eventful Friday. Theodora Mercedes would take a soothing bath. Her musings were not so much on the events themselves as on their effects on her. Theodora Mercedes laughed at the disheveled five, reeking of Craig's List, who slinked down the stairway seemingly moments after the trumpet call of Joshua that was her own voice. She sighed like an autumn breeze at her first glimpse of her ceilings and roof. Now she knew it could be repaired and no one would ever know of the damage who was not there at the scene. Most importantly, Theodora Mercedes was thankful that almost no one was hurt. The guest bathroom had been a mess and Consuelo had already cleaned it up. Again, unless you had been there, you would never know what degradation had occurred there.

Doña Theodora came down the stairs in a royal blue dress, set off by her magnanimous smile, ancient sapphire earrings, and upswept hair. She had reconquered and had dominion over her equable bearing. In short, Theodora Mercedes was restored. Her entrance into the dining room was executed with renewed aplomb and had its desired effect. The guests, her family, and Consuelo were mesmerized, and she kept everyone in that state throughout the meal.

Dinner that night was a smashing success. The beef was simple and spectacular. The merlot may as well have been Château Mouton Rothschild, 1982, except that it sold for $7.99. Consuelo's pastel de tres leches was intoxicating with flavor. Raul Theodore was calculating the square root of the new number of utensils and serving pieces, twenty-three, while chewing each bite exactly ten times. Barrington and James were clearly in love. Innocenta and Bart were in lust, although their demeanors promised more. Theodora Mercedes Silverton Vigil was proud, happy, in possession of a signed promissory note, and content—despite the fact that Alfonso Pedro Silverton Hoffmann would make a full recovery.

CHAPTER TWO
Innocenta Perpetua Vigil Silert

Innocenta Perpetua Vigil Silert had finally gotten a moment's peace and dropped into a dream-filled slumber. She saw her happy childhood in Santa Fe and the face of her father, now with the angels—or somewhere anyway. Innocenta climbed into her father's lap, her throne. Intuitively, Innocenta knew that she was her father's favorite child, and her throne was her favorite place. Her heart dwelt there like the flicker that nested in the eaves of their front porch. It was home. The bliss-dream gave way to her little, unusual brother running towards her. Father was now gone. Barrington embraced Innocenta and planted a huge brotherly kiss on his big sister's mouth. He was only three years old. Innocenta noticed that Barrington was wearing her Sunday shoes and laughed lovingly with her heart and mouth. The kiss continued, harder and suffocating. Innocenta began to panic and awoke like a cornered cat.

Bart, who had also drifted off, roused and rolled over to kiss the sleeping Innocenta. In exchange, Innocenta struggled, gasped for breath and brought her knee up with such force Bart's breath escaped in one enormous grunt. Innocenta inhaled and Bart folded himself into a fetal position, fearing that both of his testicles were ruptured. Innocenta, now free of her dream and free to breath, came to a horrifying realization. She had just drop-kicked her lover from a prone position.

"I'm so sorry! I'm so sorry!"

Bart was rolling forth and back while moaning and folding himself tighter.

"I was dreaming! I couldn't breathe! I am sooo sorry!"

Another minute elapsed before Bart took a breath and in the muted tones of a convalescent whispered, "OK, OK! Let me catch my breath."

This was not a fitting ending to a night of bliss with this fireman whom destiny had directed to her bedroom. Innocenta had not felt so woman-like in several years. Since the disappearance of her now late husband, she had been only a mother and a daughter. Although she was devoted to both, this night reawakened somnolent imperatives of nature and womanhood.

21

Innocenta wrapped her naked body around Bart's. Bart began to relax and unfold like one of Theodora Mercedes' extra bridge chairs. He was breathing quickly and shallowly, very unlike the heavy breathing of the night.

Bart pasted a smile on his face to show his forgiveness and managed to get out, "What happened?"

"I was having a beautiful dream when suddenly I couldn't breathe. I panicked. I didn't know you were kissing me."

Innocenta felt terrible. Perhaps he would not want to see her again.

"OK. I understand. Can I see you again?"

Innocenta, taken aback by the unspoken meeting of minds replied, "Of course, ¡querido! You can see me again."

The mood hit the wall when a piercing epithet rattled the house like a sonic boom from downstairs.

"My mother!"

Innocenta and Bart began moving like silent film comedians trying to put on their clothing. Garments that did not have the pleasure of making their accustomed places were stuffed into pockets. Bart started to rush out when Innocenta issued a near-silent scream, "No!" Bart bounced off the door and landed atop Innocenta on the bed. There was a moment of mutually startled silence followed by the rich laughter that only spontaneity creates.

"We need to walk downstairs slowly, as if nothing has happened here, and greet my mother. God knows what could be wrong."

As they entered the upstairs hallway, Bart grabbed Innocenta's hand. Just as quickly she slapped it away, felt guilty, and shyly smiled at Bart. They descended separately.

The scene downstairs is well-accounted. Bart awoke slumped in an overstuffed chair, his face a New Mexico sunset as he realized he had done something so unmanly as fainting in the face of a strong, angry woman. Bart wanted to be somewhere else—anywhere, home, a bar, the fire station—no, not the fire station! Then he saw Innocenta, laid out like a princess in a fantasy, so beautiful, so alluring. Bart moved to her like a stalking cat, descended to one knee and gently kissed the pale lips. Innocenta opened her eyes, recognized her lover, and smiled.

"Bart!"

Innocenta kissed him back. Observing Bart as if for the first time,

Innocenta noticed his radiant face, wildly uncombed hair, and that his shirt buttons were not matched to the correct buttonholes. Innocenta laughed.

"What?"

"You should see yourself, Bart."

"Innocenta, you're holding your brassiere in your hand." Then Bart smiled back.

Innocenta shot into a sitting position and looked at her hand as if it held a snake.

"My mother!"

"I think, Innocenta, she figured everything out as soon as we walked downstairs. She's an amazing woman!"

"Frankly, she is. We better go face her again. I promise not to faint again!"

Bart was relieved to know that Innocenta was innocent of the knowledge of his fainting as well.

After confirming that Bart was to return for dinner the following evening, Innocenta drove her mother to the hospital. Alfonso Pedro Silverton Hoffmann was not quite himself, just as a running, headless chicken is not quite himself. Theodora Mercedes would wait. Innocenta drove home to ensure that the children got to school, retrieved her mother's book, an exposé on the political construction of the New Testament, grabbed her newest magazine, *The Raising Gifted Children Quarterly*, and returned to the hospital. It was a stunning Friday noon and Innocenta wished to enjoy the day more fittingly, but her mother was waiting.

Alfonso was fully roused by three p.m., although still with multiple IVs and monitors connected to him. Theodora Mercedes first verified that Alfonso was lucid and healthy. He was. Then, Theodora Mercedes unleashed the dogs of war, her tongue, on the pathetic limp-minded Alfonso. She returned forty-five minutes later with a filled-in promissory note for Alfonso to sign. Alfonso was many things and stupid was not counted among his virtues and attributes. He signed unquestioningly. Theodora Mercedes expressed her best wishes for Alfonso's timely recovery, asked Alfonso to convey her salutations to his parents, and turned to her daughter without a word. Innocenta quickly bid Alfonso goodbye and turned to follow. They drove home.

Just before Friday dinner, Innocenta watched as Barrington and James returned for the occasion. She greeted them enthusiastically, and they returned the greeting in the same currency of goodwill spiced with delight. Bart arrived at six-twenty and kissed Innocenta more passionately than Innocenta deemed appropriate. They may have made love all night, but they were now on her mother's front porch. Innocenta did not feel the need to entertain the neighbors, nosy or otherwise. Neither did Innocenta wish to flaunt certain things in front of The Very Catholic Consuelo and, especially, Theodora Mercedes.

Dinner was the most memorable in Innocenta's memory. While Theodora Mercedes was in the kitchen ensuring that The Very Catholic Consuelo's *pastel de tres leches* was up to standards for serving to guests, Bart asked Innocenta on a date for tomorrow night. Innocenta would have to ask her mother to watch the children but was confident that this was probable.

After dessert, Innocenta and Bart retired to the front porch where Bart's urges made themselves apparent. Innocenta allowed a few brief kisses, then sent Bart home for the night. Bart walked to his car awkwardly, sporting an enormous, miserably unsatisfied erection.

Upstairs, the children were playing in their rooms. The two Unremarkables were playing on their Game Boys. This was the kind of activity that suited them well, but Innocenta frequently enforced the completion of homework and read to them from the classics. Not that Innocenta would put it quite this way, but she often wondered whether she was casting pearls before swine. She persisted in thinking the best of The Unremarkables and continued her periodic reading sessions.

Raul Theodore was doing his homework despite the fact that it was a Friday night. He did not wait to be told or for the pressure of the last minute.

"Raul Theodore, how are you doing tonight?"

"Fine."

"Are you bothered by the excitement of yesterday morning?"

"What excitement, Mother?"

"Oh, nothing. Did you enjoy meeting the firemen?"

Raul Theodore gave her a rare look in the eye, "Yes, especially Bart and James."

Innocenta shuddered inwardly as there seemed to be no apparent reason for Raul Theodore to single each of them out of the crowd.

"What do you like about Bart?"

"He was nice to you. I saw him hold your hand."

With that, Raul Theodore gifted Innocenta with a very rare smile. Innocenta burst into tears. Raul Theodore reached his little hand and touched his mother's wet cheek. Innocenta wept even more and hugged Raul Theodore almost breathless. Ten minutes later, she was gone. Innocenta was in her bed asleep and headed for strange, intriguing dreams.

When Innocenta had been asleep for about two hours she stepped into another world. Her father was asking about the children. When Innocenta had visions of Father, his was always a benign presence and she climbed onto her throne. Father asked about Bart. Innocenta lost the vision of her father's face as a warm mist enveloped them. She realized that this manifested Bart's love. Innocenta's heart was now in her hand beating with an erotic pulsation. She realized that this was a sign her growing love for Bart.

"Father, I am in love once again and it feels good."

"I know Angel. That is why I am leaving you tonight. You have no further need of me." Innocenta was unprepared for this.

"Father, no!"

But her father was already gone and she could hear his voice say, "I will always love you, Angel," and then Father's voice vanished into silence.

Innocenta awoke at eight on a Saturday. Equally amazing, her children were still asleep—except Raul Theodore who was working on expressing Foucault's power analytics into a mathematical expression. As Innocenta had no universal idea what this might be, she patted his amazing head, tightened her robe, and went downstairs. Theodora Mercedes and The Very Catholic Consuelo were already discussing grocery shopping for the day. Innocenta was energized by a remarkable night's sleep, her father's undying love, and the love of Bart. She volunteered to do the grocery shopping. Theodora Mercedes and the Very Catholic Consuelo looked as if a puff of chamiza pollen could knock them down.

Innocenta simply said, "Let me shower and get dressed."

When she turned around, Theodora Mercedes and the Very Catholic Consuelo made the mistake of making eye contact and the absurdity of what just happened caused them to erupt into laughter. Innocenta, who could hear this, just smiled. Nothing could ruin this miraculous day.

By nine-thirty, Innocenta was maneuvering her Volvo through the unholy parking lot of Universal Foods. The supermarket was the biggest, most popular, and expensive grocery in Santa Fe. The family only shopped there for specialty items that could not be purchased elsewhere. Innocenta secured a grocery cart, moved quickly past the temptation of the expensive cut flowers, and headed for the produce section. While picking tomatoes her peripheral vision picked up a celebrity, someone whose name escaped her, squeezing avocados at the opposite bin. She looked odd, disheveled, disturbed; she was looking at Innocenta. No, she was looking *through* Innocenta. Instinctively, Innocenta raised her hands to eye level to ascertain whether she had become invisible. Was the gift at work? Innocenta had inherited the gift of vision from her mother. The gift followed the third daughters of the line and only the third daughters. The visions came on their own schedules and, presumably, for their own reasons. Why an unnamed celebrity should be squeezing avocados and gazing through her on this day was a mystery to her, but she neither questioned nor feared the visions. They were as much a part of her as her blue-green eyes. Innocenta swung around to see what the celebrity was staring at and saw something in her peripheral vision. Just as quickly, the image moved beyond her sight. As the celebrity seemed to have no agenda that involved Innocenta, she moved on but felt just as if she had been pushed.

Innocenta turned into the organic foods aisle and spotted a mother with a toddler in a stroller, not a rare sighting in Santa Fe or any other market. The mother seemed to be in high spirits, but the child had a dark aura surrounding her. The aura disturbed Innocenta; it had the dark, sour shades of death to it. Innocenta moved to say something to the mother when it occurred to her that the mother was unaware that the child was dying. She stopped, looked away as if she had just witnessed a fatal car crash, and began breathing quickly and shallowly. Innocenta had to ask herself why she was being shown this. Was she tacitly being asked to speak to the mother? Why was she elected to this ugly task? Innocenta could only hold off panic by leaving the aisle. She accepted her situation reluctantly and decided that she would not buy rice today. Her emotional equilibrium off balance, Innocenta pushed her cart to the magazine rack. She picked a monthly at random and began paging through. Several miserable minutes later, Innocenta decided to speak to the mother. She searched the entire store—they were gone. She asked the store manager to help her search. It was fruitless; they were gone and no one recognized their descriptions.

When Innocenta approached the long checkout lines, she was

emotional and certainly no longer cared about groceries. A man and a woman, in line ahead of her, were locked in a silent mental struggle, each glancing menacingly at the other but only with their minds, each oblivious to Innocenta's gaze. The shoppers, who were staring at magazines, electronic readouts, or conversing with companions, turned their attention to Innocenta. Innocenta realized that she had taken her gift of sight for granted. Her behavior, especially the look on her distressed face, betrayed her inner world. Innocenta quickly turned away and looked at her groceries as if nothing had occurred.

Innocenta's small grocery basket rang up at ninety-two dollars and seventy-three cents and fit into her two canvas bags with room left over for a gallon jug of milk. No wonder her family shopped elsewhere. Innocenta dodged the rude drivers and the ridiculously laidout parking lot and made it to her Volvo. In the empty parking space next to her car, a young man and young woman were conversing, flirting, really, but standing about ten feet apart. The gift told her where this was headed.

Innocenta stopped, turned to the left and smiled at the man, turned to the right and smiled at the woman, then confidently declaimed, "Get a room."

The young people burst into embarrassed laughter and Innocenta decided that, at least, the gift had a sense of humor.

By the time Innocenta got home with the groceries, her energy had been sapped like a vampire's blood-meal.

Innocenta walked in the back door into the kitchen and Theodora Mercedes asked, "Why was that woman so angry?"

The Very Catholic Consuelo hurried out to dust the parlor. Innocenta was always surprised by her mother's abilities (in every way).

She walked past her mother, put down the groceries, and turned to face Theodora Mercedes, "I don't know. The gift only lets me know so much. Do you know why she was so angry?"

"I'm fairly certain, no very certain, that she was misdirecting her jealousy."

Innocenta shot her the "Please continue" look.

"Don't you see, she wanted to be with her husband and her lover?"

"Which one, Mother?"

"Why both."

Innocenta was defenseless and confused, sat on a chair, and just laughed. Maybe the gift was sometimes just comic relief for those with vision. Innocenta thought that a pretty good gift. Theodora Mercedes laughed too. She enjoyed these special encounters with her third daughter.

Raul Theodore informed Innocenta that Foucault's ideas contained some flaws that made a mathematical model more difficult.

"I might have to devise three universal constants to make it work. I will show you by dinnertime."

"That's wonderful, Raul Theodore. I am looking forward to seeing it."

Of course, Innocenta was astonished at her son and had no idea what this model might look like.

Entering through the back door, Barrington and James grabbed some apples and went upstairs. Innocenta, now also upstairs, could hear a rhythm above her and was happy for her little brother. Barrington was due. Innocenta fell asleep in her chair.

The mist appeared to Innocenta and she expected Bart. She knew her father would not return.

The angry woman put her nose to Innocenta's face and demanded, "Why didn't you take my side, you bitch!?"

The nasty surprise bolted Innocenta awake and she ran to her bathroom to urinate. As the woman didn't follow, Innocenta felt it was safe to go check on the children.

The Unremarkables were playing chase in the yard under the supervision of Theodora Mercedes, who was stringing beans. Raul Theodore was scratching equations in the sand box, oblivious to the world of activity surrounding him. It was a typical Saturday afternoon for the family.

"That angry woman is certainly nasty!"

"What?"

"What she said to you a few minutes ago! What a rude woman!"

Innocenta needed a cup of coffee and did not reply.

The Very Catholic Consuelo looked wary as Innocenta entered the kitchen.

Crossing herself while she was turned away from Innocenta, she asked, "May I get you something?"

"No, no. I'll get it. I need a cup of coffee."

The Very Catholic Consuelo fingered her rosary in her apron pocket and counted the minutes until Innocenta vacated the kitchen. The Very

Catholic Consuelo continued her work and began saying the entire rosary. It would take her, with interruptions, the rest of the afternoon.

By five o'clock, Innocenta was in the shower getting ready for her date with Bart. As she washed, her hands involuntarily moved the sensuous soap and soft water around her sensitive body. Innocenta could not help thinking about Bart—both in love and in lust. The shower was beginning to cool as Innocenta ran out of hot water and she quickly finished up. She dried herself just enough not to track water, opened the door, and walked stark naked into her bedroom. Innocenta heard a noise and looked up. James and Barrington were on her roof making repairs. Innocenta and Barrington made eye contact and they both screamed like air-raid alarms. James, shocked visually and audibly, lost his balance and fell through the hole in the roof. He landed on Innocenta's bed, bounced once, and landed on the floor at her feet looking straight, so to speak, up at her crotch. Innocenta screamed again. James screamed but didn't move—he was stunned by the events of the last two seconds, let alone the stun of the fall. Barrington shielded his eyes. Innocenta ran back into the bathroom. James escaped through Innocenta's bedroom door. Barrington scurried down the ladder. Innocenta sat on the commode, then jumped up, unprepared for how cold the seat cover was. She cursed. She cursed again. It would take Innocenta twenty precious minutes to recover from this misadventure that took a mere twenty seconds from beginning to blessed end.

When Innocenta came down in advance of Bart's arrival, James and Barrington were sitting at the dining room table talking over coffee. Both quickly stared at their cups and went silent. Innocenta decided to take charge of the situation; she was a third daughter of the line.

"So, don't you think I look fabulous for a woman of . . . forty-ish?"

All three burst into laughter with the men agreeing that, yes, she did indeed look fabulous. Briefly, Barrington considered specifying Innocenta's age, but wisely thought better of it. He did not have the gift," but possessed other insights to see where this could lead. They talked about how long the roof repairs might take, whether they could give Innocenta a heads-up before they started working on her roof again, and made general, pleasant conversation while Innocenta waited for Bart.

Bart arrived promptly at six. He was freshly shaved, wearing an open-collar shirt that looked brand new, and a sport coat that also looked brand new. He carried flowers. Barrington and James greeted Bart and then quickly excused themselves. Innocenta, delighted at every sight described, kissed Bart on the cheek and bade him sit down. Innocenta asked Bart about his day while focusing her mighty mental powers on Bart not asking about hers. Bart had worked at the fire station, gone to the gym, and preened for this moment. He mentioned nothing about shopping. Innocenta complimented Bart on his appearance, said nothing about shopping (his or hers), and suggested that they go.

Bart drove a smart Subaru, standard issue for Santa Fe. Unlike most Santa Fe Subarus, Bart's was spotless inside and out. He clearly took pride in his automobile. Innocenta was impressed. A meticulous man would potentially make a meticulous husband. Their sex had been meticulous, much to Innocenta's pleasures. Bart was a man of great promise. They had dinner at a popular road house, always a favorite if unimaginative.

When they were seated, Bart said, "I wanted to take you to Hanoi, but I wasn't sure that you liked Vietnamese."

"Bart, this is fine. But I also love Vietnamese food. Perhaps next time?"

Innocenta was pleased that Bart took her to a sure-fire favorite and brought up more adventuresome fare for the future. Innocenta had explored world cuisines with her mother since she was a small child. Bart showed great promise. Bart ordered chicken enchiladas with "Christmas," both red and green chile sauces. Innocenta ordered the Cobb salad with raspberry vinaigrette while Bart reached over for Innocenta's hand. Their conversation was light and flirty while they awaited theirs orders. Innocenta admired his large firm/gentle touch and they conversed while looking into each other's eyes. Was Innocenta in one of her dreams? Were Bart's eyes shallow or deep pools? There were no mists or dead people, so Innocenta concluded that this experience must be real and that Bart's eyes were indeed deep pools. Innocenta reluctantly loosed Bart's hand as their meals arrived.

When they were leaving, Innocenta excused herself to the ladies room. Looking in the mirror, there was a large patch of iceberg on her front teeth. Why hadn't Bart mentioned it? Mortified, Innocenta removed it and rinsed her mouth. She checked her clothing. Her blouse had vinaigrette on it.

"Shit!"

She rubbed some water on it, but it was there for the evening and there was nothing further to be done. Wait! She had her grandmother's antique broach in her handbag. Innocenta affixed the broach strategically and was satisfied with the result. Bart, in the men's room, found red sauce on his new shirt and followed the usual procedure. Why hadn't Innocenta mentioned it? When Bart emerged, Innocenta noticed green sauce in Bart's cleft chin. Without a word, she reached into her handbag, found a Kleenex and gently wiped his chin. Everything moved in slow motion as they stared into each other's eyes and the simple wiping of his chin became an erotic act. They kissed on the spot. As they turned to leave, Bart noticed toilet paper running all the way back to the ladies room stuck to Innocenta's left spiked heel. He deftly placed his foot on the paper and it was liberated with no further battle or Innocenta's knowledge of it or embarrassment.

Bart drove Innocenta to a local night club to listen to salsa music and, perhaps, dance a little. Innocenta hadn't been on a date like this since her late husband had courted her. She found the music entering her through the middle of her fit body, slowly gaining both weight and lightness and causing her to sway.

Innocenta grabbed Bart, "Come on. Let's dance!"

The last song, designed to bring everyone back to earth, was *Endless Love*, played slowly and editorially to a salsa rhythm. The club announced last call. Neither had even ordered a drink. On the drive home, Innocenta peered up through the Subaru's window and spied the Milky Way. It was familiar and new all at once. As a child she could lie in the grass and look up at the splendor and brilliance of the galaxy and wonder wondrous thoughts. Why had she not done so in so many years? Was it marriage, being a mother, too busy, or simply malicious compliance with adulthood? None of that mattered; she required more.

"Bart, can you stop somewhere where we can look at the stars?"

"Sure," and he drove to Museum Hill.

The car came to stop and Innocenta stepped out. She leaned against the car's hood and leaned back. Bart leaned back next to her, close enough to touch her hips and shoulder. There are men and women who require a statement; "Isn't it beautiful?" or, "The stars seem so far away." This man and this woman needed no words. They looked at and loved everything in sight and within touch, except the car. Innocenta kissed Bart on the mouth. Bart reciprocated with a long deep kiss.

Innocenta finally broke away, "Do you see where Scorpio's tail ends?"

"Yes."

"Now look a little to the left. That's the center of the Milky Way galaxy."

In the dark, Bart stared at Innocenta in admiration. He had not looked at the stars since he was a child.

"Now, take me home, Bart."

Innocenta and Bart, sneaking into the house at two a.m., despite the creaking stairs and unbearable quiet, made it undetected to Innocenta's bedroom, or so they thought. Things were moving faster than Innocenta intended (not meaning on the stairs) as compared to slowing Bart down on Friday night. But this felt right. It felt destined. Innocenta felt confident that her dreams would acquit her decisions. They made love for an hour, then Innocenta and Bart turned over on their backs. Innocenta realized that she could see the Milky Way through the hole in the roof. Bart was looking too and they broke into involuntary smiles. Innocenta fell asleep in the crook of Bart's arm. When she awoke at dawn. Bart's arms and legs were completely wrapped around her. Innocenta loved the feel of his hairy chest on her back and the strength of his limbs on hers. She wished she could lay here for an hour. Slowly, Bart roused from his slumber.

He kissed her sweetly, gently. "Innocenta, may I ask your mother for your hand in marriage?"

Innocenta barely contained her glee but coyly responded, "Give me until noon to think about it. Yes. Yes, Bart, you may ask my mother but it is a decision I can make on my own. I am the third daughter of a line of third daughters. We have strengths you cannot guess. I will marry you."

Bart was the first to emerge from the bedroom. He encountered James coming down from the third floor. "Good mornings" were exchanged and each broke into a friendly grin. They descended like old buddies. They were two hearts in the right place.

When everyone had been seated around the huge table Bart tapped his fork on his coffee cup.

Bart made a show of clearing his throat. "Mrs. Vigil,"

"Please call me Theodora Mercedes."

Bart wondered if he could actually bring himself to do that, so he continued thus, "I have only known your daughter, Innocenta, for two days but I am deeply in love with her. I believe that Innocenta is also deeply in love with me."

Barrington, James, Innocenta, and, in the kitchen, Consuelo, all smiled without any mocking intent.

Bart continued, "I would like your permission to marry her."

"Young man, please call me Theodora Mercedes. Bart, with all due respect for you, I have no need for outdated traditions or cheap sentimentality. Why don't you just ask Innocenta? She can make this decision for herself."

Bart was surprised at this but turned to Innocenta in the chair next to him.

He was already holding her hand. "Innocenta, will you marry me?"

Innocenta, feeling playful, replied, "Well, this is a big decision. We'll have to go around the table and get everyone's blessing."

The vote went around the table in a clockwise direction, the direction of good fortune, and was affirmed. Affirmed by everyone except by The Unremarkables who each replied, "I don't know."

Raul Theodore yelled, "Yes, we are missing a third daughter of a line of third daughters!" at the top of his little lungs.

Even Innocenta's jaw dropped, Barrington gave an audible gasp, and James looked at Raul Theodore as if he could see something the others could not. Theodora Mercedes looked at Raul Theodore with no surprise and great pride. In the kitchen, The Very Catholic Consuelo, listening at the door, crossed herself quickly and dropped to her knees with a moan to recite the Apostle's Creed. Only The Unremarkables had no reactions.

"Well, I accept, Bart. Yes, I will marry you on one condition; will you give my children your name?"

"Yes, of course!"

There was an awkward silence and Innocenta began to take on a mild look of panic. She looked at her mother who merely looked back questioningly.

"Bart, what *is* your name?"

"Bartram Alexander Rael de la Madrid."

"Bartram!?"

Everyone broke out in laughter, Bart turned a New Mexico sunset color again, and Innocenta kissed him on the lips.

The breakfast turned celebratory for everyone except The Very Catholic Consuelo who muttered to herself every time she entered and exited the dining room. Theodora Mercedes would periodically glare at her, but she was too happy to follow through with anything more severe. She would chastise The Very Catholic Consuelo later, not about her muttering, but about her poor opinion of third daughters of the line.

33

After breakfast, Theodora Mercedes took Bart aside, "Bart, I'm pleased that you are part Jewish as the only other Jewish part of our family will die out soon."

Bart looked completely bumfuzzled, "Ma'am?"

"Bart, surely you know of the story of the Crypto-Jews of New Mexico."

"No."

"I'm surprised being that your name includes Rael."

Bart still looked like a man wandering in the desert.

"Bart, what happens to 'Rael' when you put 'is' in front of it?"

Bart looked up and to the right, "You get 'is' 'Rael'?"

"Say it faster."

"Is-ra-el."

"Faster!"

"Israel! Israel, do you mean that my family generations ago were Jews?"

"More than that, Bart, they were Crypto-Jews; Jews who were pretending to be Catholics in order to escape the Inquisition. They were so desperate that many came not just to the New World, but to New Mexico, to escape the bloody persecutions. You couldn't travel much farther within the empire than New Mexico. Even so, they had to continue to practice their religion and rituals in secret. The Inquisition did bring its persecutions here. The fervor of the Inquisitors was driven by faith to go far and wide to accomplish their grisly mission."

Here, Theodora Mercedes paused.

"So, that's the general story. If it's true for you, then you bring new Jewish/Spanish roots to the family."

Bart was thoughtful for a few ticks of the tall case-clock.

"Why is this important to you, Theodora Mercedes?"

Theodora Mercedes was delighted that Bart finally demolished the name barrier, "It's not. It's just that it brings more variety, new roots, different thinking to a family that could go stale otherwise."

"Well, I really don't know if I'm Jewish or not. It might have to remain a puzzle. But, Theodora Mercedes, what did you mean when you said that the only other Jewish part of your family will die out soon?"

"Bart, that's an observation that I cannot discuss further and needs to stay just between us."

"Yes, Ma'am," and Bart re-erected the name barrier. Theodora

Mercedes was inwardly amused at the re-erection of the name barrier when Bart, who was walking away, suddenly turned.

"My grandfather's name was Moises Aaron."

"Yes, that's Moses in Spanish. It may or may not be a clue."

"Good day, Ma'am."

With that, Bart went off to work.

Innocenta and the three children came back downstairs dressed for church.

"Where's Bart?"

"Off to work. Didn't he tell you?"

"Yes, it slipped my mind because I wanted to show him off at church. It was selfish of me."

"Innocenta, he's quite a man. I wouldn't be so hard on myself if I were in your position." Theodora Mercedes gave her daughter a wink, Innocenta blushed, and the four started off to church.

Theodora lept to her feet, "Wait! I'll go with you."

The sermon that day, on ethical eating, was based upon "The bovine that wants to be eaten," from *The Restaurant at the End of the Universe*, by the late great philosopher, Douglas Adams. Theodora Mercedes and Innocenta enjoyed it very much and were discussing it with the President of the church board when the children came running. They had made world maps of the major religions out of construction paper. Raul Theodore covered his construction paper with equations describing the various land masses in relation to their distances from one another. His was the more artful composition. Innocenta praised them all. In her mind, Theodora Mercedes was savoring a hot, juicy steak.

Bart came to the house after the family had had dinner. It had been a long shift at the fire house. He and Innocenta sat in the backyard, holding hands, talking, observing the stars, and stealing the occasional kiss.

"Innocenta, may I ask you a question that is none of my business?"

"You may as well try, Bart. What is it?"

"I know that after your late husband left you never had another man in the house. Yet, you are so responsive and giving, as if sex were an important part of you."

"Yes, go on."

"How long did you live with your husband, George, and not have sex?"

"Three years, Bart. From the time he learned that Raul Theodore was diagnosed as "special." That he would never play ball with him. That they would never rebuild the lawnmower engine. He pulled away, beginning with me. Then, he just disappeared."

"And that was how long ago?"

"Three years."

"So, little Raul Theodore is nine, and you have not had sex for six of his nine years."

"Yes."

"Innocenta, how did you manage?"

"Bart, sex is wonderful but not the most binding force in the universe. There are things in a marriage, in life itself, much more important *and* binding than sex."

"But after he left, then was killed, didn't you need a man in that way?"

"I sometimes thought about sex, but it never was the major preoccupation. Basically, I just forgot about it until you reawakened that part of me."

"And now?"

"Oh, Bart, I thought I would never feel like a woman in that way again. Not only that, we seem to be well matched."

At this Innocenta blushed but Bart could only intuit this, not actually see it in the darkness.

"I think I understand. You have put sex into a new perspective for me. But I still love having sex with you!"

"Me too, Bart!" They shared a lingering kiss, then watched the stars once more.

The air grew chilly. As Innocenta and Bart rose to go inside, Bart asked another question,

"Innocenta, is anyone in your family Jewish?"

Innocenta was surprised and looked worried. Was Bart a bigot?

"No, no! I may be part Jewish myself. It's just a curiosity question."

"Oh. My Uncle Reigh and his son, my cousin, Alfonso Pedro Silverton Hoffmann, are ethnic but not practicing Jews. In fact, they're members of the Social Liberal Church. They live in Albuquerque. Do you know them?"

"No. I was just wondering."

Bart opened the back door, and they entered the house through the kitchen. The Very Catholic Consuelo was eavesdropping and finishing the dinner dishes. She smiled as they walked through. As soon as the door to the dining room swung back, The Very Catholic Consuelo said three Hail Marys.

That night, between the setting of the moon and the milky white of dawn, Innocenta began to dream. A soothing blue mist appeared and just hovered for a while.

The mist opened like the curtain at Radio City Music Hall and the Mormon Tabernacle Choir was chanting, "Lies! Lies! Look into her eyes! Lies! Lies! Look into her eyes! LIES! LIES! LOOK INTO HER EYES BEFORE HE DIES!"

Without warning, the stage was replaced by a black mask, inches from Innocenta's face. She could make out no features except horrible, green eyes boring through her.

The mask opened its evil mouth and a susurrate voice spoke, "I WILL TAKE HIM!"

Innocenta screamed and shot up in bed.

Bart awoke with the scream but before he could ask what was wrong, Innocenta cried, "Death! Death! Death!" and fell into Bart's arms.

Innocenta could not calm herself. Bart held her, alternating between tightly and loosely depending on Innocenta's agitation. Innocenta would not, or could not, speak. She was overwhelmed. Just as her life reached a new pinnacle, Bart would be taken from her.

Theodora Mercedes rushed into the room.

"Innocenta! Innocenta! It's not what you think! Bart is in no danger! Innocenta! Innocenta!"

She shook her daughter hard, palmed Innocenta's face and turned it towards her own.

"Innocenta, the dream will come true, but not for Bart. It is meant for someone else."

Between renewed tears and hugs, Innocenta begged, "Who will die, Mother?"

"That, I cannot tell you" Theodora Mercedes replied calmly.

Innocenta, with wide, frightened eyes, asked, "Cannot or will not, Mother?"

"All right, then, I will not. Be happy that it is not Bart. It cannot be changed."

Theodora Mercedes walked out.

Before sunrise, Bart left for the fire station. Innocenta, still trembling from the night's terror, got her children ready for school and walked them out. Barrington and James came down, asked Theodora Mercedes what the night's commotion was all about, but she was silent.

James ushered Barrington out to the porch, "Don't ask anything else. I sense disaster somewhere but not closeby."

They both skipped breakfast and went to their respective workplaces.

Innocenta returned from walking the children to school. The air and exercise had done her some good. Innocenta was calmer now and surprised that she was able to see for herself that it was not Bart who faced death. Innocenta went about her routine contemplating the possibilities, but the gift did not provide more insights. She was satisfied that the immediate household was not in danger. Still . . .

The children were home by three. The Unremarkables went to the backyard to play. Raul Theodore looked more distant than usual, even for him, and went straight to his room. Innocenta followed him upstairs. Knocking quietly, Innocenta let herself into Raul Theodore's room. He was sitting in his chair staring out the window. A normal day would have him on the floor working out some fabulous mathematical equation. Innocenta knelt next to her little one.

"Raul Theodore, what's wrong?"

In another unusual gesture, he looked straight into his mother's eyes. Innocenta held her emotions back.

"Why are the other children so mean?"

In the following ten minutes, Innocenta managed to coax out that other children were teasing, picking on, and generally making Raul Theodore's school life unhappy because of his quiet, unusual nature and mathematical gift. Later, Innocenta would verify these facts with The Unremarkables. As Raul Theodore was talking, Innocenta's memory opened back to a similar experience she had had in the fourth grade. She had recently become aware of the gift and had shared her visions openly with other children at school. What followed was parallel to Raul Theodore's experience. Innocenta remembered sharing her troubles with her mother. Theodora Mercedes had told Innocenta a story, of sorts, that made everything easier to take until her maturity and understanding caught up with the gift. Perhaps, a similar story would help.

"Raul Theodore, come with me."

Innocenta led him by his little hand to the dresser. She moved the mirror to the floor so that Raul Theodore could see himself from toe to cowlick.

"Raul Theodore, look at yourself in the mirror. Now, take off your shoes and look again."

Raul Theodore wordlessly did as his mother asked.

"Now take off your socks and shirt and look at yourself again."

Innocenta continued in this manner until Raul Theodore was in his Lion King underwear, looking at himself in the mirror.

"Now, what do you see?"

"I see me."

"That's right."

"Do you like what you see, Raul Theodore?"

"I guess so."

"I love what I see. You are a kind, smart little boy who loves his mother and his mother loves him."

In a half-moment, the gift and ordinary insight merged; Innocenta put two pieces of a puzzle together that she had never joined before. Raul Theodore was not a female, *but he was her third child.* The gift had manifested itself in Raul Theodore's interior ways and uncanny abilities with mathematics. Why had this never occurred to her before? Now the story assumed much greater importance.

"Now, look into your own eyes, Raul Theodore. Look past your body, face, eyelashes, your blue-green irises, and look into the dark spot in the middle of your eyes. Move closer to the mirror and look as far into your eyes as you can. Are you looking, Raul Theodore?"

"Yes."

"Look deeper. Now, as you look, think about all the things you and I love about you. What do you love about you, Raul Theodore?"

"I love me. I love Nana. I love everyone in our house."

"Yes, that's good. What else do you love?"

"I love you."

Innocenta could not help herself; her smile covered her entire face.

"Thank you Raul Theodore, I love you too. What else do you love about *just you*?"

"I love school. I love my teachers. I love listening to other people talk.

I love to play with numbers. I love mathematics. I love having blue-green eyes."

"That's right, Raul Theodore. Do you think that the other children see you like I see you or how you see you?"

"No."

"That's right too, Raul Theodore; they can't see you through your eyes. They can't see that you love your family, school, and teachers. Especially, they can't see that you love to listen more than talk. They can't see how much you love numbers. They can't see how much you love mathematics. They cannot see the gifts you have because they cannot see you through your blue-green eyes. You are a remarkable, loving little boy with special gifts *they may never see*. But you see them and I see them. And we both love Raul Theodore and his special gifts."

"Does Nana love me and my special gifts?"

"Of course she does! Now, when you go to school, remember that you have these gifts that the other children do not see. When they tease you, smile, feel pity; that's like feeling sad for them because they cannot see your gifts. Then just go about your day without noticing them and think about your numbers and your mathematics."

"Will I feel better, Mother?"

"Yes, Raul Theodore, you will."

"Can I go play in the sandbox now?"

"Yes, but not in your underwear!"

Innocenta left Raul Theodore to get dressed and come downstairs. By halfway down, she felt a blush of shame at her fears and behavior earlier in the day. Others had bigger problems and faced taller mountains than she. Someone somewhere was even facing death. When she entered the kitchen, Theodora Mercedes looked at her with tears in her eyes and gave her daughter a long silent embrace. Innocenta was expecting it.

CHAPTER THREE
Alfonso Pedro Silverton Hoffmann

Alfonso Pedro Silverton Hoffmann could not function properly confined to a hospital. First, there were his physical injuries at the caprices caused by soft water and poor judgment. Then, his aunt, Theodora Mercedes, had effortlessly terrorized him. The wounds to his psyche, invisible to all but the most discerning, would take more time and care than one hospital stay. The very moment his attending doctor proclaimed him fit enough to go home, Alfonso got dressed, checked out, and took a cab home—all the way to Albuquerque. A normal person would have left a day earlier than the doctor's proclamation, but Alfonso never, ever left anything to chance. When he arrived at his parents' east foothills home, no one was present to greet him. Angelica Gertrudis and Reigh, Alfonso's parents, were at the hospital in Santa Fe learning of his discharge. As they knew their son to be of persistent habits, he would have his house key. They were wrong. Somewhere in the chaos of family, firemen, burning bushes, and MICUs, his key was misplaced and never made its way back to Alfonso's pocket. Angelica Gertrudis and Reigh decided to visit Theodora Mercedes and her family as long as they had driven so far. They had a lovely lunch of *chiles rellenos* and a lazy dog's life afternoon enjoying the backyard air like spring wine.

Alfonso Pedro Silverton Hoffmann had never been locked out of the house. He sat on the front steps with his luggage and promptly went to sleep. When he awoke hours later, his bald scabby pate and face were sunburned by the relentless New Mexico sun, and he was parched. This was not an ideal situation for a man just discharged from the hospital. Alfonso reviewed his situation but didn't move. His parents drove up just at sundown.

There was a cheerful, tearful reunion accompanied by admonishing words concerned with Alfonso's properly communicating his return. Prophetically, Alfonso announced, "Next time."

Angelica Gertrudis salved his face and pate while filling him with iced tea. She was not satisfied with Alfonso's well-being until he excused himself to the bathroom. Angelica Gertrudis listened by the bathroom door to assure herself that Alfonso had made an urination sufficiently copious to indicate rehydration. She finally could breathe. Angelica Gertrudis made a quick *chilaquiles* dinner washed down with kosher wine—some habits stayed with Reigh. Alfonso was not served any wine and made do with iced tea. After dinner, Angelica Gertrudis sent Alfonso to bed.

Alfonso's bedroom never looked so good. His twin bed was madeup by his mother following his aunt, Theodora Mercedes', visit. The Power Rangers bedspread was a smooth sea of blue with nary a ripple on its surface. The tops of his dresser and student desk were dusted, polished, and restored to orderly expectations. "Cleanliness is Next to Godliness" was still on the wall and appropriately straight and level. The collage of Marc Chagall's stained glass windows, The Twelve Tribes of Israel, was next to the picture of Jesus that Alfonso's parents had presented him when he turned seven years old. Alfonso was proud of his heritage. He would have been disappointed to know that the actual windows are illuminated by artificial light, such sacrilege, and that Jesus' followers had murdered millions of Jews over twenty centuries. But Alfonso was either ignorant of the facts or preferred not to consider them. He was at peace with his two halves. Alfonso changed into his freshly ironed pajamas, climbed into bed, and promptly dropped off. It had been a week since Alfonso had known such peace.

Somewhere between the setting of the moon and the first light of dawn, a blue mist appeared to Alfonso. He thought it was pretty, pleasing, like his bedspread. The mists parted and the stage of Radio City Music Hall appeared with the Mormon Tabernacle Choir chanting. Alfonso smiled in his sleep; he had always loved choral music, and, despite his poor tenor voice, sang enthusiastically at the Social Liberal Church of Albuquerque.

Alfonso then actually heard the chant, "Lies! Lies! Look into her eyes! Lies! Lies! Look into her eyes! LIES! LIES! LOOK INTO HER EYES BEFORE HE DIES!"

Without warning, the stage was replaced by a black mask with horrid green eyes, inches from Alfonso's face.

The mask opened its evil mouth and a susurrant voice spoke. "I WILL TAKE HIM!"

Alfonso screamed and shot up in bed. In Santa Fe, his cousin Innocenta was doing the same thing. Alfonso's scream woke his parents, and they came running into his bedroom. Alfonso rarely had dreams or nightmares. Now, he was trembling and unconscious.

At Presbyterian Hospital, the doctors admitted Alfonso. He was still fragile, and the shock of the dream sent him into a deleterious overdose of adrenalin hastily followed by out-of-whack electrolytes. Alfonso would recover from this setback, but the doctor insisted on keeping him overnight. He was hooked-up to another round of IVs to ensure that his hydration and salts were rebalanced. Angelica Gertrudis felt light-headed and leaned on Reigh's arm. She refused any treatment for herself, but the staff wheeled her out to the car in a chair. At home, both Angelica Gertrudis and Reigh slept badly.

Alfonso Pedro Silverton Hoffmann's nurse that night was an attractive, petite, dark-haired young woman. She had beautiful large, brown, doe-like eyes. Leah Rose Naphtali, "Call me Leah," was unusually attentive to this sun-burned, bald, scabby, thirty-something, single man who lived at home with his parents. She suspected he had money. However, Alfonso was in no condition to appreciate her attention as he was happily sedated. Nurse Leah kept Alfonso's pillows fluffed. She did not wait until his saline bags were empty; she replaced them prior to the last drop donating itself to Alfonso's recovery. Nurse Leah ignored the old gentleman sharing the room due to a mild cardiac incident. The old gentleman finally exhausted himself, dropped off, and left her in peace to attend the prized specimen in the next bed.

The following morning, Alfonso came out of his mild sedation, opened his eyes, and saw a complete stranger peering back at him. Shakily, Alfonso lifted one hand to touch the face. It was real. Alfonso let out a breath.

Nurse Leah reared back, told herself that stunningly bad breath could be sweetened, and said, "Good morning, Mr. Hoffmann."

"Do I know you?"

"I am Nurse Leah of Presbyterian Hospital, where you have spent the night. Now you know me! How do you feel?"

"Pretty good actually. What happened?"

"The doctor will explain that to you when he comes in. May I send your parents in?"

"Yes, of course!"

Angelica Gertrudis and Reigh together explained what had happened

43

to Alfonso the night before. Alfonso was clearly astonished at what he heard; his brain chemistry had scrambled his memory. Doctor Kaufman entered, examined Alfonso while conversing with him, then turned to his parents, and pronounced him "Fit to go home; to take it easy for a few days." Nurse Leah, who had gone off duty, still attended to Alfonso, and offered to get a wheelchair. She helped Alfonso get dressed while checking him out prior to his checking out. Nurse Leah slipped her name and phone number into Alfonso's coat pocket. Alfonso was thrilled as his nurse and family walked and rolled to the pick-up area.

Angelica Gertrudis, eying Nurse Leah with suspicion and jealously, although she would never admit to the latter, said, "I can wait here for his father to bring the car around. I'm sure you have other duties."

"Oh, I'm off duty. I don't mind waiting."

Alfonso, still groggy, and unused to being at the center of things, was riding cloud five. Cloud nine was yet to come.

For the next three days, Angelica Gertrudis, the mother grizzly bear, watched Alfonso like a cub. Alfonso was untroubled by dreams. On Monday, she allowed Alfonso to go to work only after countless admonishments and contingency plans were firmly planted in Alfonso's memory. Alfonso had no trouble driving to work. His co-workers, who had missed Alfonso because the work was backing up, greeted him cordially, but were merely relieved to get the bottleneck widened. For his part, Alfonso dived into the work with the initial enthusiasm of Lucy and Ethel standing before the chocolate conveyer. Unlike Lucy and Ethel, he was not overwhelmed by the tasks before him. Alfonso had a great day. It was all chocolates to him.

A tireless, undistracted worker, Alfonso had caught-up with the work by end-of-day Wednesday. Feeling the satisfaction only an accountant could feel, he began gathering his belongings: lunch bucket, Binaca, keys, coat, pepper spray, Bic pen, and discovered a piece of torn paper in his coat pocket. Alfonso had to read it twice, put it down, and reread it a third time before it fired the correct neurons, and he recollected what this was. He smiled, and then drove home.

By Friday, Alfonso was thinking of calling Nurse Leah. On Saturday, Nurse Leah called Alfonso at work. She obviously got the number from his file. This was not playing by hospital rules, but Alfonso was too attractive to Nurse Leah not to bend the rules. The conversation was awkward. Alfonso was as familiar with this terrain as he was with the trails on Sandia Peak. He had never been on that mountain either. Nurse Leah took the situation into her control and did all the talking. Somehow, Alfonso had a date that night. As he had never had a date, Alfonso drove home with his mind in the ether. He stopped in his driveway, shocked to be home. Alfonso rushed inside to confide in his parents.

"Stay calm."

"Take a shower."

"Use some of your Dad's cologne."

"Pick her up on time."

"Open the car door for her."

"Take her to a nice restaurant."

And so on and so forth; Alfonso was as ready as he would ever be for his first date. He drove to Nurse Leah's apartment. Alfonso was three and one half minutes early. He waited in the car. At precisely seven, Alfonso rang the doorbell. Nurse Leah asked Alfonso inside, made him comfortable, and poured them each a Cosmopolitan—a cocktail Nurse Leah considered a lost art. Alfonso rarely imbibed alcohol but went with the flow of events in a cheerful, compliant way.

What happened next was a long stressful process over which we shall draw a curtain of charity for poor Alfonso. It should suffice to say that Alfonso was alternately shocked, delighted, and challenged—repeat cycle as necessary. Alfonso entered this house merely an adult. He emerged a rooster.

Nurse Leah straightened Alfonso's tie and asked, "Where shall we go to dinner?"

Alfonso loved Franny's, everyone does; however, Franny's was not a restaurant where one took a date. Off they went with Alfonso oblivious to the question of whether Franny's was a suitable venue for a first date, especially given its prelude. Nurse Leah had no complaints and seemed to enjoy herself.

When Alfonso drove Nurse Leah home, he walked her to her door as instructed by his parents. Nurse Leah planted a long, deep kiss on Alfonso that left him winded.

"See you again, Alfonso."

Alfonso noted that this was not presented as a question.

"Good night," and Alfonso returned to his car and drove home—now on cloud nine.

The house lights were still on when Alfonso reached home. His parents did not stay up past nine or nine-thirty, so, naturally, Alfonso thought, "What's wrong?" Angelica Gertrudis and Reigh were in blue light watching a re-run of *The Jerry Springer Show*. Alfonso gave a visible shudder at the sight and flashed back to his debilitating dream.

"Are you all right?"

His mother got up from her chair to help him in.

"Yes, I'm fine."

It was not such a big lie.

"Sit down. We're watching Jerry Springer!"

Alfonso sat down in his usual spot and pretended to watch two women assault each other. His parents pretended not to be bursting with questions, and pretended to be entertained by the assaults.

Alfonso grew restless, "Well, I think I'll go to bed. What time is church tomorrow?"

"Ten as always."

"Good night, then."

Angelica Gertrudis and Reigh sat alternating their sights between Jerry Springer, Alfonso's bedroom door, and furtive glances at each other.

Angelica Gertrudis spoke, "I think it went well."

"Yes. Let's go to bed."

And they did.

At work, Alfonso's colleagues noticed some changes. Alfonso might arrive at seven-thirty-two instead of seven-thirty. He might leave work on an equally varying schedule. He was wearing cologne. He would sometimes lose sight of his work and stare vacantly into space. The gossip machine went into overdrive, but Alfonso never noticed it.

When it went into hyperdrive, the woman in the closest cubicle to his own, Julie Ann, asked Alfonso, "What's new?"

As Julie Ann had never done more than good morning and good night him, Alfonso looked around to ascertain, as any good accountant would do, to whom the voice was speaking.

When Alfonso realized that Julie Ann was speaking to him over the cubicle wall he lamely could only cough up, "Pardon me?"

"I said what's new?" Julie Ann smiled.

The office murmur dropped to the sound of the air being conditioned. Goggle-eyed, "What . . . do . . . you . . . mean 'what's new?'"

There was giggling in the background following by shushing.

"We never talk. You seem different lately, so I was wondering what's new in your life."

"Oh."

There was long pause. Alfonso was totally unsure about how to answer. Finally, he said, "I'm wearing cologne."

The entire office erupted into laughter, and Julie Ann disappeared on her side of the wall.

The following weeks were a snow flurry of activity in the middle of June. Alfonso had never been as productive at work, despite his bouts of staring into space and the whispers behind cubicle walls. His dates with Nurse Leah were as varied as they were frequent. Alfonso's savings were slightly diminishing, *but he didn't care*. He was a rooster. Father Reigh was unimaginably happy. He had more time alone with his wife, and his son finally had the full life he needed. Only Angelica Gertrudis was not entirely happy. She saw less and less of her fledgling, knowing that with every date Alfonso became more independent. Angelica Gertrudis knew in her heart that she could not hold Alfonso in her nest forever. Let's face it; he had outgrown the nest by many years. Alfonso might even need a new bedspread.

Alfonso, being a man of predictable habits, had problems working Nurse Leah into his well-ordered life. Nurse Leah managed those problems for Alfonso with ease. Angelica Gertrudis had trouble acknowledging new signs of life in Alfonso's laundry. She mentioned this to Reigh.

"Angelica Gertrudis, he's a grown man. This was overdue. Just ignore it."

Not to speak of it further is not the same as ignoring it. Angelica Gertrudis did the former.

One evening in July, while Nurse Leah and Alfonso were lying in bed exhausted from their labors, Nurse Leah popped the question, "Fonzie, can I borrow some money?"

"Borrow money? How much money? Are you in trouble of some kind?"

"No. No trouble. I just get a little behind on my rent sometimes."

"Oh. How much do you need Leah?"

"Five hundred."

Alfonso wrote her a check. Nurse Leah insisted that he make it out to

"Cash." It was the beginning of a beautiful financial relationship. Alfonso got a relationship, and Nurse Leah got financing.

Alfonso lending Nurse Leah money started him thinking. The only money he ever spent on Nurse Leah was dinner and a movie. Alfonso started buying Nurse Leah gifts. First, it was a simple silver bracelet. Then it was turquoise earrings. This went on with Nurse Leah's undying gratitude with each gift. The money lending continued as well. Nurse Leah suggested pieces of jewelry for the proximate gift. Alfonso, only too happy to make Nurse Leah happy, was happy for the suggestions. And so it went until the day that Nurse Leah suggested that Alfonso should give her her own debit/ATM card to save everyone time. Alfonso was not stupid. He knew that this was risky given that he and Nurse Leah had only been dating for a short time. But love, or infatuation, was stronger than prudence and good judgment. They went to the bank together.

Theodora Mercedes had a duty. As the third daughter in a line of third daughters, each with the gift, she was obligated to consult with her sister. Innocenta dropped her mother at the Rail Runner station, and Angelica Gertrudis picked her up in Albuquerque. They lunched at The Cornichon. They laughed when they remembered that as children their parents had taken them to California. Somewhere near the coast was a little drive-up restaurant with a giant metal sculpture on top. It was called The Enormous Artichoke. Neither of them could remember anything about the food, only the delightful oversized artichoke. When their laughter subsided, Theodora Mercedes looked gravely at her sister.

"Angelica Gertrudis, I have had a disturbing vision."

Angelica Gertrudis was always ambivalent about the gift. She neither wanted it nor was repelled by it. In instances like this, she was curious.

"Tell me."

Theodora Mercedes told about the vision, its effect on Innocenta and her interpretation of it, and what she believed it actually meant.

"I believe that your son, Alfonso, is in danger."

Angelica Gertrudis was silent.

"When did this vision take place?"

"I can tell you exactly: the night of June 1. Sister, what's wrong!?"

Angelica Gertrudis had fainted.

Theodora Mercedes drove Angelica Gertrudis' car back to the Hoffmann house. Angelica Gertrudis had refused any treatment by the paramedics and insisted that she wanted to go home. Reigh was frantic at the story of his wife's collapse. She refused to go to bed but settled into her chair.

"Please tell Reigh of your vision."

Theodora Mercedes told an abbreviated but articulate version—no sense in wasting details on someone not of the line.

"What's to be done about it?"

"Reigh, I don't know. Let me ask you this; do you know where Alfonso is now?"

"He's at work."

"And later?"

"He will probably be with Nurse Leah. He's always with Nurse Leah."

"Then Reigh, Nurse Leah may be the key to keeping Alfonso from harm. Will you please drive me to the Rail Runner?"

That evening, while Alfonso and Nurse Leah were cosseted under the sheet, Angelica Gertrudis and Reigh were planning to intervene. By midnight, they had "a plan." They would need a police detective friend and a gun. They had neither. OK, they would start with the gun in the morning. Angelica Gertrudis and Reigh went to bed anxious for their son; but they had "a plan." Both slept uncomfortably with strange dreams and chanting occupying the space where sound rest should have dwelt. Neither awoke refreshed, but there was work to do. They had to save Alfonso.

CHAPTER FOUR
Barrington Wilson Silverton Vigil

In one week, Barrington Wilson Silverton Vigil had gone from an obscure paleolinguist, working on an esoteric project, and closeted homosexual to being the happiest man in Santa Fe. He was "out" to his family, had a boyfriend, and had no secrets, at last, from his mother. Barrington was confounded by the measure of his underestimation of Theodora Mercedes. She not only approved of his relationship, but she appeared to revel in it. In the most embarrassing moment of his life, his mother met his boyfriend *and* their lover. Theodora Mercedes had kept her composure during this moment and Barrington was sure that he had seen a flash of lust cross her face when she met James. Or had he? Barrington would never know with certainty as he would never revisit that moment again—at least, not with his mother.

Now, lying on his bed with these thoughts, he rose and went to his desk. Barrington got his diary out, smiled as he replayed some memories, opened it, and began to write:

One week, and I am still in love with James. I have been with him four times in seven days. James makes me feel like my life before him was so, what's the right word??? Meaningless! Yes, I had that love affair in Guanajuato. Gustavo was warm and giving, but how did I know it was not the real thing? I really do not know. James is so different. It feels like we have always known each other, yet we discover new things every time we're together. More. It feels like we have been together before— another lifetime??? It feels right, anyway. God, I love this man!

My work project is daunting me more and more each day. The people from San Idelfonso Pueblo are trying to help, but this project is hopeless. We have identified words from the San Marcos Pueblo that are already known. Yes, the hill near the ruined Pueblo is named Chalchihuitl, but this may be an Uto-Aztecan word in an Eastern Keresan language area. In any case, this name was never lost to history. So why am I doing this? What's the good? We will never be able to reconstruct this dead dialect. Even if we do (like that's likely), what's the point? Will anyone ever speak the San Marcos dialect on a daily basis??? NO! There must be a better way to use my skills and knowledge. This project just isn't it. I love having total control over what I do. I know it's a luxury few working people have. I have to make a decision—soon!

The important thing about this week is—I am not afraid anymore. I never realized how much fear I lived in until now. But I'm not afraid anymore.

But Barrington was delusional. Having lived most of his life with two or more strong women, Barrington thought himself an equal cog in the fine-tuned machine that was the Silverton-de Baca House. He had no true sense of how different he was from the women. Barrington, if asked, would have pointed to his homosexuality as the prime suspect in defining how he was different, or even "weaker," than Theodora Mercedes and Innocenta. In reality, Barrington was slowly drowning in the deep end of the swimming pool. He had started at four years old and had stayed there since. Yes, he had accumulated some years but only recently had gained a single-foot on a firm step.

It was the Fourth of July. The family was gathering in Albuquerque to celebrate Independence Day. The family crowd forced Barrington's parents to stay overnight in a motel that had a pool. Barrington's three older sisters could swim. Barrington was essentially a toddler, told by his father, "Stay away from the deep end of the pool!" Barrington thought he was doing as he was told. He liked the buoyancy of the water and its warmth. While bouncing up and down on his toes, he was imperceptibly moving towards the sloping bottom that ended in the deep end. Without warning he was gasping for breath, panicked, and the increasing slope was pulling him farther into deep water. Only his eyes, fixed on his father, could tell what Barrington was experiencing. His father, thinking himself wise, let Barrington go on his slide toward deep-water oblivion "to teach him a lesson." Just before Barrington caught what could have been his last breath, his father pushed him roughly to the shallow end. "That'll teach you!"

Barrington could never express the trauma of being taken by surprise by an unrelenting slope and choking water, let alone the unremitting helplessness. The lessons Barrington actually learned were to panic and to hate the man who had knowingly prolonged his torment. He never trusted his father again. A love died the same day that a life was saved and the Law of Unintended Consequences decisively asserted itself.

What Barrington couldn't appreciate was that he had spent the next quarter century bouncing on the sloping pool bottom just short of drowning. Even the strengths of Theodora Mercedes could not protect him from himself. As a child, he was short for his age, pretty, "artistic," and "brainy"—the adjectives that mean one thing to adults were labeled bats others used to beat the helpless Barrington. His father's death neither helped nor diminished his suffering; his father had withheld his love early on. Perhaps he recognized that Barrington, the toddler, was gay. At least he would not have to look at the man who almost let him drown "to teach him a lesson." Barrington retreated. Life got worse. He took drugs. Life got worse. He panicked. He got high on alcohol and marijuana. Life got much worse. Barrington was at that slippery slope for most of his life. Only Theodora Mercedes' aggressive actions when he was a junior in high school had saved him. He went to rehab and counseling. Theodora Mercedes took him to both five days per week for two years. While he learned to cope more effectively, Barrington never confessed his self-perceived sins: hating his father, being pretty, smart, queer—and hating himself for all of it. At least he quit the bad habits and got straight As in school.

If Barrington could see Innocenta the way she really was, then he would never have thought himself an equal. In truth, Innocenta was the artist of her life; specifically, a painter. Innocenta was mistress of her palette and brush. She would have described her life as a paint-by-numbers canvas, but she was more complex an artist. Innocenta was modest and masterly. Even when she married, Innocenta was painting-in an expected part of the picture. There were colors of her own choosing for the wedding, other colors for the new in-laws, still more for the children. When her marriage failed, Innocenta was painting in sorrowful Lenten purple. When George left her without a word, the brush strayed outside the lines and formed a prominent streak on her canvass. It was only when the streak was brushed that she realized the love had died. Had Barrington been a painter, he would have thrown the paints and brushes out the window. The canvas would have been burned. But Innocenta used the streak of purple like an exclamation point, and then surrounded it with the blue of hope and the green of better tomorrows. She then put a sunny yellow glaze over the whole effect to signify her conquest over paint and life. Innocenta would then take this canvas of her mind, hoist it up the mainmast, and sail to a new destiny of her choosing; Capitan of her ship. No, Barrington was nothing like Innocenta—to say nothing of Mother.

Barrington was not afraid anymore. What this meant, but not clearly to Barrington, was that for now he could stop asking, "Why me?" He had his family, James, a job he loved, and all the more welcomed due to its tardiness, acceptance. He put down his diary and went to his open window. He looked up at the stars. Why had it been so long since he had looked at the stars? Barrington craned his neck up and left. He saw Altair. How many years had passed without Barrington *seeing* Altair? Many a mere glance at the sky had not included recognition or appreciation. Barrington wasn't sure whether to laugh at himself or cry at lost opportunities. He was too happy to cry; he laughed at himself. Surely, tomorrow's sky would be a shade of never-before-seen blue! Barrington went to bed and slept peacefully.

Sunday morning, James and Barrington met the rest of the family at the Social Liberal Church. James was spiritual but not particularly attracted to daunting dogmas or their dogs. The Social Liberals were an attractive bunch, but James thought they needed to work on their messaging. They stressed a lack of unified belief and, certainly, no dogma. James could see that Social Liberals were more than this and that their message lacked a core. Why didn't they stress their responsible search for truth and the mutual support in that search? Surely, that would make a stronger, more compelling and attractive message. But, this was not something James felt compelled to fix. For now, he was content to appreciate the open and accepting atmosphere.

Barrington held James' hand throughout the sermon, "Wake Up and Live!" based on words of the seer, Bob Marley. The minister discussed how some people get into a rut; the rut causes them to complicate their minds with hate, mischief, and jealousy. But each rut is an opportunity to look up, unbury one's thoughts, and live one's vision. Hence, "Wake Up and Live!" To James, this resonated with his Diné upbringing and spiritual view of life. One's life was either in balance or out. If out, you could be in a rut; Diné curing rites could put a person back in balance. James was happy with the resonance and impressed that this family had brought him here. On the Navajo reservation, he might be attending a mainline Protestant service filled with the white man's dogma (only if he bothered to attend). Here, he sat in a congregation of free-thinkers who quoted a black, Jamaican, Rastafarian sage.

Over lunch, Barrington asked James what he thought of the service.

"I greatly enjoyed it. The people don't seem to mind us, or frankly, even notice us. The sermon was very good."

"I'm glad you felt comfortable, James. The church is pretty important to our family and (pause) I hope you become a part of my family—someday."

Then Barrington laughed nervously. Had he been too bold to speak so frankly and so soon? What if James felt pressured and ran away from him? Barrington blushed, and he felt like a fool.

"Why are you embarrassed, Barrington? Your thoughts are honorable and welcoming."

He allowed himself a slight smile here.

"I am open and look forward to tomorrow and the next day. But for now, let's enjoy the present."

Now, Barrington smiled with pleasure at James' words but continued to blush, as Barrington would put it, "like a girl." They ordered water and coffee, and then perused their menus.

"Barrington, can I ask you a question about Social Liberals?"

"Sure, what?"

"Well, we Navajos are not people who talk a lot or unnecessarily, so I understand a certain measured quiet and respectful distance."

"Yeah?"

"I do notice that when the congregation gets together they barely talk to each other. There are a few conversations, but those strike me as between people who will talk together regularly. On the rez, we would *never* think of not greeting our elders, immediate families, our clan members, or our tribal leaders. Yet, this group of people seems to isolate from each other even though they are attending the same church and hearing the same message. I don't understand."

"Oh that. Social Liberals are a strange group. That's all. Somehow, most of them never developed what you would call 'social skills.' It's a mystery to me too. There are lots of people in the congregation whom I've known my entire life, yet they rarely, oh hell, they *never* greet me. When I was a kid, I thought they hated me just like everyone else. My mother assured me frequently that it was *not personal*. Of course, I didn't believe her, so she told me to observe them ignoring everybody. It was true. They didn't, and don't, talk to anyone. It wasn't personal. It's funny, but in a way, it made me feel normal in that group. That's odd, isn't it?"

"Maybe not so odd."

"So, my answer is: it's not personal, and Social Liberals are high on social justice but have zero social skills—it's just the way it is."

"I accept that, but it's mighty odd."

"Let's order!"

"OK, but one last thing. I really like the congregation and what it stands for. Imagine, using Bob Marley as the basis for a sermon! I like it there, Barrington."

"I'm glad. I like it there too. Let's order."

That afternoon, Barrington took James to the Language Institute. He showed James his work in progress on the San Marcos dialect.

"The people from San Idelfonso Pueblo are nice and try to help, but this project is hopeless. Even if I could reconstruct this dialect, what good would it do? There is no more San Marcos Pueblo or people. Why am I doing this?"

"You are really handsome when you speak passionately, Barrington."

"What?"

"You are—"

"I heard you crazy man!"

"Crazy, huh? Crazy enough to grab you and kiss you!"

James made his move towards Barrington, and Barrington flinched.

"Someone might see us!"

"It's Sunday, no one is here, and what do you care—I thought you were out?"

Barrington's response was muffled by a passionate kiss.

By three o'clock, they were in James' studio. James was showing Barrington his latest project. It was a commission from a Northern Pueblo showing the tribal leaders of 1680 being led in revolt by Popé. The clay model was small, but the finished larger-than-life bronze would stand in the immense lobby of the Pueblo's new hotel. James betrayed his emotions when describing the piece.

There was a pause, "And can you imagine; they asked a Navajo to do this sculpture. I am humbled and so proud all at once. We Navajos, the Apache, and Comanche were the Pueblos' worst enemies. Look at us now!"

James looked down with humility. Barrington, with his Silverton-de Baca intuition, understood. He silently hugged this incredible man.

"Navajo men aren't supposed to do that."

"Do what?"

"Almost cry."

"My Navajo man can do that whenever he needs to. No other Navajo need ever know. God, I love you, James!"

James was so proud of being loved by Barrington that he teared up. James and Barrington were breaking every rule they thought they knew. Yet, it felt good, right, fulfilling. A revolution was playing out in two dancing spirits. Had they been painters instead of a paleolinguist and a sculptor, they would now be painting outside the lines—and doing so with childlike enthusiasm.

That evening, before dinner was served, Theodora Mercedes, at her most powerful and hypnotic, read Walt Whitman to her assembled family. "The Untold Want" is singular among Whitman's poetry for its brevity and simple message. It has only two lines and the second was Theodora Mercedes' favorite of all his lines; "Now Voyager, sail thou forth to seek and find." The line had been her mantra, her touchstone, since she first read it in high school. It was the inspiration for some of her boldest decisions, course corrections, and revolutions of thought. The family was silent, taking the poetry in, and wondering, "Why this? Why now?" They knew nothing of the line's history with Theodora Mercedes. After the last word Theodora Mercedes was silent and appeared to be meditating. Innocenta, Bart, Barrington, and James all seemed to understand with astonishing simultaneity—they had all left port "to seek and find."

How did Theodora Mercedes convey, as with numinous powers, this clear-as-water message to four at once? The gift had more to offer than any of them imagined. But how could they imagine? Only Innocenta had any knowledge of the gift and its metered-out secrets. As the message reached her, Innocenta had a starburst revelation—the gift would someday be hers alone, and she would inherit its ways and untold depths. She wondered if she would handle the gift in its full flower as gracefully as Theodora Mercedes. This was not an unreasonable question. Innocenta knew that her mother was extraordinary.

The Very Catholic Consuelo walked in with the first course, artichokes with curried mayonnaise for dipping, and thought that she had interrupted a séance. Although her hands were full, The Very Catholic Consuelo crossed herself in her mind and started reciting *The Lord's Prayer*. Theodora Mercedes shot her that disapproving look, and The Very Catholic Consuelo hurried out to finish the second course and adjust—OK, hide,—her attitude. Barrington, who avidly followed the unspoken messages between his mother and The Very Catholic Consuelo, was amused and eagerly

56

awaited the cook's return. The rest of dinner was delicious and almost uneventful.

Raul Theodore announced that he was working out the half-life of Element 128.

James, losing his poker face, searched his memory of the Periodic Table, leaned over to Barrington, and whispered, "That element hasn't been discovered yet!"

Barrington, usually impressed but not too distracted by his nephew's announcements and results, turned from James and stared at Raul Theodore. Raul Theodore was already well into his calculations and couldn't see him.

That evening, Barrington and James excused themselves and ascended to the third floor. Barrington led James to the window, and they crowded themselves into the frame to examine the stars. A coyote cried in the distance, magnifying the effect of the quiet between lonely calls.

"That one straight up is Altair. What do Navajos call it?"

"Sometimes, just Sister Star; sometimes, just beautiful. Right now, it's just beautiful."

An hour later, in their spent relaxation, cuddled together under the sheet, James asked, "What would you like to do?"

"About what?"

"About your project."

"Oh. I don't know. I can't see continuing with the San Marcos Project."

"What are the best uses of your skills?"

"What do you mean?"

"One reason I am a sculptor is that I studied engineering, including metals. So I have a certain artistic talent and knowledge of specific materials. So, I sculpt in metal. I'm asking you the same question but about you."

"Yes, what a great question. Maybe you put in words what I am struggling with."

There was a pause while Barrington let the revelatory question, twist its way through the dusty volumes of his mind.

"It helps to discover the right question, James. Thanks. This will help me but I need to think before I can answer."

Waking up refreshed, Barrington discovered his bed empty and James emerging from the bathroom fully dressed.

"Barrington, I'm skipping the gym this morning and going straight to my studio. Our visit there yesterday gave me some ideas I need to act on before I forget them."

Barrington sat up in bed, "I was just going to say the same thing! I'm going straight to work. Your words of wisdom gave me the kick in the pants that I needed."

They kissed and James left.

On his way downstairs, Barrington ran into Innocenta, "What!? No Bart?"

"No. He was preoccupied with something last night and went—something about confronting his father. I don't know . . . Where's James?"

"Left for his studio; he has some ideas he wants to work on. I'm off to the language lab myself."

Barrington greeted his mother, Theodora Mercedes, and The Very Catholic Consuelo as he grabbed an apple and headed out.

Barrington changed CDs in his car. He needed Bob Marley's *Natty Dread* album to see what he needed to see. By the time he pulled into his parking space, the apple was uneaten and Barrington knew what to do, other than eat the apple. He bounced out of his car with renewed vigor for his professional direction.

Friday night, James took Barrington to a high-end restaurant near The Railyard for wine and dinner. Barrington was told to dress up but was not told of their destination. Barrington wondered, "What's up?" but contentedly went along. How bad could it be? The ambience at The Cutting Board was subdued, plain, and elegant. The hostess showed them to a table in a cozy corner. James ordered Vueve Cliquot.

"Wow! I love Vueve Cliquot. What's the occasion?"

"Not yet, Young Man!"

Barrington ordered the braised osso buco. James ordered the Muscovy duck breast. They shared each other's entrees without any embarrassment and savored, giggled, and, by their behaviors, were the only patrons there. Chef Jeff Florham came out to greet them. Not only was James a well-known sculptor, a Santa Fe celebrity, but word had gotten to the kitchen how much enjoyment was being had at table three. James introduced Jeff and Barrington. Jeff sat down and ordered cognacs for all of them despite it being a busy Friday night. They made pleasant small talk, the chef listened to renewed kudos for his cuisine, then excused himself and left. James paid, and they exited.

James drove to Museum Hill. They got out of the car and found a bench in the courtyard of the Museum of International Folk Art. James the Tall put his arm around Barrington and tightened the space between them. They gazed at the stars in silence. The Milky Way was particularly luminous and mysterious.

"Do you see that cluster of stars?"

"Yes, the Pleiades; the Seven Sisters."

"We call them *Dilyéhé*, the Sparkling Particles. They are associated with many aspects of Navajo cosmology, but most importantly, at least in my opinion, they are the center of the skies. They represent order, the power of the Black God, and the illuminating power of the god."

"Black God?"

"The Black God is a good god; a powerful collection of demi-gods. Hence, again, the center and the power of the gods."

"That's beautiful, James."

Barrington could not help believing that this was leading somewhere. The entire evening was leading *somewhere*. Barrington looked at James' profile, waiting.

"Barrington, when we went to your language lab and my studio on Sunday, our connections became deeper for me. We are linked hogan to hogan, our houses. We are merging spirits."

Barrington looked at James' profile in rapt admiration as James continued speaking while looking at *Dilyéhé*.

James then turned to look at Barrington directly, "Barrington, I don't know what the proper term is. I want to be with you for the rest of my life. Will you accept this ring as a symbol of our friendship?"

"Friendship? James, I love you!"

"Yes, I love you, but am afraid to name it in case you do not feel the same."

"James, I love you and feel the same way. I never want to be without you. I want us to be like *Dilyéhé*, always together and shining. I accept your ring but I don't have a ring for you!"

"I took the risk and made matching bands."

James smiled and it appeared that he finally breathed. He produced two rings which shone in the dark but were otherwise undetailed. Each put the other's ring on their respective fingers. They kissed passionately and teared up. Barrington and James were overcome by emotions and by being drawn up to join *Dilyéhé*.

Later, in Barrington's room, they examined their rings. They were gold, inlaid with black opals, jet, turquoise, and a bright green garnet. Of course, James' was much bigger in circumference.

"You made these!?"

"Yes. It was easy once I decided on the design. I worked like crazy all week to get them done. They were polished this afternoon."

Barrington gazed at and was lost in his ring for half a minute, then from far away, "No words."

James smiled. "You have the heart of a Navajo."

Saturday morning, Barrington and James stayed in their room talking. Barrington explained that he had abandoned the San Marcos Pueblo Project and had spent the week doing some research.

"In 2008, a Native American of Alaska died. She had the unlikely name of Marie Smith Jones and was the last known speaker of Eyak. When she died, Eyak died with her."

Barrington would now devote his skills to preventing a recurrence locally. He would now apply his skills in helping the San Buenaventura Pueblo preserve its North Tiwa language. While the orthography was in place, more of the vocabulary and grammar needed to be captured. The tribal leaders were enthusiastic as less than fifty people still spoke the language.

"There's all that work to be done, grants to apply for, then creating the curriculum for teaching the children and adults. After that, I'll record their myths and other stories so that the children can read them for themselves in their original language. The tribal leaders even want me to translate some classics into their language."

"Barrington, that's incredible. You found it!"

"Yes, I did. I couldn't have done it if you hadn't spotted my problem and clarified my thinking."

"This will do so much good for Native Americans. Another language will be preserved. Barrington, you make me so proud for you!"

Barrington's grin threatened to engulf his entire face.

"I have been busy too."

"Yes, these beautiful rings were a lot of work."

"Yes, but that was, what's the cliché—a labor of love? What I mean is that your visit to my studio got me to thinking that my design for Popé and the leaders of the other Pueblos was not right. I studied Rodin in art school and chose the *Burghers of Calais* as my inspiration. But after our visit, I realized that it just didn't work. The burghers are scattered in the sculpture and only unified by their shackles and dejection as they go to their deaths. Look at this."

James went to his gym bag and pulled out a clay model, many times smaller than the finished sculpture.

"I rearranged the figures into a phalanx with Popé at the head and larger than the rest. But they not only form an arrowhead, they are touching. Each chief has one hand on his weapon and the other on the shoulder of the chief in front of him. It's more symbolic of their strength and solidarity. See how the entire sculpture tapers from Popé, larger-than-life, at the head of phalanx to the women at the back supporting their leaders? It's a more powerful form in countless ways."

James was beaming.

"James, that not only makes so much sense, it's also more beautiful than the model I saw in the studio."

"You did it."

"Me!?"

"When we were in my studio, our spirits danced. That's when I knew how much I love you, and it made me look at the old model with new eyes."

"That's very powerful, James."

"I've already met with the tribal leaders, and they prefer the new design!"

The intimate interplay was shattered by a child's voice reciting a long number at ear-shattering volume. Evidently, Raul Theodore had finished calculating the half-life of the yet undiscovered Element 128. It had taken him a week and the Sparkling Particles danced in the night.

"That must have been one huge problem to solve!"

"That's not the only one, Barrington. I am going to the rez tomorrow to visit my mother. I want you to come with me."

Barrington, to hide his panic, abruptly had to urinate and ran to the toilet. He returned and verified, "You want me to come with you because you're going to tell your mother you're gay."

"Yes."

"Holy Mother of God!"

James broke out in laughter at this surprising Catholic oath. They laughed together and fell into each other's arms unknowing that little Raul Theodore's thundering voice was not the only catastrophe awaiting.

CHAPTER FIVE

Theodora Mercedes Silverton Vigil

U nlike Barrington who preferred the romance of a handwritten, book-bound diary, Theodora Mercedes Silverton Vigil kept her journal on a state-of-the-art iMac. She was recording the state of her family, updated to this very same cheerful, sun-filled hour. Raul Theodore had solved, at least to her satisfaction, theoretical problems orbiting an undiscovered element. The Unremarkables, thank heavens, were still predictably unremarkable. Barrington and James had exchanged handmade rings of subtle beauty in symbolic, mutual union. They had made a trip to the rez to visit James' mother, although she had no knowledge of any outcome of that exhausting journey. Innocenta and Bart were spending time together, still in the throes of courtly love despite their declarations to marry. The Very Catholic Consuelo had only needed correction once during this entire week, thus marking this an unusual week. In short, The Silverton-de Baca House continued to rest on its considerable foundations solidly, upright, and in proper order. Theodora Mercedes insisted—no ensured—that this house continued to operate in an open-minded, equable, and finely tuned custom. No racehorse, Silverton-de Baca House was her show horse. And, Theodora Mercedes' equable nature would be tested again.

Theodora Mercedes had switched to email. She was writing to her minister at the Social Liberal Church with a pithy suggestion for a sermon, the wisdom of Kurt Vonnegut. Theodora Mercedes had finished her greetings to the minister when The Very Catholic Consuelo came running into her study without so much as a knock.

"There is a man downstairs demanding to see you. He is very angry Doña Theodora!"

Theodora Mercedes could hear heavy feet in solid boots pacing downstairs.

"Who is this man, Consuelo? I will not go down unless I know who he is and what he wants. I don't give audience to ill-mannered men who practically break into my house. Find out or show him out!"

Theodora Mercedes was mentally bitch-slapping whomever the intruder was. The Very Catholic Consuelo, recognizing the cobra-poised-to-strike look in Doña Theodora's eyes, froze. She was afraid of the man, but she was more afraid of Doña Theodora. She turned and slinked out like a frightened cat, reclosing the heavy door behind her.

Theodora Mercedes could hear yelling downstairs, a man's voice but no other, followed by quick and heavy footfalls coming up the stairs. The blood shot to Theodora Mercedes' face and woe awaited he who entered. Then he did—trailed by The Very Catholic Consuelo like a rag mannequin behind him. Theodora Mercedes had reached the center of the room when the door swung open with such force it hit the doorstop and bounced shut again. She was certain that it hit whomever it was in the face. Then, nothing happened—nothing for a full minute.

Theodora Mercedes strode to the door and opened it. Sprawled before her was a late-middle-aged man laid out like a corpse on top of a struggling Very Catholic Consuelo. The man clearly had been stunned by the heavy oak battering and was holding his nose. His face was splattered with blood. Now the blood ran over onto The Very Catholic Consuelo's cheek and she screamed and struggled violently, but he was like dead weight. Theodora Mercedes strode to the bathroom, retrieved a towel, threw it on the man's face and rolled him off the panicked maid.

The Very Catholic Consuelo was unsure which to do first, breathe without the dead weight upon her or swipe at the blood on her face. She did both, without benefit of any decision, badly, and thrashed about like a rag doll. Theodora Mercedes got another towel, wet it with cold water, and returned to place it on The Very Catholic Consuelo's face. The mild shock worked its intended magic, and she calmed down while wiping her face.

"Consuelo, take this man downstairs and get him cleaned-up. Please change your clothing. It makes a bad impression, and I would prefer that this beast, whoever he may be, not get a bad impression of my house."

Theodora Mercedes rued that there were no other men in the house. She had to help the maid get the man to his feet, lean him on The Very Catholic Consuelo, and start them down the stairs. At her feet, Doña Theodora could see a copious amount of poinsettia-colored liquid seeping into her pre-embargo Persian hall carpet. She retrieved yet a third towel, soaked this time, and placed it on the offending pool. Theodora Mercedes washed her hands thoroughly and returned to her study. As she approached the door to enter the study, the face of man, made of facial oils, appeared on the door about head height. Theodora Mercedes burst into laughter, entered the study, and collapsed into her chair. As she was a mass of circulating chemicals, not the least of which was adrenaline, Theodora Mercedes simply sat and focused her energies on reclaiming her equable demeanor.

Twenty minutes passed. Theodora Mercedes' chemical mix was approaching normal and there was a tiny knock on the study door.

"Come in."

It was The Very Catholic Consuelo, newly cleaned up, who opened the door. Theodora Mercedes leapt to her feet, rushed past the maid, closed the door, and then turned around. Saying nothing, she embraced Consuelo and held her; just held her.

"Consuelo, I am so sorry this had to happen to you. Are you all right?" she asked as she eased Consuelo into her own chair.

Consuelo burst into tears. Theodora Mercedes sat on the chair arm and continued to hold her respected, non-blood family member.

After five minutes or so, The Very Catholic Consuelo attempted to return to form, "I cleaned him up. He's drinking coffee in the kitchen. I had his name but now I can't remember it!"

"That's fine. Let's go down together and meet this man who frightened us. You have no need to be afraid anymore."

The last statement needn't have been said. The Very Catholic Consuelo knew her mistress well.

"I think that you should first introduce yourself, apologize for your barbaric behavior, and pay to have my carpet cleaned of your precious blood."

The man started to slam the cup on the table, seemed to reconsider, and calmly sat the cup down. He was bandaged, bruised, and his eyes were showing signs of turning black. Theodora Mercedes put her hand to her mouth to stifle a smile. The man looked beaten and pathetic. The man noticed and appeared to smile back.

"Serves me right for my temper," he muttered.

"Pardon me?"

"Uh, nothing. My name is Alfredo Bartram Rael de la Madrid."

Theodora instantly made his identification.

"I came here to discuss—no, tell you—to leave my son alone."

"What do you mean, 'leave him alone?'"

"I mean bringing up the past. We are good Roman Catholics and have been for generations. Bart knew nothing of our converso past until you put your big nose where it doesn't belong. Now Bart keeps asking questions, trying to dig deeper into what was forgotten history. He was raised and continues to be a good, practicing Catholic. You have done my family no good."

Theodora Mercedes sat down, "Mr. de la Madrid, would you like more coffee?"

"Yes, please."

The Very Catholic Consuelo was only too happy to jump to this task for a fellow believer, instantly forgiving him his previous trespasses. Theodora Mercedes, never missing anything however subtle, was not pleased with the celerity of her maid's attention to this man.

"Isn't your son, Bart, about forty years old? Wait! Don't answer yet. You are treating him like a child, and he is most emphatically not a child. Doesn't he have every right to know of his history, his heritage, to take pride in his family and its persecuted and illustrious past? Now, you may speak."

"Mrs. Vigil, what you say may be true, through your eyes. But you are not a part of my family. You have no right to push this subject. My wife and I have worked tirelessly to keep these things quiet, to raise the children as good Roman Catholics, and to forget the past. It is none of your business!"

"Mr. de la Madrid, while I can see your point—only to a certain point—you are not being reasonable. First, the cat is out. Second, Bart is a man and I still say that you are treating him like a child. Third, how do you know that he already didn't suspect, or know, or would have found out about the family past without my help?"

"I don't care whether you think I'm reasonable or not. Bart is my son and you are interfering in my family business. Please, please, stay out of this."

"Mr. de la Madrid, I need to ask you an important question. If you choose to answer, then I promise you that your words will not leave this room."

Mr. de la Madrid shifted uneasily in his chair, "Yes, go ahead."

"What are you so afraid of? What is so shameful?"

Mr. de la Madrid looked up and far away. His eyes got dewy and he swallowed some coffee.

"Mrs. Vigil, I told my children that their grandfather had passed away before they were born. My wife and I pursued Roman Catholicism with the eagerness of true believers, because we are. I am a Knight of Columbus. People think that times have changed, that people are more open and accepting. But they don't know the old Roman Catholic community. Whatever the archbishop may say or not say, the old guard would shun us if they knew of our background. There wouldn't be anything outward or obvious. People would forget to invite me to meetings. We would be left off the altar decoration duty list—by accident of course. I will be asked to help clean up after the Santa Fe Fiesta procession instead of marching in it as always."

"Your fellow church members don't sound like good Christians to me."

"That, again, is none of your business! They would be acting out of timeless traditions that have never died out."

"Fair enough. I don't have a right to judge other people, but you must admit it gives anyone cause to wonder about their motives."

"Perhaps. Do you think the Jews would be any more welcoming?"

"I wouldn't know."

"Well, they would not! Ask any Jewish convert. There is always an undercurrent that keeps them from being fully Jewish. People are people, no matter what."

"Why did you mention your children's grandfather?"

"I grew up in a very small village north of Taos. I will not name it for a reason—you will see. My parents were secretly practicing Jews. Ours was the only family left who clung to the Dead Law of Moses, as they say. When my mother died, I left. I became a Roman Catholic, met my wonderful wife, and embraced my faith with all my heart and soul."

"And your father is *not* dead, is he?"

"No. Now I'm afraid that Bart will dig far enough to find that out, then go find him. What do I do then, Mrs. Vigil?"

"I haven't the wisdom to hazard an answer, Mr. de la Madrid. I meant no harm and I promise you that this subject is dead between me and your son. If Bart brings up the subject, then I will change the subject. I promise."

"Thank you."

"Under the circumstances, Mr. de la Madrid, I ask you for your forgiveness and please do not worry about my carpet."

"Fair enough, Mrs. Vigil. Let's forgive each other and not part as enemies."

"Excellent. How is your nose?"

Mr. de la Madrid started to laugh. It hurt him mightily and he grabbed his face.

When he recovered he said, "Who would have guessed that that heavy door could pack such a punch?" Then he turned to The Very Catholic Consuelo, "I am very sorry to have barged-in like a rabid animal. I hope I didn't hurt you. Please forgive me."

The Very Catholic Consuelo merely smiled and nodded in agreement.

When Theodora Mercedes and The Very Catholic Consuelo were alone, they had coffee together.

"Consuelo, how do families get so complicated? It's sad what that man feels."

"I wouldn't know, Doña Theodora, but I feel for him and his discomfort."

"Why don't you take the rest of the day off, Consuelo? Didn't your niece just have another baby?"

"Yes! Number five! I would love to go help her."

"Go. By all the Gods of the Americas, you've earned it today."

The Very Catholic Consuelo cringed at the reference, grabbed her handbag, and left with a heartfelt thank you.

Theodora Mercedes nursed her coffee for a while longer and said to herself, "God, I love doing that!"

Theodora Mercedes was now alone in the house. She walked over to her sofa and lay down to relax and review the two-scene, one-act play that was performed that afternoon. The coffee prevented her from drifting off. Thirty minutes later, there was a gentle knock at the back door.

"What on earth . . . "

An ancient pick-up truck was parked in her side-yard and a very old man in a yarmulke stood at the door. Evidently, he was wearing the tallit with its special twined and knotted fringes known as tzitzit attached to its four corners. The fringes stuck out below his shirttails. Theodora Mercedes blanched.

"Are you all right?"

"Yes, I was just drowsy, that's all. You must be Mr. Moises Aaron Rael de la Madrid. Please come in."

"And you must be Mrs. Vigil, my grandson's future mother-in-law."

"Yes. Coffee?"

"No, thank you. I have one, and only one, cup every morning. But if you have tea . . . "

"Of course. Please sit down. No, not that chair. Take the armchair, please."

The teapot was heating.

"Did you drive down today?"

"Yes. I have work to do on the farm, but speaking with you has some urgency."

Theodora Mercedes was not ready for this, "Where is your farm, Mr. de la Madrid?"

"We call it San Bruno, but it doesn't really exist. It's just a collection of small farms and ranches north of Questa. In fact, we go to Questa to pick up our mail."

"I am a native and I've never heard of San Bruno."

"Like I said, it's not really even a village. Mrs. Vigil, my son has contacted me because he is afraid that his son, Bart, will find out that I am still alive. He wants me to ensure that Bart will never find me."

"Yes, I recently learned the truth of your family—at least your son's truth. How can I help, Mr. de la Madrid?"

"I wish to find Bart first."

Neither spoke, but they looked into each others' eyes for a few ticks of the kitchen clock. Only they knew what they were searching for.

"Your son will be unbelievably angry with both of us. He is the most guarded man I've ever met about who he was and who he is now. We will both pay dearly."

"How can I pay more dearly than I have already? Bart is forty-two years old by my reckoning, maybe older. I have never even laid eyes upon him. I feel like Mark Twain."

Theodora Mercedes laughed at this coy reference.

"It is one thing to upset your son, but Bart is engaged to my youngest daughter. I wouldn't want to jeopardize their relationship."

"If Bart is anything like his father or his father's father, then he will be stubborn, tough, and resilient. He will not just survive the ordeal, he will thrive with it. I want to meet him. I want to know him a little and then disappear again. I don't wish to ruin anyone's life. My son is stubborn. I complied with his wishes for almost five decades. How many years do I have left to me? Do you know what it's like not to know any of your grandchildren? To hell with my son. I would like to meet Bart."

Theodora Mercedes had never known such inner conflict in her life. She felt her equable nature oozing out in her tears. How could she turn down this ancient man who had been deprived of the love of his grandchildren? What price would her family pay if she got further involved? What harm would she do to Bart if she got involved or stayed out?

"I'm sorry to upset you. You are my only link to my grandson that I know. Alfredo mentioned to me that you were the reason this all started. I, an old man alone in this world, need you to follow through. Perhaps you owe it to us all, even Alfredo, to finish what you have begun."

"Never in my life would I have imagined the world of locked doors that would be behind an idle question; a mere curiosity. Now, I can't take it back. Yes, I'll help you, Mr. de la Madrid."

Theodora Mercedes found Bart's cell number and called.

"Bart? What time do you get off work today? Good. Can you come straight over to the house—no stops, it's important . . . No, no, everything's fine. Innocenta is out with her girl friends and will pick-up the children as usual. But, I need you to come over here straight away . . . Yes, I can hold . . . Oh, I see. I'll put the coffee pot on now." She hung-up the phone and turned to the ancient converso. "He's on his way now."

Theodora Mercedes showed the old man the bathroom and her private study. She brought him more tea, and then went downstairs to wait for Bart. Bart was at the back door in ten minutes.

"Whose old truck is that? It must be from the early fifties!"

"Bart, come in, sit, and be quiet a minute."

Theodora Mercedes chose her words carefully as she explained acts one and two of her day. She left out the bloody parts for now. Bart listened while sinking into his chair. He never touched his coffee. As Theodora Mercedes approached the end of act three, Bart straightened up and looked at her incredulously.

Theodora Mercedes led Bart to the door of her study, took a deep breath, and ushered Bart in. She said nothing but looked at each in admiration and respect, then quietly retreated, closing the door behind her.

Innocenta arrived about an hour later. The Unremarkables went into the backyard to play. Raul Theodore went straight to his room to do his homework. Theodora Mercedes called Innocenta into the kitchen. How to begin? What should the middle sound like? How would this end, if that was the appropriate word?

"Bart's father came to see me today because he's angry that I brought up possibly being Jewish since he's a devoted Catholic. All his children think his father is dead, but he's not; then the grandfather came to see me because he's not dead, and he and Bart are in my study meeting for the very first time."

Innocenta took a few moments of processing time to understand the stream of consciousness that was clearly a condensation of a very long day.

Finally, "They're upstairs? I've got to . . . "

"Sit down, Innocenta. This is their very private time together. When they are ready to come out, only then will we follow their leads. You should not interfere, Innocenta. Not even the Gods of all the Americas know how much is happening up there after almost fifty years of lies and separation. Promise me you will not go near that door."

Innocenta could easily sense the wisdom of her mother's admonishments.

"I think that this would be a perfect time for a long bath. But you'll call me as soon as that door opens, won't you?"

"Of course, my dear, sweet daughter. I'll even watch the children."

Innocenta headed for the bath. Theodora Mercedes checked on The Unremarkables first and then headed to Raul Theodore's room.

"Sweetheart, what are you doing?"

"Hi, Abuela. I'm trying to find Stephen Hawking's error. I think it's at the one millionth of a second point after the start of the Big Bang."

"Really? Why do you think so?"

"Because if he were correct, then the universe would be much cooler than it is now. It would be much less than three degrees Kelvin that has been measured."

"I see. Let me know if you need anything Raul Theodore."

The boy was already lost in his calculations and did not respond. Theodora Mercedes just looked at him. He was short for his age like Barrington had been before his growth spurt. His large blue-green eyes were in deep space, moving rapidly back and forth, forth and back. Raul

Theodore's fingers moved slightly, like butterflies resting but not quite still. Theodora Mercedes wondered if his fingers were part of the calculations. She would not, however, disturb his calculations and instead patted his light brown head and slipped out of the room.

Theodora Mercedes went back to the kitchen to finish preparing the dinner that The Very Catholic Consuelo had begun. No sooner had the vegetables escaped the prison of the refrigerator, than there was a knock on the back door.

"By the Gods, not again!"

Alfredo Bartram Rael de la Madrid was standing on her back porch. He was clearly irritated but doing an excellent job of keeping that genie bottled.

"That's my father's truck! Where is he? You said you would stop interfering!"

"Wait! Just wait, Mr. de la Madrid. Come in and sit a minute."

Mr. de la Madrid sat in the same chair he had occupied earlier.

"Not long after you left, your father appeared at my back door. He came to find me because it turns out that *you* let the cat out of the bag."

"Me?"

"Yes, you! By telling him to stay away from Bart you piqued his curiosity and his need to connect with his grandson. I kept my word to the best of my ability but your actions have brought them together!"

"Is that Bart's car out front?"

"Yes. They are upstairs in my study getting acquainted whether you like it or not. How could you be so cruel?"

"Cruel?"

"You kept a grandfather and his grandchildren from ever knowing each other. No birthdays, no first steps, first teeth, graduations, and no love to share. Mr. de la Madrid, they are together now, and there is nothing you can do about it! If you want to go up and make an ass of yourself, then that's one choice."

"And what, Great Buddha, would be my other choice?"

"Your poor sarcasm does not do you justice. Your other choice is to go up and make the very best you can of a situation that you no longer control. Mr. de la Madrid, you no longer control this. It has moved beyond you."

Even if Mr. de la Madrid had made mistakes, he was an intelligent, thoughtful man. He sat agitatedly for an eternity, then stopped fidgeting.

71

Theodora Mercedes waited, staring at his profile intently.

"Does my father still drink tea in the afternoon?"

"Yes."

"May I have a cup?"

"Yes, Mr. de la Madrid, you may!"

"You better start calling me Alfredo."

"And I am Theodora Mercedes."

"Pleased to meet you, Theodora Mercedes."

"Yes, likewise."

Theodora Mercedes and Alfredo sat in silence sipping their tea. Alfredo was clearly taking measure of the situation that had moved its orbit.

"I would like to go up and make the best of the opportunity. I give you my word as a good Catholic that nothing ugly will happen."

"Alfredo, I would have taken your word as a man or as a friend, but I'll take your word just as you offer it. Let me tell them you're here first. There has been an excess of shocks today. Let's not add one more."

"Good idea. I'll wait here until you come back."

Theodora Mercedes led Alfredo upstairs, knocked on her own study door, ushered Alfredo in, and then left without attempting to notice too much.

After her bath, Innocenta was incredulous about act four, especially missing it. Every twitch of her muscles urged her to rush into the study. But she didn't. She and her mother fed the children at seven—they could wait no longer. Neither of the women was hungry but they sat at the dinner table watching the children eat, frequently looking up to the study. One can imagine being a fly on the wall. What does it look and feel like knowing that there is a sister fly on the wall?

At eight-thirty, the children were in bed. Innocenta went into her bedroom and closed the door. There, lying on her bed was Bart.

"Innocenta, I just came in. I have so much to tell you but I'm exhausted. Can you lie down beside me?"

She lay her head on his shoulder, watching Bart look straight up until he at last closed his weary, worldly eyes and began breathing slowly and deeply. Innocenta stealthily arose and went downstairs.

Theodora Mercedes was sitting alone in the living room.

"Mother, you look exhausted!"

"They just left. Alfredo and his father left arm-in-arm. They went to

Alfredo's house to spend the night. I think it's going to be a long one for both of them. I'm going to bed."

As Innocenta helped her mother up the stairs, she could hear The Very Catholic Consuelo come in through the back door. She smiled as she heard the final line of act four, "Ay! No one washed the dishes!"

Chapter Six
Alfonso Pedro Silverton Hoffmann

Alfonso Pedro Silverton Hoffmann thought his parents, Angelica Gertrudis and Reigh, had been acting peculiarly for some time. Had it been only days, or had it been weeks? In any case, his mother insisted on asking him questions about Nurse Leah; what was she like, who were her people, was there anything "different" about Nurse Leah that he would like to talk about? Angelica Gertrudis seemed not to accept the ordinary nature of Nurse Leah and Alfonso's relationship. Certainly, this required a suspension of disbelief that someone of Alfonso's limited experience and insight could actually realize what a relationship of "ordinary nature" was.

Alfonso had been certain that he saw his father at times outside the office, maybe, outside Nurse Leah's apartment, perhaps—he wasn't entirely sure. Initially, Alfonso thought it equally likely that he was imagining these sightings. Now, his accountant's mind gave the odds slightly in favor of the imaginings. Alfonso was a reluctant box turtle. Moreover, he had never had to stick his neck out and ask his parents if everything was OK.

What Alfonso didn't know was that since Theodora Mercedes' visit two weeks prior, his parents had taken what they believed to be *decisive action*. Angelica Gertrudis watched Alfonso's every move and mood at home. She would cook his favorite dinners in vain attempts to keep him at home. Angelica Gertrudis would ask him if he would like to accompany her to the grocery store on Saturdays. This had always been one of Alfonso's favorite pastimes. He could find the best buys per ounce on canned tomatoes faster than Angelica Gertrudis could put on her reading glasses and find the information for herself on the tiny print of the shelf talker. Alfonso liked looking for new, exotic foods. When the oriental foods section went in at the supermarket, Alfonso was fascinated by the sauces and condiments that he knew he would never try. His favorite at one time was tiny, tiny ears of corn stuffed into a glass jar. Imagine! But, these days Alfonso would politely decline Angelica Gertrudis' invitations to accompany her; Nurse Leah would be expecting him. The box turtle was in full rut. Alfonso thought it odd that his mother could be so, so—insistent, even to the point of annoying him; not that Alfonso would *ever* show annoyance to his mother.

Reigh had taken more and more time off work. He taught his classes, skipped faculty meetings, cancelled office hours, and came under the scrutiny of his dean. One day after Theodora Mercedes' visit, Reigh had bought a cheap used car. He would follow Alfonso undetected. Reigh paid exactly one hundred dollars for an American Motors Pacer. Its original green was so faded and calicoed by the New Mexico sun that it could have been deliberately camouflaged by the military. The Pacer was the box turtle of its day. How it was still running was a mystery known to no one. Reigh would park this monstrosity around the corner at the end of a cul de sac. The residents of the cul de sac would see this box turtle drive up, park, and a middle-aged man get out and hurry away. Then it would be gone. Then it would be back. Reigh *was* a respectable looking man. Only this prevented the neighbors on this street from calling the police to report "suspicious activity."

Reigh had found that tailing Alfonso was rather fun and wicked. Frankly, the exhilaration of playing detective was offset by the torment of believing that something fatal would befall Alfonso. It was an inequitable trade. Reigh longed in his heart for the days, only recently, that he did not worry about his son; the calm predictability of each mundane and welcomed day. He wanted Alfonso to regain his vanilla life so that he and Angelica Gertrudis could resume theirs. He missed his students. So did Angelica Gertrudis, but neither tortured the other by actually saying so. Reigh maintained his surveillance while risking his employment; the consequences of not doing so were too high. Yet, what if Theodora Mercedes were wrong?

Theodora Mercedes was surfing the net when the gift asserted control over her vision. She was as awake as the birds outside her window and here were the hideous green eyes again. The blue fog enveloped her and she expected the Mormon Tabernacle Choir to resume chanting. Theodora Mercedes saw Angelica Gertrudis and Reigh following Alfonso and an unknown woman. Was this woman an agent of destiny? They were in the woods; where she could not tell. She was robbed of her breath when the black aura appeared surrounding Reigh. While Theodora Mercedes had never seen this before, she recognized it instantly for its symbolism. Had she misinterpreted the original vision? Was this a new vision? Did this add to or supplant the first vision? Theodora Mercedes could not afford the luxury of sorting this out. She needed to get to Albuquerque.

Reigh had a flash of brilliance. Not going to the police based on a vague premonition from his sister-in-law was a good decision. But why not go to the police and just have Leah Rose Naphtali checked out? Reigh knew a detective who had taken one of his drawing classes. It took a trip to his office, but Reigh found the man's name, Det. Sgt. Willard Adelante. Reigh remembered the man well upon seeing his name again. Adelante was short, balding, had a mottled complexion and loved to draw. He had a natural talent that had neither been realized in school nor reinforced by his parents. These types of students made Reigh angry because they had never been recognized and encouraged. Adelante had received Reigh's attention with unnecessary gratitude. Reigh would contact him immediately.

Alfonso continued to be the object of curiosity at work. The office staff thought of Alfonso as a fly, wings pulled off, for their amusement. A box turtle would have been too, too boring for this wanton murder of crows. The crows were betting on every conceivable aspect of Alfonso's unknown life. Did he have a girl friend? Was it a boy friend? Would they ever meet her/him? Was the friend a complete geek like Alfonso? How many new clothes would appear? When would Alfonso lose the comb over? The ever oblivious box turtle stayed completely unaware of all of this mischief at his expense. While Reigh and his heavily disguised Pacer were watching from a short block down the street, Julie Ann popped up over the cubicle wall.

"Where ya going tonight, Alfonso?"

"Pardon me?"

"Where are you taking your new girl friend? It is a girl, isn't it?"

Twittering could be heard amongst the crows.

"Yes, it's a girl."

Someone in the background could be heard, "Yes! You owe me twenty bucks!"

"Shush!"

"What was that?"

"Oh nothing, Alfonso, just ignore it. So where you taking her, hmm?"

"Uh, The Rain Room."

"The Rain Room! Gosh, that's really expensive, Alfonso. This girl must be special."

"Yes, she is. I need to get back to work now."

"OK. I've never been to The Rain Room."

Anyone else would have recognized an obvious come-on, except Alfonso.

"Neither have I."

Julie Ann shook her hair, gave Alfonso a reappraising look, and then disappeared on her side of the wall. Alfonso went back to checking the balance sheets unaware that money was exchanging hands throughout the floor.

"Say, Fonzie, why don't we do something different this Saturday?"

"Sure. What?"

"Let's take the tramway to the top of Sandia Mountain and have a picnic."

"Oh, I don't know Leah. . ."

"Why? What's wrong with that?"

"Nothing's wrong with that. It's just that it sounds pretty scary."

"Honey, millions of people have taken that tram and lived to tell about it. It'll be fun! We'll sleep late, and then you can go home and change. I'll take care of the picnic."

"Oh, OK, Leah."

Det. Sgt. Adelante remembered Reigh well and fondly. No other person had given him lessons so well explained, examples executed like photographs deconstructed before his eyes, words that caressed his artistic soul. Yes, Adelante remembered Reigh, or Assistant Professor Hoffmann, very well. Reigh found him at the Northeast Substation working in an unsolved-murder task force. After exchanging updates, Adelante became childlike in his eagerness to show Reigh his drawings. A sketch of the Albuquerque Volcanoes was executed with the sparse drama of the desert captured through a fervid eye in textures, shades, and terrain. They examined several more. Reigh evaluated the drawings as being overly meticulous at the expense of life. In effect, the drawings looked dead.

"You should add some people to your sketches. They not only give dimension and scale to the surroundings but an expression of a complete landscape with its characters, follies, and failures."

"That may be why I never sketch people, professor. I have seen the character, follies, and failures in abundance. My drawings are pure, without the taint that humans inflict on the natural world."

"I understand, but not all human influence is negative. Can't you picture your own children (did he have any?) climbing these rocks or being captivated by these petroglyphs?"

"You are my professor. I want to say yes, but I would say it only to please you, professor."

"We should discuss this more, perhaps another time."

Reigh explained his business, not failing to omit how naïve Alfonso was, or his and Angelica Gertrudis' attempts to intervene undetected. Even the Pacer was confessed to.

Adelante laughed so hard he was nearing wetting his pants. "A Pacer! You've got to be joking! I haven't seen one of those pigs in years. Is it here? I would love to see it!"

"Actually, it looks like a very poor rendering of a turtle. I'm sure you could have designed a better looking automobile with your skills."

"Maybe! Is it here?"

They went out to the police parking lot where Adelante did a complete inspection while guffawing the entire time.

"I'm sorry, professor. The thought of you tailing your son in this, it's even uglier with age, it's too comical. I don't mean to embarrass you, it's just—a Pacer!"

The laughing began again where it left off while Adelante escorted Reigh back inside the substation.

Adelante plugged "Leah Rose Naphtali" into the computer. Numerous photographs popped up as well as a number of aliases, including her present one.

"Her real name is 'Lotus Namaste Kilborn Geier.' Geier—that means 'vulture' in German; a hobby of mine, the origin and meanings of surnames. Anyway, Lotus seems to be from New York state and the child of hippies, judging from her name. She's not a nice person, professor. She is wanted for various thefts, fraud, petty crimes, a plethora of fake IDs, and has been questioned in four states."

"Questioned for what?"

Adelante looked at Reigh gravely. "For being associated with money and people who have disappeared."

Reigh's throat tightened up and his face colored like a cardinal's cloak. Adelante moved Reigh's lean, athletic frame to the floor and called for water. The paramedics next door were called. Reigh's blood pressure was very high but dropping.

"Do you take medicine for high blood pressure, Mr. Hoffman?"

"No, never have. I think my imagination just worked a little quickly. It was silly. Can you help me up?"

"Mr. Hoffmann, we're going to leave you here for a few more minutes until we're satisfied that your blood pressure is safe."

"Fine. Where is Adelante?"

"Right here, professor."

"They are taking the tramway to the top of Sandia Mountain today."

Adelante maintained a stony, unmovable expression. This was not the time to display his thoughts.

"Well, when you have been certified as healthy by these gentlemen, let's talk some more."

"Now, Fonzie, you're just being silly. I told you, I *have* to run some errands. They have to be done today. . .Yes, I'll meet you at the picnic grounds on the rim trail. . .Yes. . .It's the only one up there. Just take the tram and I'll be there on the next car or the next. I won't leave you waiting long. . .Because I don't know exactly how long my errands will take. Besides, the views are breath-taking from the rim. . .Yes, I'm sure. . .Yes, I *will* be there. Don't forget your warm coat. It can be chilly up there even in summer. OK, I'll see you there. Don't disappoint me, Fonzie. . . Yes, I love you too and can't wait to show you how much."

The errands had already been run. Alfonso's bank accounts were empty and Leah had booked a flight from Amarillo to New Orleans in the name of one of her aliases. Leah had friends in The Big Easy. She had just enough time to drive east on I-40 and continue on to the parking lot under the communications towers on top of Sandia Mountain, take care of business, then drive to Amarillo. Leah dropped her cell phone into her handbag and drove out of the bank parking lot smiling.

"Picking Theodora Mercedes up at the train station? Angelica Gertrudis, you've got to get to the tramway. They're going up to the top. I have a horrible feeling about this. . .Angelica Gertrudis, I'm afraid. . .Just bring her. You don't have time for anything else. Just get there, Angelica Gertrudis. I'll see you at the top."

Det. Sgt. Adelante and Professor Hoffmann took a brisk pace to Adelante's police cruiser. They beelined, lights off, to the tramway station.

Alfonso was witless trying to choose between puking and dying of fright. Sandia Mountain loomed above him like a menacing wave. Alfonso was certain that he knew what the residents of Sendai, Japan felt as they caught their collective breath, horror-struck, as the tsunami raised its head to consume them. The tram had just left the station and Alfonso had a tight grip on the handhold. He refused to look out the windows, to say nothing of looking down. The car swayed, mocking him with every puff of wind and passing of the towers. Just near the terminus, Alfonso lost it and puked into the plastic bag he had brought just for this inevitability. The other passengers flew like turkeys out of the rank-smelling car. Alfonso waited until they were all gone. The operator, who had seen this many times before, waited for him compassionately, grabbed Alfonso's arm and helped him onto firm ground.

"There's a trash can right there, sir, and a restroom inside. I hope you feel better."

Alfonso could only manage a nod of thanks, dropped the bag in the can, and ran into the men's room. Had Alfonso escaped with the turkeys, the upper-end operator in the control booth would have spotted him. He had been alerted to watch for Alfonso. Not seeing him exit, the operator went about his business which included a fine young lady inside the booth. His attention had been divided only momentarily anyway.

"What do you mean you don't know if Reigh is in danger too? Is he or isn't he?"

Theodora Mercedes tried to reason with Angelica Gertrudis. The gift was erratic, fragile, and capricious. How could she explain this to someone who had no personal knowledge of the gift and its unpredictability? The conversation, never moving forward, continued until the tramway terminal was in sight. They parked and bought two tickets.

Alfonso had reached the fork in the trail when Reigh and Adelante landed at the top of the tramway. The attendant in the booth had not seen anyone fitting Alfonso's description. Adelante, all too familiar with human nature, noted that under the circumstances the young man would hardly have taken his eyes off the fine young lady.

"Professor, he may be up here. That young man wouldn't have noticed if Elvis had left the tram. Let's follow the trail to the north along the rim. Most people go that way."

Angelica Gertrudis and Theodora Mercedes were on their way up. Alfonso, much to his discomfort, took the trail to the left along the rim, looking for the picnic grounds and moved at the speed of turtle. The trail approached the edge, and then turned away from the cliff as it went north. Alfonso found that he was drawn to the edge despite his fears—like someone who hates blood and guts but drives slowly past an automobile accident. As much as Alfonso backed away, he was drawn again to the edge. Leah was right, the views were spectacular. Mount Taylor, to the west, looked like Alfonso could touch it if he reached out far enough. The thought sent shivers through him and he drew back from the edge. Now fascinated, the turtle found a spot with a rock to sit on, several shelves of rock below him (in case he slipped), before the cliff-face became a sheer precipice. Alfonso sat, his blood pressure went down, and he took deep breaths of the fragrant mountain air.

"Got a light?"

There was a man's voice behind Alfonso. The startled Alfonso leaped up and turned. A smallish man with a moustache and fedora was holding a cigarette. He had unusually green eyes.

"I don't smoke. Sorry."

"That's OK. I should quit anyway. It shortens your life, ya know?"

Alfonso took a hard look. "Leah? Leah, what are you doing in that get-up? Are those contact lenses? Where's lunch?"

Leah pulled a gun.

"Oh, Fonzie, we had fun didn't we?"

"What do you mean, Leah? Is that a gun?"

"Oh, Fonzie, you're the dumbest man I ever sank my claws into. Of course, it's a gun. It's a Smith and Wesson lady's gun. It packs a wallop while fitting neatly into my handbag. I'm gonna use it to kill you unless you do exactly as I say."

"Leah! Why? I thought you loved me!"

"Loved you? Oh, Fonzie, I *used* you. You're such a desperate loser all it took was sex to capture you. You got sex and I got all your money. I finished emptying your accounts and you won't need money where you're going."

"Where am I going?"

"You really don't understand yet, do you? You're going to jump off that cliff."

"What? No!"

"Jump, Fonzie, or I'll shoot you first then dump you over."

Adelante and Reigh approached them stealthily and nervously through the trees while this was enacted. Angelica Gertrudis and Theodora Mercedes, two middle-aged matrons, had climbed and descended the trail as fast as they could, not knowing where they were going. Rounding a boulder, Angelica Gertrudis caught sight of Alfonso one hundred yards distant. She could see no one else.

"Alfonso!" she screamed with all her power.

Alfonso didn't react right away because of the distance. When his head turned, Reigh jumped like a predator onto Leah's back.

Adelante, not expecting this, reached but couldn't grab Reigh's coat.

Alfonso turned back toward Leah because of the noise just as Reigh hit Leah at full speed. The impact caused Leah to pull the trigger as the gun lurched up. The bullet entered just below Alfonso's left eye, killing him instantly, and propelling him backwards just enough to fall over the cliff. He landed a few feet below on the first shelf. Reigh and Leah had the momentum to sail out over the shelves into clear, fragrant, mountain air and disappeared from sight.

Reigh, realizing that his son was dead, morphed from saturated fear for his son to cold, green hatred for this wonton predator. He held her like a fish eagle holds a trout in its unrelenting talons; he held her close; he held her until his last thought was of her certain death as he heard the crushing of her skull, the snapping of her bones, and burst of her entrails beneath him. Reigh died satisfied.

The double memorial had an overflow attendance. Reporters were there. The story was sensational and would sell double the usual number of newspapers. University peers, students, all the local family and friends, all the Santa Fe family and friends, even some of Reigh's estranged family appeared. Angelica Gertrudis was not fit to meet the estranged relatives. They had not earned any consideration from her. She shunned them in her grief. Many people wept openly. Det. Sgt. Adelante wept artistically and was disconsolate. Alfonso's supervisor attended as did Julie Ann, the only two of the murder of crows to do so.

The testimonials for Reigh were abundant and moving. He was well respected and even loved. Only Innocenta and Barrington spoke on Alfonso's behalf. When the memorials were over, the reporters became frenzied. Barrington and James had to shield the family to get them out quickly and with no interviews.

"How do you feel, Mrs. Hoffmann, with your son and husband

murdered?"

Animals, stupid animals. How would they expect the mother and wife to feel? Later, Angelica Gertrudis had the remains of her husband and son cremated. She had yet to decide on boxes, urns, burial and whatnot.

"I know what you're thinking."

"Is this the damned gift speaking to you?"

"No, this is just the intuition of a sister. I will not let you do what you're thinking."

"How can you know what I'm thinking? Go home now. I don't want you here!"

Theodora Mercedes waited. It had been four days since the double memorial. The cremated remains were on the dining room table.

"Angelica Gertrudis, the gift is not what you think. It is not a window into everything, everyone, all of the time. I do not command it in any way. You believe that I should have been able to see everything that happened before it happened, then prevented it. None of that is in my power. The gift is not in my power. It does as it wishes, Sister. At this moment, I wish it belonged to someone else, but it doesn't. You cannot blame me for things well beyond my sight or imagination. *It just doesn't work that way.*"

Angelica Gertrudis was silent for some time. Her tears had all dried up two days ago, and she was still heavy with unspeakable grief. They were both silent for the rest of the day.

The following morning, Angelica Gertrudis found Theodora Mercedes packing bags.

"So, you are leaving."

"No, we are leaving."

Angelica Gertrudis just looked at her sister vacantly with no strength to even protest.

"Come into the kitchen with me, Sister."

She led Angelica Gertrudis delicately by the arm to the kitchen table. Two coffees were poured. The two sisters just looked inquiringly at each other for several minutes.

"Your plan won't work Angelica Gertrudis. You will retire from teaching, which you love, put these two urns on either side of the mantle, and spend the rest of your days slowly dying in this house. I know you have considered suicide, but I will have you committed before I allow you to do that. Angelica Gertrudis, your grief is unimaginable. Not a soul knows what you must be going through. Certainly, I don't. But now, no one loves you as much as I do. You must let me think for you for now."

The minutes ticked by while Angelica Gertrudis stared into her coffee cup. Theodora Mercedes wondered what she saw in the dark brown depths.

"You're pretty smart. If I weren't so sad and tired, I would be angry with you for being so damned accurate. What do you propose?"

Two days later, Angelica Gertrudis was installed in Raul Theodore's room. Raul Theodore was moved to the guest room. It would be a lark for the nine year old to fly up the stairs to the third floor. Angelica Gertrudis could share Theodora Mercedes' bathroom. Innocenta's was already doubly occupied on too many occasions. No one could know that Raul Theodore's move to the guest room was prophetic. Angelica Gertrudis, settled for now, didn't know yet that this was where she would live for the rest of her life.

The very next morning at nine, Det. Sgt. Adelante knocked on the front door. He had left Albuquerque at seven that morning in order to arrive early but at a decent time. Theodora Mercedes was surprised when The Very Catholic Consuelo announced him. She told the housekeeper to run and fetch Angelica Gertrudis immediately.

"Det. Sgt. Adelante, I'm surprised to see you so soon. Would you like coffee?"

"Yes, Ma'am. Black, please."

Angelica Gertrudis came down dressed, but not in colors one would describe as cheerful. She greeted her sister and Adelante.

"I came to give you an update."

Theodora Mercedes leaned forward in her chair. Angelica Gertrudis was unmoved.

"We found Ms. Geier's car, some plane tickets to New Orleans, and lots of incriminating evidence. We even found the withdrawal receipts for when she cleaned out your son's bank accounts. All of that is evidence, including the huge pile of cash she had under her trunk floor covering. The New Orleans PD found her address based on phone numbers we got off her cell phone. It appears that she periodically lived in a commune-like house down-river from the French Quarter. Some place called Bywater, on Lesseps Street."

"Lesseps, why does that sound familiar; the vampire?" asked Angelica Gertrudis.

"Anne Rice, dear, you're thinking of Lestat."

"Vampire, well that sure describes this Geier woman and maybe all those ghouls living on that street. Anyway, they searched the place and found enough evidence to convict her of multiple unsolved murders in four states. There were personal possessions of her victims and lots of withdrawal slips. It looks like she kept those as souvenirs or trophies of her conquests. In any case, it will take months to sort everything out. I talked with the district attorney in Albuquerque. As long as we have the withdrawal slip, there's no reason to hold on to the money. We have lots of police witnesses who saw it, counted it, and verified that those very bills were paid from your son's accounts. Anyway, as Ms. Geier is dead, there will be no trial, just a formal inquest. I don't see that your son's money won't be returned to you in a matter of months. Mrs. Hoffmann, she took out nine thousand dollars a day for twelve days. That's one hundred-eight thousand dollars. Mrs. Hoffmann, your husband was a fine man. Your son was an innocent victim. She was a vile and evil woman. I'm glad she's dead."

Angelica Gertrudis said nothing or even moved. She stared into corners of her soul and into foul mists known only to her. Theodora Mercedes politely wrapped up the conversation, thanked Adelante profusely, and showed him out. She came back and sat with her sister.

Finally, Angelica Gertrudis took a sip of coffee and smiled. "I know what to do now."

Two weeks later, Angelica Gertrudis and Theodora Mercedes were standing on the Highway 64 bridge over the Rio Grande Gorge, the rest of the family giving them time and space together. They prayed each in her own way, then the immediate family gathered tightly together, and Angelica Gertrudis committed Alfonso's ashes to the winds, cliffs, and waters. Then she did the same with Reigh's ashes. The entire family was crying silently; the wailing was long over.

On the return to Santa Fe, Theodora Gertrudis stopped and gave the bronze urns to some Native Americans selling jewelry beside the road.

"Solid, high quality bronze; make some fine jewelry, please."

Raul Theodore wondered aloud how many calories it required to melt that much bronze. Angelica Gertrudis patted his little light-brown head, looked into his sparkling blue-green eyes, and smiled. The innocence and beauty of extreme youth worked its magic on her.

She said, "You'll tell us when you finish your calculations, won't you

Raul Theodore?"

He gifted her with a rare direct look and smile.

Theodora Mercedes squeezed her sister's hand. She knew Angelica Gertrudis would persevere and, perhaps, thrive. She, Theodora Mercedes Silverton Vigil, would see to it. A daughter of the Silverton-de Baca House had returned to the home in which she was born and the stars, having dimmed themselves in grief, decided to shine brightly that night.

CHAPTER SEVEN
Innocenta Perpetua Vigil Silert

Innocenta Perpetua Vigil Silert awoke to find that she was alone. The afternoon and evening before had been filled with the comings and goings of Rael de la Madrid men. No comedy of entrances, exits, and slamming doors; this was a family in a struggle for the heart of its identity. Innocenta had put her exhausted mother to bed and then retired herself for a second time. She slept badly. Voices whispered in the inky turbulence of shallow sleep; Innocenta had no idea what had transpired in Theodora Mercedes' study. Her subconscious filled the void with flowing and ebbing smokes from emotions on fire and words aflame. Now, she lay there weary. Innocenta grabbed her robe, stepped into the second floor hall, and heard her children playing.

"It must be Saturday."

In one week, her cousin, Alfonso, would meet green-eyed death.

Downstairs, Innocenta found her mother and The Very Catholic Consuelo drinking coffee in the kitchen. Good mornings were exchanged, and the cook got Innocenta a cup.

"Mother, you look good this morning. I didn't sleep well, but I must have been asleep when Bart left."

"Bart left about an hour ago. He said he was going straight to his father's house."

"It did seem from Bart's, what should I call it, serene expression, that it wasn't as ugly as I imagined it would be, at least for Bart."

"Innocenta, I wasn't there, but I can assure you from sixty-seven years on this earth, living my entire life in this small town, that every known emotion was expressed last night. But, I do think it ended well. The problem is that there are always so many things to be said that whatever is happening at the de la Madrid house, most of those emotions will be revisited this morning."

"And I think I'm the one who's tired. Damn it, Mother, why do you look so good this morning?"

"Innocenta, the only investment I had in yesterday's dramas was empathy. There was nothing I could do or change. Whatever was supposed to happen, happened without my help. So, I worried a little for everyone's wellbeing, I mean emotionally, and had a good night's sleep."

"So, what do we do now?"

"Do? Nothing. We go about our Saturday as always. Whatever else happens, it will likely come to us."

Innocenta showered, gathered the children for breakfast, and they ate as a family.

"Where's Barrington, Mother?"

"I don't know. I suppose he spent the night at James' house."

"They're certainly an island of calm lately. James is lucky to have found Barrington."

"Innocenta, Barrington is luckier to have found James."

Innocenta was offended by her mother's remark and chose not to address it directly.

"What do you mean?"

"Have you ever gotten the impression that James was lost or had been lost?"

"No. James comes across as mature and solid, like he's always been strong and steady."

"Yes. And our Barrington?"

"I see your point, Mother. Well, they're both pretty lucky, then, aren't they?"

"Yes, they are! I'm delighted for both of them."

Innocenta ensured that the children had their baths. All three were old enough to bathe themselves, but she did watch Raul Theodore as he was "distractible." Innocenta followed a pattern: ears were checked for missed or excess earwax, remedies were made, the spaces between toes were checked for unscrubbed dirt, and wash cloths reappeared. As each child was approved, each dressed in comfortable Saturday clothes. It was a magnificent early June day.

The Unremarkables played chase through the front and back yards. Raul Theodore was kicking his soccer ball, making marks in the sandbox, then repeating this over and over. This was his pattern when multitasking. Innocenta, watching from the kitchen window, had no notion of what Raul Theodore was calculating now.

By eleven, Innocenta was being driven crazy by the silence from Bart.

What was going on? Was everything all right, or did the harmony of the previous evening take on some sour notes? Blue notes would be fine. She hoped the sour ones were short lived. At noon, Bart drove up in his sparkling clean Subaru.

"It was incredible, Innocenta!"

"Wait! Wait! Let me get my mother."

Theodora Mercedes left the kitchen at a quickened pace without sacrificing any dignity. She sat next to Innocenta. Bart was bursting.

"My grandfather is ninety-six years old! Can you believe it? He still farms, raises sheep, and drives his truck. All my brothers and sisters came over first thing this morning. You can't imagine the excitement—we all thought he was long dead. I never dreamed of a family reunion like this. My sisters all cried."

"Bart," Theodora Mercedes interrupted, "What did your mother do?"

Bart visibly deflated while the tall case clock stared back at him. He didn't hear ticking—more like "Tsk, tsk, tsk."

"Mom seemed really confused. She cried at times, but I don't think they were 'tears of joy.' Then she laughed a little. Sometimes, she just worried at my father and grandfather."

"Do you think that your mother was trying to reassemble a puzzle that had been jumbled up?"

Bart thought.

"Yes, maybe the picture she and my father had made was being—re-arranged?"

"Watch out for her, Bart. She could easily be the forgotten one in all this excitement. Her life has been turned upside down too."

"Yes, thank you, Mrs. Vigil."

Theodora Mercedes was silent and exasperated by the return to formality, but this would wait for another time.

"Anyway, we all got to meet *abuelo*; even most of his great grandchildren were there. He told stories about my father, our *abuela*, and life on the farm. We heard about our ancestors who spread throughout Northern New Mexico and Southern Colorado. He doesn't know if any descendents are still living or where they are. The family has been here for at least fourteen generations."

Innocenta wedged herself into the flow, "Ours too! I'll bet we're intermarried at some point."

"Oh, with that many generations and such a small population, it's probable."

Both Bart and Innocenta looked at Theodora Mercedes with clear surprise.

"But it would have been early as the conversos married within their own secret community. The de Bacas would have branched away at least two centuries ago."

"Mother, are you speculating, or do you know?"

"At least two centuries ago, we counted Raels and de la Madrids in the family tree. Those names disappeared from our line during the first half of the nineteenth century. But, this is just history, children! The main thing is to get back to Bart's story."

"Mother, your little history lessons can be like Raul Theodore's calculation outbursts."

All three laughed with good humor at the comparison.

"Anyway, Bart . . . "

Bart continued telling stories of his grandfather's childhood, the grandmother he could never know, and a father's hidden past in a lonely corner of New Mexico.

"He's driven back to San Bruno . . . "

"The non-existent village!" Theodora Mercedes chimed in.

They shared smiles and comic relief once more.

"He's invited all of us to his farm this Saturday. He gave us directions, and nearly everybody's going. I want you, your mother, and the kids to come."

"Nearly everybody?"

"I'm not sure that Mother will go. If she doesn't, Dad won't either. But, I have six days to work on them."

Innocenta seemed willing to go, but Theodora Mercedes hesitated. Her reservations remained unspoken, but she felt that this was a gathering suited for the immediate family and not for other uninitiates.

"I'll see and let you know, Bart."

Innocenta watched as Bart drove off. He went home to shower, nap, and change clothes. Bart was taking Innocenta to dinner at a romantic continental place on Galisteo Street quietly away from the Plaza. In the few minutes they had alone, Innocenta felt Bart's energy. It was not just heightened; it was changed. To Innocenta, it was as if sunflower yellow was washing onto the canvas of Bart's life; but it came in swirling, dancing with the other colors, creating new shapes, shadows, and rhythms. It also seemed to Innocenta that Bart's subconscious was working in the background, working out the new shapes, shadows, and rhythms. Dinner would be an extraordinary event.

Raul Theodore was at his computer on the Internet.

"Raul Theodore, what are you looking up?"

"I'm trying to find a theorem that describes the effects of the time-space warp of lighting a wooden match. For example, if I light the match in the kitchen, then how is the sand in my sandbox affected? But I can't find anything suitable."

"So, what do you do next?"

"I'll just have to work it out for myself."

"Will that be fun for you, Raul Theodore?"

"Oh yes! I have all summer to work out the fine tuning!"

"Well, have fun."

Innocenta left the room shaking her head. Raul Theodore had gone from a no-longer-progressing two year old to a brilliant nine year old who communicated well (when he chose to speak), and was kind, cheerful, and loved soccer. Innocenta noted that he was speaking more frequently and seemed happier. She went downstairs to check on The Unremarkables.

At twelve-thirty, the phone rang.

"Mrs. Silert, please."

"Speaking."

"Mrs. Silert, this is Raul Theodore's school principal, Anthony Abendaño. Do you have a few minutes to talk?"

"Yes. Is anything wrong?"

"No, Mrs. Silert, I guess you could say just the opposite. I know it's a Saturday, and there are only three more days of school until the summer break, but may I drop by your house?"

"Yes."

"I can be there in an hour."

"Fine, I'll be expecting you."

Innocenta put down the phone and thought to herself, "How much more excitement can we cram into this week?"

Innocenta found her mother in her study. She was listening to Berlioz's Messe Solenelle. Theodora Mercedes had several passions in her

91

life: authenticity in people (especially herself), anything but Abrahamic religions, working with the congregation's Social Justice Committee helping the poor and homeless, expressing herself in writing, good order in her house, the blues, and classical music. She had particular fondnesses for opera and string quartets. Most paradoxically, she was especially partial to liturgical music. The paradox was more than met the ears; if she were jubilant, she listened to Mozart's *Requiem Mass*—a profoundly sad work that focused its energies on Mozart's own impending death. If she were disturbed, she listened to the *Verdi Requiem*, a raucous celebration of life. If pensive, then Arvo Pärt's St. John Passion might meet her needs. Only Theodora Mercedes knew why she chose the *Berlioz* today. Theodora Mercedes turned the music down, listened to Innocenta's story, and agreed to come down in an hour.

When Innocenta opened the front door, she was surprised to see three people standing on the front porch. Principal Abendaño stepped in with his companions as Theodora Mercedes rose from her chair and met them at the door.

"Mrs. Vigil, good to see you."

"Principal Abendaño, how gracious of you to say so."

"This is Supervisor of Public Schools, Dr. Patricia Ilfeld, and Dr. Francisco Williams Roldán of the University of New Mexico. This is Mrs. Silert, Raul Theodore's mother, and Mrs. Vigil, Raul Theodore's grandmother, whom I know well."

Theodora Mercedes was forced to suppress a smile and continued the gracious beginnings by having them all comfortably seated and calling for coffee.

"So that's the long and the short of it. Raul Theodore is a genius, we would like him to attend the University of New Mexico, particularly to audit advanced mathematical studies, and the state will pay for boarding, round-the-clock supervision, and general care on campus."

"Dr. Ilfeld, I do appreciate your candor in describing the State of New Mexico's poor standing in education and the great opportunity proposed for Raul Theodore's education."

Here Innocenta paused and looked into each person's eyes starting with Principal Abendaño and ending with Theodora Mercedes.

"However, my answer is an unequivocal 'No.' While the opportunity is, indeed, priceless, I have to think of the entire well being of my child. He has grown from a disconnected toddler to a happy, studious, brilliant boy. The school has been cooperative, and it's clear to me, and I'm certain my mother would agree, that his stable family life is a significant and important contributor to his progress. So, while your offers are breathtaking and generous, my answer will not change."

"But Mrs. Silert . . . "

"My answer will not change."

The tall case clock looked on with amusement at this standoff while each tick magnified the discomfort of three of the five.

Dr. Roldán released the tension, "Mrs. Silert, I appreciate more than you know your position as Raul Theodore's mother. He is, indeed, fortunate to have you and your family to nurture and support him. Perhaps I can offer a compromise that nurtures his brilliant gifts and continues to provide him his invaluable support system. The university would be willing, no, *enthusiastic* about providing Raul Theodore a very advanced computer here in his own home. He would be provided with direct access to university classes, data bases, and real-time tutoring with our mathematics staff. Raul Theodore would get advanced studies and keep his strong family life."

"Mother, would you bring down Raul Theodore? Thank you. Let's just ask my little genius what he thinks. More coffee? No? Well, he'll be right down."

Raul Theodore was bewildered by the assembly in his living room and retreated into his "shy" mode. Innocenta coaxed him into looking at her while she explained the proposal. She paused to let him cogitate the entire proposition and its implications as he understood them. Raul Theodore looked up and to the right for a full minute.

"Will I have access to Stephen Hawking's, Jim Hartle's, and Neil Turok's equations? I have many questions and concerns."

Dr. Roldán, not repressing his dumbfounded reaction, practically stammered his reply, "Yes, Raul Theodore, you would. Those and much more."

"How about Juan Maldacena?"

"Of course, virtually anyone you can think of."

"OK. Can I go finish my calculations now?"

"Yes, but only if you thank these nice people for these gifts."

"Thank you."

Raul Theodore flew up the stairs as only a nine year old could.

"Mrs. Silert, I will be in touch with you this week. We can arrange the installations at your convenience. I hope that you and Mrs. Vigil are as excited by this as we are at the university."

"Thank you, Dr. Roldán. I can't say that I am excited just yet. I need to see how it affects Raul Theodore. Perhaps, I'm now being too protective. I'm sure that he will love his new computer and all that goes with it."

Innocenta smiled broadly and extended her hand. Thank you and general good wishes were exchanged, hands were cordially shaken, and the trio left.

Innocenta and Theodora Mercedes turned to face each other. Where to start? Intuitively, they decided on a beautiful way; they both broke out in giddy laughter. Mother and grandmother both raced, so to speak, up the stairs and fawned (he would say "annoyed") and cooed over Raul Theodore for the next thirty minutes. Theodora Mercedes led Innocenta downstairs, pulled a bottle of Vueve Cliquot out of the wine cooler, and they laughed and toasted to Raul Theodore and all his innumerable virtues.

Innocenta spent the rest of the early afternoon playing with The Unremarkables. At four o'clock she took a much needed nap and slept like a cowhand who had spent the day rounding up mavericks. Yes, she even snored. Innocenta's sleep included a visit from the gift. The mists were multicolored swirls that seemed to dance joyously until they parted just enough for her to briefly catch sight of a shrouded body. But the mists kept dancing, and Innocenta did not feel pain, sorrow, or horror—just a disconnected experience.

When Innocenta awoke it was quarter to six, "Damn!"

She ran to the bathroom to wash her face, apply daring amounts of make-up, perfume, and get dressed for dinner. Emerging triumphant onto the second floor landing, Innocenta could hear a Bach Cantata filtering from behind Theodora Mercedes' closed study door. It was six-thirty. She glided down the stairs a diva.

The children were finishing dinner under The Very Catholic Consuelo's eagle like supervision.

"Thank you, Consuelo. I overslept, but I was so tired."

The cook nodded agreeably and poured Raul Theodore more milk. The children seemed content and evidently had stuffed themselves with homemade fried chicken with all the fixings.

"Is there any champagne left in that bottle?"

"Yes, I recorked it and put it in the fridge. Shall we have another glass?" It was Theodora Mercedes walking in at a most theatrical moment.

Innocenta grabbed the bottle and two champagne glasses, and she and her mother headed for the expansive front porch. They spoke little and sipped the Vueve Cliquot, but their thoughts were everywhere.

Finally, Innocenta broke the silence. "What do you think it means?"

Theodora Mercedes looked at Innocenta while draining her last sip.

"Another death, clearly, but not one that affected me very much. I felt empathy, but it was not upsetting. What do you think?"

"Mostly the same except that I didn't even feel empathy. It felt like it was someone I don't actually know."

"Interesting. We live with life and death, always, whether we pay heed or not. All deaths affect us differently. Here comes Bart!"

Bart kissed Theodora Mercedes first and greeted her by her double first name. Theodora Mercedes puffed her feathers with happiness at this act of familiarity.

"By all the Gods of the Americas, I hope this sticks!" she thought to herself.

Innocenta received her kiss from this fine man with pride and gratitude.

"We're out of champagne!"

"What are we celebrating?"

"I'll tell you at dinner. Good night, Mother."

Bart ordered grilled polenta with rosemary gorgonzola sauce and champagne for appetizers.

"Bart, tell me what's going on in your head and heart. I can't imagine the last twenty-four hours you've had."

"Well, first, I'm still drained! What a journey this has been. This even beats my troubles at UNM."

"What troubles?"

"I couldn't pick a major for two years and thought that I was the most defective person in the school. I quit dating for a while. Then I dropped out of sports. I was so confused. I loved too many subjects to pick just one."

"What did you do?"

"I talked to my dad. He asked many questions but never once told me what to do. I went back to school, and my decision just came to me. I declared my major in Public Administration and contacted the Santa Fe

Fire Department. I wanted to work for the people. Someday, I hope to be fire chief for my hometown."

"That's a great story. Not many people can describe their struggles so lucidly. But, what about the last twenty-four hours?"

"My life and family have been muddled. I used to think that we were good Catholics for generations. It gave my views a certain narrowness, never requiring much thought. Now, I find out that I'm also equally Jewish."

"Does that bother you?"

"Oh no, but I have had to sort my feelings and my view from inside. I'm proud of all of it. The problem is that neither religion, Catholicism or Judaism, really suits me. I want to go with you to your church. It's much less confining, not defining me without my acquiescence, and, from what you say, allows me to choose my own beliefs."

"Holy Mother of God! This is out of left field!"

They both laughed with gusto.

"Well, that's quite an epithet coming from a life-long Social Liberal!"

"Yeah, my brother has the same problem."

They laughed again.

"It must be some programmed holdover from the family line. Otherwise, I don't know where it pops out from. Anyway, you don't feel Catholic or Jewish?"

"No. You know what, I feel like a grown-up. All the things that have always bothered me about the Old and New Testaments strike me as pretty equal in both of those religions. I don't believe in a personal god, a wrathful god, heaven or hell, or all the 'ya must do it this way' stuff. I have never shared this with anyone, Innocenta, but I have spent the last twenty years studying most religions. As a Catholic, that means I'm going to hell!"

Bart laughed heartily and Innocenta shushed him (it was a small restaurant).

"You know, if you put fifty Social Liberals together in one room, you would have about seventy-five belief systems."

Bart smiled, "Sounds wonderful! Can I be a Buddhist Social Liberal?"

"Yup. Just ask my mother."

"Really!? I will ask your mother. So, the bottom line is this—I forgive my parents, especially my father, for what they did, I am ecstatic about meeting my grandfather—ecstatic. I feel like a more complete person, but

I can't relate to either Catholicism or Judaism."

Then, purposely, dramatically, "I declare my independence!"

The foursome at the neighboring table broke out into applause. Bart turned New Mexico sunrise pink and wanted to sink below the table. The foursome felt self-conscious at over-hearing Bart and embarrassing him and returned to their plates.

The nearest man turned to Bart, "The *frito misto* is wonderful!"

Bart recovered and replied, "Thanks for the recommendation."

Bart continued with small stories about his father's childhood that his grandfather had told this morning. Everyone in the de la Madrid family (well, most) was excited about trekking up to *San Bruno de los Conversos* (as his grandfather had referred to it). Innocenta expressed her enthusiasm for the trek as well. Over coffee and dessert, Innocenta related the story of the visit from the educators and the decisions made.

"Raul Theodore is an extraordinary kid, and you are an extraordinary mother. I'm so proud of both of you."

Innocenta beamed.

"Let's go home and sit in the backyard. I feel the stars calling us."

The stars were noisy with enthusiasm, swirling with energies, beckoning, and unspeakably beautiful. Innocenta and Bart sat holding hands and pointing out exceptional stars and interesting constellations.

"That group is our family. See, nine stars, just like us."

"I hope I'm a good enough star to be up there with you."

"Oh, Bart."

Innocenta kissed him tenderly and whispered, "You are a star, Bart, my shining star. God, I love you! Let's go to bed. It's been a very long day."

The following morning, Barrington and James emerged. Everyone had a rowdy breakfast together and headed for the late service. The sermon was entitled "The Gospel of Thomas; Meeting Jesus Before He Was Christ."

The Gospel of Thomas was one of the many banned books, deemed heretical by the bishopric wing of the early Christian Church, lost, and then found nearly complete at Nag Hamadi. It presents sayings of Jesus without associating the stories, miracles, and other apocrypha that were added later to orthodox, "acceptable" gospels. In The Gospel of Thomas, one meets an enlightened human named Jesus who, like the Buddha before him, needed no person or gods to intercede on his behalf. He knew the ineffable because he willed himself to and realized that the message of love defined heaven on earth. The sermon ended with Saying 113:

"His disciples said to him, 'When will the kingdom come?' He said, 'It will not come when it is expected. They will not say, 'Look here,' or 'Look there.' Rather the kingdom is spread out on the earth and people do not see it.'"

The minister omitted the phrase "of the father," after "the kingdom," as it was anachronistic for the twenty-first century.

Neither Bart nor James had ever heard any sermon like this. This gentle message from the Middle East seemed to have been lost—they were empowered to create heaven on earth if only they would will themselves to see and act. Bart was so stunned that there was no violence, threats of damnation, no "God the Father," and no mention of "salvation" that he just sat in the pew for a few minutes. Innocenta had to go back and retrieve him.

"Wow! Now, I really know that I'm not in a Catholic church. None of it was about the afterlife or supernatural stuff. It was just here, on Earth, now. And it was beautiful."

Innocenta led him into the narthex to introduce him to other congregants. Bart felt right at home.

Bart's cell phone rang. He was embarrassed because he had neglected to turn it off; it could have rung during the service. Bart glanced at his phone and stepped outside to take the call. As the congregants were dispersing, Innocenta found Bart in the garden weeping.

"My father just called. Grandfather's neighbor, the lady who checked on him every day, called. She found Grandfather dead. He went to sleep and never woke up."

"Oh, Bart, I'm so sorry."

Bart cried softly, the child in him guiding his tears out through the ducts and into the glare of extinguished dreams. Innocenta got a ride home with Barrington and James while Bart drove straight to his parents' house.

Innocenta, Theodora Mercedes, Barrington, and James attended the funeral. The Rael de la Madrid family assembled by erratic arrivals at the cemetery. Theodora Mercedes went straight to Alfredo's wife, introduced herself, and stayed next to her. The oldest daughter joined them on her mother's right. Alfredo was being physically supported by Bart and another brother. Alfredo wept bitterly, and Innocenta was fearful that he would faint—or worse. Someone whispered to Innocenta that there would be no traditional gathering afterwards—most unusual for a Hispanic family, and a measure of the depth of their grieving. Bart and James were split when Innocenta joined them and locked her arms into theirs. There she stayed for the entire service. Innocenta and Theodora Mercedes each discovered, as always, that the gift had only partially lifted its veil. They *were* affected and wept openly.

Moises Aaron Rael de la Madrid was buried next to his wife in Santa Fe's Jewish cemetery. Except for Bart's parents, everyone in the family was surprised that she was there. Grandmother's grave had been blocks away, but they never knew it. There was not a dry eye to be seen or an unbroken heart to be felt. Innocenta had never laid eyes on Moises Aaron Rael de la Madrid despite his being only one door away just a few days ago. There was an emptiness in her that she now understood from her vision. Innocenta was mourning not ever having met him and not being properly able to feel what was tearing at her future husband's heart. But her spirit was closer than she believed; they were both mourning the loss of chance only offered once—Innocenta to meet and get to know Moises; Bart to touch his grandfather one more time and hear one more story.

CHAPTER EIGHT

Barrington Wilson Silverton Vigil

Barrington Wilson Silverton Vigil slept fitfully in anticipation of visiting James' mother, never reaching full REM sleep. James endured a strange, disquieting dream that seemed to last an entire morning.

When James was five, he was taken to his first Protestant Sunday school class on the reservation. James was frightened but maintained a passive expression. The school room was no bigger than the family hogan (in which they never lived), in every aspect cold in climate, and ruled by a Dominionist with pasty skin. James would have been terrified by now; his mother had left him there, except for one, saving grace—a poster of the crucifixion. Not being a Roman Catholic or even Hispanic church, the crucifix was not what James would later see in such institutions—the bloodiest, goriest nailing the imagination could conjure up. No, this was a beautiful Italianate rendering of manly perfection, in countenance and body, pale, pale pink with blond hair and no excessive body fat. James took one look and decided he could stay for a while; he was the most beautiful object he had ever seen. He had no understanding at all of the stirring in his loins but James knew with no instruction required that he really liked what he was feeling. James knew that the Jesus must be in pain, but that made him all the more erotic. He was not old enough to understand this paradox and felt guilty, just as he was meant to feel. James was reprimanded several times for not paying attention. Later, when his mother asked what was discussed, James, was utterly perplexed—he had no idea how to respond. His mother, seeing his reaction, let it go.

And now, all of this came back in James' dream with one spectacular exception—it was Barrington on the cross. Barrington had grown (in a late growth spurt) to nearly six feet, one inch, had dirty blond hair, and a beautiful body. James was disturbed by this both horrid and beautiful vision—what could it mean? Barrington and the crucified Christ had nothing in common. Why was Barrington up there? Before James could sort all this out, Barrington opened his eyes and looked right into James'.

This mixing of images and swirling of life and death startled James awake. Barrington stirred but never fully awakened, so James lay there letting his mind relax from the disquieting vision. He was awake for an hour before his mind and body let go, and he found a peaceful slumber.

In the morning, neither Barrington nor James said anything about their fitful nights. At James' request, they had skipped Sunday service at the Social Liberal Church. James said it was to get an early start, but Barrington thought that this did not sound convincing—it had that chalky undertaste of something unpleasant disguised. Barrington attributed this to James' being nervous about the purpose for this trip.

They each had an overnight bag; Barrington's was leather, expensive, and stylish, whereas James' was canvas, marked-down, and utilitarian. Had she been up, Innocenta would have said, in one of her most vulgar of sayings, that they were leaving "at the butt-crack of dawn." In her absence, Barrington filled-in the comment on her behalf much to James' amusement.

A reserved man, James rarely laughed aloud but was caught off-guard. "Your sister says that?"

"Yup. Ain't it great? She comes up with some zingers. It's very un-Silverton-de Baca when she does it."

"Well, whatever; I think it's funny."

"Not only that, she blames me for the "Holy Mother of God" phrase, but it's hers; I can assure you."

Beginning a road trip with a good laugh was a good start, particularly given the night each had had.

They were in the shadows of Sandia Mountain when the sun rose. James then headed west on Interstate 40. Neither discussed the impending encounter with James' mother. James sensed that Barrington was avoiding the subject; he would wait.

Barrington had been in James' truck for over two hours and had to attend to nature. They pulled off at Laguna, completed their biological needs, and then stopped to admire the little Pueblo. The Pueblo occupied a tiny hillock in a narrow valley with a tiny church at the top of the mound. Most of the buildings were whitewashed.

"Did you know that this Pueblo has less than four thousand people?"

"The town is certainly small."

"Yet, the Pueblo owns two large companies. One operates all its retail and services, including three casinos. The other is a construction company that has offices in Albuquerque, Texas, Jordan, and Iraq. They do a lot of construction work in Iraq."

"This little Pueblo?"

"Yup, this little Pueblo. A lot of this was fueled by uranium mining on Pueblo lands, but they are very organized and successful."

Less than two hours later, Barrington and James were sitting in the restaurant of the El Rancho Hotel in Gallup. They had a late breakfast and then toured the mezzanine to see the pictures of the movie stars. The El Rancho had housed everyone from John Wayne to Katherine Hepburn while they made movies in the area. It was quaint, interesting, and a welcomed break from the travel. Barrington had never been there and would never forget this incongruous outpost of Hollywood. They jumped into James' Ford F250 and continued on to Window Rock.

"Can we talk about your mother?"

"Thought you were never going to ask. My mother lives in Window Rock, in an assisted-living place."

"Is she disabled?"

"No, not at all. She doesn't pay for services she doesn't need, so for her, it's simply a retirement home. When my father died, she was lonely and already had friends in the place. So she moved in and has lived there ever since."

"How long has that been?"

"Um, close to ten years. She loves it, plays bridge, bingo, gossips, or whatever old ladies do together, and still bowls."

"How will this conversation go?"

"I don't really know. I'm her youngest, but she never badgered me about getting married. My hope is that she will take it well."

Barrington kept silent and waited for James to continue. Nothing else was offered, so Barrington asked, "What if she doesn't take it well?"

James remained silent still and kept driving. Finally, as they were approaching Window Rock, "I don't know. I've never had a big disagreement with my mother. I just hope that we can talk about it."

"James, why do you have to talk about it at all? Lots of people don't discuss their intimate lives with their parents. What if it just serves to upset her and nothing good comes of it?"

"I can't believe that my mother would reject me as her son because

I'm gay. It just wouldn't be her. As to why I have to tell my mother, you should know that already."

"You mean because of *my* mother's demand that people be authentic?"

"I wouldn't have put it that way, but yes, authentic. I just would have said that your mother is loyal to the truth and intolerant of deception."

"Is your mother like mine?"

"No, we have just always had a very straightforward, honest relationship—except for this."

Barrington let it go. It became clear to him that it was important for James to be honest with his mother. Barrington simply had to accept that.

James slowed his truck as they entered the outskirts of Window Rock. The sprawling unruly mix of commercial buildings, manufactured housing, strip centers, and the like made the town look like many western small towns. Window Rock was the administrative center for the Navajo Nation, the largest reservation in America. James pointed out the Navajo Nation Council Chamber, a handsome building of stacked native rock and timbers.

"That's an impressive building. It has dignity about it. Did you go to school around here?"

"No, I attended grammar school in Chinle then went to the Navajo Academy in Farmington."

"Navajo Academy? I never heard of it."

"It's now known as the Navajo Preparatory School, but its mission is more or less the same; to get promising Navajo kids ready for college. After that, I went to the University of Arizona, as you already know. Well, Barrington, here we are."

James had pulled into a parking lot covered in chip seal. A nondescript low building stood before them. A flagpole flew the Stars and Stripes, and the flag of the Navajo Nation with its outline of the reservation, the four sacred mountains, and the distinctive rainbow overarching it all. Barrington stopped to admire it and to make out its details.

Inside, they signed the visitor register.

"You better wait here until I either come and get you or run out."

James delivered the line with utmost calmness and serenity. Barrington's eyes widened and James let a smile grow on his face.

"I'm just kidding!"

"You . . . get outta here!"

They both chuckled as James retreated into the complex. Barrington sat down on a couch and then it dawned on him that he had no idea how long James would be gone. He closed his eyes, exhaustion and a full stomach overpowered him, and Barrington was sound asleep in a few minutes.

James found his mother playing Bingo.

"Hello, Mother." James continued to greet all the ladies around him with the same traditional greeting.

"James, what are you doin' here? I'm in the middle of playing Bingo. Got good cards too!"

"I came to talk with you, Mother."

"Not now, James, I need to win this. It's today's jackpot, three free games of bowling for four!"

"OK, Mother, I'll wait in the back until you win."

James had no need to ask if his mother had won. When the last letter/ number was called, she yelled "Bingo!" so loudly that Barrington could hear it in his sleep. This led to a confusing dream.

Mrs. Many Farms led her son to her apartment where they sat outside under the shade of a locust tree.

"What brings you here, Son? Is everything OK in Santa Fe?"

"Yes, Mother, everything's fine. I have enough design and construction work to keep the money flowing, and the art market is strong."

James then took the opening to tell his mother about the commission to sculpt Popé and the tribal leaders. He told her the whole story.

"Who's Barrington? It sounds like a character on Masterpiece Theater."

"No. He's not a character; he's a friend, a very good friend. Mother, that's what I came to talk to you about."

James stopped here as verklemption took him by surprise.

"James, are you finally going to tell me about the two spirits in you?"

"What?"

"In Navajo tradition, some people are recognized as being of two spirits, not just one. They are *nádleehé*, 'one who changes or is transformed.' They possess, or are possessed by male and female spirits, neither heterosexual nor homosexual. *Nádleehé* occupy both genders and traditionally must choose one or the other. These days, there is less reason to choose and more reason just to be you. But the white man has poisoned our minds with his ideas. I took you out of that church when I heard that man talk about homosexuals as perverts going to hell. I didn't want my little boy to hear that and be hurt by it. But the poison has spread. *Nádleehé* are now often treated by our own people like the white man treats homosexuals. It is a sad change for us. I was glad to see you leave for boarding school and then college. I wanted you to be well adjusted and happy, James. It was better for you to be off the reservation. Did you have any problems at the Navajo Academy?"

James the Awestruck had said nothing, attempted to process as fast as his mother spoke, and now failed to recognize a question.

"James? Did you have any problems at the Navajo Academy?"

"Oh, no, I was bigger than most other boys; taller anyway. It wasn't bad."

"That's good. If you had had problems there, I wouldn't have known what to do next."

"Mother, do you mean to tell me . . . "

"That I've always known you are gay? Yes, James, of course. I'm your mother. I watched. I listened. I first saw two spirits when you were in the first grade. Little boys are seldom comfortable with little girls. You liked everyone, especially girls. Then one day, I had to get you out of my Sunday shoes before your father saw you. He had already been poisoned by the white man's thinking. I hid your true nature from him. It wasn't actually that hard, you were very athletic. You still look very athletic, James."

James was mute in deep thought. Had he known it, James would know that his underestimation of his mother was mirrored in Barrington's underestimation of Theodora Mercedes.

"Mother, I don't know what to say."

"Then tell me about Barrington. You are finally in love, aren't you?"

James turned bright red through his tawny features and suppressed a very embarrassed smile.

"Mother, I would like you to meet Barrington if you would like to meet Barrington."

"He's here. I like that James. You secretly had faith in me. I would be honored to meet, to meet your—what do you call your relationship?"

"I guess he's my 'partner.'"

"Your partner; is he nice?"

"Really nice, Mother."

"Good looking Native American or white man?"

"Good looking white man of Hispanic background. His people have been in Santa Fe since just after the Pueblo Revolt. Good family too."

"Well, I better meet him. You know bridge starts in another hour, and we intend to mop the floor with Mrs. Tsiniginnie and Mrs. Begay."

"Barrington! Wake up."

James gently rocked Barrington by the shoulder. Barrington awoke, looked at James and spoke,

"I had the strangest dream. I don't know where I was, but someone in the distance yelled 'Bingo!' or something like that. How did it go?"

"It was amazing and perplexing. Mother has always known and she's OK. Actually, she's more than OK; she wants to meet you."

"Well, we better not keep Mother waiting."

"James was right; you are a good looking man. I am James' mother, Mrs. Many Farms of the Butterfly Clan, born for the Piñon Jay Clan. Actually, we tend to go longer on this, but you don't need to be bored by it. It's a Navajo thing. I am very pleased to meet you, Barrington."

"I'm very pleased to meet you, Mrs. Many Farms. How are you today?"

"Wonderful. Won the jackpot at Bingo this morning and I'm going to win at bridge in a little while. Most importantly, my son came to see me and seems to be happy. Do I have you to thank for that?"

Barrington grinned and looked at James, who was blushing.

"I would like to think that I have added to his happiness. James is a happy person anyway, hardworking, and full of artistic talent."

"I'm glad you think so. He could draw well as a small child. Are his latest sculptures good? I haven't seen any for some time."

"Yes, his sculptures are beautiful and James is justifiably famous for them. Did he tell you about his Popé project?"

"Yes, and he gives you some credit for making it better. You seem to be well-matched spirits. I hope you feel your spirits dance together. I can see that they do."

"Yes, Ma'am, I do feel our spirits dance. James makes me happy, and I sincerely hope I make him happy."

"I think so, young man, I think so. May I ask who your people are?"

Barrington looked to James for guidance, "Your family names."

"Oh! (feeling stupid) I'm from the Silverton–de Baca line."

"Very good. I hope you are proud of your lineage."

"I am, Ma'am."

"You must come back to visit again. But bring pictures of some of James' sculptures. Can I leave that to you?"

"Yes, Ma'am, you can, I promise."

"Good! Now gentlemen, I want you both to escort me to bridge. When the other ladies see you tall, handsome men on my arms, they will be green with envy. Navajo modesty is overrated. I will be the talk of the house, and I will never contribute a word. I especially want Mrs. Tsiniginnie and Mrs. Begay to see us. I want to shake them up so that we can beat them at bridge."

James and Barrington did as Mrs. Many Farms asked. It was true. All heads turned, and the entire room went silent. Mrs. Many Farms beamed at everyone and seemed to encourage speculation without saying a word. Both James and Barrington kissed Mrs. Many Farms on the cheek and promised to return. They exited quickly.

Barrington and James reached the lobby to sign out and found two of James' brothers looking at the sign-in register. James' oldest brother Samuel and the middle brother (of five), Phillip, lifted their eyes and conversation to James' own eyes.

Samuel slowly spoke. "Jimmie, I didn't know you were in town. I've heard rumors about you from Santa Fe. They say you're one of those Nancy Boys. What are you doing here, Cocksucker?"

"Sam, Phil, good to see you. We were just leaving."

"Who's this, your girlfriend? Let's see" and he turned to look at the register as Phil blocked Barrington, "Barrington. What kind of cocksucker name is Barrington?"

"Just shut up, Sam. Leave him out of this!"

"Like hell I will, cocksucker! So, Barrington, do you suck my brother's cock or just take it up yer ass?"

"Sam! I said leave him alone!"

Sam threw a muscular punch and caught James in the jaw in a glancing blow. James, taller, younger, lither, moved quickly, grabbed Sam's arm, and used his momentum to throw Sam to the floor. Phil surprised Barrington with a punch to the stomach and he went down like a cheap piñata. But, that put Phil at James' advantage, landing a left hook straight into Phil's right eye. Phil was knocked backwards and hit his head on the sign-in counter. He went down. Sam was now up and grabbed James from behind in an arm lock. One look at this and Barrington recovered. Seeing his lover in the arm lock spurred incalculable rage, and Barrington landed a round-house kick to the small of Sam's back. James and Sam went down, and Barrington kicked again before Sam could recover. He grabbed James and pushed him towards the door as Phil, in one last vicious effort, kicked James in the groin. James doubled over and Barrington kept him moving.

When they got to James' truck, Barrington was in full flight mode, "Give me the keys! Give me the keys!"

As James reached for his left pocket, Barrington pushed his hand out of the way and retrieved the keys himself. Sam and Phil were coming out as Barrington got James into the passenger seat. Because Sam and Phil were waddling like overweight skunks, Barrington had enough time to get into the driver's seat and start the engine. They roared off just as Sam reached for the passenger-side door handle. The truck wheeled him around and flung him into Phil and they went down in the parking lot.

Barrington exceeded the speed limits and got to the bitter edge of town. He pulled behind a gas station building.

"Are you all right?"

"Yeah, my balls don't hurt as much as my hand does. You?"

"I'm fine. He just surprised me."

"I'm so sorry, Barrington, I'm so sorry!"

"It's OK, James, you didn't plan this. Let me see your hand."

James' hand was skinned from the middle to the outer knuckles from hitting Phil's eye socket. The blood was starting to coagulate, but his hand, shirt, and jeans were covered in blood.

"Do you have a first-aid kit?"

"Yes, behind your seat."

Barrington fished around with his hand until he felt a handle. Five minutes later James' hand was bandaged but not cleaned up.

"That will have to do."

"I'm fine now. Let's get out of here."

Barrington drove out and was now calm enough to keep within the speed limits.

"Where did that kick come from? I think they call it a round-house kick."

"I saw Innocenta do one. She was being pestered in high school by a gang member who insisted that she was going to be his girl friend. He wouldn't take 'no,' or worse, for an answer. One day he showed up on our front porch. Innocenta went out, there was a lot of shouting, and he tried to grab her. She was too fast for him and gave him a round-house kick right in the you-know-whats. He wasn't as tough as my sister and never bothered her again. It was so cool! I asked her to teach me that move. She hung a twenty-pound sack of potatoes from a tree limb and that's what we practiced on. Consuelo was really put out. We bruised all the potatoes and they were all over the yard because we battered the hell out of the burlap sack!"

"Your sister is one incredible woman."

In Gallup, Barrington pulled into a doc-in-the-box place.

"God, I hate these places. Let's get this over with."

The wait was almost an hour, but finally James' hand was cleaned, disinfected and properly bandaged—no stitches required.

Barrington drove them back to the El Rancho Hotel. The desk clerk looked at them oddly; a white man and a bloodied Indian.

"Is everything all right, gentlemen?"

"Everything's fine. We would just like to check in and rest."

"Fine. One room or two?"

"One, king bed, please."

The hotel clerk had no doubt seen it all and heard it all; he was unphased by this request.

"I can let you have a very nice mini-suite. It's away from the street and has a nice sitting area as well—no extra charge."

It was at this point that Barrington realized that the clerk was gay.

He smiled and replied, "That'll be fine. Thank you."

The clerk responded with his best flirty smile, which Barrington pretended not to see.

Barrington's history of "Why me?" kicked-in with paranoiac insistence. He parked James' truck in the back. Having been in an unexpected fight, Barrington's imagination painted ugly pictures of the two brothers following them and finding them in Gallup. It would take several hours for Barrington to return to his new-found adulthood. But for now, Barrington was afraid again.

Neither man talked while Barrington pulled off James' boots, socks, bloody jeans, and stained cowboy shirt. Barrington looked at the shirt. It was lush with embroidery, piping, and blood. He estimated that it had cost James at least one hundred and fifty dollars. James had dressed-up for his mother. When Barrington realized this, he buried his face in the shirt and cried. James, now stretched out on the bed, looked at his lover with guilt and empathy. He had never anticipated the ugly encounter, much less its effect on Barrington. James reached up and tenderly pulled Barrington down into his embrace while Barrington continued to cry out his fears in copious silent tears.

At seven minutes after seven, James awoke. He and Barrington had slept for three hours. Barrington was still in his arms. James gently roused him.

"Hey, I'm starving."

Barrington found himself in his lover's strong embrace. With great literalness, his position braced his courage, and he found that he "was back."

"What a day! I need to eat a horse to fully revive!"

They laughed with the ease and gentleness of people in the presence of two spirits dancing.

Barrington sat up. "Your clothes! We can't go out with your clothes looking like . . . "

"Like I was in a fight?"

They laughed again.

"Those are some brothers you have."

"Yeah, I had no idea they would be anywhere around."

James looked far away, to a hurtful place, and said nothing more for a few seconds.

"James, it's not your fault. It's over."

"Yeah, for now. We promised to visit my mother again."

"Well, James, at least we'll already know that two welcomes will be possible next time. We promised your mother, and I think she'll hold us to it. I don't want to disappoint her. Do you?"

"You amaze me, Barrington. You endure the terrors of meeting my mother, survive an unexpected fight, take care of my wounds, and you're ready to do it again."

"OK, let's not get carried away here. Can we at least wait a few months?"

"Good idea. What about dinner?"

"What about your clothes?"

"It just so happens that I brought an extra pair of jeans and a shirt. I was so nervous that I thought I would sweat through my clothes. So, I brought extra everything."

"Amazing! Let's get showered."

"Where can we get dinner and a drink—not too far away?"

The evening clerk listed several bar/restaurants within walking distance. They picked the closest one and walked down one block. By ten, they were tipsy, fed, and walked back to the El Rancho. The next morning, neither would remember going to bed. Barrington awoke with a slightly sore stomach. James' hand was throbbing. They made haste back to Santa Fe with Barrington driving.

Barrington and James stayed at James' house for the next week. James' hand was healing, and neither of them talked about the previous Sunday.

On Tuesday, Barrington brought up a subject common to gay men, "James, when was the last time you were tested?"

"I don't know; a year maybe?"

"Why don't we go down to the clinic tomorrow afternoon and get tested together?"

"OK."

They didn't know yet that they would be attending a funeral Wednesday morning.

Moises Aaron Rael de la Madrid's funeral was a sobering, shadowing event despite the New Mexico sun. Barrington was heartbroken for the family, especially Bart. Barrington and James held Innocenta between them during the service. She wept quietly the entire time for her lover's shattered heart. None who were present would ever forget this day, but not necessarily for the same reasons.

That afternoon, Barrington and James changed their clothes and drove to the clinic. The modern tests only take a couple of minutes. They were led as a couple into a testing room, their fingers were sanitized, pricked by a needle, and a drop of blood was collected from each. James, who had been pricked first, was pronounced "negative." James and Barrington grinned with happiness and relief.

"Mr. Vigil, I'm sorry, but you've tested positive for HIV."

Barrington slumped into a faint as the potentially devastating news had not been expected. James leaped to him and held him up. The nurse put cold compresses on Barrington's forehead.

"No! No! It can't be true! You have to test me again. The test must be wrong!"

"That's not likely, Mr. Vigil. But as you have tested positive on this quick test, there are many tests to come. I'm sorry."

James managed to get Barrington scheduled for the next round of tests for the following week. He led Barrington to his truck. Barrington buckled his own seatbelt but otherwise looked and moved like a dead man. His eyes were hollow, glassy, and focused in the badlands of his soul. His skin looked like gray paper. Barrington had aged ten years in just a few minutes. James was heartbroken for his lover but couldn't find any words. Barrington stayed at James' house for the rest of the week, a battered spirit folded in on himself. He spoke little and ate less. James would hold him at night, but Barrington was in a spot where loneliness kept him in its claws.

On Friday, Barrington spoke, "You're going to leave me, aren't you? I'm diseased and you're going to leave me, aren't you?"

"What!? I'm not going anywhere, Barrington. I still love you. This doesn't change anything. We'll fight this together. I'm not going to let my love go so easily. Please don't ever say that again. We'll fight it, Barrington, we'll fight it!"

"What if I die?"

"Barrington! We're all going to die!"

"Not like this. Not with this disease."

"Barrington, you are not going to die. That's ancient history. The nurse said that HIV is 'a manageable infection.' Please, just get a hold of yourself. I know how sad you are, but I'm here, and I'm not going anywhere!"

"You still want to be in a relationship with me?"

"Yes, with no hesitation, Barrington."

Barrington, who had been dry-faced all week, burst into tears and James gathered him into the fortification of his arms.

On Saturday, Barrington was still depressed but was functioning enough to cook James' dinner. James was still at his studio when Innocenta called with the news of Alfonso's and Reigh's deaths. The news of Barrington's favorite uncle dying and his strange, quirky, but loved cousin dying by murder put Barrington into a different frame of reference. He had an infection; others were dead or had lost their entire family. Barrington ached for Aunt Angelica Gertrudis. How could she possibly bear this? It seemed impossible to Barrington that anyone could survive this much butchery and horror of the heart. The triple tragedy put Barrington's catastrophe in a new perspective as he put down the phone. He drove to James' studio.

Barrington told James the entire sordid story of the Hoffmann family. He described what Angelica Gertrudis and his mother must have seen. James was too stunned to speak. First, the confrontation in Gallup, then the de la Madrid tragedy, and now this—all in one week.

James and Barrington both were teary when at last Barrington spoke. "James, I'm so ashamed. I've felt sorry for myself all week, but my infection is nothing compared to what the de la Madrid and Hoffmann families have suffered. I feel like an idiot, a selfish idiot."

"Barrington, you deserved to grieve. It was quite a shock to you. These other events put it in a new perspective, that's all. In a macabre way, these deaths have been good for you. Just when you think your world has crumbled and you wish you were dead, things much, much worse come along and right your head and heart. Now, I think we can deal with your infection with level heads. And, we'll do it together, Barrington. Now, what about your family? They need you."

"They need us, James. Let me go home and talk to Innocenta. She'll know what to do and how to help."

"OK. Let me finish up here, and I'll meet you at your house later."

After retrieving his dirty clothes and shaving kit from James' house, Barrington drove home. Innocenta was sitting in the kitchen with The Very Catholic Consuelo. They were drinking tea. Innocenta rose to greet and hug Barrington. He held her as she cried.

"Mother had to see the whole thing too. I feel so bad for them. And poor Uncle Reigh and Cousin Alfonso, dead! It's so horrible."

"I know. It's unimaginable. How did Mother sound?"

"She was rattled but strong, just like a third daughter of the line is supposed to be. She'll phone later. A police detective was there and was a friend of Reigh's or something. He's going to help her with the arrangements."

On Wednesday, Barrington drove himself, Innocenta, and James to Albuquerque. The funeral, because of its sensational nature, was a frenzied affair. Barrington and Innocenta both spoke about their uncle and cousin. Afterwards, Barrington and James had to hustle Theodora Mercedes and Angelica Gertrudis out of there because of the press. They comforted the women at Angelica Gertrudis' now empty house. Reigh's good-natured conversation was missing, and Alfonso's enduring (to some) weirdness was apparent only by his odd bedroom. Barrington and James spent a few minutes in his room looking at Alfonso's treasures. They were now fossils of a past life and looked forlorn and lifeless. There was a peculiar heaviness to Alfonso's space. Perhaps, his bedroom was in mourning too. Who knows what happens in objects and spaces that we in our hubris perceive as inanimate? Barrington remarked that the Chagall windows "looked sad."

"They always looked so happy to me before."

James kept his thoughts closed but knew that emotion imparted meaning to art. That effect was occurring now but Barrington would only realize it later. For now, James avoided sounding like some Native American sage. By his silence, James only proved that he was.

The trio left the two women at the Hoffmann house. It was difficult to leave. They all knew that Theodora Mercedes was facing the biggest challenge in her life—how to keep Angelica Gertrudis moving through her unspeakable grief yet causing her to will herself to persevere and keep living. The enormity of the task was daunting, but they knew that if these goals were possible, Theodora Mercedes was the best woman for the job. Nevertheless, their hearts went out to her.

In Santa Fe, dinner was bitter-sweet as the trio tried to be cheerful for the children. The two Unremarkables seemed untouched by the events. Raul Theodore sensed that something was amiss and kept staring at his mother. Tonight, his calculations did not seem to be rooted in mathematics or physics. Innocenta, despite her grief and show of cheerfulness, observed Raul Theodore in return. She discovered new depths in him that she never knew existed. Innocenta grabbed him and hugged him until he protested and squirmed out of her grip. Innocenta was smiling now.

After dinner James asked, "Barrington, what would you like to do?"

Barrington led him into the backyard and they sat in the chairs between the trees. "James, I think that I need to just look at the stars."

They sat mostly quiet, holding hands, and looking to the complexity of the Milky Way for meaning. If it was there, neither said so. Without a word, both got up and went to bed. The Milky Way continued in its churning path across the sky, keeping to itself its secret knowledge and ineffable beauty. They couldn't know that it too was also weeping.

CHAPTER NINE
The Very Catholic Consuelo

When she was born, The Very Catholic Consuelo was an eccentric combination. She had been born into a family native to the organized dust called Ascension, Chihuahua. Her grandfather Leopoldo had been converted to a polygamist Mormon sect by a proselytizer from nearby Colonia Diaz. This was just before the entire Mormon colony was forced to emigrate back to the United States in 1912. The Mexican Revolution had produced a not surprising lack of tolerance for Americans in Mexico. The polygamist Mormons fared no better or, perhaps, worse due to their poor marrying habits as seen by the Mexicans. Moreover, they were not Mexican citizens but were given a reasonable time to go back—a few weeks. Leopoldo, a disingenuous man who saw a continuing opportunity to satisfy his desires, decided to emigrate as well. He waited a reasonable length of time after Colonia Diaz was emptied, sacked of its remaining goods, and burned to the ground by locals who delighted in seeing the Mormons go. Leopoldo, who should have been shocked as he watched, instead participated wholeheartedly; such was the character of this man. He let a few months pass, then Leopoldo moved his family to Cuidad Juárez, applied for legal entry, and waited with his first wife and two "sisters-in law."

Upon entering El Paso, Texas, Leopoldo took a job in a laundry—a job he was lucky to get. Erroneously believing that polygamy was still legal in the United States, he estimated that it would take him three years to save enough cash to continue the move to Utah. Leopoldo was not only ill-informed but dull, unlucky, and unobservant as one-by-one his wives escaped his filthy clutches. Like many selfish, egotistical men, Leopoldo could not fathom why his wives should flee him like this. He never learned that his first, and only legitimate, wife had fled to her parents' house in *Gómez Palacio, Durango.* The others went east and north. Sister-wife Alicia went to San Antonio, Texas, joining countless members of her extended family there. Alicia would disappear into this friendly city. Sister-wife Xochil, whose name Leopoldo never got around to Mormonizing, fled north to Santa Fe.

Xochil had grabbed enough cash to board a bus. The vehicle was shabby, rusty, rattled without mercy, and its bald tires rolled on faith alone. The journey took four excruciating days during which Xochil banged her head twice and puked out a broken window. When she arrived, her back was so sore she exited the bus stooped like a woman fifty years her senior. In Santa Fe, she went to the cathedral and threw herself and her story on anyone who would listen. Father Jones, a priest assigned to the cathedral befriended her, and Xochil was taken in by nuns for the next few months. Coincidentally, she also managed to land a job in a laundry while preparing meals for the nuns out of gratitude. The nuns, used to simple meals, enjoyed Xochil's meals such that they bordered on sinfulness while avoiding gluttony. Her reputation as a cook grew outside the walls of the convent. When the archbishop's cook/housekeeper retired, Xochil was promoted. Xochil liked Archbishop Pitaval immensely; however, she was not fond of the priest who had befriended her when she first appeared in Santa Fe.

Father Jones had had relations with the now-retired cook when she was young. Later, when the cook was in early middle age, he abandoned her and had relations with her daughter. The cook never learned about this ultimate of betrayals.

In Xochil, Father Jones saw a beautiful, petite young woman alone in the world whom he believed owed him some favors. The new cook was grateful, but her gratitude had limits. Having been falsely betrothed to the loathsome Leopoldo, Xochil was twice-shy of any man's advances. But an ordained priest repelled Xochil beyond the realm of words and her newly restored faith. She was no fool like Leopoldo, who was blind to his wives' plans and actions to escape him. Xochil recognized the subtle advances and feigned a convincing nonrecognition of the signs. Father Jones stepped it up. Xochil found that she would have to glide, slip, duck out of Father Jones' grasp. Finally, biology and wickedness overpowered the priest, and he confronted her in her quarters.

"Xochil, why do you evade me? You would not be here if it were not for my help. I only ask for an easy favor to show your gratitude to me."

Xochil felt like the Beast was addressing her from hell. Her fright at his soothing words and burning eyes produced a seizing up of her will. Paralyzed, Xochil watched as Father Jones crossed the room to take her.

116

Once upon her, Xochil reacted with physical fury, but Father Jones was stout and strong.

Afterwards, he lay panting upon her while she cried softly, waiting for this base and heavy man to roll off her.

"There, there, that wasn't so bad, was it? It's not like you were a virgin. After all, your sin was the greater by living in a polygamist marriage not recognized by God."

Xochil could not locate the words to express her revulsion of this man and his cleverly reasoned rape. When Father Jones left her, Xochil cried as if something in her had died. A bath to wash the Beast off her did nothing to help. Vowing to never let herself be taken by Father Jones or any other man, Xochil was resolved.

One week later, Father Jones approached her again in the kitchen. Xochil grabbed a chef's knife and held it behind her. She warned him, but vaguely, at first. Father Jones sneered at her. She warned him more directly. Father Jones came at Xochil; she brought the knife forward and stabbed him in the crotch before he even realized that she was armed. The knife pierced his scrotum, severing his left testicle. Father Jones stifled his pain and wrinkled himself onto the floor like dirty laundry.

Xochil threw him a towel, looked at him with a pure hatred, like that of molten steel, and said, "Why, Padre, you have fallen on a kitchen knife. Let me call the archbishop to help you!"

"No! You bitch! Call nobody, you bitch, you bitch!"

Father Jones pulled the knife out of his pants, tossed it in the sink, held the towel closely, and limped out the way he had come. Xochil cleaned up his abhorrent fluids and disinfected the knife. She was not as satisfied as she expected to be as she slipped the knife back into the rack. The knife was clean, replaced into its position prior to its new purpose, but she was a changed woman. Xochil, who loved her life in Santa Fe, found that her hatred extended to the church that tolerated such a man. Her faith in the archbishop Pitaval, oddly, did not waver. He was a decent God-fearing man. But the institution was tainted forever by Father Jones.

The story was that Father Jones was working in his own kitchen and had an unfortunate accident with a knife. Doctor Reveles suspected that there was more to the story of this remarkable wound than met his ears and eyes—there was no bloody knife in the kitchen. Doctor Reveles was also physician to the retired cook and her daughter. He said nothing but thought much.

Doctor Reveles looked at the bandaged priest with contempt, "I hope you don't develop an infection, Father Jones. It would be very difficult to treat, and you would likely lose your capacities as a man. But, of course, as a celibate, this would mean little to you. Keep some ice on the wound but keep it dry. I will be back tomorrow to change the bandages. Good evening, Father Jones."

Doctor Reveles was amused that Father Jones would suffer the pain of the wound, the pain of ice on his genitalia, and whatever humiliation he had already endured. Doctor Reveles left the priest's house with a smile on his face.

Xochil would never learn whether Father Jones properly healed. In fact, he kept an unreasonable distance from Xochil from that day forward. Unfortunately, Xochil would later learn that her one encounter with the Beast had also left her pregnant. Her stomach showed nothing but her cycle stopped. Xochil was grieving at this loss and had no idea what to do. She continued with her duties, kept silent, vomited in private, and worried. Four months after her assault, Xochil saw herself as being out of options. She went to the archbishop

"Archbishop, I have a very bad problem."

He encouraged her to speak.

"I have been taken against my will, raped, and I am pregnant."

"Xochil, did you go to the police? This beast must be caught and punished."

Xochil sighed when the archbishop used the same term to refer to her attacker.

"This beast is someone of prominence in the town. It would be worse for me than for him if I came forward. I will not go to the police, Archbishop."

"What do you wish to do, Xochil?"

He reached out to hold her hand. Xochil reacted with a quick, fearful retraction of her hand, then realized what she had done. She reached for the archbishop's hand and he, slowly this time, reached towards hers.

He held her hand like a tender, easily bruised flower and looked into her eyes. "What do you wish to do, Xochil?"

"Father, I have no idea!"

Xochil collapsed to her knees and buried her face on the sleeve of the archbishop's cassock. It was the first time since the rape that all her emotions poured forth in a bitter, wordless torrent. The archbishop, a man accustomed to using words to console others, kept his words to himself. He allowed Xochil to run out of tears, and stop shaking with fear and rage.

"Xochil, let me think about this for a few days. If you are adamant about not going to the police, then so be it. The beast will be punished eventually; God sees everything. But, I need to think about how to help you. Will you give me a few days?"

Xochil was standing again, wiping her tears on her apron, "Yes, Archbishop, of course."

"Fine. I will come and find you when I am ready."

Xochil left the archbishop feeling strangely better—the effect of confessing one's sins, although Xochil would never have equated the last twenty minutes with being in an actual confessional. Nevertheless, the result of her unburdening herself relieved the tightness in her chest, and she slept well for the first time in weeks.

For two days, Xochil kept her mind on her tasks. Father Jones only got near once when he had an audience with Archbishop Pitaval. He did not look at her and she certainly did not look in his direction. Father Jones was with the archbishop for a long time. When Xochil returned from the market, he was still there behind the protective shield of the heavy pinewood doors. Xochil never saw Father Jones leave. She was in the kitchen preparing the archbishop's dinner. Xochil would never see the Beast again. She would not see that he exited the archbishop's office in tears, red-faced, and stooped-over with shame. The next day, there were rumors of Father Jones' sudden disappearance, and he was, indeed, nowhere to be seen in town. On the third day, Archbishop Pitaval found Xochil cleaning his sitting room.

"Xochil, may I speak with you?"

"Of course, Archbishop."

He sat her in a leather chair that Xochil felt was well beyond her station—she was now at a point of self-humiliation. Could she have stopped Father Jones early on? Should she have been more vigilant and not let herself be cornered in her own room? Could she have fought harder? Did she have to stab him? Her endless doubts were beating down her confidence and self-respect. Xochil was uncomfortable in the leather chair.

"Xochil, is something more wrong today?"

"No."

She dared not risk more words as she could easily betray doubts better left to herself.

"I can only think of two courses of action, Xochil. One is to move back to the convent and have the baby. You can put it up for adoption, and the sisters will care for it until that time. Two, you can get married, have the child, and raise it yourself."

"Marry!? Marry who?"

"I know a very good man. He is a widower and a good Catholic. He is lonely and loved his deceased wife more than anything except God. Without giving any details, I have approached him, and he is eager to love again and to help you."

Xochil, expecting nothing but words to make her feel better, was nonplussed by two practical, if unattractive choices. Her complicated life was potentially more complicated now. Xochil had no idea even what question to ask first. The archbishop could see her overloaded mind in her frightened eyes.

"Xochil, I am having lunch tomorrow with a guest at one o'clock. Please make something nice like your wonderful chicken enchiladas. We will eat in the dining room."

"Yes, Archbishop, as you say."

"You may go, Xochil. Think about what I have said."

"Yes, I will, Archbishop."

The following day, Xochil went about her day as usual with the exception, not too unusual, of preparing lunch for two in the dining room. The archbishop normally ate his lunch in his sitting room even when he had one or two guests. Contented to be working for a man she respected, Xochil took extra measures in setting the table and preparing lunch. She used only tender white chicken meat. She made the sauce with extra care, handpicked the tomatillos, and tasted until Xochil deemed it perfect. Each grain of rice was perfect, gently colored by tomato, didn't stick to its neighbors, and was flecked by tiny pieces of red pepper, carrot, and green peas. She chopped the cilantro with extra enthusiasm, with no bruised leaves in sight. Xochil ironed the tablecloth and napkins with military precision. The lunch would be grand for her "hero," the archbishop.

At two minutes to one, the doorknocker echoed in the entry. Xochil, for reasons unknown to her, was expecting a new priest who would replace the now-displaced Beast. A short, fit, sun-bronzed man in clean work clothes was on the steps.

"I'm sorry, did I startle you, Miss?"

"No, Sir, I guess I was expecting someone else. Please come in. Are you here to lunch with Archbishop Pitaval?"

"Yes, I hope I'm on time."

"Of course, come right this way."

Xochil showed the man into the archbishop's sitting room, and then turned to announce him. But who was he?

She turned again. "I'm so embarrassed, I forgot to ask your name, Sir."

"Martín Algodones de Maria."

"Thank you"—and she turned to announce Mr. de Maria.

Xochil warmed the plates, the sauces, put the condiments on the dining room table, and returned to the kitchen to dress the cabbage salad. When she heard the conversation between the two men move into the dining room, Xochil started her train of dishes beginning with homemade cold, pickled, spicy vegetables known as *jardiniera*.

"Martín, have you met my very fine cook and housekeeper, Señorita Xochil?"

"Only in passing a few minutes ago, Archbishop, I am very glad to meet you, Señorita Xochil. If I am not mistaken, your name, Xochil, means 'blossom' in the Nahuatl language."

"Yes, Mr. de Maria, it does."

Xochil was astounded that anyone north of the border would know such a thing.

"Excuse me while I bring the other dishes."

Xochil thought that Mr. de Maria was a very nice man and could easily see how the archbishop could like him.

While in the kitchen, Xochil could hear the archbishop and Mr. de Maria discussing the food. Although she could not hear every word, Xochil heard enough words and enthusiasm to know that her food pleased the archbishop and his guest. In a period of time fraught with pain, doubts, and a pregnancy that potentially put Xochil's future into severe chaos, she needed this small triumph. She rinsed the platter, gently placed it in the rack—then Xochil took in the coffee and *pan dulce*.

When lunch was cleared, Archbishop Pitaval asked Xochil to remove her apron and join him and Mr. de Maria in the sitting room. Xochil, not knowing what to think, felt panicky but assured herself that nothing bad could happen in the archbishop's benign presence.

"Xochil, sit down please, here in this fine leather chair."

The archbishop was at his most affable. Xochil, despite her misgivings about her worthiness to sit in a chair of this quality, did as she was told.

"Mr. de Maria is the best furniture maker in Santa Fe, Xochil. He made the chairs we are sitting in."

Xochil looked to Mr. de Maria, who was blushing, "These are beautiful Mr. de Maria. You are what we call an *artisano*."

"Thank you. I try to put a little of everything my father taught me into each piece. He did not just show me the crafts, but drilled in me the love of the materials and passion for the finished work."

"Xochil, do you recall the conversation you and I had yesterday?"

The abrupt change of topic and its direction was a jolt. Xochil felt her chest tighten and her face shine like a Santa Fe morning. She said nothing, but nodded, hoping that this would not go farther in front of this stranger.

"Xochil, please try to relax. I know you are upset and frightened, but I am trying to help you."

The archbishop let this sit with Xochil for a few moments.

"Mr. de Maria is the widower and good Catholic that I was telling you about yesterday. I asked him to lunch so that the two of you could meet."

Mr. de Maria, unaware of Xochil's true identity, stared into his lap and assumed the colors of a Santa Fe sunset.

"I deliberately kept your identities concealed from each other so that you could be your natural selves. I apologize if you are now shocked and embarrassed, but it seemed to me the best way to introduce you."

Xochil stood up and turned to run out of the room. She knew the archbishop's words made sense, but she was humiliated just the same. The archbishop let her go.

The archbishop found Xochil at the small, battered kitchen table just sitting. She wasn't crying or producing any other dramatic emotions. Taking a chair, the archbishop sat and folded his hands on the table.

Xochil looked up at his kind face, "Mr. de Maria seems very nice, Archbishop. I would like to get to know him a little better."

"That is most reasonable. I wouldn't have expected less of a fine woman like you. How would you care to do that, Xochil?"

"Perhaps we could meet again, when I'm not working or distracted by the archbishop's needs."

"If I give you tomorrow off, will you meet Mr. de Maria for, say, lunch?"

"Yes, the morning sickness has passed. Actually, Archbishop, I find that I am always hungry."

For the first time in months, Xochil laughed out loud with the archbishop joining her.

Xochil and Mr. de Maria made short courtship, both by necessity and by choice. They were well matched. He was as kind and devoted as he was described to Xochil. She never knew how the archbishop had described her, but Mr. de Maria called her beautiful, clever, resourceful, a great cook, and most importantly to Xochil, he said that he *admired* her. "Admired," such a simple and direct word. When completely unexpected and, frankly, needed, it is a word infused with magic, majesty, and borne on wings. It was, perhaps, the last word Xochil ever expected to hear applied to her.

Archbishop Pitaval married Xochil and Martín quietly two weeks later. Two parishioners who were in the cathedral waiting for confession were asked to step into the chapel of *La Conquistadora* to act as witnesses.

The chapel was the only remaining portion of the second church built on this site. It was raised of adobe in 1714 and incorporated into the stone cathedral finished in 1884. It still houses a statue of the Madonna, the oldest in the United States, brought to Santa Fe from Spain in 1625. The small icon, carved of elm wood, was old even before its arrival to Santa Fe. It is revered, and its calming powers worked on Xochil from within. She was at peace throughout the brief ceremony. *La Conquistadora* conquered in manifold ways, many unseen but certainly felt by her people.

Mrs. De Maria moved to her new house within walking distance of her work. Martín was even more than Xochil expected. A man who has lost a beloved wife and still has a lifetime of love to give keeps his love in the present. As Xochil's belly grew, he would listen with his ear to her navel to feel the kicking. On market days, Martín accompanied Xochil in order to carry the groceries. Five months later, The Very Catholic Consuelo's mother was born.

Flor Estela de Maria was born into a loving family. Martín never treated the little girl as anything less than his own issue. Xochil took her time warming to the girl. She was the living, eating, pungent, laughing, crying reminder of the worst moments in Xochil's life. But Martín took such joy in the girl that Xochil was drawn into the love triangle by its powers alone. In a few months, the trio were inseparable, and no lack of love was evident or actually wanting. Xochil took Flor to work with her often. When she was weaned, Flor often accompanied Martín to his shop where both the apprentices and the patrons delighted in the raven-haired, dark brown-eyed little girl.

Xochil had been married for two years. In that time, she had never had relations with her husband, and he never intruded into her bedroom. The day came when Xochil no longer equated sex with rape, at least not with Martín. Eventually, they produced two more children—a red-headed girl and another raven hair, but a boy. Xochil showered her children with kindness and admiration. It was the best she knew how to do. Martín was just Martín—he was a natural-born father and husband. Xochil was sad for him that he never had children with his first wife. She believed that Martín would have been even happier with two families.

Flor attended Sunday mass regularly with her father and then eventually with her siblings in tow. While Xochil's piety never wavered even throughout her ordeal with the Beast, her religious habits died with the rape. Even so, Xochil wanted her children to grow up with religious habits until, like her, they could choose paths for themselves but without her particular circumstances. Archbishop Pitaval never said a word to Xochil. He accepted that she seemed pious but needed to distance herself from the church. This was difficult for the archbishop as Catholic doctrine insisted that to stay away from the sacraments, including Mass, were grievous sins. Knowing the events that led to Xochil's schism from the church created a boundary that intuition proclaimed he should never cross. Losing Xochil completely, even as his cook/housekeeper, was an option that was unacceptable to Archbishop Pitaval and, he believed, to his Lord. At least, Xochil was physically close to the house of God and his servant. It was the best he could do. But Archbishop Pitaval cursed the day and the Beast who attacked Xochil.

When Flor was twelve years old, she expressed her fears for her mother's immortal soul. She cried because her mother continued to commit the sin of not going to church while working directly for the archbishop himself. The irony of the situation, reasons unknown, was not lost on the very bright Flor. Xochil tried numerous ways to explain to Flor that not attending Mass was her problem and not Flor's. No explanation worked.

Flor was as devout as Xochil was adamant. Faith and psychological forces were in combat. Martín stayed out of the religious fray and only spoke to Flor in private. Flor would ease up on her mother like a dog that knows its bone is in another's possession, even though it will not give up the bone. Flor was a dog waiting for its time. When Flor's fears raised her emotions to the surface, the battle for the bone of sinfulness versus freedom would begin again.

The house had been quiet for several weeks, much to Martín's relief, when, without notice of any kind, Xochil appeared to be getting dressed to attend Mass. Not a soul in the house uttered a word. To speak, breaking the spell, may have meant ruining a momentum that progressed under its own forces.

"Well, what are we waiting for? Let's go to Mass."

Flor held her mother's hand for the entire walk to church. Xochil slipped a snow-white mantilla over her head as they entered through the great doors of the cathedral. The last thing Xochil expected was the comfort, the familiarity, the warm inner feeling of attending Mass. She spent the first half of Mass resisting these feelings and was determined to hang onto her bitter emotions associated with the church. By the transubstantiation, Xochil gave in. A single tear rolled down Xochil's face towards the end of mass. She was thinking of how Archbishop Pitaval would have been happy, moderately, of course, to see Xochil's return. But although he was not saying the Mass that day, he was there. Archbishop Pitaval moved to deliberately greet Xochil at the end of the service. Xochil's face colored and, uncharacteristically, the archbishop embraced her. Both were reluctant to speak; there was the awful risk of saying the wrong thing. Regardless, a communication passed between them.

Flor grew quickly into a young woman of shapely curves, erect bearing, and perfect school grades. Had it been the custom at the time, Flor would have gone to college. But during the 20s and 30s, it was not the custom for Santa Fe. Briefly, Flor considered the convent—the sisters would have greatly welcomed her. But Flor was a product of a passionate and undisciplined man she never knew (or knew about), and a passionate disciplined woman she did know. Her beauty, brains, and confidence had to come to full flower under the auspices of a gentle loving father and a mother who imparted kindness and admiration on her children. Flor was the envy of other young women of Santa Fe, although she was too self-effacing to realize this. As for the men, Flor was most certainly aware that they fawned on her like awkward first-antlered deer. Flor would only entertain her friends, men and women, at home. She did not fear people, but was a prudent person in congress with others. Martín and Xochil spoke of her prospects at night in the bed they now shared. Would she marry? Whom would she marry? Would she choose not to marry? If she didn't marry, then what did that mean? They allowed themselves the speculative questions but refrained from speculative answers. Flor was a woman of solid substance who would move in alignment with her unique bearings on life. For now, that was enough for Mr. and Mrs. de Maria.

Jean Claiborne Pépin came to Santa Fe with his parents. Jean's grandparents and their people had been in Quebec for generations until the Pépins tired of the infernal, interminable winters. They chose Louisiana because at least some of the people spoke something close to French. They were warmly welcomed by the Cajuns but overestimated the similarity of languages. Jean's parents grew weary of the malicious, interminable summers and picked Santa Fe as their destination for a milder climate. They chose well.

Jean was twenty-six years old when he met Flor at the open-air *mercado* on a Saturday in 1931. The next day, he looked for her at church in the cathedral. There were two Masses on Sundays, but which one did she attend? Jean attended the later Mass and never saw Flor. The following Sunday, Jean attended the early Mass and made a nuisance of himself searching for the beautiful Flor. He was a wayward giraffe, not a first-year buck, in laced-up shoes and his black suit of clothes, with a stretched and nutating neck. It had never occurred to Jean just what he should do if and when he found her. Flor was there with her family attending to the miracle of the Mass, not looking for Jean or any other man of this world. As the congregation was leaving, Jean spotted her and then moved strategically into her path. The giraffe voluntarily placed himself in the charge of the lioness. Martín was the first to notice a tall, strikingly handsome young man directly in his daughter's path. He followed Jean's eyes. They were smoldering with desire and searching for badly needed eye contact. Alarmed, Martín grabbed both Xochil and Flor by the arms and headed toward the side doors.

"Martín, what are you doing? We're almost to the door."

"Uh, there is a customer standing there that I don't want to see just now. Let's go this way."

"Martín, what have you done? I don't see any of your customers."

"It's someone you don't know; please just follow me."

Jean understood. In not planning what he should do if he found the beautiful Flor, his eyes did what came naturally and alarmed her father. Jean watched as the opportunity slipped out the side door. He had the good sense not to follow.

Jean spent the next week during all of his free time searching for Flor's father. It didn't occur to Jean until after he had made the identification at the farmer's market, that the farmer's market had been second only to the church in identifying Martín. He wondered in how many aspects of love he was blind. It certainly blinded his common sense twice in one week. The first farmer he asked identified both Martín and Flor; Jean resolved to visit the furniture shop of Mr. de Maria.

When Jean entered the shop, Martín looked up and stiffened visibly. Jean took his turn at imitating the New Mexico sunset with his face. He stared at the floor as he slowly approached Mr. de Maria.

"Sir, do you make furniture here?"

"What does this look like, a candle?"

Martín was holding a turned wooden chair leg. The images were not lost on Jean. He took a step back, exhaled what had been held breath, and inhaled.

"Mr. de Maria, my name is Jean Claiborne Pépin. I came to offer my apologies for my dreadful behavior last Sunday. I saw whom I believe to be your daughter at the market one week ago. She is a striking woman, Mr. de Maria. I am sorry if my eyes alarmed you."

"Well, your eyes did, young man! My daughter is a woman, not an animal for the taking!"

"I know, I know, I am so sorry, sir! I was, how do you say it—*encantado* with her beauty. It was stupid of me, Sir. I meant no harm."

"I have never seen you before, and this is a small town."

"Yes, sir, my parents and I have just moved here from Louisiana."

"Do you live with your parents?"

"Yes, why do you ask?"

"So that I'll know who to go to if you ever need correcting for your abominable behavior."

Jean thought he was going to faint; he couldn't imagine his shame if this ever were to occur. Martín's directness was Jean's undoing.

"Sit down, Mr. Pépin, and tell me more about yourself."

Relieved to be sitting, Jean relaxed enough to converse. Martin found that Jean was French-Canadian via the bayous. His parents had done well in the cannery business and retired to Santa Fe. Jean was their only child and a child of their old age. Jean himself was a man of business, self-taught. He had managed the cannery from the age of nineteen until his parents sold it. Jean had applied for a job with the state government but knew that without the proper "entry," his prospects of landing a job were nil. Forty-five minutes later, Martín found that he liked Jean. He seemed sincere, hard-working, honest and, possibly, ambitious. Jean never once mentioned Flor.

"Mr. Pépin, would you like to actually meet my daughter? Her name is Flor Estela de Maria. She will be in church on Sunday at the early mass. I suggest that you attend the late one. Flor works in my shop part-time. She will be here on Monday. I suggest that you come and order a piece of furniture from her. I will be watching you."

"I will be here at seven!"

"We open at eight. You will not appear before eleven."

"Yes, Mr. de Maria, eleven sharp; not one minute earlier!"

"Good, I suggest you order a settee. They can be complicated and will require many questions and options. And remember, Mr. Pépin, I will be watching!"

After church on Sunday, Martín instructed the family to walk home alone. He had some business with Archbishop Daeger, Pitaval's successor. Forty minutes later, after coffee and much reminiscing about the retired Archbishop, Martín walked out with the Archbishop Daeger's promise to use his considerable influence to help Jean Claiborne Pépin.

On Monday, Martín went to the shop as always knowing that Flor would follow later. When she arrived, he was waiting on spouses who desired an entire suite of parlor furniture. This was a substantial order that Martín would have tended to personally in any case. He was still with the clients when Jean arrived. Martín ensured that he made eye contact with Jean as he entered. Jean looked right back at Martín and gave him an acknowledging nod—I know you're watching.

Flor thought that Jean looked somewhat familiar but passed this off quickly. She went straight to business. Now Martín was in a quandary—

how could he give important clients his full attention and eavesdrop on Flor and Jean? He learned quickly that he couldn't do both well and switched his attention to his livelihood. Besides, no one was as mature and trustworthy as Flor. Martín would have to rely on nineteen years of solid upbringing and maintain his faith in Flor.

"Hello, I mean, good morning."

"Good morning. How may I help you?"

The conversation began and proceeded innocuously, but the two young people seemed to enjoy the interchange. Before all the decisions were made regarding the settee, a messenger came from the governor's office. Jean was needed as soon as possible in the capitol. Jean was astonished that the messenger should know his whereabouts, but this was a small town.

"I'll come back later and finish the order. May I ask your name?"

"Certainly, if you don't see me, then ask for Flor."

"I am John, spelled J-E-A-N in the French manner."

He left with the messenger but kept looking back as he walked down the street. When Jean ran into a streetlight pole, he bounced off and decided that he had better look straight on and prepare for whatever was coming.

Jean got a job as a secretary to a secretary to a secretary of the Department of Natural Resources. It paid little, but he had mysteriously obtained entry. When he returned that afternoon, Martín joined in the completion of the sale.

"Mr. Pépin, are you new to town? Do you have a family? Have you employment? Perhaps, as you and your parents are new to town, you have few friends and relatives here . . . Yes, I see, then will you and your parents do us the honor of dining at my house on Wednesday evening? Yes, well, that is good isn't it? I look forward to meeting your parents. I'm certain they are fine people . . . Oh, they are Catholic . . . yes, how fine!"

"Father!"

"Well, we will see you all on Wednesday! Oh, let me write down the address and time. Good day, Mr. Pépin!"

With that, Jean left with triumph in his step and a glow in his heart— and not just for Flor.

"Father, what are you doing!?"

"Doing? Why, Flor, doing my Christian duty and reaching out to strangers. Do you object to Christian principles?"

Flor merely turned and stepped into the street facing in the direction of Jean's pheromones.

There are such men and women who are content to live in the moment without pushing, pushing to the next moment unnecessarily. Such people were Flor and Jean. Their friendship grew quickly, as did the friendship between the two families, but the courtship was an exotic tropical plant that only flowered when every nuance of its cultivation was in perfect harmony. The courtship between Flor and Jean was stimulated by the light of romance, watered by the wine of patience, and fertilized by a genuine friendship until it became clearly harmonious. It took two full years for Flor to realize the blossoming of the courtship. When Jean had at last the sheer guts to ask, Flor surprised the world by saying, "Yes." In a lightning strike of double happiness, Jean was promoted during the same week.

Archbishop Pitaval had died in 1928. His successor, Archbishop Daeger, retired at the end of 1932. As Xochil was still cook and housekeeper to the archbishop, it was Archbishop Gerken who married Flor and Jean in 1933.

"Ladies and gentlemen, I am privileged to introduce Mr. and Mrs. Jean Claiborne Pépin."

The wedding was followed by a combination of French and Mexican foods and drinks in feasting proportions. Needless to say, with two of the supreme cuisines of the world, the celebration was as just short of depravity as it was joyous and inebriated. Even the archbishop attended and appeared to enjoy a little too much local wine. However, much to the disappointment of some, there were no fights at this celebration. Despite this glaring omission, everyone had a delightful time.

Jean was well liked at the capitol and noted for being bright and resourceful. He thought nothing of raiding another department's stores, say of typing paper, when his department ran out. As sharing resources was simply beyond the ken of other departments, he would wait until everyone had gone home, requisition by moonlight, and, mysteriously, everyone had typing paper the next morning. Jean also returned an equal amount of paper by moonlight when his department's supplies were restocked. Jean reasoned that no harm was actually done, people could continue to work, and everything evened out reasonably. No one asked unnecessary questions, but smiled suspiciously when Jean would pass.

However, Jean did not make much money. Yes, his salary was paid promptly at noon every other Friday, but he could hardly afford much beyond food for his table. As a consequence, Jean and Flor lived with Jean's parents in an adobe not far from the de Marias. From all the evidence, both families believed the marriage had been arranged by God himself. They had never seen two people so compatible and so in love. The unexpected was in the lack of progeny. A lack of lust was not an issue, although they hardly advertised such a delicate thing. It simply didn't happen.

In 1952, at the astounding age of forty, Flor became pregnant. When she grew at a rate that alarmed her mother and mother-in-law, the doctor was called back. Dr. Reveles was the son of the earlier Dr. Reveles and much in demand for his medical skills and bedside charms. He was unmarried, and the rumors went about that he had no need of a wife, much on the order of "if you get free milk, then why buy the cow?" With Flor, he was the perfect gentleman. Moreover, Jean towered over him by four inches. Besides, Flor was pregnant.

"Mrs. Pépin, you have twins in your womb! There are two heartbeats. Here listen."

Dr. Reveles let Jean put the ear pieces in for himself, but the doctor's hand placed the membrane on Flor's stomach.

"Oh, there are two, very faint but definitely two!"

"Twins must run in one of your families."

Everyone in the room looked to everyone else; no, twins ran in neither family. Fortunately, it never occurred to either Xochil or Martín to wonder if twins ran in Father Jones' family. (They did.)

Consuelo Margarita de Maria Pépin was born six minutes after her twin sister, Carmela Ascension de Maria Pépin. It was clear from the day of their births that they would be spectacular. They had Flor's raven hair and womanly facial structure and high-noon blue eyes—eyes even bluer than Jean's.

Carmela was the more outgoing of the two. Consuelo was more unusual because no one could remember anyone in the family being as shy as she. As they grew, Carmela was the clown, and Consuelo was either in her father's arms or hiding behind Flor's skirts. Both were excellent students, except for the obvious personality difference. As a result, Carmela was the preferred student as she charmed everyone who would give her a minnow's weight of attention. Consuelo was content to be unnoticed.

By the time the twins were twelve, they were startling in their beauty. They began to develop Flor's curvaceous body; the raven hair was long and luxuriant, the perfect skin paled next to the midnight hair, the eyes—oh the eyes—were arresting for their lapis lazuli color and intensity of gaze. Consuelo had only two friends, but very close friends. Carmela counted everyone she met as a friend. They reached the extremities of introversion and extraversion, but they were also close to each other. Consuelo could have completed most of Carmela's sentences had she the will to do so. Carmela was protective of her "little sister."

Consuelo and Carmela inherited the family's devout nature. They were fixtures at Sunday Mass and sometimes on weekdays as well. Neither missed their weekly confessions. Both were popular with the nuns and the priests with whom they associated. Because of the clear extremes in personality, everyone assumed that Consuelo would choose the convent. While Consuelo was devout, everyone misinterpreted what they saw and believed. Consuelo was enamored of one man, Oscar Padilla de la Mancha.

Oscar was one year ahead of the twins, but at St. Michael's High School, a star athlete, and handsome in the *mestizo* manner. He had high cheek bones, café au lait skin, dark brown eyes of great depth, and the twins' raven hair. Oscar was quiet and accomplished at school and acquired a full scholarship to the University of New Mexico. How could Consuelo not be enamored of this specimen of manhood?

What Consuelo did not know was that Carmela harbored an equal passion for Oscar. The rule of opposites attracting each other was in full play. Carmela and Oscar had been seeing each other in secret—not that anything shameful was occurring. Perhaps, the secretiveness of the relationship enhanced the enjoyment of it—that is usually the case.

The hapless Consuelo was literally floored when upon her graduation from Loretto Academy, Oscar proposed to Carmela. Not a soul could fathom the real reason Consuelo fainted. Was Consuelo ill? Did she have food poisoning? Was it an innocent shock? Just what had happened to cause Consuelo to faint? Flor was secretly praying that Consuelo was not pregnant, despite the fact that her better sense told her that that was not possible for Consuelo.

Consuelo never confided a word to anyone, not even, or especially, to Carmela. When she saw Oscar and Carmela together, her stomach would churn with great violence. Still, she kept her feelings to herself. The wedding took place in the chapel of *La Conquistadora* as had her parents' and grandparents' weddings. Midway through the ceremony, Consuelo, the maid-of-honor, had to excuse herself and exited the Chapel quietly. She vomited in the baptismal font (a sin she would later confess) because that was as far as she could get before nature forced its upper hand. Consuelo threw some flowers into the font to cover her sacrilege (a sin she would later confess), rinsed her mouth, and returned to her place on the dais. She structured a smile on her face as Carmela looked at her questioningly. Consuelo produced no further incidents at the ceremony or the raucous reception (would Carmela have it any other way?) except for getting stupefyingly drunk. Jean, having never witnessed his younger daughter possessed of spirits (of multiple persuasions), led Consuelo off to her bed. Consuelo passed out as soon as she was prone and only arose when the need to vomit awakened her.

Carmela and Oscar left the next day for Albuquerque to set up house off campus. Consuelo looked to a summer without her twin and a shattered life beyond. As an act of pure will, Consuelo took a full-time job in Santa Fe's only flower shop. She reasoned that by forcing herself to interact with the public she could overcome some of her shy nature and learn the art of conversation. The proprietor, a friend of the Pépin family, had misgivings; Consuelo's shyness was legendary. But Consuelo, now that Carmela was gone, was considered to be the most beautiful girl in Santa Fe. Surely, that couldn't be bad for business, could it? Mrs. Rosas took the chance and Consuelo braced herself for the challenge. There was method to this madness of hers. Consuelo divined for herself that proper preparation would give her a sporting chance at being successful. She made lists of phrases; greetings for various parts of the day, opening phrases, phrases for pauses, closing phrases, phrases of parting. Moreover, Consuelo loved the flowers and took real pleasure in learning their names. Mrs. Rosas was so pleased, and dumbfounded, that she taught Consuelo the art of flower arranging.

Consuelo worked in the flower shop for three years, fending off manly advances, dealing with grumpy customers, and generally enjoying herself. A regular customer, a Mrs. Vigil, was a favorite as she was intelligent and made for the most interesting conversations. Mrs. Vigil could talk on any subject. Consuelo was fascinated by her. There was no subject that Mrs. Vigil could not shed light upon or utter a sharp opinion. Consuelo was in love for the second time in her life. She began to slip extra flowers into Mrs. Vigil's bouquets, add a ribbon, throw in some baby's breath for contrast.

One day, Mrs. Vigil came into the shop for two dozen roses for her retiring cook/housekeeper. During the transaction, Mrs. Vigil asked offhandedly if Consuelo, whom she now knew quite well, had knowledge of anyone looking for a cook/housekeeper position. She paid well, the job came with its own quarters on site, and Mrs. Vigil lived in one of the most famous houses in all of Santa Fe. Consuelo replied that she did not know of anyone offhand, but would ask around.

"Be sure not to mention my name and emphasize that the woman must be well qualified. She must be an extraordinary cook and a meticulous housekeeper. Well, you yourself know, Consuelo, how particular I am about my flowers. I am equally particular about my table and my house. Now, how much was that, Consuelo?"

"Four dollars and sixteen cents, Mrs. Vigil."

"Four dollars for two dozen roses. I shall have to have words with Mrs. Rosas!"

But, she paid and left.

The following morning, there was a knock at Mrs. Vigil's back door.

"Why Consuelo, what a surprise. What brings you here—come in, come in."

"Mrs. Vigil, I have come about the job."

"Really, so soon, have you found me a suitable candidate?"

"No, I mean, I would like to be your cook and housekeeper myself."

"Consuelo, what are you talking about? You have a perfectly wonderful job for which you are very well suited."

"That's true, but that does not entirely satisfy my needs. I have learned to deal successfully with my shyness, converse with strangers, and I know a great deal about flowers. Frankly, Mrs. Vigil, I would find working for you much more interesting."

"You had better sit down, Consuelo. Have you not thought about marriage? It becomes very difficult to meet suitable men as a live-in. Don't you want to get married and have children of your own?"

"I did once, Mrs. Vigil, I did once. But that's in the past and the love of my life is gone."

"Gone as in dead?"

"No, gone as in unavailable."

"Oh, Consuelo, there are other men."

"Maybe so, but not for me. Mrs. Vigil, I am a great cook. I learned from my mother and Creole French grandmother who learned from their mothers. I can cook Mexican, Spanish, French, and Creole dishes. I love to cook. Your house will be as spotless as your flowers are perfect. Mrs. Vigil."

"Consuelo, what does your family think of this idea?"

"Mrs. Vigil, I am nearly twenty-two years old, in full control of my faculties, and can make my own decisions. I only have to give Mrs. Rosas a reasonable notice before I start working for you. Mrs. Rosas has been very good to me, and I can't just leave her without a helper."

"No, of course not. Consuelo, are you quite sure about this?"

"Yes, can I start just as soon as Mrs. Rosas replaces me?"

"Yes, dear, you can. I can see that you are a strong, resolved woman. You will fit nicely into my house. But, I must warn you, if you come into this house, I will treat you like a member of my family. That may be good . . . or, not so good. Have I told you about being a third daughter in a line of third daughters? No? Well, that can wait."

Mrs. Rosas found a suitable girl to replace Consuelo within two days. Consuelo and Mrs. Rosas spent the next three days training the girl. Consuelo declined to take her pay for the final three days of her work. On Monday, the drop-dead gorgeous Consuelo stepped off the main stage of Santa Fe and onto the private stage of Silverton-de Baca House. She had two suitcases, her catechism, rosary, and two hats with her. Theodora Mercedes showed her to her room and private bath. They were actually spacious compared to her small bedroom and shared bath at her parent's home.

"Do I wear a uniform, Mrs. Vigil?"

"Uniform? Consuelo, this isn't the nineteenth century. But you had better wear this apron to protect your clothes. And, please call me Theodora Mercedes."

The apron was embroidered linen, of high quality, and ironed to within perfection. Consuelo put it on.

In a nod to her own sensibilities, she addressed her new employer, "How do I look, Doña Theodora?"

"Very special, Consuelo, very special."

Consuelo Margarita de Maria Pépin began her new life where, eventually, she would also be known as The Very Catholic Consuelo—but not by Theodora Mercedes.

CHAPTER TEN

Theodora Mercedes Silverton Vigil

Theodora Mercedes Silverton Vigil was shelling peas with Consuelo and listening to *A Worcester Lady Mass*. The music was soothing and Consuelo marveled that her pagan employer could still enjoy sacred Christian music. She saw this as part of the consolation for working in a non-Catholic household, but her thoughts about this masked the true depth of her feelings on the subject. They were preparing large trays of hot food to take to the homeless shelter that evening. It was an exercise in which Theodora Mercedes always participated with the Social Justice Committee of her church. Consuelo was an eager contributor. It did not matter to Consuelo that Social Liberals were behind this effort. She loved helping the poor and helping Doña Theodora. It was early in the day. Innocenta was at the gym and the children were playing in the yard or computing something extraordinary.

"Consuelo, I have been meaning to ask you a question for quite a while. If you had known about 'the gift' would you have come here anyway?"

Theodora Mercedes asked this while never looking up from her hands.

Consuelo looked up from her peas and searched her employer's face, "If I had known thirty-some years ago, I would never have come into this house."

"And now?"

"The gift, as you call it, is often disturbing because it catches me offguard and has some other-worldly qualities. But, it also seems to be harmless or benign. It tried to warn you about your nephew. I don't see it the same way anymore. I'm a Catholic, but I'm not stupid or drunken with religion or needless fears—I'm not a child anymore, either. You do have a gift, but it's not like reading *Macbeth* with witches stirring cauldrons."

"Well, I'm relieved to hear that you don't believe I'm a witch!"

"Would a witch listen to this beautiful music?"

"Hmm, maybe not, but I do," and she winked at Consuelo. "Did you know we were Social Liberals before you arrived?"

"Oh no, I assumed, wrongly, that you were a Catholic like most

Hispanics. At first, I thought that you didn't believe in anything and that that was true for all Social Liberals. It took me four or five years to understand that there's a match between your actions and your spiritual beliefs."

"And what do you believe now? Don't worry, your membership in this family doesn't depend on your answer."

"I think that you and your family live like good Christians, yet you don't believe that Jesus Christ is your savior. It worries me sometimes."

"Do you think that I'm going to hell?"

Consuelo had to stop herself from making the sign of the cross. It was a life-long habit that she had outgrown, but muscle memory continued to react before she could stop it—most times.

Consuelo smiled sheepishly and bravely continued, "I think that hell is an interesting concept with no souls in residence. Please don't ever repeat that. I will deny you three times if you do."

They both chuckled.

"So, do you think Shakespeare believed in witches?"

"I read Macbeth in high school and then again last year. It had been too long since I had read Shakespeare. For most of my life I didn't know what to think. It puzzled me and challenged my beliefs, and I never gave it much thought after the first reading. But then last year when I reread *Macbeth*, it dawned on me—the three women *believed that they were witches*. That made a huge difference. There are lots of people, crazy or not, who believe that they are something they imagine or, let's say, out of the ordinary. The rest of those scenes are just theater. I think Shakespeare had fun with his audience, but who knows what audiences thought in Shakespeare's day? Now, you probably think that I did think you were a witch until last year, but, no, I didn't. If I did, I would have run out of here long ago."

Theodora Mercedes had stopped shelling peas during this soliloquy and watched Consuelo with barely concealed pride. When Consuelo was introspective like this, Theodora Mercedes saw how incomparably beautiful she still was; raven feather hair, traffic-stopping blue eyes, fair skin, and depths she rarely showed to anyone except Theodora Mercedes.

"Consuelo, you never cease to amaze me." Theodora Mercedes reached out and touched Consuelo's hand, "If I ever had another daughter, Consuelo, I would want her to be you."

Consuelo, who had her own biological mother, nevertheless was overwhelmed emotionally by this honor.

"And I would be happy to be your daughter, Doña Theodora."

"Well, there's a problem; I would have to have been ten years old when I gave birth to you! Perhaps you should be the younger sister I never had."

"Either way, I'm flattered. Of my two older sisters, I think that I prefer you."

Theodora Mercedes didn't need her legendary astuteness to realize that there was undoubtedly an enormously interesting and probably sad tale behind this statement. She kept her thoughts off her face and tongue.

Innocenta walked in the back door, greeted the women, and headed deeper into the big house.

"I have had enough of shelling peas. We have plenty of time to prepare for tonight's feast. Take off that apron, grab your handbag, throw on some makeup, and let's go shopping! Chico's is having a sale!"

Consuelo started to protest, but recognized the tone of a woman on a mission. She popped into her bathroom to freshen up and was ready when Theodora Mercedes came back downstairs. Without her apron and a little daytime eye shadow, Consuelo's eyes reflected the royal blue of her cotton dress. Theodora Mercedes got the Honda sports car out of the garage, put the top down, and off they went—surrogate sisters continuing a day of bonding by shopping.

Innocenta had thrown her sweaty clothes into the washing machine, slipped on some loose shorts and a T-shirt, and went looking for the children. The Unremarkables were playing hide 'n seek with a cottontail that had wandered into the yard. They were rare in town and The Unremarkables, in rare audibles, squealed with enchantment. The rabbit didn't show as much enthusiasm for the game as did the children, but stayed in the yard.

"Where's Raul Theodore?"

With as much ennui as they could muster, they responded in the time-tested manner: "Upstairs in his room."

Innocenta could hear Raul Theodore singing to himself in his idiosyncratic manner, which others might call repeating monotones. This was always a sign that Raul Theodore was deeply entranced in some calculation that could take Innocenta's breath away.

"Do you know anything about the 'Anti-de-Sitter/conformal field theory correspondence'?"

Innocenta took a few precious seconds to replay the question and answer in the time-tested manner, "No, do you?"

"Yes, but I am wondering if it's that accurate a prediction of black hole behavior or whether he just got close."

"Oh, I see. Who is it that just got close?"

"Juan Maldacena. He's a very good theoretical physicist, but I think I found a missing component in his calculations."

Innocenta asked herself for the thousandth time whether she would ever truly get used to these conversations with her rare child.

"Would you mind if I just stayed in here and read my book?"

"No."

Raul Theodore returned to his chanting and calculations while Innocenta just stared at him. He was oblivious to her.

Innocenta forgot the book in her lap and watched Raul Theodore for some time. Was he *really* her child? His chanting and his moving fingers, like butterflies each thinking their own thoughts on his hands, moved at differing rhythms from each other and from the chanting; as if his chanting were coming from a raven far above. In some Native American traditions, the raven was a helper of humankind. What raven was at work here in little Raul Theodore? Innocenta asked herself if her son was related to Albert Einstein. Maybe all men and women who seemed otherworldly were, in fact, closely related. The Buddha begot Jesus who begot Clara Barton who begot Gandhi. Alcibiades begot da Vinci who begot Newton who begot Neils Bohr who begot this Juan Maldacena person. Perhaps Shakespeare begot Dickens and Whitman, who begot Irving and Kingsolver. Or, maybe they were all related from the same seed. Where did the seed originate? Oh my god, what about the musicians; Monteverdi, Bach, Vivaldi, Telemann, Mozart—yes, Mozart—and Beethoven, Brahms, Puccini, and Saint Saens? And what about the painters and sculptors, novelists and poets, philosophers and theologians? The potential list of people and their accomplishments made Innocenta feel like she would fry her brain at any moment. Aliens? Superhumans? Beings beyond her ken, in any case.

Innocenta watched Raul Theodore's eyes. They were moving rapidly back and forth much like Innocenta imagined REM sleep to be. But he was awake—or was he? Was Raul Theodore the latest exhalation of an alien race salting our humanity with individuals who were capable of taking great leaps of thought, art, and faith? Did the gods speak through him, to him? Maybe, these remarkables were like the aspen grove high up on Tesuque Peak, thousands of acres of individual trees *but not so*. They were one great organism connected by a common root system unseen, subterranean, scarcely believable. Were all these people like the deceptively individual aspen trees? And where did Arthur C. Clark and Theodora Mercedes Silverton Vigil fit in? Surely, they were also deceptive aspen trees.

In an unwanted flash of insight, Innocenta realized that the metaphor of the trees extended to her and the people around her. Perhaps, The Unremarkables were hackberries, Barrington a cottonwood, tall and breakable, maybe she was a ponderosa pine. Who knows? How could she know?

Innocenta watched Raul Theodore's eyes; like REM sleep they were, conversing with—gods? She observed his fingers like butterflies; multiple lives connected to each hand. His chanting like a far off raven conveying messages only the aspens could comprehend. Conscious of the metaphors, Innocenta wondered if she really knew her son. Without the metaphors, Innocenta would have next to nothing. She thanked the cosmos for the metaphors allowing her to imagine her son.

Innocenta reassessed her dead husband—perhaps this child really was more than he could handle and not just an excuse to bail-out of his marriage. Now she would never know. All Innocenta knew was that she was immeasurably stronger than the late George. She sighed and wondered when Bart would come along.

When the phone rang, Innocenta's hackles raised up on the back of her neck. At first she thought something was wrong with the children, but Raul Theodore was asleep on the floor and The Unremarkables could be heard tickling each other on the second floor. Innocenta ran to catch the phone before it went to the machine. As she reached for the handset, the gift informed her of the call of a *rara avis*.

Theodora Mercedes and Consuelo had finished shopping and were enjoying coffee and croissants at Croissant on Guadalupe Street. The elder of the two had spent less than two-hundred dollars on herself, but three-hundred dollars on her surrogate sister. Consuelo would protest these extravagances on every shopping trip, but nothing short of being penniless would stop Theodora Mercedes. In a way, Theodora Mercedes saw this as a form of compensation for pulling Consuelo off the marriage market without her express intent to do so. Then there were also those withering looks to atone for. Consuelo would have made a model wife and mother, indeed, her potential was limitless, but she had chosen a unique path of her own accord. Still, Theodora Mercedes would ask her, once in a blue moon, if Consuelo had ever regretted her decision.

"Doña Theodora, I have never regretted anything in my life, least of all counting you as someone close to me."

And that was that—the same answer every time.

Without warning, Theodora Mercedes moaned. Consuelo, thinking the worst, leaped to her feet. The other customers turned to stare and found two magnificent women, one standing and the other looking somewhat forlorn. Theodora Mercedes was not crying or looking stricken.

"Doña Theodora, what's wrong!?"

For a few ticks of the tall case clock back in Theodora Mercedes' parlor, she said nothing.

Then, "Consuelo we must get home. We will have a visitor soon."

Consuelo's heart began to slow down, and she gathered their hand bags.

"A perfect day will suffer an attempt to ruin it, but I will not allow it to happen. Nevertheless, we must get home, Consuelo."

Theodora Mercedes smiled at Consuelo who now realized that the gift had spoken and an immovably strong woman had answered.

Barrington and James walked in just as Innocenta put down the phone. Angelica Gertrudis was descending the stairs.

The three noted that she looked pale as she turned to them, "Grandmother Prattle is on her way!"

"Who is Grandmother Prattle?"

"James, you had better sit down. You, too, Barrington, I'm not sure you've ever heard everything you should know."

Barrington had never seen Innocenta this way. Not even when her husband had left or when the news was received of his death did she look like this. She was flushed with anticipation. Wordlessly, Barrington sat on the couch next to James. Angelica Gertrudis, withdrawn since losing her family, sat in an armchair.

"She was born during the Great Depression, a not-too-distant relative. Her given name is Genoveva April Parral Boswell. She was a spoiled only child. Genoveva was not liked by our other grandparents. She was a willful, selfish brat. When she was only fourteen, Genoveva was wearing make-up and seeing men many years her senior. Remember that this was the nineteen-forties, and this would have made her a cheap, racy girl. Somehow, she managed to avoid getting pregnant until she was seventeen. The man, Seymour Atkins, a war veteran, came from a moneyed family, and hadn't counted on this. Genoveva's parents forced the issue, and Seymour was forced to marry the girl. Mother calls it the only shotgun wedding in the family's history, but who knows? Anyway, Seymour married Genoveva when she was six-months pregnant, but Genoveva lost the child. Seymour waited about a year, moved to Reno to establish residency, and then divorced her. Meanwhile, Genoveva had hooked up with other men and got pregnant again. This time the poor schnook was our grandfather. Henry Angel Silverton Vigil, our grandfather, also came from a moneyed family—stop me if you see a pattern—and did the honorable thing voluntarily. They were married for sixteen years and had two children. The first one was Daddy, Angel Silverton Vigil. The second is our aunt Norma."

"Wait, are you saying that Dad was younger than Mother?"

"Yup. But remember, Mother is sixty-seven now but looks fifty-five at most. Back then, she probably looked the same age as Dad. But back to the story. Henry died young and Genoveva was back on the market, so to speak. Then she met Haskell Murray Evans Prattle, again from a wealthy family, and according to Mother, set her sights on him. There was a problem this time."

"She got pregnant again?"

"No, he was already married. Genoveva claimed she was pregnant. Haskell never had children with his wife and saw an opportunity to have an heir. But, he would have to divorce his first wife. It got ugly, and his first wife made out well. Haskell managed to convince the court to let him pay a lump sum rather than alimony. Genoveva had a fit because she knew that Haskell could just forget to pay the alimony, but, by agreement, a lump sum would have to be paid to finalize the divorce."

"Wait! How come I've never heard this stuff about Grandmother Prattle before?"

"Mother thought you were too young to hear all these sordid details about your grandmother. Besides, she loved Dad and didn't want you to think less of him because of his mother. After Genoveva remarried, it didn't matter anymore and Mother just moved on. Then Daddy died young, too.

142

Besides, Barrington, why would Mother tell you this stuff?"

Angelica Gertrudis, who had been listening intently, nodded in agreement.

"OK, I can see that she wanted to put Grandmother into the past and keep her out of the present. Is that why I can only remember seeing Grandmother a few times in my life?"

"Yup, Mother kept her at arms length to keep her influence at a minimum. I think that Dad agreed with her. I don't think Dad was very close to his mother anyway."

Innocenta paused here, "I actually think that if Dad had been capable of hating anyone, the closest he ever got was his own mother."

Angelica Gertrudis closed her eyes and nodded again.

"Whew!"

"Yeah, sweet old Dad; whew!"

"Where was I?"

"Haskell, the divorce, and the lump sum payment," replied James.

Innocenta, Angelica Gertrudis, and Barrington looked at James and realized that he was fascinated by this juicy tale. Two of them smiled at James, who blushed with every capillary in his face.

"Yes, Haskell paid his first wife the money, then married Genoveva. A short time later Genoveva miscarried."

"Wait a minute! How do we know that she was really pregnant? She could have faked the whole thing just to ensnare Haskell."

"That's what Mother thinks! She thinks Genoveva did whatever she had to do in order to get Haskell and Haskell's money. Haskell surrendered half of his assets and never earned enough to replace what he lost in the payment. Then Haskell died under mysterious circumstances. So Genoveva was married three times, all three times into money, and has lived well."

Angelica Gertrudis registered her opinion by rolling her eyes, then looking into the carpet.

"What mysterious circumstances?"

"Some kind of car accident, but I don't really know."

"So Grandmother's name is Genoveva April Boswell Parral Atkins Vigil Prattle?"

"No, Genoveva April Parral Boswell Atkins Vigil Prattle," corrected Angelica Gertrudis.

"Oh, by all the gods, what a story; now I really want to meet this woman!"

"You already have, Barrington, just not of late. Stick around, James, this could be fun. I just hope Mother gets here before Grandmother Prattle does."

The Honda could be heard in the driveway, the sound then amplified by the enclosure of the garage. Theodora Mercedes came roaring in with bags of purchases and stopped short when she saw the assembly.

"Well, I see that the gift has been doing its job."

Innocenta stood to help with the bags, "Not really; she called."

"Here, I bought you a silk blouse."

Innocenta knew better and gave the corresponding look.

"OK, I bought it for me but you can have it. It's quite lovely."

"Thank you, Mother."

"Have you been briefing the others? How are you feeling today, Angelica Gertrudis? Are you ready for some excitement?"

Angelica Gertrudis smiled broadly for the first time, "I wish Reigh, especially, were here. He would really get a kick out of what's to come."

Theodora Mercedes teared up to see her sister so alive after a prolonged period of stoicism. She went to Angelica Gertrudis and hugged her tightly to her bosom.

"Sister, you're smothering me!"

Theodora Mercedes released her, and took a deep breath to keep from crying, "Well, I wonder what this visit is all about?"

Theodora Mercedes was not ready to field the group's questions. When nothing happened for thirty minutes, everyone in the house went about his or her own business. Angelica Gertrudis joined her sister and Consuelo in getting restarted on the trays of food for the unfortunates in the shelter. No one spoke much except to coordinate the food preparation—the anticipation caused unspoken speculation and a small amount of tension. Barrington and James were drinking beer in the backyard. Bart was probably still at the fire station and Innocenta hoped that he would arrive for the upcoming festival atmosphere.

At precisely three o'clock an ancient Chrysler Imperial limousine pulled up to the front of the house, its smoke and rattles engulfing the vehicle as its brakes screeched to a stop. Everyone in Silverton-de Baca House was alerted and made every effort to appear nonchalant while heading towards the front door. No one was fooled. Innocenta pinched Barrington, who broke out in loud laughter. Theodora Mercedes shushed them all.

A young, clean-cut man emerged from the driver's door, opened the passenger door some eight feet behind him, and then proceeded to the trunk. Out came an old-fashioned bentwood and cane wheelchair, possibly an antique. The young man wheeled it around to the door. A middle-aged woman in a pretty flowered blouse got out and immediately leaned back into the door.

"That's Aunt Norma," Theodora Mercedes whispered.

An equally middle-aged man emerged from the opposite side of the vehicle. He was unbearably skinny and dressed in a shiny blue suit and black cowboy boots.

"That's Phil, Norma's husband. Phil hasn't worked in over twenty years; they sponge off her."

"Mom, why are you whispering? No one can hear you through this oak door."

"Shush!"

While the young man held the chair, the other two helped an elephantine shape dressed all in black out of the car and into the wheelchair. There was much pulling and conversing as they worked at this improbable task. An enormous woman was finally seated, and something hairy was placed on her lap. Had the woman been able to stand, a kind description would have said; mammose in front and callipygous in back. But her true circumstances were that every part of her was spread by gravity, to be held in place only by groaning wood and cane, assisted by stout but compliant clothing. Genoveva's pale hands looked like afterthoughts at the end of what should have looked like sleeves but seemed to appear from nowhere in particular.

"I don't know how she expects to get into this house; we don't have a wheelchair ramp."

Theodora Mercedes led the household, sans children, out to the front porch. Four large concrete steps shielded them from the argosy progressing below. Genoveva rode as if she were in a phaeton, regally if pompously, instead of a wheelchair. Phil pushed while Norma and the young man with a gamp, a huge umbrella, trailed like escort ships. They finally reached the foot of the stairs, the New Mexico sun blazing in its June glory, with no shadows for the fleet to rest in. At least Genoveva had her mammoth umbrella.

"Genoveva, what brings you here? I haven't seen you since your last husband committed suicide and we had that strange funeral."

"The coroner stated that the cause of death was deferred, probably accidental, Theodora Mercedes—you know that!"

"Yes, but we both know what really happened, don't we?"

Neither woman was in possession of the all the facts.

In 1977, Haskell had driven his aging Buick Skylark toward the Grand Canyon. He had every intention of committing suicide to escape the grasp and nagging of Genoveva. Haskell had briefly flirted with the idea of killing her, but discarded it as far too complex an adventure for his exhausted nerves. No, suicide it would be. He started out in one of the most ferocious monsoon seasons in memory. The air conditioning of the Buick hadn't worked for years, and Haskell had some windows open. Haskell approached the Grand Canyon from the quiet side, Highway 64 West. He broke through a pounding rain into the heat and clear air of the well-watered high desert. The humidity was stifling. Haskell slowed his speed and opened all the windows. Just west of Desert View, Haskell stopped the car, got out and looked over the side of the canyon. The first drop was easily one thousand feet to a steep slope followed by another drop of indeterminate descent. Haskell sat down to contemplate his fate. He lit a cigarette and inhaled deeply the rich, killing smoke. For eighteen years, Haskell had refrained from smoking, but when he made up his mind to kill himself he went out, bought a carton of Lucky Strikes, and then headed west. He never uttered a word to Genoveva about his leaving or purpose.

Haskell got back into the Buick Skylark, pulled his suicide note from under the front seat, placed it on the dash, then lit another cigarette. Haskell backed as far as he could into the pines, put the car in drive, and pushed the pedal to the floor. With such a running start, Haskell was at one-hundred-miles-per-hour when he sailed over the precipice. A powerful gust of wind caught the Buick, blasted the suicide note into space, and rolled the car starboard. Horrified, Haskell watched his suicide note sail off, never to be found. The Buick hit the rocks with such momentum that it folded over on itself, wheels up and wheels down, creating a tiny compartment where Haskell, clearly dead, was mashed and encased. The ball of steel, rubber, and fading paint disappeared over the next edge.

Unbeknownst to Haskell, he had been observed, too late, by a Grand Canyon employee on her way to work. She pulled over, looked over the edge and saw . . . nothing. She drove to the nearest ranger station to report.

The remains of the Buick and its contents, were so far down the canyon that it was easier for rescue teams to ascend than descend to attain it. So precariously was it perched that they could neither move it up nor down. The rescuers were flummoxed. In an act of desperation, they hauled up a small, portable Honda generator and a Shop Vac. They hooked everything up, got the generator going, identified a suitable opening in the wreckage, and sucked Haskell's viscous remains out through the hose. The Coconino County coroner opened the Shop Vac, took one look at the grisly goo inside, closed it back up, and made his pronouncement: Deferred, probably accidental, despite the witness's testimony. Perhaps the coroner thought he was doing the right thing; there was no suicide note. Wherever Haskell's spirit now resides, he is still kicking himself for opening the windows and watching his suicide note vanish. What good is a spectacular suicide if no one ever knows about it, can appreciate its glory, or knows what your last words were? Theodora Mercedes was fairly sure that Haskell's spirit was still in the Santa Fe area, possibly even the exact address. Genoveva had managed to get Haskell quickly buried in the Catholic Cemetery before anyone could ask too many questions about the unusual cubic coffin—it held the Shop Vac with all its Haskellian contents.

"What is that in your lap, Genoveva, some beast, or has your pudenda prolapsed as a sign of your dissolute life?"

Genoveva's retinue cringed, and Theodora Mercedes' children pulled their chins down so that their mouths couldn't open.

"This is Pierre, my Pekinese. You always were a rude woman to me, Theodora Mercedes."

"Are you saying that deformity is a dog? Were real dogs too expensive?"

"Now, Theodora Mercedes, stop this. I came here in good faith to offer you and your family an invitation. This is Norma's grandson, Diego. He is to be ordained this Saturday in the cathedral by the archbishop himself!"

Theodora Mercedes recognized this for what it was, the crowning achievement of Genoveva's sinful life; offer up a great grandson to the church in this life and hope for absolution in the next.

Diego looked up for the first time and attempted a smile. He was about six feet tall, had very dark brown hair, impeccably coiffed, a heavy but close-shaven beard, and beautiful doelike eyes.

Barrington's "gaydar" went off in milliseconds, and he turned to James and whispered, "He's gay."

Diego, equally gifted with this particular type of insight, flushed and stared at the back of the wheelchair while the gamp wavered.

Theodora Mercedes, unusual for a woman, also possessed gaydar and missed not one beat. "Diego, I'm very happy to meet you. Are you absolutely sure that you have the vocation?"

Diego merely nodded assent and refused to make eye contact with anyone.

"Are you sure that you're not doing this because other people expect you to?"

Now Diego looked apoplexic and only managed to stammer, "Yes, I'm sure."

His voice trailed off tellingly, and Theodora Mercedes thought her heart would break for this handsome young man.

"What do your parents think of this choice and, by the way, where are they?"

"Both my parents work in their hardware store. I think that they are supportive of whatever I do."

"I see. Well then, we will have to attend to witness your ordination and offer our support." She turned to Genoveva. "We will see you on Saturday."

"There is also a reception following in the cathedral hall. Even the archbishop will make an appearance."

"Well, Genoveva, now I wouldn't miss this if we had hurricanes, tornadoes, and earthquakes all in the same day. While I believe that there's a chance, I think it's small. See you at the ordination and the reception, all of you!"

Genoveva smiled as if she had won the battle and the argosy made the slow turn of an admiral's fleet and headed toward the tired Chrysler Imperial. Everyone on the porch stood hunting-heron-still and watched as the entire choreography was performed in reverse. As Diego closed the trunk and turned towards the driver's door, he looked at Barrington and smiled. Barrington read this, probably quite precisely, that Diego found him attractive, and he grinned back lasciviously. James didn't miss this and looked hurt and inquiringly at Barrington.

"Don't worry, James, I was testing my theory. You're the only man for me."

"Consuelo, I saw you standing behind the open front door. Was I awful?"

Consuelo smiled at being put so on-the-spot and replied truthfully, "Yes, but only a saint could have held her tongue around that . . . kind of woman."

"That kind of woman—the devil in me would like you to be more specific, but I love you too much to press the point. So, we are all agreed that I am not a saint?"

In unison, the entire group replied, "Yes!"

Everyone, even Consuelo, laughed and giggled.

"Mother, you're not really serious about attending!?"

"Serious, of course, I'm serious about attending *both* functions."

Everyone looked at Theodora Mercedes with the concern one expresses for a loved one who has lost her mind.

Theodora Mercedes stared back; they were still all standing in the entry hall, "Barrington, if you were starring on Broadway in *How to Succeed in Business Without Even Trying*, do you think any of us would miss it?"

"Broadway, wow . . . "

"Barrington, come back; do you think we would miss it?"

"No. I sure hope not."

"If Innocenta were starring in *Sawn Lake*,"

"*Swan Lake*, Mother; I think you're excited."

"Yes, yes, *Swan Lake*. Would you miss it?"

Everyone nodded and murmured that, of course, they wouldn't miss it.

"Children, this is the same thing! It's theater, grand, high theater in the cathedral. We'll see all the pageantry and rituals of another time with the Grand High Poobah himself performing. James, clear your calendar for Saturday, I expect the whole family to arrive in grand style. Everyone will dress up in their finest attire. We're going to the theater!"

Everyone broke into enthusiastic chatter. Consuelo was slightly more subdued. She had never looked at Roman Catholic matters in this way. Theodora Mercedes illustrated a new way to view the customs of their family's past; great theater in a great setting, the Cathedral Basilica of Saint Francis of Assissi overlooking Santa Fe.

The rest of the day was hectic as the four women prepared the food for the homeless shelter. No slumgullion for the homeless, Theodora Mercedes was preparing baked boneless chicken in white wine sauce with fresh peas and carrots. Angelica Gertrudis and Consuelo worked on two pans of gooey, rich macaroni and cheese made with real extra sharp cheddar and toasted panko on top—just as they would make it for themselves. Innocenta made two gallons of fresh salad, although she was expecting Bart that evening.

By five o'clock Theodora Mercedes, Angelica Gertrudis, and Consuelo were nicely dressed and placed the food into Innocenta's Volvo, borrowed for the evening. They checked-in, got help with the trays of food, and spent a delightful evening greeting and feeding people who needed them. It was an uplifting way to top off an eventful day.

Home by nine-thirty, the three women sat in the backyard sipping wine, laughing, talking about the hilarity in the front yard, and generally enjoying the company. They speculated about Saturday's upcoming events without treading too heavily on Consuelo's beliefs. At ten o'clock a noise could be heard above them. All three looked up to find Barrington and James crammed into the third story window. They seemed to be enjoying the night air and sharing the stars.

"Doña Theodora?"

"Yes?"

"That scene you played out on the front porch today . . . "

"Yes?"

"It was great theater!"

All five howled with laughter and the men disappeared back into Barrington's room. By ten-thirty, the women were quiet, holding hands in an arc mirroring Orion's bow, and searching the stars for hidden beauties and sparks for their apperception.

CHAPTER ELEVEN
Barrington Wilson Silverton Vigil

Barrington Wilson Silverton Vigil was driving parallel to the sparkling Chama River, a spectacular road through russet canyons, chalky bluffs, verdant fields watered by the high water table, and parenthesized by the Jemez Mountains to the south and the foothills of the Southern San Juans to the north. The meeting with the tribal leaders had been as successful as the previous three in taking practical steps to preserve the North Tiwa Language of San Buenaventura Pueblo. Barrington's story about Marie Smith Jones had been a saddening wake-up that Native Americans were being assimilated into the larger culture even on their own lands—and losing parts of their own culture. The tribal leaders had easily agreed to own the project, thus making it a tribal effort and not one imposed from the outside. Barrington knew that this was always a key to effective efforts with the tribes—or any group. He, Barrington, would gather the necessary resources and help apply for funding, although not under his name, but the Pueblo's. The tribal leaders were enthusiastic and sober about saving an irreplaceable part of their heritage.

Barrington should have been pleased—success normally bolstered anyone's frame of mind. By the time Barrington was ten miles down the road from the Pueblo, he was lost in the scenery. Two miles later, he was lost into himself again. A successful meeting was drowned, not in the Chama, but in a river of uncontrolled thoughts. The Chama, cliffs, mountains, and cornflower blue skies disappeared as his brain drove via its automaticity, and Barrington was thinking of lab results.

Barrington had been staying at James' house most nights. He was avoiding his mother, even his sister Innocenta, for that matter. They were too "gifted" and too normally intuitive for him to deal with just now. Barrington was consumed with his medical diagnosis and did not have the reserves to deal with the family knowing of his condition as well. It chewed on his mind, attention, nerves, and his relationship with James. Barrington was letting the virus win. Last night, he had returned to his mother's house late to avoid encountering anyone still awake.

Barrington was ignorant of his Aunt Angelica Gertrudis' lack of sleep, and she heard him arrive. Angelica Gertrudis kept to her chair and the unread book and listened while Barrington tiptoed into his room up one more flight. Like most people who have smashed heart-first into extreme loss, Angelica Gertrudis was suffering the onslaught of the chemicals that cause unrelenting grief. The overdose had produced an insomnia like she could never imagine—an overwhelming fatigue unaccompanied by any sleep. She grew wearier day by day, hour by hour. The chemicals had killed her appetite. A fit woman, she had nevertheless lost fifteen pounds and looked like a run-down runway model. Angelica Gertrudis had stopped coming to the dinner table. Theodora Mercedes had taken up tray after tray, but Angelica Gertrudis would taste the food, feel disgusted by it, and simply move the food around to make it look like she had eaten. Theodora Mercedes was neither fooled nor ready to force feed her. She had images of imprisoned geese—foie gras—when she thought of forcing Angelica Gertrudis to eat. Maybe time, solitude, and her sympathetic ear would take care of it. But if they didn't, then what would Theodora Mercedes do?

Barrington couldn't sleep or eat either. Food made him nauseous and sleep eluded him regardless of what he tried. Sometime after two a.m., Barrington got out of bed and descended the stairs in his boxer/briefs. Angelica Gertrudis waited until he was on the ground floor when she ventured out to spy, yes, spy—that was the correct word—to spy on her nephew. She too had intuition despite her own physical and emotional infirmities, and recognized someone else troubled and lonely.

Barrington was not in the house. Angelica Gertrudis peered out through the back windows until she found Barrington on his knees, sitting on his heels, in the center of the charred remains of "Barrington's Garden," staring into the night. His cheeks glistened with tears, and he was as silent as the constellations that rarely gave up their hard-earned secrets. The spirits of butterflies and piñon jays hovered around his head, but neither she nor Barrington could see or perceive them. As Angelica Gertrudis watched, Barrington lifted his arms and held his open hands up as if imploring to his god—what, she thought, what? In a time when Angelica Gertrudis had every right to think and feel only for herself, her heart reached out to Barrington. She sensed his isolation and grief but was powerless to help or intervene. She could not even help herself. What could she do but watch, empathize, and maintain her own isolation? If Angelica Gertrudis had any tears left, she would offer them up to Barrington. But her tear ducts had dried up just as she was drying up inside. Angelica Gertrudis walked up each riser with increasingly heavy steps and went back to her chair. She was still awake when Barrington came back up and, later, when he left the house again.

It had been two long, tortuous weeks of waiting since Dr. Asher's nurse had drawn nine vials of blood. Barrington was stunned to see so much blood emptied through his own vein. James had talked to him the entire time to keep Barrington distracted, but to little effect. Barrington tuned James out, not rudely or willingly, but out of the continuing insult and distraction of the virus that had made his body its home. The ten-minute event was for Barrington more of the same devastating news. This afternoon, Barrington would pick up James, and they would go straight to Dr. Asher's office to get the results.

"Do you want me to drive?"

"I want to pretend that I'm fine and can drive myself, but I would be lying. I don't know what Dr. Asher will say or how I will take it."

"OK, let's go in my truck."

The trip was short. Had Barrington been aware of Innocenta's comparing him to a cottonwood tree, perhaps he could have appreciated its nuanced implications. Like a cottonwood, Barrington was reaching for the skies to stay in touch with his life force. He was desperately keeping himself rooted in the current realities of twenty-first century medicine. Cottonwoods are tall, stately trees that rot from the inside. An ancient or damaged tree may sigh heavily one day and a major limb, easily three feet around, will snap without warning, and one third of the tree may crash to the ground. There was damage in Barrington that about equaled the weaknesses of cottonwoods. It had surfaced many times, and pieces of Barrington had come crashing to the ground. Unlike a cottonwood, which has been known to kill people sitting below, Barrington hadn't killed anyone yet. Barrington wondered just how much more buffeting from the stifling zephyrs of his private hell he could take.

"Your blood is normal in every way, and you are most definitely HIV positive. Your T cells and CD4 counts are within the normal range. That's a great result. Your liver function, red cell counts, oxygenation levels, kidney functions—they are all normal. Your viral load is at one hundred thousand copies per milliliter."

"One hundred thousand!"

"Actually, Barrington, that's not that high. I know it sounds like a lot, but some men come in here with one to three million copies per milliliter. This probably means that this infection is recent because in most healthy people the virus doesn't do well at first. Then, when it's established, it begins to replicate exponentially. We can deal with this, Barrington. The protocols are very effective and there are choices in case you have side effects."

"Protocols?"

"Protocol just means a daily set program of usually three medicines that work together to suppress the virus; this, coupled with regular visits to your specialist. I hope that you will allow me to be your HIV physician."

Dr. Asher described the various medicines and how they worked. James, and even Barrington, thought they were fascinating even as Barrington was horrified at the thought of taking the meds for the rest of his life. But what other choices did he have? Santa Fe was overflowing with homeopathic healers, faith healers, *curanderas*—every imaginable alternative to modern drugs. Even James believed that a Navajo curing ceremony was not an alternative to a successful and easy-to-take modern protocol. Barrington was not a natural gambler, and rolling the dice with his health was out of the question. A decision was made—Barrington would take two pills per day every morning. He should see no side effects, and the viral load should plummet to undetectable within sixty days.

"Dr. Asher, what's this?"

Barrington lifted his pants leg and pulled down his sock. His ankles and shins were covered in starbursts of blood under the skin. James was unaware of these, and his calm demeanor changed as a great sadness and shock overcame him.

"Barrington, you never showed me this!"

"I know, James; it just started a few days ago. I was pretty freaked and didn't want you to be freaked too."

"That, Gentlemen, is called petechia. It's caused by inflammation caused by the infection. Don't worry, Barrington, it looks much worse than it actually is. As the drugs take effect, the rash will go away, but it will continue spreading for a while before it starts to recede."

"What do you mean 'a while'?"

"Two or three weeks; as the drugs build up and infiltrate your body, the inflammation will never completely go away, but the petechia will."

The three discussed the protocol, contingencies, and a continued testing schedule for another half-hour. Barrington left with scrips for the medicines, and he and James walked across the parking lot to the clinic pharmacy.

"Barrington, I think you should visit my psychologist, Dr. Edelman."

"*You* have a psychologist?"

"Yes, there's nothing wrong with that. I still visit her about once every six months for what I call a tune-up."

"I didn't mean that there is anything wrong with seeing a psychologist; I only meant that I was surprised that you see one."

"Cause I'm such a rock; a strong stoic Injun?"

Barrington could see that he touched a live wire. "No, no, not because I stereotype you; because you just don't strike me as anyone who ever needed one. Don't be angry with me, James, I couldn't take that just now!"

James reviewed his hurt and turned to appreciate that no harm was intended and, more importantly, that Barrington couldn't carry any more burden than he already had.

"I know, Barrington, I didn't mean to snap. I had lots of issues with my homosexuality—lots of issues. Dr. Edelman listened and showed me that there were other ways to react and to accept without guilt and to just be happy to go ahead and live the life that was legitimately mine. Once I let go of living up to everyone else's expectations, like being straight, it got a lot easier. But I needed help, Barrington; I needed someone like Dr. Edelman. Now, you're having a terrible time—what harm would it do to talk with her?"

"I don't know. I never thought of seeing a psychologist about this. Let me think about it, James."

"OK, just let me know when you're ready. Dr. Edelman isn't accepting new patients, but I know she'll make space for you if I ask her."

"I had a psychologist help me for the last two years of high school. I was abusing alcohol and marijuana and had lots of issues, not just being gay. It might be time to go back or try your doctor."

The conversation stopped there of its own inertia, and James drove them back to his house with almost no conversation.

Almost no conversation, but Barrington's inner voice was relentless in its tirade spoken into its own reflection; his experience in the motel swimming pool, the resulting hate for his father, the emergence of his gay nature, the resulting hate from his father, his inexorable drowning in the deep pool of depression, his tormentors in school, his substance abuse, and his repressing his "real" life from his dear mother, Theodora Mercedes; the one person who could have helped him. Barrington was lost in the convolutions of his life, contemplating that which wounds one from within. The reliving was too much; Barrington rolled down the window and dry heaved while crying profusely. James, alarmed and panicky, tried repeatedly to get Barrington to tell him what was wrong. Barrington was unable to answer until he regained control of his heaving guts and was able to breathe again. But Barrington's response to James was simply to cry silently. James realized that his lover's emotional fragility was dragging Barrington down without Barrington's acquiescence; Barrington was no longer in control of Barrington. James turned the truck around, and drove back to the clinic.

Then, James drove Barrington back to his house. It made no sense to take him to Theodora Mercedes' house. Barrington needed to rest and let the valium do its work in Barrington's brain and more importantly, his soul. By the time they drove into James' driveway, Barrington was groggy, and James helped him into the house and into bed. Dr. Asher said the valium would let Barrington sleep for at least twelve hours; it was a large dose.

James was drained and beaten with stress and worry for Barrington. He sat in his armchair and drank wine until his nerves were suitably numbed. James, always a careful and casual drinker, had never drunk alcohol with this express purpose until today. James went up to the bedroom; he undressed, went to the bathroom, forgot to brush his teeth, and climbed into bed next to his stricken lover. James wrapped his naked body around this man whom he loved and held him, just held him; wrapping Barrington's arms in his arms, warming Barrington's legs with his own legs, taking any position that felt like a shield against the demons and fears that threatened this wonderful, but hurting, loving man. James cried because he felt so maddeningly helpless and fell asleep at long last.

Angelica Gertrudis was drinking coffee in the kitchen.

"Where is Theodora Mercedes?"

"She is in her study writing her journal, I think."

Angelica Gertrudis mounted the stairs knowing not a thing about what she would say.

"Come in."

"Do you know what is troubling Barrington?"

Theodora Mercedes looked up from her monitor and understood that an unnamed unease in her now had a source.

"He has been blocking me out. He has even been staying away from this house to shield himself from me. I sense that Barrington is trying to protect me from something, and he's very adept at repressing his thoughts enough to keep even me out. The gift has been no help if that's what you're wondering."

"Did you know that he often comes home late at night and leaves early? It's clear that he wants to be, or just is—alone. In the early hours before sunrise, I have seen him in his garden. His face glistens with tears, but his agonies are silent. He sits in his underwear, sometimes naked, in his little garden appealing to higher powers. If my heart weren't already broken, it would break for him."

"Angelica Gertrudis, I don't know how to help him. He's not in high school anymore. Whatever it is, he must have very compelling reasons for isolating himself. I wonder if he's still working. I wonder when, or if, he will let me know what is eating him from the inside. Barrington is a complex man, Angelica Gertrudis, made more complex from so many years keeping himself imprisoned inside. Oh, Angelica Gertrudis, you don't need this burden now! Let me deal with this. You need to take care of yourself, Sister."

"Maybe so, but I have lost enough for one lifetime. I don't want to lose Barrington too!"

The two sisters embraced, their eyes welling up, noses running, each feeling helpless and not needing words to express it. They didn't move or relax their mutual embraces for several minutes.

"Four to the sixth power divided by the square route of C!"

The mood was broken by Raul Theodore blasting the solution to something utterly unknown to the household.

"Well, Angelica Gertrudis, there is still some life in this house that requires our immediate attention! Oh, wipe your eyes and nose; we can't walk out looking like this."

James was working downstairs in his studio when Barrington awoke the next morning. Barrington had a valium hangover and had no memory of returning to the clinic, taking two valium pills, or the ride home. In fact, Barrington was surprised to wake up in James' bed after a few strange minutes of wondering where he was. James had left a large glass of water by the bed. Barrington leaned-up on one arm and drank. There was a nasty taste in his mouth, and he drank more. By the time Barrington had finished the glassful, he felt the urge to go. He took his time acclimating to sitting, followed by acclimating to standing. When he was ready, he made his way with great care to the bathroom.

Barrington leaned in the bathroom doorway and saw James sitting on the side of the bed.

"How do you feel?"

"How do I look?"

"Uh-uh. You tell me first."

"I feel slept in, like I'm waiting for the rest of me to wake up. Do you know anything about that? I also looked in the mirror. If I had the strength, I would scream then throw the water glass through it for lying so horribly."

James smiled; some of Barrington was back.

"Come back to bed."

Barrington tried to walk with authority over his body, but James met him halfway and eased him into the bed.

"You don't remember yesterday?"

"Some, I was in San Buenaventura early and left by noon. Then, I think we went to the clinic. Then it gets fuzzy, but I suspect it's supposed to be fuzzy, right?"

"Barrington, you went into overload, emotionally and who knows what else. I took you back to the clinic, and they gave you valium."

Barrington was silent. James had more, he could feel it somehow.

"I already called Dr. Edelman. She'll see you today as a favor to me. Barrington, I think we're both over our heads here. Please go talk to Dr. Edelman."

Barrington lay back and put his hands under his head. He looked at James for a while, then looked at the ceiling, then past it to sights out of James' range.

"I am over my head, James. I am also truly sorry that you have been dragged into this awful place."

"Barrington, that's what love is all about; being there for the person you love. I've told you, we'll fight this fight together. We're stronger together, but we need help."

"God, I love you, James. Yes, I'll go see Dr. Edelman today. You can't carry me by yourself while I slog my way through this."

"OK, babe, your appointment is at four-thirty. She's adding an appointment just for you. Do you feel like taking your meds right now?"

"Sure, my stomach doesn't feel bad, it's just my groggy head."

James brought Barrington's two pills and more water. Barrington examined them first as if they were new species of insects to be studied, catalogued, and admired.

"One blue and one white and they apparently do a lot of magic."

Barrington swallowed them simultaneously while James replied, "I'm all for magic; your magic and those beautiful little pills."

Barrington slept off and on for the rest of the day. It was not just the aftereffects of the valium at work; it was the combined weight of all his new problems being released from his overly stressed body. He needed rest and recuperation and to face his fears with Dr. Edelman.

Angelica Gertrudis was trying to follow Raul Theodore's abstruse explanation of some oblique problem in something called String Theory. Evidently, he had created a thought problem just for the fun of it.

"String theory—are you sure that's what it's called? Maybe it's 'Strong Theory' or something like that."

Raul Theodore looked at his great aunt incredulously. "No, it's called String Theory."

"OK, I'm sorry, Raul Theodore, you obviously know more about this than I do. Can you explain more? Start from the beginning."

Raul Theodore spent the next hour and a half explaining theoretical physics, then specifically String Theory. Then he explained his thought problem and why it was just fun and not something that solved an issue or outstanding problem with the theory. Angelica Gertrudis sat patiently, working feverishly to pay attention; after all, she had asked. She followed the large concepts, lost the track in the details, but Raul Theodore would circle back to the large concepts to go to his next subtopic.

Angelica Gertrudis was unaware of when or how she stopped listening to String Theory and instead listened to a rather fascinating little boy. She watched his eyes, mannerisms, the rising and falling of his voice, the increased vocal speed when he was explaining something he truly liked, and the unworldliness of his complex mind. Unbeknownst to him,

Raul Theodore made his great aunt smile and feel how much life was contained in him. She watched and listened with the wonder of someone who has discovered not just a new species, but a glorious new species. Raul Theodore was an exotic bird; she felt like the first European explorers who found the Birds of Paradise in New Guinea—the colors, extravagant feathers, the sounds, the complex mating rituals. Angelica Gertrudis was falling in love with this exotic species made up of a single specimen, this boy. He reminded her of her own exotic boy, Alfonso, not in a sad way, but in an exalted way. By the time Raul Theodore came to the arbitrary end of his explanation, Angelica Gertrudis was crying tears of joy for rediscovering the beauty of his life—and her own.

"So, that's it, but I left out the really complicated parts."

Angelica Gertrudis laughed, "You did? Well, that's really something because it sounded very complicated to me. Raul Theodore, you can actually see these things in your head, can't you?"

"Yes," and he looked at his aunt quizzically. She understood the look and the silent intent, "You mean that you don't?"

"Honey, I can't see what you see, so you'll have to see them for both of us."

"OK, I'm hungry."

"Oddly enough, so am I. Let's go downstairs and raid the refrigerator!"

Theodora Mercedes was in the kitchen with Consuelo planning her annual summer solstice celebration when her sister and grandson walked in hand-in-hand. Angelica Gertrudis was smiling; really smiling.

"We're famished. We just took a trip through the universe on a string and we're famished."

Raul Theodore giggled at her joke.

Theodora Mercedes was glued to her chair as she watched her sister call out the names of available goodies for her and Raul Theodore to eat. They settled on leftover roast beef, made into sandwiches with horseradish, Swiss cheese, mayo, and lettuce and tomato. Consuelo volunteered to make the sandwiches, but Angelica Gertrudis would have none of it. She and Raul Theodore would make them themselves.

Barrington got dressed slowly, the moves of a man who knows he must do something, but is stalling for time.

"B, we need to go in five minutes."

"Did you just call me B?"

"Yup; B."

"I've never had a nickname before; Mother wouldn't allow it."

"Don't you like B? I kinda do. B; it's strong but brief."

"I kinda like it because it came from you. It's silly, but I like it a lot."

"Good, B, now we need to get a move on."

"OK, but be careful around Theodora Mercedes. She may not like it."

Barrington buried his fears and trotted out to James' truck.

"I feel a lot more together today. Maybe this isn't necessary."

"Barrington, we both know it is. I'm glad you're feeling better, but you need to help both of us."

"So, when I'm in big trouble, then I'm Barrington again?"

They both chuckled and there was no further argument.

James waited in the vestibule reading women's magazines, longing to hear what was being discussed but not wanting to actually listen. The hour dragged. When James heard louder, animated voices, he recognized that the session was ending. The door opened. Barrington had cried and recovered in the short hour; he was smiling.

"Thank you, Dr. Edelman."

"You're quite welcome. I'll see you tomorrow at four-thirty, OK?"

"Yes, Ma'am, I'll be here."

"Bye, James, good to see you."

"Same here, Dr. Edelman."

"Tomorrow, huh? Sounds like it went well."

"I know that you know that I know that you are dying to hear what we talked about, but I'm not telling."

"No, I'm not!"

"Yes, you are."

There was a long pause while James felt totally outed. "OK, I am dying to hear, but I also know that it's private. Did she have to force you to talk?"

"You're prying!"

James chuckled.

"No, she didn't have to 'pry' it out of me. You forget that I had two years of this in high school. I know the drill *and* the expense. You have to walk in and start talking; otherwise you waste time and money. I like her, James; I like her a lot. We have to drop by Dr. Asher's office to pick-up some prescriptions. She called him while I was in there."

"What are you picking up?"

"Something called Cymbalta and clonapiszam or something like that. They're brain drugs that will help me get through this. Dr. Edelman said it's pretty clear to her that I'm going through a prolonged period of stress and depression. I guess these will help lighten the load."

Barrington took the first doses right in the pharmacy, and then James drove them home. James baked some chicken and vegetables and set the table. Barrington came down and looked at the food with skepticism. He ate slowly and sipped at his wine. He barely consumed half of his food.

"I think I'll go upstairs and read."

"Good, what are you reading?"

"As a matter of fact, I'm reading a Navajo mystery; something light, adventurous, and informative."

"Good choice. I'll be up after I've done the dishes."

Before James could get upstairs, he could hear Barrington vomiting in the bathroom. His stomach was still in turmoil. James knew that this would take a little more time. He stalled downstairs, listening as Barrington brushed his teeth and gargled. James wanted to help preserve Barrington's dignity. When it got quiet upstairs, James went up.

"You OK?"

"Yeah, my stomach's just a little out-of-sorts. I'm going to have to go home late tonight and get some fresh clothes."

"You going to work tomorrow?"

"Yes, I need to; it'll do me good to work on the project."

At midnight, Barrington arose and drove home. James arose with him, planted a lingering kiss on Barrington and, with his eyes alone, wished him strength.

Barrington entered the house and mounted the stairs quietly and with enough love in his heart not to wish to wake anyone. Angelica Gertrudis was in her room, listening, waiting, and wondering. At about three in the morning, she heard Barrington descend. She waited; then went down to the same window as two days earlier. In the waning moonlight, Barrington was sitting in the same position, naked, reaching up towards whatever compelled him. Angelica Gertrudis decided to go out.

Barrington was rapt in reveries of pain and loss, his cheeks shining a cold, pale indigo, his naked body a study in black shadow and blue light placed like a scab on a cauterized wound.

"Barrington, why are you crying? What are you doing out here night after night?"

Barrington had not heard Angelica Gertrudis approach and was startled. His tears stopped like they had brakes applied to them.

"Huh, Aunt Angelica Gertrudis, I didn't hear you! I . . . I'm naked!"

Theodora Mercedes was at her opened bedroom window, listening, observing. She could see the spirits of butterflies and piñon jays attending to Barrington, but also that neither he nor Angelica Gertrudis could see them.

Angelica Gertrudis ignored his lack of clothing and his protest,."What's wrong Barrington, you are so sad and alone?"

"Nothing, nothing, please leave me alone!"

"Did someone die?"

"No."

"Is someone sick and going to die?"

"No, no, nothing like that."

"Are you ill?"

Barrington considered his choices and decided to answer in the most truthful way he knew, "No, not really."

His aunt paused to think, "Are you upset about Reigh and Alfonso, Barrington?"

Now, Barrington was caught in a trap. He could lie or he could tell her the truth.

"No, I'm not crying for them either."

"Then what is so bad that you come out here night after night and cry and look so lonely and despairing?"

Barrington did not want to tell his aunt his troubles, especially naked in the middle of the night.

"Nothing, Aunt Angelica Gertrudis, just nothing."

If Barrington could see his aunt, he would have seen her blood rise up with the emotion of someone truly injured, "Nothing! Nothing?"

Her bony hand reared up to its full height illuminated by the blue moonlight while Barrington watched but didn't move. She hit Barrington so hard he tumbled over sideways and Theodora Mercedes gasped when the sight and sound careened up to her. Barrington stayed where he was, said nothing, put his hand on his cheek, and looked up in fear of his aunt. The attending spirits drew back.

"Did that hurt? Now you have something to cry about! No one is sick, dead, or dying and you can't tell me that anything is wrong!? Cry about that or, at least, cry like a man for my husband and my son. But don't cry about nothing, Barrington, don't ever let me see you cry about nothing!"

She turned in anger and disgust and stormed into the house. In her room, she massaged her frail hand; she had struck Barrington with the animal force of her outrage. Now her palm and fingers were swelling and stinging.

Theodora Mercedes stayed at the window for a few minutes and watched as Barrington righted himself and stayed in the garden. Now he cried in a humbled position, head down, arms and hands on his thighs, the profuse tears of a man who knew he had debased himself through his own weakness. The slap had flung his irrational fears out his right ear and into the darkening night where they belonged. The spirits drew close, closer than they had hovered before the great slap, but he still could not see them. Barrington found his balanced spot between Angelica Gertrudis' extreme grief, legitimate, real losses, a level of pain beyond his imagining, and his comparatively manageable infection. Barrington was ashamed of himself. He decided in those waning moments of this night that he would face this infection with bravery and James at his side. Theodora Mercedes went back to bed.

How would he handle his aunt? Barrington would have to give this some solemn thought tomorrow; this could not be hurried—he hadn't the wisdom to hurry it. He got up, and walked slowly up to his third-floor bedroom, and lay down. He slept until eight.

When Barrington came down, fully dressed for work in smart khakis and a golf shirt that showed off his physique, his mother, aunt, and Consuelo were having coffee at the kitchen table. Theodora Mercedes and Angelica Gertrudis looked up expectantly; Consuelo, sensing that something was afoot, looked at Doña Theodora.

"Good morning everyone! How's your hand, Auntie?"

"Why it's fine. What should be wrong with my hand?"

"Nothing, I guess, just asking. Well, *adios*, everyone, I'm off to work."

By the looks on everyone's faces, Barrington guessed that no one moved or spoke for several minutes at that table.

When he arrived at the institute, Barrington stretched up to the streaking clouds of fair weather. He knew he would have some backsliding, but he also felt confident that he could and would prevail. Dr. Edelman, James, and a large scoop of courage would see him through. Barrington

164

charged through the entrance to challenge the day.

At, Silverton-de Baca House, Angelica Gertrudis was proclaiming her hunger. Could Consuelo make a big breakfast? Theodora Mercedes just watched and listened. Was her sister taking a corner in her recovery? Consuelo whipped up a New Mexican breakfast smothered in Christmas. Angelica Gertrudis ate it slowly; her stomach had shrunk. Then she drank a small glass of milk.

"I think I need a nap."

Theodora Mercedes was still silent as she watched her sister head not upstairs, but to the chaise lounge in the backyard. She moved it to the shade of the *zelkova serrata*, stretched out, yawned, and went to sleep.

Theodora Mercedes reviewed the previous day, night, and morning events in her head. It seemed an unavoidable conclusion that Raul Theodore had helped Angelica Gertrudis and that Angelica Gertrudis had helped Barrington. The house was fixing itself without her acquiescence or control. She marched upstairs to find Raul Theodore. Even if he was in deep calculations, which was likely, she intended to smother him with kisses.

At four-thirty, Barrington and James were at Dr. Edelman's. James brought his book this time, a story set in India of forbidden love between an Untouchable man and an upper class woman. He knew it would end badly. James was able actually to read it as Barrington seemed so much better today. When he had tried to find out what had changed, why Barrington was better, Barrington had just smiled and played coy. Whatever it was, James was supportive of it. Barrington emerged from the conversation with yet another smile on his face.

Barrington took James to an Italian bistro, the kind with black table cloths and napkins, dim ambient lighting, and romantic candles. It was one of Barrington's favorite restaurants and, not insignificantly, Barrington was fairly sure he could keep down Fettuccini Alfredo.

Afterwards, Barrington drove James to Theodora Mercedes' house where they joined the women in admiring the stars. Angelica Gertrudis looked at Barrington for some time in the darkness.

Finally, she said, "Despite all the calamities that have befallen us, we still have much to be thankful for."

Everyone was flabbergasted by this unexpected pronouncement from a woman who had every right to be depressed, if not suicidal.

"Yes, Auntie, especially thankful for family; you, Mother, Consuelo, Innocenta and Bart, wherever those two are tonight, James, me, and the children. We do have much to be thankful for."

Theodora Mercedes was breathing in relief as the entire group went their separate ways through the house to their beds. She waited at the bottom of the stairs to watch Barrington and James ascend hand-in-hand with Angelica Gertrudis in tow. They left her at her bedroom door with kisses from both of them. Theodora Mercedes' heart was gladdened, and she went up herself.

"Barrington, I'm so proud of you."

"Not out of the woods yet. I know my pattern, and I'll be back and forth on this, so don't stray too far."

Barrington searched James' eyes for understanding and found it. That night they made love for the first time in over two weeks and the constellations approved.

Chapter Twelve
Theodora Mercedes Silverton Vigil

Theodora Mercedes Silverton Vigil was smiling, enjoying a lucid dream. She was in her thin, summer nightdress reaching up to a twilit sky with just enough sunset afterglow to give the fabric a rosy color. Theodora Mercedes was stitching together one of three rips in the sky with wisps of mare's tail thread. She could see well past the sky, and her vision reached behind her as well. Theodora Mercedes knew that both the gift and her ordinary insight, that which others might call "intuition," were both at work. As always, she did not know where one stopped and the other began. Theodora Mercedes could hear Aaron Copeland's *Saturday Night Waltz* nearby. Moreover, she could hear it coming, faintly, through the third rip. The choice of music created a calm, introspective atmosphere to the scene.

The dream had begun *in medias res*, but Theodora Mercedes knew that she had ripped open the sky herself. Now, Theodora Mercedes stretched up to reach the last stitch, knowing that she had now repaired two of the three. The third rip, smaller, wider, frayed just slightly, was out of her reach. Looking with all her resources into the rip, Theodora Mercedes could see the dense blackness of space. Slowly, the stars revealed themselves with their pure light. Not needing the gift to interpret these signs, Theodora Mercedes knew that her actions or words had torn the sky into skies. She also knew that two of the rips equally could be healed by her. But what meaning did these visions suggest? What about the third rip? Then, with gentle motion and a chorus of *Amazing Grace*, Theodora Mercedes was borne back into her own bed, pillow, and cool sheets. She awoke refreshed.

"I believe that this is going to be a fascinating day," she said to no one in particular. That morning the house was alive with activities and anticipation of today's ordinations. Consuelo was making a huge breakfast for everybody—Bart and James were also in residence. Between tasks, Consuelo would rush back into her room to examine her wardrobe. Should she wear the cerulean dress? Perhaps, the red—no, no—no red. The three-piece ensemble that Doña Theodora had bought her on their last outing together? Which hat? Consuelo rushed back to the kitchen before the chorizo burned.

It was Saturday, but Theodora Mercedes insisted that everyone dress up; they were attending grand theater in two acts. She hoped it would also be great theater, perhaps *opera buffo*, but was also distracted by last night's vision. Was she part of great theater—certainly not by any of Theodora Mercedes' intentions? She pushed her breakfast around her plate, lost in thought. Afterwards, she helped Consuelo and Angelica Gertrudis pick their outfits. While Angelica Gertrudis was better, she was still grieving.

"I really don't know if I feel like going, Theodora Mercedes."

"Sister, it will be a wonderful distraction. All you have to do is show up. I'll bet Genoveva is spending her next to last dime to put on an impressive banquet after the ordination."

"But what about the people offering their condolences?"

"Angelica Gertrudis, you know that the less you say, the quicker they will leave you alone. Here, wear this lovely dress with the stripes. It will show off your lovely figure. Do you have a hat?"

Angelica Gertrudis was amused by all this determined distraction and shook her head, "No."

"Oh, that's all right. I have a hat that will go well. I'll be right back."

By eleven, Theodora Mercedes had assembled the entire household in the parlor for head-to-toe inspection. No one representing the House of Silverton-de Baca would look less than spiritually noble, an image of their respect for theater and for other's religious beliefs. Theodora Mercedes invited the others to drive to the cathedral if they wished, but she would walk with her sister and Consuelo. They got into their training shoes, put their heels into Theodora Mercedes' bag, grabbed umbrellas to ward off the June sunshine, and off they went.

Traffic, pedestrians, and dogs gave way to this procession of handsomely turned-out women. Theodora Mercedes was attired in dark blue silk and wide-brimmed dark green straw hat with blue silk peonies; Angelica Gertrudis in vertical red, vermillion, and subtle black stripes with a black belt (showing off her slim waist) and black straw fedora with one red silk rose, and Consuelo in a multihued three-piece silk outfit and white, traditional *mantilla*—some habits do die hard—of crocheted fritillary butterflies.

Only the infestation of tourists seemed oblivious to three of Santa Fe's most illustrious, beautiful, and colorful citizens. They stayed focused on buying trinkets and taking pictures so that they would remember where they had been. Less interested in the city's glorious and old history and more interested in common pursuits, the tourists at least took notice of the stunning cathedral. They frequently entered wearing shorts, tank-tops, and sandals, and attempted to take flash pictures in the sanctuary. Santa Fe had few, if any, summer mosquitoes but suffered swarms of this particular pest. The residents often wished for a deterrent spray for this plague, but alas, none had been developed yet. Moreover, their local economy depended on them.

"Did Mrs. Arguello make it over?"

"Yes. She arrived right on time and parked herself in the shade to watch the children."

"I suppose she brought her own tea."

"Yup, even offered us a sip. Bart, Barrington, and James tried it and when we got into the car pronounced it undrinkable."

"I should think so. Did you tell them what's in it?"

"No, I'll let you tell them."

The three walkers had now finished exchanging their shoes. Consuelo's attention was on the coming religious service; Theodora Mercedes and Angelica Gertrudis were focused on live theater.

All seven walked into the darkened sanctuary and were jostled by bodies and pummeled by shoulder bags. Theodora Mercedes took the lead, and they all followed her, snaking through the throngs of visiting insects. The three walkers took the second pew, reserving the first one for Diego's immediate family. Bart, Innocenta, Barrington, and James sat immediately behind them.

Theodora Mercedes turned to Bart and asked, "How did you enjoy Mrs. Arguello's tea?"

"It was awful! I had to gulp down the glass in order not to insult her," he replied as Barrington nodded his agreement.

"How much did you have?"

Innocenta replied, "Oh, I got out three of the kids' juice glasses. She was very sweet and insisted that they all try it."

"Have you any idea what's in it?"

Bart looked slightly distressed. He wasn't sick, but was anticipating hearing a gross recipe in response.

"I thought not. She makes it out of the finest Japanese green tea, *sinsemilla* flower heads, *jamaica* flowers, and lots of sugar. Did you get all that?"

Bart played the list back slowly in his head while Barrington started giggling uncontrollably.

"Oh shit!"

"Shush, Bart, we're in somebody's church!"

"Are you telling me that there was pot in that tea?"

Theodora Mercedes chuckled, "Well, Bart, it should enhance the theatrical experience today unless it puts you to sleep. Barrington, hush! James, he's stoned. What am I saying, you're stoned! Still, you had better keep him quiet."

James was doubled over with laughter while covering his mouth with both hands—he and his partner were loaded in a church.

"Well, Innocenta, since you let them drink it, you will need to babysit three children after all. Shush, all of you!"

Bart was still processing and had yet to react.

Just before the noon hour and the start of the solemn proceedings, the tourists were annoying Theodora Mercedes. She stood up, walked to the front of the main aisle and started to admonish the tourists, herding them toward the back, explaining, as if to school children, that religious services would be starting at any moment and that they should show the proper respect. The docents, impressed by this bossy woman who made their jobs easier, finished herding the beasts out. By now, Bart was laughing uncontrollably and saying something garbled to Innocenta about someone named "Babe." This was lost on Innocenta. This was also a good thing.

Since before the seven had entered the cathedral, a choir had been practicing the hymns in start-stop fashion. Unlike the church choirs of the past or performance choirs of the present, this was a modern, each-enthusiastic-chorister-for-his-or-her-self type of assembly. They relied more on spirited delivery than precision, volume over nuance, individualized performances rather than a cohesive sound.

"By All the Gods of the Americas, I wish they would shut up!"

"Mother!"

"Well, honestly, have you ever heard such a noise?"

By luck and, perhaps, the gods' intercessions, celebrants began entering from the sacristy.

The main doors swung open again, and Genoveva and company progressed awkwardly but triumphantly down the main aisle like the Doge of Venice barging down the Grand Canal. The first ordeal was the mutual acknowledgment of Theodora Mercedes and Genoveva.

"So glad you could make it—oh, look at all these people!"

"We wouldn't miss your show for anything, Genoveva!"

Sardonic smiles whose chief attributes were the baring of teeth were exchanged. Now, the ordeal of getting Genoveva into the pew began. It took Diego's parents and grandparents to hold the wheelchair and move the expansive marshmallow flesh into the primary spot in the pew. It was breathtaking, and Diego's father wheeled the chair to the back of the massive nave. When Theodora Mercedes finally took a breath, she was assaulted by an insect-killing cloud of Tabu, the worst scent in the modern history of perfumery. Genoveva must have applied the entire bottle—everyone knew the stuff was cheap enough. Consuelo looked faint, Angelica Gertrudis appeared ready to vomit, and Theodora Mercedes grabbed both ladies' arms, moving them several aisles back. At least they were still on the main aisle.

"Holy Mother of God," cried Consuelo.

Both sisters looked at her, totally surprised as Consuelo had never been heard uttering such a thing. To hear it from her in a church left them awestruck. Four pews ahead, Bart was laughing in a loud voice between attempts to ask what the overpowering smell was. Innocenta had to poke his ribs to get him to shut up. Barrington and James slid down the pew until Tabu was a fetid memory. Innocenta dragged Bart down and sat him next to her brother.

"You three better behave! I am not missing this!"

Evidently, Innocenta had enough authority that her three charges became quiet.

The tourists were all either locked out, or some modern miracle had actually occurred; it was dead quiet. The minor celebrants looked to the main entry, evidently anticipating something—a colossal knocking three times. Everyone stood, the doors swung open, and the retinue of the archbishop—several priests, a monsignor, and four ordinates—entered to fanfares followed closely by a raucous hymn with organ accompaniment. The sounds overpowered even the stench of Tabu. The archbishop entered last, clearly enjoying his station, smiling beatifically at everyone on either side of the aisle, and proceeded to his throne on the dais. The four ordinates, one middle-aged and three young men, took places facing the altar. Consuelo crossed herself as the archbishop passed, while Theodora Mercedes looked aghast at the pomp and pageantry.

Angelica Gertrudis tapped her sister on the shoulder. "You're the one that said this would be great theater."

Theodora Mercedes wiped the disapproving look off her face and smiled beatifically back at the archbishop. Her mind was picturing rips in the skies, still unspecified, and she smiled even more broadly. They all sat down.

Most of the ordination passed without further incident. Bart mentioned to Innocenta that the ritual was following the basic plan of the Latin Mass with several extra flourishes thrown in for the ordinations. She only nodded, not speaking, as Innocenta was fascinated by the whole thing.

For the most part, the three stoned men were well behaved until what turned out to be the halfway point. "Holy Mother of God, I'm hungry!"

This was Barrington's sole contribution to the solemn rite while the other two contributed their complete agreement. Innocenta shushed as Genoveva looked back across one empty pew with a peevish countenance.

When the pillows were brought out, the family all looked perplexed. When the ordinates lay face down on the floor with only their faces on the pillows, the family looked on as if Hitler had invaded Poland to the accompaniment of a bad choir. Even Consuelo gasped. Theodora Mercedes stood up to get better view of the scene and actually leaned into the aisle. Angelica Gertrudis was trying to yank her back and down but abandoned the effort before she ripped her sister's sleeve. Theodora Mercedes ignored the clearing of throats behind her until she was satisfied that she had verified what her eyes had perceived. When she sat, at last, Angelica Gertrudis noted that her demeanor was changed—Theodora Mercedes was outraged at this humiliation of grown men at the hands of a superstitious faith. Had she been made to watch the prostrated men one more second, Theodora Mercedes would have walked out and smoked a cigarette next to the statue of Archbishop Lamy. But she wasn't, because the men finally arose, and she didn't smoke anyway. Nevertheless, Theodora Mercedes was ripping at the firmament above throughout the rest of the service.

Mercifully, the service ended—with rapturous applause for the men, now full-fledged priests of the Roman church. Theodora Mercedes stood, not applauding, and searched for Diego to look him in the eye. The commotion and attention ate several precious minutes before Diego's eyes found Theodora Mercedes'. Diego was transfixed far more than even during his ordination, and she held his gaze for a half-minute. Theodora Mercedes then turned and walked towards the exit followed by Angelica Gertrudis and Consuelo. She was silent as they walked to the banquet hall, but a smile fertilized her face as they neared the entrance.

Angelica Gertrudis had often seen that look. "Theodora Mercedes, what are you thinking? Don't you make a scene!"

"What scene? What are you talking about? I am enjoying myself more than you believe is possible!"

"Yes, that's what I thought."

Innocenta had shepherded the hungry boys straight to the banquet hall, forsaking any ham-handed congratulations which would have required sobriety and sincerity. While the boys pounced on the hors d'oeuvres trays without benefit of adult supervision, the wait staff looked on with amusement and secret knowledge—they had seen this before. While the herb-induced gluttony gained momentum, Innocenta discovered that the tables had place markers. She and Barrington were at one of the main tables with their grandmother, Genoveva. Theodora Mercedes' name was found at the very back of the hall with an obstructed view. Innocenta did some surreptitious rearranging involving not looking at what you were actually doing while simultaneously smiling at anyone nearby. Theodora Mercedes and Angelica Gertrudis were now seated with Genoveva. She, Innocenta, was now seated with the three stoned boys in the Gulag of the hall. Everyone would now be safe except Genoveva.

The three women entered and looked about, spying Innocenta, Bart, Barrington, and James in the back. They waved. Consuelo could not find her name tag, and she took a seat next to James. Theodora Mercedes and Angelica Gertrudis found their names, made themselves comfortable at their assigned table, and ordered chardonnay. As somehow, all the deviled eggs had disappeared, the wait staff offered the ladies canapés and fine cheeses with grapes. Theodora Mercedes rose several times to greet the few people with whom she was acquainted, and introduced her sister. The ordinates and their families arrived at last. Genoveva was nowhere to be seen. At last, after a dramatic interlude following the entrance and seating of the monsignor and the newly minted priests, Genoveva deigned to enter the hall. The Doge's barge arrived with all the pomp of Venice minus the red and gold flag of St. Mark. When the procession stopped at the table, Genoveva saw that Theodora Mercedes and Angelica Gertrudis were seated and well established.

With fire in her eyes and the baring of teeth with no hint of a smile, Genoveva remarked, "I don't recall seating you at my table . . . "

Her words drifted off as a hint that she required Theodora Mercedes to complete the thought. Theodora Mercedes, unaware that place markers had been changed, rose to the bait with her own,

"Well, it must have been your absent-minded good nature to honor us by sitting us here. And what pleasure we will take at sharing your table."

Genoveva grinned maliciously while she pondered whose perfidy had contrived this calamity.

Once again, the ordeal of getting Genoveva seated took place before the entire assembly—just the way Genoveva liked it. Instead of moving to a stationary chair, she stayed in her ancient wheelchair, but the challenge of proper placement took a few enchanting minutes. When she was finally positioned, Genoveva could hardly reach the table due to the long, curved arms of her chair. Moreover, the foreshortened arms and extended girth of Genoveva prevented a closer approach. The stationary chair was returned, examined to ensure that it was up to the task, and the full ordeal recommenced with much grunting, flatulence, and creaking of strained bentwood. Genoveva's ribs, or something close, were jammed up against the table and her voluminous breasts rested on the table where her plate should be. Diego's father ran off with the wheelchair and didn't return for a full ten minutes. He returned reeking of cigarette smoke and sporting a calm demeanor. Everyone was introduced, or reintroduced, all around as the salads came out.

Theodora Mercedes noted that Genoveva was seated where she could survey the entire room and, more importantly, the entire room could survey her magnificence. Theodora Mercedes was placed where she could see past Genoveva and straight onto the table of honor. Seated there were the monsignor and the four ordinates, two on either side of him. Theodora Mercedes watched all five carefully, noting the ordinates' discomfort and the monsignor's idea of holding court. The monsignor seemed to all but ignore the middle-aged gentleman and spent his time in animated conversations with the three young men. Theodora Mercedes could hear more fabric tearing.

Genoveva, convinced that Theodora Mercedes was staring at her, persisted in glaring back at Theodora Mercedes while flatulating in stuttering sounds like Velcro separating itself. Theodora Mercedes never took notice as her attention was ten feet farther out. This lack of reaction caused Genoveva to glare even more frighteningly, flatulate even more loudly, and her frustration caused her to attack whatever food was placed before her.

"I ordered the trout! Take this chicken away!"

The wait staff and their nostrils were being chewed up by the aggressive cloud along with her meal.

"I'm out of tea!"

At the Gulag, Consuelo found herself in the amusing company of Innocenta and three men. The rest of the table was empty. They joked, ate, drank beer, ate more, joked again, and generally entertained Consuelo.

"Consuelo, I never noticed how really beautiful you are."

This was Bart speaking.

"Yes, I've known you my whole life and it seems like I've never noticed how Hooloovoo your eyes are."

All went silent while they attempted a recognition of the word "Hooloovoo."

James asked, "What's Hoobalu?"

"No, Hoovooloo; no, no Hooloovoo. It means 'a super-intelligent shade of blue;' I read it somewhere."

Consuelo blushed with full vigor and nodded gratefully. It had been many years since men of any age had been so open about her outward appearance.

James just looked at her in admiration. "If I were straight, I might make a pass at you! Good thing I'm not!"

The entire table broke out in riotous laughter that even distracted Genoveva. Consuelo decided that gay men were more charming and less threatening than straight men. She was having a ball as Genoveva's day was tanking.

Just as Genoveva's rancor was about to peak, someone was tapping a glass. She turned to find that it was the monsignor himself doing the tapping. He was standing and about to address the assembly. Genoveva quickly assumed her most pleasing, alluring smile and made delighted eye contact with the monsignor. The monsignor, noticing an overly-painted enormous red-wigged woman who reminded him of Newt Gingrich in drag smiling at him, forgot what he was about. There was an unexpected pause while the monsignor's senses recovered from the onslaught, and he resumed tapping his glass.

When he had everyone's attention, the monsignor launched into a long speech about the four priests, serving God, and blathered on for a good, or bad, twelve minutes; one minute for each apostle. It was soporific if you were close by and stupefying in the Gulag, where the effects of cannabis were wearing off and the effects of beer and wine were growing. Mercifully, the speech ended with no one's being physically hurt. However, no one could ever properly gauge the psychological damage inflicted by the monsignor's speech whatever its content.

When applause died down, the monsignor was reseated, Diego found that his great aunt was sitting next to him. She had brought her own chair.

"Congratulations, Diego, you must be proud and happy."

"Yes, I am, thank you."

"I wonder, do you have any free time this week, Diego?"

"Free time?"

"Yes, free time; I would like you to be my guest at my beautiful and historic home."

"Oh, how nice. I don't report to my parish until Friday. I could come on, say, Tuesday."

"Perfect, dress like a civilian—it's your last chance, and bring an overnight bag. The family would love to get to know you."

"Why thank you, Aunt Theodora,"

"Actually, I'm your great aunt and please call me Theodora Mercedes."

"Yes, Ma'am; I mean Theodora Mercedes. See you Tuesday."

"Lovely, enjoy the rest of your day."

Even Angelica Gertrudis, watching this without benefit of sound or a vision, could hear fabric ripping.

Theodora Mercedes introduced herself to the other ordinates and the monsignor, shaking hands and smiling with genuine affection for these good-hearted men. As she made her way back to her table, she encountered the Genovevan Cloud. In an instant, Theodora Mercedes understood the need for the over-compensating cloud of Tabu—not that it worked. Genoveva was ripping out a fresh toxicity as Theodora Mercedes walked by, and that was when she realized that her mother-in-law could not hear herself.

For a brief moment, Theodora Mercedes' heart went out to Genoveva—until Genoveva spoke. "Well, what nastiness were you up to at that table!? You have no business going up there! You're not even supposed to be sitting at my table!"

"Oh, I see that I have arrived just in time for the cake and coffee! What a lovely banquet you have hosted, Genoveva. I'll bet it was expensive."

"Thank you, but as a matter of fact, it was a cooperative venture that I coordinated with the other three families."

"Oh, I'll bet you did coordinate it! Well, let's have our lovely cake and coffee."

Theodora Mercedes knew that Genoveva would have surreptitiously coordinated a four-way banquet in which the lion's share was paid by three of the four families. Genoveva was the Mae West of Santa Fe arithmetic. Genoveva continued to glare and flatulate as the final course was served.

As people started leaving and stopping by the head table to offer last-minute congratulations, Theodora Mercedes waited until the monsignor stood. She thanked everyone at her table, showered Genoveva with empty compliments, took Angelica Gertrudis by the arm and navigated to the monsignor. Genoveva watched her every step, unable to rise up and tackle Theodora Mercedes.

"Theodora Mercedes! Theodora Mercedes, I know you're up to something! I'll thwart you, Theodora Mercedes, I will!"

She continued in this vein until she looked like an apoplexy was imminent. Her family, used to these episodes, casually moved to get the wheelchair and end the entire event. Theodora Mercedes giggled like a school girl as she walked away.

"Your Grace, do you have a minute?"

"Yes—I'm sorry; I don't recall your name."

"Mrs. Vigil. I know your offices are in Albuquerque, but I have an urgent matter to discuss with you. Do you have any time in Santa Fe this week?"

"As a matter of fact, I do have business in town and will be staying the entire week. I have a cancellation tomorrow. Is that too soon?"

"Not at all, Monsignor, I'm flattered that you would see me so soon."

"You did say it was urgent?"

"Yes, it is urgent. What time shall I be in your office?"

"If you can call my local assistant tomorrow morning—I don't recall what time the cancellation is. I'll let her know you'll be calling and to schedule you in that time slot. Will that work for you?"

"Yes, thank you, Monsignor; that will be fine. I'll see you tomorrow."

The walk home included only Theodora Mercedes and Angelica Gertrudis. Consuelo rode with the others after verifying that Innocenta would be driving.

"Theodora Mercedes, what's going on? I know that something is going on."

"What's going on is the death of freedoms. At least two men are involved who either may be miserable forever or have a chance to see their real choices. What kind of an ethical person would I be if I knew that they couldn't see those choices and I did nothing about it?"

She stopped and looked at Angelica Gertrudis. "Sister, all I'm going to do is talk. The rest is up to them. There are two of them, so I estimate my chances of success at fifty percent. Conversation is a small price to pay if I can help to two wandering souls."

Theodora Mercedes turned, took her sister's hand, and began walking again. Angelica Gertrudis was about to speak when she saw tears streaming down her younger sister's face. Whatever Theodora Mercedes perceived as her duty, it was having a profound emotional effect. Angelica Gertrudis squeezed her sister's hand and walked in silence and solidarity in service to Theodora Mercedes' duty. They stopped on the front porch. Theodora Mercedes wiped her eyes, blew her nose, and put on a cheerful Santa Fe spring face.

"Do I look all right?"

"Oh, Sister, you look beautiful!"

They entered the House of Silverton-de Baca.

Consuelo had already changed clothes, and Mrs. Arguello had gone home. The three men were taking naps demanded by an afternoon of excesses. Innocenta could not be found.

"Innocenta!"

There was a pause. "Yes, Mother?"

"Are you busy?"

"Yes, Mother!"

"Too busy to come down and stop us from yelling up and down the stairway?"

There followed another pause, "Yes, Mother, way too busy! Can we talk later?"

Theodora Mercedes quickly recalled that when she was young, her late husband would occasionally smoke a little pot. He invariably became loving, and they had some of their best sex at those times. This was followed by a most refreshing nap. Now, it dawned on Theodora Mercedes that four adults were busy retracing her footsteps, so to speak.

She decided to shut up and let them be, when out of nowhere in his best outside voice, Raul Theodora proclaimed, "I've solved Goldbach's Conjecture!"

The two sisters looked at each other, and Angelica Gertrudis spoke."Well, then, we better go up and hear about it before the whole house does!"

They giggled and went upstairs to Raul Theodore's room on the third floor. They were certain that after hearing Raul Theodore's solution, they would also require naps.

Theodora Mercedes consulted with Consuelo on the need for and the size of dinner. They decided that a small snack would be adequate after the overeating typical of a banquet. Consuelo would put out fixings for build-your-own sandwiches and make macaroni salad. It would be ready at six for the children and anytime for the adults. Then they agreed that they needed naps.

Theodora Mercedes was having another lucid dream. She was in her comfortable jeans, a cotton blouse, and barefoot. Her lustrous salt and pepper hair flowed with the breezes. She reached up to touch the sky. The repairs were still there and the third rip was still open. *Saturday Night Waltz* was still playing so quietly that she felt carried on its notes. Theodora Mercedes touched the second repaired rip. It was soft, yielding, looked like a long ago healed wound, and it welcomed her touch. She looked around her and thought she might float to the other repair, becoming conscious of her freedom to roam, in her dreams and in her life. She knew that she had exercised myriad choices in her life, often with controversies that still did not perturb her compelled direction. Theodora Mercedes grinned in her dream for having the wisdom early to realize that she had true choices. For all her mistakes and triumphs, Theodora Mercedes knew that she was living her life to its fullest and freely. She had chosen at the age of ten to leave the Roman Catholic Church, run off with her second cousin, the only man she ever loved, and chosen to watch over her family, keeping them close without ruling over them.

Two wandering clouds neared. These she knew as the monsignor and Diego. They were not mare's tails; they were rain clouds. What was their rain? When would they rain? What meaning would the rain contain? The two clouds merged, each with one of her repairs, but seemed to keep their separate identities. Theodora Mercedes saw this as a good omen; the monsignor and Diego would be torn, repaired, and at one with their healing. These would be their exercises of their freedoms. In the first dream, Theodora Mercedes knew that she must rip open and repair the skies, but she didn't know exactly where, when, and who would be involved. After the two-act play of this afternoon and this latest dream, she knew exactly what she must do. Her sense of well-being embraced the firmament above; then Theodora Mercedes exercised her freedom to return to her bed and leave her dream. She slept soundly until the sounds of laughing children awakened her.

CHAPTER THIRTEEN
Theodora Mercedes Silverton Vigil

Theodora Mercedes Silverton Vigil awoke on Sunday morning, peered out her bedroom window and saw real mare's tails clouds high up in the mid-June sky. Her sixty-seven years in Santa Fe told her that these were harbingers of the monsoon season. She also smiled as they reminded her of the double dream. Theodora Mercedes grabbed a light robe, brushed her hair, and descended, barefoot, to the kitchen. Innocenta and Consuelo were already drinking coffee and gossiping about the two-act theater of yesterday.

Consuelo started to get up to pour Doña Theodora some coffee.

"Good morning! No, no, just sit; I can get my own coffee."

She grabbed her favorite mug, poured, and joined the other two women at the kitchen table.

"This wooden table is pretty, but it would be nice to have a cheerful tablecloth on it, don't you think?"

"We have the vinyl one," replied Consuelo.

"No, that's just for picnics. We need something in cotton, easy to wash, and something with a seasonal print. Anyway, what did you two decide?"

"Decide?"

"Was it good theater in two acts, or was it great theater in two acts?"

"Oh, I think it was great theater all the way. There were entertainments and shocks throughout both acts."

Consuelo smiled and nodded in agreement.

Theodora Mercedes replied, "Well, I agree, if reluctantly."

"Why reluctantly?"

"The sight of those poor men being humiliated by prostrating themselves was almost more than I could bear. But the pomp, pageantry, and costumes were splendid in their Renaissance look—except for that dreadful choir."

The two women nodded and chuckled in agreement.

"What do you think, Consuelo?"

Consuelo, who usually would be uncomfortable about now, swallowed

181

her gulp of coffee. "I think I agree with you. I've never been to an ordination, and I was shocked. I understand the concept of subordinating oneself to God, the word, and the hierarchy, but that was out of another century. However, the costumes were wonderful. I would love to have an opera dress made from the archbishop's brocade."

Both sisters smiled.

Theodora Mercedes was expecting less from Consuelo. "Consuelo, you never cease to astound me. How was your luncheon way in the back?"

"Oh, Doña Theodora, I have never laughed so hard in my life. The men were so funny, and I could see you and Genoveva interacting, but it was all like pantomime because we couldn't hear anything. I had the best time."

"Well, how was the food?"

"Oh, the food was awful, but banquets sometimes are. Even the coffee was bad. The cake tasted like shortening."

"It was shortening!"

They all laughed.

Angelica Gertrudis raised an eyebrow. "Do you think the monsignor meant for you to call today; it's Sunday?"

"Hmm, maybe this is just another workday for them. Well, there will be no harm in calling even if no one answers."

Theodora Mercedes rose and ascended the stairs to Google the monsignor.

She descended a few minutes later, "It turns out that if the archbishop is in town, his assistant and the monsignor work those days, whatever days of the week they are. The rest of the time, the assistant works for the parish."

Consuelo added, "Yes, when my grandmother worked for the archbishop, he still headquartered in Santa Fe. I recall she often worked odd hours. She really loved that old gentleman."

"Anyway, I have an appointment at ten in the morning tomorrow—two hours if I need it."

Angelica Gertrudis raised both eyebrows and cocked her head in Theodora Mercedes' direction. "And will you need two hours, young lady?"

Theodora Mercedes took up the challenge, "Perhaps—maybe longer. Which service are we going to this morning?"

"We're too late for the early one."

"I'll go up and start knocking on doors," Consuelo volunteered.

Innocenta and Theodora Mercedes were alone in the bright morning kitchen.

"Was that your first experience with a stoned man?"

"Mother!"

"I remember when your father would smoke a little pot, by All the Gods of the Americas, we had fabulous sex."

"Mother, it's unnatural talking about sex with you. Can you just please let it go?"

"Innocenta, you are such a prude. Are you sure you're my daughter?"

"Very funny, Mother."

Then, abruptly changing the subject. "I hear the others; do you want to ride with Bart and me?"

"No, I have another idea in mind. I'll meet you there."

"Consuelo, would you be interested in attending more live theater today?"

"What live theater?"

"I thought that you might find it interesting to attend the Social Liberal Church, just once, no further obligation."

"As a devoted Catholic, I would be risking my immortal soul to do that."

"Yes, that's the dogma, but what to you believe?"

"Oh, what the hell; let's go! Don't expect a Social Liberal Road to Damascus from me."

They chuckled, Consuelo grabbed her bag, and they hopped into the Honda 2000. Consuelo was alone with her thoughts all the way to church. Perhaps, thought Theodora Mercedes, she was having second or even third thoughts. If she did, Consuelo never let a facial expression or a word pass her deep plum-painted lips. They pulled up to the church, and Consuelo exited the sports car.

"It's so small."

"Yes, it's small, but important in its own way."

"It looks very plain compared to many Catholic churchs."

"Yes, but, like us complex women, others can't see our depths from the street view."

Consuelo shot Theodora Mercedes a radiant smile.

Inside, Theodora Mercedes was playing hostess, introducing Consuelo as her visiting friend. Consuelo was quiet, polite, charming in her naturally reserved way until she heard a loud gasp behind her. She whirled around; it was Innocenta. Theodora Mercedes quickly stepped between them and ushered Innocenta away.

When they returned, Innocenta merely smiled. "Welcome, Consuelo, I hope you enjoy your visit."

"Thank you. Shall we go in?"

Innocenta herded the children to their classes, and then joined the family in the pews. In the tradition of most Social Liberal congregations, the worship assistant asked if there were any visitors this day. Horrified, Theodora Mercedes realized that she had forgotten to warn Consuelo about this seemingly harmless exercise, but one that could possibly make Consuelo squirm like a beautiful creature taken out of its element.

She looked at Consuelo seated next to her. "You don't have to get up, you know."

Consuelo began with a momentary visual riposte, thought better of it, and stood up.

"I'm Consuelo from Santa Fe visiting for today." When she settled back into the pew, she colored a little and leaned into Theodora Mercedes to whisper, "Thanks a lot."

Then she looked Doña Theodora in the eye with her own laughing eyes. Theodora Mercedes gave a sigh of relief while Consuelo chuckled at the thought that it was not she who had been the most uncomfortable.

The sermon that day was particularly apt for the season, "Rational Mysticism, Opposites Attract, and Celebrating the Solstice." It was a remarkable blend of rationality without stark, empty facts; mysticism without demanding faith alone while accepting mysteries of life, the vast universe, and unanswered questions; and why honoring transitions by observing the solstice realized the need and beauty of the soul to appreciate all it could observe with every aspect of one's freedom. The minister pronounced herself free to accept and question and to claim her ground as a rational mystic. It was one of those rare occasions when the congregation actually applauded the minister; an occurrence as rare as the solstice and only offered when the brain and the heart had both been equally touched and strengthened.

Afterward in the narthex, Consuelo was enjoying coffee with the others and remarking on what a wonderful sermon it had been.

"She never mentioned the Bible, Jesus, or God."

"No, not today—although we sometimes honor Jesus for being a remarkable teacher, we do quote the Bible, and we do talk about God. Sometimes we talk about the Buddha, quote the poet Rumi, or use Gandhi as an example. But here, it's not a requirement, it's an option—to make whatever point needs to be made. Truth and wisdom come to us Social Liberals in many diverse forms."

Consuelo nodded. "That is really interesting."

She kept to herself the astonishment of having been spiritually moved without the usual tropes of her Catholicism, enlightened without the demand for blind faith. Despite her smiles and cheerfulness, Consuelo was unsettled.

When the children, at last, came running out, Consuelo grabbed the hands of the two Unremarkables and led them to the yard to play. Raul Theodore was enlightening his grandmother on his new-found ability to create an irrational form from a single piece of paper and a strip of tape.

"Oh, you made a Möbius Strip."

Raul Theodore was greatly annoyed that that which he had just invented already had a name. The implications angered him and he vowed to find out who this back-stabbing MÖbius person was. Realizing that his siblings were climbing the apricot tree outside, he instantly shifted his mood and ran out to join them.

Theodora Mercedes and Consuelo were leisurely heading back through town.

"Consuelo, are you all right?"

The length of the pause caused Theodora Mercedes to believe that Consuelo hadn't heard her.

Finally, "I feel spiritually off-balance. I am ashamed to say that I really, really enjoyed the sermon and the entire service."

"Ashamed. What's wrong?"

"Doña Theodora, you knew I was a devout Roman Catholic before you took me there. You should know what's wrong!"

"But, Consuelo, you have the freedom to believe what you believe. There's no reason that this should threaten your strong faith. I know that you are a devout Roman Catholic, so today was just a new experience to see how we live, nothing more."

"You are so wrong, Doña Theodora, so wrong."

With that, Consuelo went silent for the rest of the short ride, and Theodora Mercedes was left wondering how she had damaged someone she loved. For the rest of the day, Theodora Mercedes would stay out of Consuelo's physical and spiritual paths.

At five o'clock, Consuelo approached Doña Theodora and mentioned that the solstice celebration had not been fully planned. She suggested that they complete it this evening. Theodora Mercedes noted that the conversation began in a businesslike manner but with Consuelo's mood and manners becoming normal as the plans progressed. Perhaps the bottle of chardonnay that Theodora Mercedes had opened helped. By nine that evening, they were giggling and drinking wine in the backyard. Whatever Consuelo's immediate crises had been, they seemed to be in abatement now, much to Theodora Mercedes' ease of conscience. Bart, Innocenta, and eventually, Barrington and James joined them. Theodora Mercedes abruptly changed the subject whenever anyone approached the subject of the morning's services until everyone understood the encoded message to "leave it alone." Instead, they enjoyed a dark, iron-colored night, the stars, the camaraderie, and giggled at Raul Theodore's pique at Professor MÖbius.

That evening, Bart reported to the fire house, Barrington joined James at his house for the rest of the week at Theodora Mercedes' request, and everyone else had retired early to their rooms. Theodora Mercedes was in reverie ebbing and swirling around Consuelo and her faith, the coming meeting with the monsignor, and the fate of Diego the priest. She read her book while propped up in bed and found that entire pages would turn of their own accord as her mind had been elsewhere despite her eyes having been on the page. Turning back the pages, she would reread in futile attempts at single focus concentration, but her divided attention repeatedly conquered her. At ten-thirty, Theodora Mercedes quietly closed her book in frustration, turned out the lights, and rolled over to her left side. She stared at the blackness on the inside of her eyelids, but her conscience and the gift had her in their grasps. Theodora Mercedes was uncertain whether she slept or existed in another level of consciousness when she reached for the night skies.

The skies were as dark as any moonless night in New Mexico—velvet black. Theodora Mercedes stretched up to the sole remaining rip. Why would it not allow her to repair it? She passed through this opening like a feather buoyed only by whispers, entering a realm beyond the skies and gave a backward glance. In the surrounding blackness, the rip was lit up from the earth's reflection, itself sitting in blackness. Either the earth, an unbearably beautiful swirling blue, was examining Theodora Mercedes through a cat's eye, or she was observing the earth through the same aperture. What did it mean to be on both sides of this tear that she had inflicted on the sky? How far would she float before she returned to earth? Why a cat's eye? The repaired rips were of no consequence in this dream—this was solely about an open wound. As if drawn by the gravity of her questions, Theodora Mercedes reversed course and began floating back down to her cool bed. She returned to a restful sleep worthy of a cat.

Innocenta found her mother in her study, "Did you really throw Barrington out?"

"What?"

"I'm just kidding, Mother; he told me that you asked him to stay at James' for the rest of the week. Are you all right?"

"Yes, I did. We are having a guest tomorrow, Diego, and I want him to feel completely at home. Consuelo is dusting, vacuuming, and putting on fresh linens for his stay. As to your other question, I'm fine. I'm just thinking about my meeting with the monsignor. I was about to put on Arvo Pärt's *Berliner Messe*; why don't you grab your coffee and your book and keep me company?"

Innocenta had never seen her mother in this particular mindspace. Wordlessly, she ascended to return with her coffee and book.

"What are you reading?"

"I'm reading a book about evangelicals in Africa. They aren't doing so well. I never got around to reading it when it first came out. I think I was intimidated by its size."

"What a wonderful book! I put it as one of the best novels I've ever read."

"Well, it certainly grabbed me from the first page."

"Enjoy it."

They lapsed into silence, one reading and half-listening to Arvo Pärt, the other lost totally in thought, unconscious of the *Credo* playing in the background, mocking her doubts.

Ivan Rudolph Monsignor Szabo's assistant was a pleasant matron who seemed happy in her job. She was cheerful, well-dressed, and named Marianna.

Theodora Mercedes had already been announced; "Let me show you into the monsignor's office."

"Thank you, you've been very kind."

Marianna just smiled happily and closed the door behind her.

"Your assistant is charming, Monsignor."

"Yes, Mrs. Vigil, she is; a delight for me when I have duties in Santa Fe. Frankly, my real assistant in Albuquerque could learn a few things about keeping an equable demeanor. But, that is neither here nor there. How are you, Mrs. Vigil?"

Here, she gave a theatrical, but purposeful, pause. Theodora Mercedes was torn between two needs, the need to help Diego, and the need to satisfy her own, heretofore private, outrages regarding the Abrahamic religions, and the Catholic Church in particular. She would have to employ all her skills and self-control in this conversation. Theodora Mercedes stared lovingly into the monsignor's eyes and drew him closer. She had his attention, now she needed his heart followed by his complete capitulation to her powers.

Monsignor Szabo was puzzled by this gap in the conversation and her unwavering stare. He had only asked a typical, ice-breaking question. Why wouldn't she answer? As he wondered he was drawn deeper into her eyes; he felt her mind, her heart, her spirit. It was her spirit that mesmerized him. Theodora Mercedes' concentration enveloped the monsignor like a vine. Her tendrils held his attention, good-will, and his depths. He knew that he was hers to command; he knew that Theodora Mercedes knew that as well.

"I'm quite well, thank you."

Monsignor Szabo had nearly forgotten that he had asked the question. He nodded, but had little command over his will to speak. However, Theodora Mercedes' need to express her outrage would change that.

She surrendered to its power. "It has served us well, this myth of Christ."

Monsignor Szabo was unable to answer immediately.

"Pardon?"

"I'm quoting one of your own popes, Leo X, from the early sixteenth century. The myth, as kept alive by the Roman Catholic Church, has served it more than well, don't you agree?"

Monsignor Szabo collected his thoughts by first regrasping the present. "Mrs. Vigil, what are you talking about?"

"All this; this enormous edifice—the cathedral, the extravagant expense of keeping a bishopric and especially a Pope, financing a Vatican Bank, paying for your own country, to say little about the gold, jewels, and embroidery. Did you know my friend, Consuelo, would love to make an opera dress of the white brocade that the archbishop wore on Saturday?"

The monsignor put the full force of his will against Theodora Mercedes.

"Mrs. Vigil," exclaimed the astonished monsignor, "Did you come here just to insult me? You said that you had something important, urgent to discuss with me. Was that just a ruse to gain entry and insult me and the Church?"

"Not at all," Theodora Mercedes replied in a quiet voice. "I do have something urgent to discuss with you. But it hardly seems fair to gain an audience with a minor prince of the church and not offer up an opinion or two about the whole enterprise. I suppose discussing the business plan or questioning the logic and ethics of having an all-knowing, all-powerful God, who creates faulty humans and then blames them for his own mistakes, is also out of the question."

Monsignor Szabo, a small, pale man of slight frame, a good four inches shorter than Theodora Mercedes, now stood and leaned over his expansive desk toward Theodora Mercedes. He was battling her control over him.

His face was now flaming-cliffs red, "Mrs. Vigil, I must ask you to leave!"

"No, I can't. We have urgent business that cannot wait."

"Get out! You're not even a Roman Catholic are you? Get out, get out!"

Theodora Mercedes stood, mirrored the monsignor's stance, looked deeply into his soul and regained her grasp. "I will leave when we have discussed a matter of utmost urgency and not before. Now, please sit down."

The monsignor didn't move and his face grew alarmingly redder.

"Sit down, little man, or I'll sit you down."

Monsignor Szabo may as well have been slapped, his shock was so great. No one since his mother had talked to him in this way. Theodora Mercedes was counting on just that. As he collapsed, in slow motion, back into his glorious red leather desk chair, Theodora Mercedes mirrored his movements again. An eerie silence ensued as Monsignor Szabo's face retreated to its natural paper white—but not quite.

"Would you please take a breath so that I can verify that you are all right?"

"Mrs. Vigil, who are you and what is it that is urgent? It appears that I would be forced to have you dragged out of here unless we get this business done."

"Yes, that's probably true. However, I am fully capable of disarming any intruders."

Her voice continued to be quiet and calming and kept him in her thrall. She waited until his breathing appeared normal.

"I am a fourteenth generation New Mexican, a widow with four children, and eight grandchildren. Two of my grown children still live with me, as do three of my grandchildren. I am also a member of the Social Liberal Church, and not a very good one, I must admit."

The monsignor's face betrayed his thoughts. "Oh no, not an effing Social Liberal!"

"I'm not a very good one because we are admonished to accept others' beliefs with respect and treat those beliefs with appropriate dignity. It must be all too clear that those qualities are beyond my abilities."

"Beyond your abilities or beyond your choosing?"

He was calmer now.

"Either way works well enough for me, so you will have to decide to suit yourself. Will you promise to tell me which one you think is true before I leave?"

"Yes, especially if it will get you to leave earlier."

"Fine, that's a promise I will hold you to. Now, we've gotten off to a bad start . . . "

"You think so?"

"You know that I'm a Social Liberal and a bad one; tell me something about yourself. I can't possibly discuss matters of utmost importance with someone I hardly know."

A long pause, punctuated by deliberate breathing by the monsignor, followed.

"What would you like to know?" and he walked into her wiles.

"Well, for one thing, I noticed that when you get excited, if that's the right word, your excellent American accent takes on another quality altogether."

"Yes, I was born in Communist Hungary. I have worked very hard at losing the Hungarian accent. I never wanted to sound like Zsa Zsa Gabor."

Theodora Mercedes burst out in surprised laughter. Unwillingly, the monsignor followed suit—it was funny and her laugh was infectious.

"In a million years, I would never confuse you with any of the Gabors!"

They both now laughed willingly.

The laughter died down and Theodora Mercedes continued, "Please tell me about Hungary, it must be very beautiful."

Monsignor Szabo found that he wanted, no needed, to talk about Hungary. Theodora Mercedes was causing a willing exhumation of his past—he began his story.

"At the time, I would not have called it beautiful. The Communists were ruthless, life was hard; even the skies looked gray and depressed. All religions were persecuted, but especially Roman Catholics and Jews. I suppose you think that's appropriate."

"Not at all, my opinions on superstitious and very wealthy religions do not include persecution. I just question them vigorously. You were saying . . . "

"Yes, we had to practice our Catholicism in secret, but my parents kept losing their jobs and we lived on the edge of extreme poverty. We were outcasts."

"Did you have a good relationship with your parents?"

"Well, as good as any given that they were constantly under stress. I always did well in school and professed to be a nonbeliever to continue. Communism was the only religion. It was very hard on all of us."

"It sounds terrible. Did your mother suffer especially?"

Theodora Mercedes knew instinctively that his mother was the key to keeping him talking.

"My mother did suffer terribly. Her faith was shattered although she continued to practice in secret. She never let on that she may have stopped believing. I think she did it for me and me alone—I was an only child. In Hungary, one had to believe in something, even a decent afterlife, to get by. My father couldn't hold his own. He was never as strong as my mother . . . he beat her."

"Oh, I'm so sorry. What did you do?"

"Do? Nothing. What could a kid do? I'm the same size as my mother.

191

My father was an enormous man, strong, and dishonest with himself. Besides, my mother forbade me to interfere. She was more concerned with my safety, my studies, my faith; she suffered all the more because of him."

Monsignor Szabo's eyes welled up as he spoke about his mother.

"You must love her very much."

"Loved. She died years ago. It almost seemed to me that she waited until I had escaped and entered seminary in Rome, and then she just died; for no apparent reason, she just died. I was not permitted to attend her funeral, such as they were in Hungary in those days."

Monsignor Szabo's voice trailed off as he looked at a point on his own horizon, painfully in focus.

"Did you always want to be a priest?"

"A priest?" he laughed, "No, I wanted to write. I wanted to be Freud, Thomas Mann, and Kafka all at once and set the world free with my poetry and prose."

"That sounds wonderful. Your mother must have been so proud of you."

"No, she knew that I could only be successful if I wrote doggerel in service to the state. Otherwise, I would not be published, and I might even be imprisoned. She pushed me away from my writer friends and toward the church."

"She pushed you away from your friends? That must have hurt you deeply."

"Yes, we had to meet in secret. It was another layer of oppression, only this time, coming from my mother."

Monsignor Szabo stopped, sighed, and looked wistful.

"Was there anyone special?"

Another silence ensued until he spoke again.

"I had one very close friend in particular that she insisted that I avoid."

"What was his name?"

"Georgy, Georgy Zoltan Rozsa, my dearest friend."

"You loved him."

Here was a long break in the conversation. Theodora Mercedes could tell that he was weighing whether to continue down this too-telling line.

Then, he announced his decision, "Yes, I loved him. I think my mother knew how much I loved Georgy. But she couldn't keep us apart. We would meet in secret even from our writer friends."

"What a wonderful thing it is to love and be loved. What happened to him?"

Archbishop Lamy's French clock ticked relentlessly as Monsignor Szabo's face colored, and he was at the point of crying.

"He died. No! He didn't die—his own father killed him!"

"Oh no."

"It was my last evening in Hungary. Georgy and I went to a bar that . . . tolerated . . . men of our sort."

"Monsignor, I have a son who is gay, and I love him with all my heart."

"Gay, yes, a bar that tolerated gay men. We knew that we would not be able to make love that night because I was being spirited out of the country. My mother arranged it with the church—the church is very well organized, even under extreme duress. We were stupid. We got drunk. Toward the end of the evening, the music got to us; like fools we started dancing. The crowd turned on us. They pushed me aside because everyone in that bar knew I was leaving for seminary that night, but they beat Georgy terribly. They threw him out into the street, and someone got his father—another brute like my own father. I was hiding outside in the shadows and heard when they told him the story. Georgy was lying in the street beaten so badly that I thought he was already dead. I was crying. The men who were taking me out of Hungary found me, but I refused to leave. Georgy's father went into a rage and got down next to Georgy. He was still alive. His father started screaming at him and then beat my Georgy's head on the cobbles until it was mush!"

Theodora Mercedes gasped and rose to her feet.

"I watched as Georgy's life was ended by his own father, his own father. He brutally murdered his own son for loving another man."

Monsignor Szabo began weeping uncontrollably. Theodora Mercedes moved around the desk with her chair and held him to her chest.

Hearing loud voices, Marianna knocked on the study door. "Monsignor, is everything all right?"

"Yes. Go away, Marianna. Go to lunch right now."

"Yes, Monsignor."

He collapsed on Theodora Mercedes' breast and wept—just . . . wept.

Theodora Mercedes waited until the worst was over and lifted Monsignor Szabo's face in her hands. She kissed his forehead and wiped his tears with her delicate fingers.

"Oh, Monsignor, I had no idea. I had no idea how much you have suffered. I'm so sorry; I'm so sorry."

Her own tears rolled down her face as she tried to comfort this emotionally battered man. The monsignor was beyond her reach in emotions and visions that had long been suppressed by a will made of the iron of necessity. Finally, he righted himself in his chair and reached into a drawer for some tissues.

"I'm sorry, Mrs. Vigil, I never allow myself to revisit those days for reasons that must be too obvious by now."

He blew his nose and wiped at his eyes, but his tears continued in a heartbreaking trickle, echoing Georgy's long-ago spilled blood.

"Don't be sorry. You loved him. You have every right to feel his loss so deeply. Did Georgy love you equally?"

"Yes, if things had been different, we would have lived our lives together. We would have been writers and lived loving, full lives, Mrs. Vigil."

"Please, call me Theodora Mercedes. We have shared far too much to be formal now."

"Theodora Mercedes, OK, please call me Ivan. I have always preferred that to Monsignor Szabo."

Their faces were only inches apart and they smiled.

"How do you feel about your life—the life that you chose instead of life as a writer and with Georgy?"

"Well, you are not a young woman, so you already know. One makes the best of the life one is given. I could have let my broken heart and broken dreams ruin me. I built walls and gave myself willingly to my life as a priest. I was asked to go to Africa. I went. I was asked to come to America. I came. Now, I'm Monsignor Szabo. Except for testicular cancer, now cured—I do have one testicle left—life is pretty good."

"Testicular cancer; that's what comes from a life of celibacy. Was it worth it, Ivan?"

"How would you like to measure 'worth'? I serve God's people; I give them hope; I give their misery a reason for existing in anticipation of a better afterlife. I'm satisfied and have done well. I hope to cast my vote for a new Pope someday—as a cardinal. By most measures, I'm a success."

"But, Ivan, how can you endorse celibacy and the church's condemnation of homosexual behavior? Surely, this presents some conflict or, dare I say it, hypocrisy for you?"

"I don't have any choice, do I?"

"Why not? Why don't you have a choice? Surely, you don't approve of these rules?"

"I am a servant of the church. My duty is to enforce the church's teachings and rules."

"But you cannot possibly agree with them."

"I'm not paid to agree or disagree. I'm paid to do my duty."

Theodora Mercedes searched his face for conviction. She found equivocation.

"Ivan, you may believe that it's too late for you, but other young men are affected by these terrible rules. The history of the church is filled with married men who were priests. They were not just married to women; they were married in the church to other men. Saints Serge and Bacchus were joined in marriage. Women were also joined together. The church used to celebrate love without regard to gender."

Ivan did not know any of this; he appeared to be witnessing a miracle.

"In the eleventh century, marriage was abolished for priests for reasons of property and corruption. Title to churches and church lands was unclear; priests created dynasties to keep church properties in the family. Rome saw this as a threat to its wealth and dominion, and the easiest thing to do was to abolish married priests. Don't you see, Ivan, for centuries the church not only acknowledged love in all its forms, but celebrated and joined love in all its forms? It was only greed that caused a cessation of priests, gay and straight, to be joined, accepted, and celebrated."

Ivan was no longer returning Theodora Mercedes' gaze. She detected a slight shivering in his body. Had she loosened her grip too soon?

"Is this why you came here today, to discuss my past life and use it against me? I can't believe that you would be so evil."

"I'm not. I could tell that you were gay when I met you on Saturday. I just wanted to appeal to you because . . . Diego is also gay. Moreover, I believe that he was forced, brainwashed from an early age, to become a priest. I don't think he has ever wanted to become a priest."

"Then why did he become one? By the way, I, too, know that he's gay. One picks up on the signs. Still, being gay is no barrier to being a priest."

"No, but being miserable and feeling one's whole life as if forced into it is a barrier to being a priest—certainly a committed one. What if he hasn't your discipline? The church has been financially ruined, its reputation sullied beyond repair, and truly awful coverups have occurred because men have repressed their drives—drives that stem from biology and natural law. Do you want Diego to settle for a life or embrace one? Are you willing to gamble on his strengths and weaknesses?"

"Are you suggesting that Diego might be or will become a pedophile?"

"No, absolutely not. What I am suggesting is that neither of us, nor Diego for that matter, knows what an unfulfilled life could bring for him. We know how well you handled it. Are you so certain that you know how he will handle it?"

Theodora Mercedes relaxed her grip; the power of her appeals would be enough.

"What do you want me to do? Diego has already taken his vows. He's scheduled to report to his parish on Friday.

"Wait. Why do you think he has been forced into becoming a priest?"

"Well, first, of all he all but told me so; not in words, more in the spaces between the words. I also know that his great grandmother is behind this. He is her salvation."

"Her *salvation*? What can you mean?"

"Genoveva has the longest name of anyone I know. She has led a dissolute life based on multiple husbands, greed, and the use of sex to gain whatever she has wanted. When Diego was born, I think she decided that his becoming a priest would absolve her of her sins."

"But that's ridiculous. How can Diego's becoming a priest absolve her of her sins?"

"Call it salvation by proxy. Regardless of what you or I might believe, Genoveva believes it. So for all of Diego's life, Genoveva drilled into him that she expected him to become a priest. Now, he is, and I'm telling you, Ivan, that he is and will be miserable."

For yet another instance, Monsignor Szabo was lost in thought. Theodora Mercedes saw him becoming misty again.

"What do you want me to do?"

"Nothing much, really. Just talk with him. Suggest that you think he has doubts. Let him know that you know that he's gay. That will get his attention, and he can ask himself the serious questions. I am not saying that you should throw him out or tell him what to do. Just ask him if he chose this life for the right reasons. If he insists that he did, then so be it. If he has doubts, let him admit those, and then guide him to the best decisions for him and the church. Let me put it in a more dramatic way—don't let your life become his. Please tell me that you understand my meaning, Ivan."

"I do, I do understand. Let me think about this until tomorrow. You are asking me to go against the church in some ways. Finding priests in the 'first world' is not easy anymore. I must call the archbishop, discuss this candidly, and possibly call you tomorrow, Theodora Mercedes."

"Thank you, Ivan."

Theodora Mercedes got up to leave, putting her chair back in its rightful place opposite the monsignor's chair. Monsignor Szabo rose to escort her out.

"Ivan, for what it's worth, you are a hell of a man. You would have been a great and loving companion to whomever you chose."

The monsignor maintained a poker face and merely nodded in acceptance of the compliment. "I'll call you tomorrow. Good bye."

"Wait, Ivan, what did you decide?"

"I said I would think about it."

"No, about whether I am either unable or unwilling to accept others' beliefs with respect and treat those beliefs with appropriate dignity."

"Oh, Theodora Mercedes, as we used to say in Hungary, most disrespectfully I might add, that an idiot Bulgarian wrapped in a Romanian moron could tell that you are able to do whatever it is that you choose to do. Therefore, you are unwilling. As a child you must have been a handful."

"I agree with your assessment, and, yes, I was a handful—still am. Ivan, I think we should be friends, whatever your decision about Diego."

"The monsignor and the Social Liberal, even I am shocked. Perhaps we should deal with the immediate crisis first."

"Hmm, I am having a little celebration on Wednesday afternoon at my home. I would be honored if you could come. We're celebrating the summer solstice with a little prayer, food and drink, and thankfulness. Don't worry, we won't be dancing naked around an oak tree, just celebrating our beautiful world."

"I think that it would be awkward for a monsignor to attend such an event, don't you?"

"Yes, but you could *choose* to come. Why don't you? Wear ordinary clothes, meet my family; I guarantee that you will find them interesting, and your secret will be safe with us."

"It's a stretch, but I'll still call you tomorrow."

"Excellent. Goodbye, Ivan."

"Good bye, Theodora Mercedes."

On her drive home Theodora Mercedes wondered what the monsignor was doing, thinking, feeling; how he must be replaying the conversation. Would he revert to thinking of her as evil? She did, in fact, use her knowledge of him to gain the conversational advantage, but in the process, uncovered the long-hidden man inside the priest. Maybe she was evil, yet she didn't think so; too much was at stake. Theodora Mercedes hoped that Ivan would see the concerned human in her and not only the purposeful drive. The best she could hope for, she decided, was that Ivan could balance those two opposite motivations and see her as a complete and complex human. She sighed and mentally crossed her fingers. Theodora Mercedes did believe with all her heart that Ivan had the potential to be a great friend. She pictured them having lunch together, sitting in her yard drinking wine and discussing, or perhaps, arguing theology and philosophy.

She sighed again and stopped at the Iberian Table to look for tablecloths. Given her present state of distraction, an unusually cheerful pattern would be required to wrap up this morning.

When Theodora Mercedes arrived home with her new tablecloth and matching napkins for the lowly kitchen table, she had missed lunch. Consuelo reheated some cheese enchiladas for her and tossed a little side salad.

"Thank you, I'm famished and don't know why."

"You look like you've had an emotional day. It's kind of all over your face."

Theodora Mercedes stopped in mid-bite, "Really?"

Consuelo raised her eyebrows and simply nodded.

"It was much more emotional than I expected it to be. There is much sad history with the monsignor that I can't discuss. He's a very complex person."

Consuelo left Theodora Mercedes with her thoughts and returned to washing the casserole dish. The phone rang.

"It's for you, the monsignor!"

"Hello . . . yes . . . yes . . . oh, already . . . how did . . . oh, I see . . . oh, that's good . . . he said he's coming here . . . yes . . . yes . . . oh, you will . . . well, we'll see you Wednesday, Ivan . . . no, I left the address on Marianna's desk . . . of, course . . . thank you so much for calling, Ivan. I'll see you on Wednesday at two . . . yes, good bye."

"By All the Gods of the Americas, is Barrington's room ready?"

"Yes, all cleaned with fresh sheets and towels."

"Excellent, Diego is on his way. I must get upstairs and brush my teeth. Where's Innocenta?"

"She's at the community college waiting for Raul Theodore to complete a supervised lab. She'll be home by three." Theodora Mercedes picked up the phone.

"Innocenta, . . . no, no this not an emergency . . . I'm just a little excited, that's all . . . well, the monsignor called the archbishop, who called Diego, and probably called him before I even got home . . . I don't know . . . Diego told the archbishop that he was going crazy staying at home and was coming over here . . . well, of course he'll be welcomed early. It's just one day . . . OK, I'll see you soon."

The second Theodora Mercedes put down the phone, the light dimmed in the kitchen. Consuelo turned around in silence, left the room, and the table cloth Theodora Mercedes still clutched began to unfold upwards. The gift was asserting itself. Festooned with red tulips, pink roses, and extravagant magenta peonies, the sky-blue colored cloth stretched out and up, wafting Theodora Mercedes with it into the mare's tail clouds. Her vision morphed to floating in a blue sky with a flowered tablecloth for a sail. She reached for the rip she had caused but it stayed out of her reach. Then the gift possessed Theodora Mercedes like she had possessed the monsignor, without any mercy.

"Oh, no, it's Diego's life that I've ruined." While she experienced this horrifying conclusion, the front doorbell rang. Theodora Mercedes dropped back to her kitchen trailing printed flowers.

"What have I done, what have I done?"

Theodora Mercedes gasped for breath, "Consuelo!"

"Yes?"

"I'm going to need ice cream, lots of chocolate ice cream. What have I done, what . . . have . . . I . . . done?"

Chapter Fourteen
Innocenta Perpetua Vigil Silert

Innocenta Perpetua Vigil Silert was still reeling from the blithe query from her own mother: "Was that your first experience with a stoned man?"

She was still too flummoxed, unable to control her complexion and working feverishly not to be amused by her mother's brazenness while trying to avoid the overt embarrassment. Innocenta was suffering from the futility and the emotional work required for self control. She ran back upstairs where Bart was still getting ready for church. In even less control now that she was winded, she blurted out what her mother had asked.

Bart cut the cleft in his chin and swore."She what!?"

"Judging from the cut on your face, I think you heard me just fine."

Bart just stared incredulously at Innocenta while grabbing toilet paper to daub his chin. His face now lost its control over its color as he realized that shortly he would have to go downstairs and face Theodora Mercedes. Neither he nor Innocenta had ever known anyone like her.

Innocenta managed to snag Angelica Gertrudis and sneak the three of them out the front door while Theodora Mercedes was conversing with Consuelo. She was unaware, probably the best thing for her now-restored complexion, that her mother spied them leaving and waved.

"What are you laughing about?" asked Consuelo.

"Oh nothing, let's get ready and go."

Bart and Innocenta were at last feeling normal when Innocenta thought that she heard a familiar voice, turned around in the church's narthex only to find, of all people, Consuelo standing there with her back to Innocenta. Consuelo was already wearing her "Visitor" nametag, and being introduced to people by Theodora Mercedes. Innocenta issued an involuntary gasp nearly of the same proportions, in sound anyway, as one of Genoveva's flatulences of the day before. While there was no shriveling smell, the attention-getting effect was similar. Consuelo and Theodora Mercedes immediately wheeled around, her mother as if she were expecting Innocenta. She was, so she grabbed her by the sleeveless arm and whisked her away like a bad pâté before a guest could nibble at her.

"I want you to behave as if nothing unusual is going on. Please don't make a fuss about Consuelo's being here, you'll embarrass her, and we don't want that, do we?"

"But . . . "

"Never mind that for now. She's here, and we are not going to call a lot of unneeded attention to her, agreed?"

"Yes, Mother."

Innocenta dutifully followed her mother back to Consuelo. "Welcome, Consuelo, I hope you enjoy your visit."

After the service, Innocenta and Bart mingled until it was time to round up the children. Raul Theodore was in a petulant space, tearing up a taped piece of paper while muttering, "Möbius!" Bart took everyone to lunch at Cowhands, and Raul Theodore was distracted by a big, juicy bison burger and fries. By the time the children were home and changed out of their church clothes, he was muttering again and doing a search on his computer.

Most unexpectedly, Innocenta received a reminder call on a Sunday from a Professor Fellini about Raul Theodore's assessments. Innocenta thanked the professor and noted that she seemed anxious, as if the professor fully expected she had forgotten. Innocenta popped in when the shadows were leaning east to remind Raul Theodore that he had a supervised assessment on Monday.

"Can I wear what I have on now?"

"No, you have to wear school clothes."

"But it's summer."

"Actually, it's still spring, but you're going to school tomorrow to be tested so you will wear school clothes, OK?"

"OK. How do you spell Mo-bee-us?"

The tension in the air on Monday morning was palpable. Innocenta joined her mother in her study while Theodora Mercedes grasped at ideas in silence, during which *Berliner Messe* played almost unheard. Innocenta tried to concentrate on her novel, but her mother's reveries were distracting, and she only pretended to be fully engaged in reading. She left to get Raul Theodore ready for the ride to the UNM extension at Santa Fe Community College.

At the college, Innocenta experienced the same wanderings of any visitor to an unfamiliar campus. She finally asked a security guard, who put her on the right path to the computer labs. Innocenta and Raul Theodore were met by a student aide and then welcomed by various Doctors This and Doctors That. They never saw or met Professor Fellini. Raul Theodore was led into the lab. Doctor This—or was it Doctor That—explained that Raul Theodore's IQ and achievement levels in calculus, quantum mechanics, and general physics would be measured. The assessments would take three to four hours with at least one break. They would continue again on Wednesday. Innocenta was thankful that she had brought her book and wandered off to find a coffee machine. During the break, she bought Raul Theodore some juice and chips and then sent him back in with the student aide.

Afterwards, Innocenta stopped at the gelato shop to reward her son, but learned that yet another gelato shop had gone out of business in Santa Fe. Innocenta muttered to herself that for a nearly perfect town, it failed miserably to keep gelato on the menu. Perhaps, this portended that the apocalypse was to begin in Santa Fe—Innocenta was not amused.

When Innocenta re-entered the house, it seemed to be a different place. There was tension emanating from her mother and a second cousin occupying Barrington's room. Consuelo was distant and almost, but not quite, short with her. Innocenta imagined that little green men had invaded and had replaced some loved ones with badly programmed memes. She decided to go make a proper reintroduction to Diego. Innocenta knocked on Barrington's bedroom door.

"Hi, I'm Innocenta. I think we're second cousins," said more as a question than a statement.

Innocenta had so many close and distant relatives in Santa Fe that the exact levels of removal were often mysteries. When someone stated the exact relationship, Innocenta normally accepted it without question, even if fifty percent of the time the other person was off by at least one removal.

"Yes, I think that's right. I haven't seen your brother. I feel awkward that I've taken over his room."

"Oh, don't worry about him; he's staying with his boyfriend, James. You remember seeing the tall unbearably handsome Native American?"

"Yes." He blushed uncontrollably and, to Innocenta, needlessly.

"I just love my brother's taste in posters. Did you look at them? They're like a short history of his life. When he moved up here earlier in the year, he was selective about what he brought."

Diego wished he were an invisible, mute bird who could leap through the open window and wing into the afternoon breeze and disappear—but he wasn't. "Yup, it's quite a collection."

He stared at the floor.

"I think this band from his teenage years is quite nice—in a garish way. This poster from The Santa Fe Opera is just gorgeous. You can see how his taste is growing in sophistication. But I really think that athlete in his Emporio Armani underwear is the most interesting. It's the newest and most unexpected. Just when Barrington has grown up, he chooses this. I think it's because he became comfortable with his sexuality so late in life."

Innocenta turned to face Diego.

"Which is your favorite?"

Innocenta turned to look again at the posters.

Diego chose to lie. "I haven't really looked that closely; I've been unpacking."

Realizing that she was embarrassing Diego, Innocenta spun around and saw him still staring at the floor. "I'm sorry. I didn't mean anything by talking about the posters."

"That's OK. Everyone in this house seems to have me identified in precise detail."

"But you're self-conscious about it; I should have realized . . . "

"No, it's fine. At least everyone in this house isn't in denial about who, or what, I am. It's just that the poster—I'm not used to it."

Diego met Innocenta's eyes, still showing a high degree of discomfort, and attempted an unsuccessful birdlike smile.

"Why don't I take it down?"

"No, no, this is Barrington's room, not mine."

Another awkward pause ensued while Diego seemed to be making a decision. "Innocenta, was I put in this room for a purpose?"

"That, I don't know, Diego; but if you're not comfortable, we can move you. Would you like to stay in my room? It's less . . . provocative."

"No, I need to deal with this for reasons that I won't say. Besides, I've already unpacked. Did you know that there's an Easy-Bake Oven in the closet?"

When he produced a genuine smile this time, Innocenta chuckled. "Oh, is that where it is? It used to be mine but Barrington wanted it more than

I did. Why don't you finish and come down to the kitchen? I'll be waiting for you. Do you like wine?"

"I'm a priest; it's a requirement."

They both chuckled at this joke.

"Red or white?"

"Whatever you're having, Innocenta."

She turned to leave and Diego caught her by the arm. "Thanks."

"Thanks for what?"

"I'm not sure, maybe just for being a sensitive person."

Innocenta's eyes smiled with genuine affection; she gave him a hug, awkward on Diego's part, and descended the stairs.

"Mother, what are you trying to do to Diego? He's uncomfortable in Barrington's room, especially with that one poster."

"I'm trying to make a point, Innocenta, a crucial point. Besides, I'll bet that he gets comfortable up there sooner than you think. Innocenta, I believe that Diego is in trouble, trouble that he can't handle on his own. I think we can thank Genoveva for that. Diego needs to look at his life straight on and honestly before . . . before he gets lost."

They could hear Diego coming down the stairs. Consuelo, having already had enough of this conversation, took the liberty of exiting to the backyard, ostensibly to check on The Unremarkables.

"Hello, everyone; thanks again for your hospitality, Mrs. Vigil. I was going crazy around my other family, especially around my great-grandmother."

Theodora Mercedes and Innocenta gave Diego "please continue" looks.

"The room is lovely, but I feel bad about displacing Barrington. I hope to get to meet him while I'm here."

"Oh, you will," replied Theodora Mercedes, "He'll be here for Wednesday's festivities. As a matter of fact, we might also have a surprise guest on Wednesday. Meanwhile, Diego, don't waste another thought on Barrington. He's staying with his boyfriend, James, and is quite happy. Are you sure his room is comfortable? I could move you."

"No, it's fine. The posters were a surprise. Innocenta gave me the short history."

Innocenta broke in."Yes, the opera poster is the finest, but I think I prefer the athlete."

"Yes, I too have a preference for him. He reminds me of a young

Monsignor Szabo."

Diego flamed in the cheeks when he realized that he had just said too much in front of two very astute and intuitive women. "I mean, well . . . of course, he's nothing like the monsignor, especially the tattoos."

Innocenta saved the moment by changing the subject, "We were about to have pinot grigio. Let me get the glasses while you sit down."

Diego trembled as he sat and his color did not modulate by even half a hue.

"Diego, please relax. You are among friends here. Even though you don't really know us, we are part of your family and, more importantly, we are your allies."

Diego began to question the word "allies," but decided just to effect a smile.

"You mentioned that you have been uncomfortable at home. Can you share why?"

"My great-grandmother has gone on my entire life about my becoming a priest. Now, I am a priest, and she's still going on about it day and night. My parents and grandparents are no help; they just go along with her. Great-grandmother supports my grandparents financially, so they never say anything to her."

"What should they say, Diego?"

Innocenta put glasses of wine down, placed the bottle on the table, and silently slid into a chair.

"I don't know. First, it was to become a priest, now it's that I'm her salvation. She never stops and even cries about it. I don't know what she's talking about; I'm not her salvation; Jesus Christ is. But she just clings to me, I mean physically, and cries about my saving her. I've done everything she's ever asked of me, and I still haven't done enough!"

Innocenta counted the flowers on the new tablecloth. Theodora Mercedes looked at Diego pityingly and without disguise. In his mind's eye, Diego looked astonished at himself.

"Well, you can stay here for the entire week, Diego, and no one will bother you or expect anything. You seem to have earned a vacation before you start your work. Let me go check on the children."

Theodora Mercedes shot Innocenta a meaningful look that Innocenta did not welcome, and she left.

She had to improvise. "Diego, have you met my son, Raul Theodore?"

"No, I haven't; is he here?"

"Yes, let's take our wine and go meet him."

Raul Theodore was enthralled by reading-up on August Ferdinand Möbius and his famous Möbius Strip. He seemed less angry bee and more productive hamster.

"Raul Theodore, can we come in?"

"Yes."

"I would like you to meet someone. This is Diego. He's your . . . your . . . uh your uncle/cousin Diego."

Raul Theodore looked up with extreme disinterest but did ask, "What's an uncle/cousin?"

"It means that Diego is a relative, but I'm not sure what to call him."

"OK, hello uncle/cousin Diego. I'm Raul Theodore Vigil Silert, but you can call me Raul Theodore."

"It's nice to meet you, Raul Theodore. You have enormous and beautiful yet unusual blue-green eyes."

"What do you say, Raul Theodore?"

"Thank you, Diego, they're heterochromatic."

"What?"

Innocenta turned to Diego. "This is a new one."

"Heterochromatic. If you look real hard the middle of my iris is bright green and the outside is bright blue."

"Well, well, so they are. That's quite a word, Raul Theodore, heterochromatic."

"Yes, I like it a lot."

"What are you working on?"

"I was going to email Professor Möbius, but he's dead. So I'm going to try to calculate the amount of energy required to stop the moon in its orbit, down to at least the kilo-joules."

Diego's face gave everything away; he was beyond astonished—first heterochromatic, now this.

"Raul Theodore has many gifts, Diego. He doesn't talk much but is amazing with numbers that, no offense, could floor you."

"No offense taken; yes, I can see that. What a marvelous boy."

"Well, calculate away, but don't be late for supper."

"OK, Mom."

Innocenta and Diego took their wine glasses back downstairs and joined Theodora Mercedes in the backyard. The Unremarkables were playing in the sandbox by simply piling sand into each other's skirts. This was the usual extent of their unremarkable imaginations. Consuelo, who had been sitting on the side of the sandbox, spied Innocenta and the priest coming, found an excuse to go back to the kitchen, and exited just after the two settled into chairs next to Doña Theodora. The three adults watched Consuelo go but did not express their thoughts.

"Did you meet our little Raul Theodore?"

"Yes, but have I upset Consuelo in any way?"

"Possibly. However, she has some larger issues that may work themselves out. We're giving her the space to do that."

Diego looked over his shoulder to the kitchen door and chose to let the subject go.

"Did you find Raul Theodore to be simply amazing?"

"Oh, yes, his vocabulary alone was amazing. When he started talking about calculating the amount of energy required to stop the moon in its orbit, then it really hit me."

Theodora Mercedes feigned confusion but was actually fishing. "I'm sorry, what hit you?"

"It hit me that he is limitless in his potential, but only in limited areas. He's a living dichotomy in some ways. He's sweet, too. Raul Theodore must be wonderful to have around."

Theodora Mercedes was examining Diego through the microscope of her finely tuned mind. She did not doubt Diego's sincerity and probed for his level of understanding the real Raul Theodore. Theodora Mercedes decided to get to the point quickly.

"How would you describe Raul Theodore, especially as compared to other children?"

Diego sensed that he was being tested. He took a sip of wine.

"I would say that some people might say that he is 'special,' and possibly be uncomfortable around him. He seems to have a good heart and a great intellect. Does he have problems relating to other people outside the family?"

"He does, but we have interceded enough that the issues for him are minimized. The kids leave him alone."

"Does Raul Theodore notice that they are leaving him alone?"

"He did at first. Now, it's just normal, and it appears that he gives it no thought. Other children would be devastated by being ignored or even shunned. Raul Theodore doesn't know how to sense his isolation in that way. In fact, the word 'lonely ' would never occur to him. It's just the way the world is."

"To the extent that I can understand him, he does seem to be content. I don't know if 'happy' would be an appropriate word."

"That's perceptive of you. I have been around him for ten years and often have to remind myself that he is happy. He shows affection to us on rare occasions and we are grateful when he does."

Diego nodded his head. Innocenta watched him carefully and sipped her wine.

"Diego, Raul Theodore was born with no choices in life. He lives his life in increasingly advanced mathematics, on the computer, and largely alone. He plays a little soccer, but that's rare because the other kids don't like to play with him. His world contains about a dozen people, and he has no choice about noticing anyone else. Yet, Raul Theodore is our treasure, a rare joy and in some ways, a jewel in the family. Can you imagine a life where you have no choices, Diego? Oh, he has free will, but within a small box that defines his limits."

Theodora Mercedes let this penetrate for a while and turned to her wine. Innocenta turned her attention to The Unremarkables in their sandbox. Some of Theodora Mercedes' truths about Raul Theodore applied to them as well. Innocenta excused herself and went to the sandbox to hug and kiss The Unremarkables. Then she turned to go upstairs, leaving behind her wine. Innocenta needed to hug Raul Theodore, an act that would greatly annoy him if he were deep in calculations. He was annoyed but tolerated his mother's attentions because he knew they were important to her.

"I get it, Mrs. Vigil," Diego said firmly but short of aggressiveness.

Theodora Mercedes could not resist a riposte. "Please, don't let respect for my age impinge on our conversation just as I haven't let your being clergy impinge on it."

Diego inhaled fresh air for a moment and collected his thoughts, which were ranging over mental landscapes new to him. "Theodora Mercedes," he paused, "You have the astounding ability to combine great subtlety with the directness of a bullet. I get it; Raul Theodore has had few, if any, choices in his life, and I have all the choices available to the rest of us."

It was this last phrase that he collected during his deep breath, and it had the effect that he had sought, a useful generalization, a contrast, while lacking any labeling of Raul Theodore. It did not escape Theodora Mercedes, and she mentally thanked him for his cleverness.

"You're saying that I have always had choices that I have chosen not to exercise. Is that it?"

"I don't recall saying any of that. However, I'm glad that you think I have."

Theodora Mercedes smiled at Diego with intention, not casualness, to establish firmly that she was Diego's friend. Diego turned diagnostic and discovered that he could not resist her. Even with her laser directness Diego found that he liked this woman more than anyone he had met in a long time. He felt the same about Innocenta and noted that she let her mother do the heavy lifting. Diego did not know that this was a temporary arrangement.

There was silence for several minutes during which time Consuelo looked through the kitchen window, which was open, and tried to eavesdrop as well. Consuelo knew her mentor well, had attended her church, and now Theodora Mercedes lounged in her own backyard with a newly ordained priest—what could she be doing? Consuelo thought it would make things easier for her if they were arguing or shouting or both. But, they weren't, and, regardless of how she strained, Consuelo could not follow their conversation; however, Consuelo heard just enough. Now, Consuelo bobbed back away from the window as Theodora Mercedes was smiling at her without taking a direct look.

"How does she do that?"

It was one more mystery for Consuelo to solve on her life's journey.

Innocenta came back down, refilled the glasses, and sat again. She felt blessed to have her children. She also noted that the conversation had stopped. With no warning, both Theodora Mercedes and Diego began speaking to the other. Innocenta was surprised by her mother's surprise. They both abruptly stopped in their paths like dogs chasing sticks that have bounced behind them.

"Please go ahead, Theodora Mercedes."

She smiled and noted Diego's thirsty look, but she had only intended to ask if he was hungry. How could she satisfy his thirst without metaphorically pouring water down his throat?

Theodora Mercedes decided to punt. "Have I upset you or hurt your feelings, Diego?"

"Oh, no, you haven't."

Diego was clearly expecting more and wanting more.

"Perhaps you would like to go freshen up before dinner? We dine at six."

"Yes, I think I will."

Diego smiled at Innocenta and entered the house.

"He wants me to tell him what to do."

"Surely, you're not going to?"

"Of course not, I can only point out the obvious. He needs to think and feel his way through. Meeting Raul Theodore certainly made an impression on him. I wonder what Diego was thinking about when he was Raul Theodore's age?"

As this was not a question that required an answer, there was more silence.

Finally, Theodora Mercedes spoke. "I'm so tired, Innocenta. I'm feeling . . . depleted. I'm being manipulative with Diego, and it doesn't feel good. I've always been direct, often diplomatic, but never manipulative. At least with Monsignor Szabo I was direct—and manipulative—perhaps too direct. He could have had me thrown out at any time, but he didn't. Maybe he appreciated someone being direct. Maybe a monsignor is surrounded by underlings who never tell him what he needs to hear. I don't know, Innocenta, I don't know. I just know that I feel tired, manipulative, and depleted."

The words and languid tone alarmed Innocenta. She had never heard her mother talk this way no matter what the hardships were, including the deaths of the men in the family, Raul Theodore's diagnosis, and the tragedies that befell Angelica Gertrudis.

"Innocenta, I need you to help me with Diego. He needs us, and I need you."

"Mother, are you all right?"

"Yes, I'm just tired; so much has happened this spring."

Innocenta let the last sentence lie there for a minute, "What are you trying to accomplish with Diego, Mother?"

"I want him to realize that he has never made a free choice. I want him to realize that he has never spoken or acted except with Genoveva's words and wishes. I want Diego to choose his own life and tell the world about it in his own voice and without fear. If he chooses to stay a priest, then fine, as long as it's Diego finally making the choice. That's it, Innocenta, nothing more. But this is so important. We're talking about someone's life."

Innocenta drank this in and watched her mother's face. When had it become so careworn, her eyes bereft of that mischievous sparkle? When did the bruise-like circles appear under her beautiful eyes? Perhaps, she was just exhausted. Innocenta would watch over her with every power she could muster, even the gift if it was willing.

"I think I'll go nap in my study, Innocenta."

As she rose from her chair, Innocenta volunteered, "Let me help you up the stairs, Mother."

She instantly felt a fool as she knew that her mother's pride would never allow it.

"No!" The exclamation came out stronger than Theodora Mercedes intended, then realizing this, her voice softened. "I can manage the stairs, Innocenta, thank you anyway."

Innocenta watched her go. Theodora Mercedes did climb the stairs with strength but at a slower speed than normal. Innocenta felt a knot tightening in her stomach as she sat back down.

Dinner was simple. Consuelo prepared shrimp tacos accompanied by Mexican oregano-accented posolé and a salad composed of roasted beets, lettuce, and goat cheese. Barrington and James were not present. Bart was absent as well and was on duty for forty-eight hours. He would be off-duty at eight on Wednesday morning, the day of the summer solstice festivities.

Diego, Raul Theodore, The Unremarkables, Theodora Mercedes, Innocenta, and Consuelo had a quiet dinner. Diego asked questions about Theodora Mercedes' side of the family. The Unremarkables stared at him throughout the meal. Raul Theodore was calculating his moon energy problem. Innocenta hoped that he would not arrive at a solution during dinner, producing decibels equivalent to a rocket launcher when he announced it. She did not want to risk her mother's being surprised. This was a useless worry as Theodora Mercedes came to the dinner table looking well and with her usual energy level. Evidently, the nap had fortified her. Moreover, if anyone were likely to jump it was the on-edge Innocenta or poor, unsuspecting Diego.

"Diego, may I speak with you after dinner? It will only take a minute."

"Of course, Mrs. Vigil."

Theodora Mercedes sighed lightly; why was it always so difficult for people to call her by her given name? As the adults finished the last of the chardonnay, Theodora Mercedes got Diego's attention, and they excused themselves and entered the parlor.

"Diego, I apologize for my appalling behavior this afternoon. I was not feeling well, and I manipulated the conversation most disrespectfully. I am sorry, and I hope that you can forget it; perhaps, we can start over?"

"Mrs. Vigil, I didn't perceive the conversation that way, but I appreciate the gesture. You are asking me to think about some aspects of my life that I have been avoiding, but I think you meant no harm. Frankly, you are the only person outside of the church screeners that has ever cared enough to question my choices. While we're here, my interview with the archbishop is tomorrow. I'm not sure why he's calling me in. Perhaps you know?"

"I do. It's no different from the general subject we have discussed today. I do hope it goes well for you."

Theodora Mercedes ended this portion of the conversation quickly by reaching out and taking Diego's right hand in both of hers. They looked into each other's eyes. Diego perceived her love and missed the continuing manipulation of her ending the conversation abruptly. Theodora Mercedes perceived a lonely but gladdened heart.

That evening, Innocenta called Bart at work. She had no idea how to proceed. It seemed to her that her mother and Diego had said everything worth saying. Yet, Innocenta had promised her mother that she would help with Diego. What was left to do?

Bart listened patiently—there was no fire station action to attend—and finally said, "Innocenta, I think you should either do nothing and wish Diego well or just keep it simple."

"Simple, like what?"

"I don't know; you and your mother have the gift, you'll think of something."

Innocenta tried her best not to sound exasperated, but Bart was too perceptive.

"I'm sorry; I just don't know what else you can do. Why don't you just sleep on it?"

Innocenta paused for only half a breath. "That's the best idea I've heard all day."

They said good night and Innocenta went to bed.

Theodora Mercedes went to bed early and would be startled the next morning when she recollected her dream.

Innocenta tossed and turned like a spilled salad for what seemed like an eternity and finally fell asleep. Her last remembered thoughts were of Bart. Innocenta's vision opened with her waiting on the front porch for Bart. It was a scene from her past, her recent past, although it seemed now like so long ago. Bart arrived; they made small talk and sat down to dinner with Theodora Mercedes, Barrington, James, and all three children. Before the first course was even served, artichokes with curried mayonnaise for dipping the leaves, Theodora Mercedes had read a poem. Innocenta remembered every detail of the poem and the dinner. She smiled, and then willed herself awake.

Innocenta tiptoed into her mother's study to find some good stationery. Although Theodora Mercedes was digital in her writing and research habits, she valued the old-fashioned art of letter writing and kept good stationery in her ancient desk. Innocenta opened three drawers before she found what she needed. The paper was heavy, watermarked, and double-bordered in rich green and blue, a stylization of the family's trademark eyes. Turning on the desk lamp, Innocenta wrote a short note and ended with Walt Whitman:

> The untold want by life and land ne'er granted,
> Now Voyager sail thou forth to seek and find.

Innocenta folded the note, inserted it into its matching envelope and then addressed it. She sealed the envelope, turned off the light, and left. Innocenta climbed to Barrington's bedroom door and slipped the note under it. Diego would find it in the morning. Innocenta felt Theodora Mercedes-like as she tiptoed back to her own room and bed.

"Bart, I could just kiss you," she said aloud to the empty room.

Innocenta smiled, turned over, and went quickly to sleep in the cosseting darkness of the good night.

When Innocenta threw on her robe, descended to the kitchen, and found her mother smiling at her, she returned the smile.

"Innocenta, I had the most peculiar dream. I dreamed about Walt Whitman, just Walt Whitman, nothing else. He just kept smiling at me and pointing to the starry sky; that's all."

"Mother, I think Walt was trying to tell you something."

"No offense, Innocenta, but I would say 'obviously'."

A Cheshire cat smile appeared on Innocenta's face, and she poured herself a mug of coffee. Theodora Mercedes was left with an annoying puzzle and a smug-looking daughter confidently returning her gaze. Diego walked in.

Diego was showered, freshly shaven, and dressed in a suit and tie. His graceful movements wafted sweet lavender. His hair had a light coating of gel, providing sheen and resistance to June's breezes. He looked like a movie star, not the rugged kind, more like the romantic kind. Even Consuelo's face betrayed her admiration for his scrubbed and handsome looks despite her secret knowledge that he was on the cliff edge about his calling—she disapproved of his doubts. Before anyone could speak, Diego grinned and pulled the envelope out of his coat pocket. Theodora Mercedes looked from the envelope to Innocenta and was astounded to realize that her dream now made sense.

"Thanks for the encouraging words, Innocenta. I had never read the Walt Whitman before."

"A very wise woman once shared that one with me. I decided that it was worth passing on."

Innocenta said this without once looking at her mother. Diego, however, had enough intuition to put the pieces together and gifted Theodora Mercedes with a knowing and grateful grin.

"Are we having coffee?"

Consuelo had already poured Diego a cup.

"What time is your appointment with the archbishop?"

Both Theodora Mercedes and Innocenta turned, in shock, to face the questioner, Consuelo.

"It's at eight-thirty."

As she handed the cup to Diego, her disapproval melted away as he thanked her and took a chair. Consuelo, smitten by this young priest who reminded her of her own lost love, also took a chair.

Oscar Padilla de la Mancha had been lost to Consuelo for over thirty years. Diego was not as dark-skinned as Oscar, but there was enough resemblance that Consuelo forgot that she didn't approve of Diego. She sat at the table lost in memories that she believed she had buried long ago. Consuelo effected an emotionless face and said nothing else for the remainder of the morning.

"Do you have time for breakfast?"

"No, Theodora Mercedes, I'm a little too nervous to trust food in my stomach. In fact, I better be on my way."

No one had the bad taste to say, "Good luck." Instead, they watched as his handsome frame exited by the kitchen door, and he walked toward the cathedral.

Consuelo got up and returned to her duties but remained in her reveries of bygone days and love.

"He is more handsome every time I see him."

"Yes, Mother, he certainly is. It's strange about our having different versions of the same dream. What do you think it means?"

"I don't know. Perhaps, it just means that I was too tired. Perhaps, it means that the gift is getting stronger in you."

Neither woman voiced the observation that it could also mean that the gift was weakening in Theodora Mercedes. Innocenta was troubled by the wide variety of implications. Perhaps, her mother was tired and only tired. Theodora Mercedes was sixty-seven years old, however, that was not considered old or in decline in this family. She would not dwell on it now.

The rest of the day was magnificent. Consuelo had stopped frowning and even hummed unidentified tunes while she dusted furniture that she didn't notice was dustless. She was visualizing Oscar's unbearably handsome face, his gentle, almost wordless nature, and the love now turned to distant fondness that she still felt for him. The rancid smell of stolen love was gone.

Theodora Mercedes felt as vigorous as the day was gorgeous—brilliant skies almost peacock blue, fair weather clouds to add depth and purity, and just a light breeze to keep the air fresh. She busied herself making chicken with wild rice. Knowing that Barrington and James were expected for dinner, she could already hear Barrington exclaim, "Chicken Orloff, I love you, Mother!" The last good, thin, bright red stalks of rhubarb were up in her garden and she conjured up her own strawberry rhubarb pie recipe.

Innocenta talked with Bart on the phone twice and played with her children, alternating between The Unremarkables whom she took to the park and Raul Theodore, who was busy as a CRAY super-computer and delighted about it. Not a soul in the house heard or saw Diego when he returned. When he entered through the front door, the ground floor was vacant, so he continued up the stairs and noiselessly closed his bedroom door.

By six-thirty, everyone, even Bart, who had gotten away from the fire station for dinner, was there. When Diego heard Barrington's exclamation all the way to the third floor through his closed door, he braced himself and began his descent to the dining room. It was a long one. Diego imagined a very pleasant evening; then, he imagined himself as the sacrifice, not that he would ever compare himself to Christ, still he felt like "Diego on a spit" could be served for dinner: basted by this family knowing absolutely everything about him, flamed by questions about his meeting with the archbishop, and flavored by the sizzling fat of his melting self-confidence. He felt like running away but continued his descent to face the fires of truth. A persuasive voice in his complicated head whispered that he was safe.

Upon spying Diego, all conversation stopped, and Consuelo stopped in her tracks. Everything stopped except the kitchen door, which continued its swing back, hitting Consuelo's elbow and knocking half the broccoli to the floor with a squish. Diego entered the overly quiet room, and it appeared that his face colored up. Consuelo tried to pick up the squished broccoli while not missing any of the conversation.

"Hello, everyone."

By the time the reintroductions were completed, Consuelo was back and lingering in the dining room.

Dinner was served, and it was a casually tense affair; Theodora Mercedes merely asked how Diego's day had gone.

"Fine."

Barrington examined Diego furtively while James did the same to Barrington. Innocenta made small talk with her children and Bart, who kept staring at Diego, disconcerting Diego, but never saying a word. Consuelo tired of coming in and out and eventually brought her dinner to the dining room and sat between Doña Theodora and The Unremarkables; Diego was getting eye contact from Consuelo, but no meaningful looks or conversation. Diego constantly adjusted his chair, and, when James asked, "How do you like being a priest?" all conversation ceased as if the power had gone out of the people who were all plugged into the same surge-protector.

"Fine."

This was Diego's second word at dinner, and it was the same word as the first word. The rest of dinner was a delicate balance of Diego's becoming relaxed and the gentle banter of any family meal. By the time the second glasses of wine were being poured, Diego was smiling and enjoying himself. The sense of danger had passed.

Innocenta asked the children whether they would like their pie outside. They eagerly accepted and ran out to play and wait for dessert. When the children had left, Diego not only seized the opportunity, he became brave.

"I know that you're all wondering how my meeting with the archbishop went. We had a candid conversation, most of which is private, between the archbishop and me. I will tell you that I intend to remain a priest and will be leaving New Mexico soon."

Theodora Mercedes looked defeated, like a dog whose master will no longer throw the stick. Diego's face assumed a quizzical look as he realized that his words had upset Theodora Mercedes. Now, dinner broke up quickly.

Theodora Mercedes grabbed Bart, Consuelo, and the bottle of dry rosé, and then headed toward the backyard. Innocenta watched them go in one direction and Barrington and James go in another. Diego arose, followed Theodora Mercedes, and quickly came back with her on his arm. Theodora Mercedes, Innocenta, and Diego now had the dining room to themselves.

"My words were clumsy a few minutes ago. I have more to tell the two of you, you who have extended your hearts and counsel to me. Among the things the archbishop and I discussed is that he had an unexpectedly frank discussion initiated by Monsignor Szabo. It was important for the archbishop to share this because he wanted me to understand that he is not just my superior, but my friend. He stated openly that our common interests in what's best for the church and for me should help us be frank with each other. At first, I was shocked, but, as he questioned me about my vocation, the conversation *did* become frank. He told me little about himself and quite a bit about Monsignor Szabo. When he asked me if I would rather be a lay person, find a boyfriend, and build a life around that, he got to the heart of the matter. I have thought long and hard about my vocation since I entered your home. I don't know which life I need to live. I have nothing against being a priest, especially now that I'm educated and ordained. However, my great-grandmother complicates matters so much that I have to get away from her. I asked to be sent overseas. The archbishop is sending me to a monastery in Minnesota. From there, I might be sent to Africa or some other place in the Third World. Unless I get away from great-grandmother, I will never know whether I do or don't want to be a priest or whether I will discover another problem. So, the archbishop is getting me away from her, and I will be free to discover whether I have the true vocation."

"What if you discover that you don't have the vocation?"

"Innocenta, if that's what I discover, then I will take the next steps. But, unless I am in New Guinea or some other equally remote place, I will never find out for sure."

Theodora Mercedes' face looked relaxed; the stick had been thrown. "Diego, I am so happy for you; when do you leave?"

"I leave on Thursday. I should be in Minnesota no longer than two months." Diego paused,."I think that the archbishop is a great man for many reasons, most of which, I'm certain, I don't know, but can feel."

Theodora Mercedes continued to express a satisfied look. In fact, she felt that the solution to Diego's and her own doubts was growing favorably with every new facet of her thoughts. Diego would escape Genoveva, alone a great blessing, he would see new lands and people, he would complete his emotional maturity, and, finally, Diego would discover what he wanted out of his own life. The solution was a diamond in the rough; it had little possibility of failure even if Diego ultimately decided that he wanted to stay in the priesthood. Theodora Mercedes agreed with Diego; the archbishop was a great man. She wished that she had met him.

Innocenta wasn't nearly as sanguine as her mother. She saw a dream deferred. Didn't Diego tacitly admit to being in love with Monsignor Szabo? How did being sent away help a good man, a man who reminded her of her own brother and his travails, make peace with his unrequited love? Didn't people say, "Absence makes the heart grow fonder?" Innocenta tried to effect a poker face throughout the conversation; however, even Diego could detect her discomfort. Her jawline was stiff and the muscles taut. Theodora Mercedes scanned Innocenta's face and deduced that she did not understand the beauty of the solution.

But, Innocenta said "Congratulations, Diego. I'm certain you made the right decision."

With this statement, hollow as a store mannequin, she excused herself and ascended to her bedroom.

"She didn't seem to be as happy as she tried to sound."

"No, Diego, she isn't. Innocenta needs some time to sort out the difference between your feelings and her own. She cares about you very much. Right now, she feels that you're making a mistake, but she quickly will see that you now have your life in your hands. Frankly, she believes in love. If that's enigmatic for you, then I'm sure that you will deduce my meaning on your own later. I won't belabor the topic. Let's go join Consuelo in the night air; I have another bottle of this wonderful dry rosé."

Consuelo, who had been listening from the kitchen, ran out the backdoor quickly and quietly, and sat in her chair. Diego looked up the stairs as they passed, wondering what Innocenta was really thinking.

Innocenta was sitting in her chair looking out over the street. Sending Diego away, still a priest, seemed to avoid the issues as she understood them. Innocenta had sensed that Diego was one of God's creatures at the end of his rope; this Third World journey felt like desperation's desolate destination. Diego was in love with Monsignor Szabo; didn't this love deserve to live and live in the light of day and truth? Innocenta felt sorry, yes, sorry, for both of these men. Her naïveté about the Roman Catholic Church made Innocenta's solution seem easy; two men who loved each other would get together and buck the system. The system was an anachronism that required active, revolutionary changes. These two men were the perfect seeds to sprout those changes. Why didn't they charge forward? She could find no satisfactory answers. Frustration and restlessness eventually compelled Innocenta to head for the backyard. Theodora Mercedes had stopped Bart from charging upstairs, and he had returned to the fire station.

"You opened more wine; that's wonderful; I need another glass."

Innocenta sat as Consuelo poured.

"We were just enjoying the stars and discussing how fascinating a place like New Guinea must be."

Innocenta replied with a weak smile, no words, and took a frustrated gulp of wine. Theodora Mercedes decided that she would risk an oblique approach to Innocenta; she couldn't watch her for long in Innocenta's agitated state.

"Sometimes, in life, the thing that seems to be your 'want,' is really a substitute for something else. People often believe that they are in love with another person, but that is a positive emotion put there because the person is so tired of a negative emotion. The negative emotion pulls the person down so much that any substitute that looks good at the time seems better."

Theodora Mercedes watched Innocenta during her entire speech. Innocenta was not connecting with her words yet. Consuelo quietly got up to leave, but Theodora Mercedes put her hand on Consuelo's forearm, indicating that she should stay. Diego sensed that more was afoot that exceeded his skills and kept silent.

"Do you remember when Barrington escaped into addiction?"

"How could I forget that?"

"Do you think that addiction was attractive to him, or was it just an illusion?"

"It was an illusion. When you got him into psychotherapy, he worked-out the issues, and got off the crutches."

"Yes, and when your husband, George, left, did he leave for a better life?"

"Not really. He couldn't take the pain of having a son that was not an average kid, so he left the pain behind. Frankly, I don't think he had any destination in mind except getting away and drinking." Innocenta paused."I don't think that working in the molybdenum mine provided any great solace. In effect, he drank himself to death."

"Drinking himself into an early death was an accidental and permanent solution to a problem that should have been fleeting."

No one spoke for several minutes.

"Innocenta, I thought that I would never love again when Oscar Padilla de la Mancha married my sister. I was wrong, Innocenta. I found more love in this house than I ever believed was possible. But when Oscar broke my heart, I was determined, at least initially, to enter the convent."

Both Theodora Mercedes and Innocenta looked at Consuelo in astonishment. She had never been this forthcoming about her private life.

"We're talking about Walt Whitman, aren't we?"

"Yes, if that's what makes sense to you."

"Mother, I think that you are cleverer and wiser than I will ever be. I think I'll go to bed and think about Walt Whitman's words. Good night, everyone."

She stood and gulped the last of her wine.

"Innocenta, don't be so sure about your conclusion. Sleep well."

Innocenta was as disconcerted as a tourist who has boarded the wrong train and sees another country screaming by. The primacy of lost love continued to churn in her mind, blocking out other paths that could ease her mind. At last, Innocenta fell asleep. Innocenta was wafted up into the sky where a great sailing ship met her. She sailed through the air to a fantastic island filled with tropical trees, flowers, waterfalls, and people. Children grabbed her hands and led her into a village where she was welcomed, an honored guest. The chief emerged from the largest hut. It was Monsignor Szabo.

The people bowed their heads in reverence to him, and the monsignor spoke. "Welcome, Innocenta, to the Unexpected Port. Some visitors stay here too long."

He had no sooner finished when Innocenta was borne up again. There were three rips in the sky. Two had been stitched back together with stringy cirrus clouds she recognized as mare's tails. Innocenta felt peace emanating from the clouds. She looked to the third rip, and Innocenta felt nothing from it. Then, as quickly as it began, her vision of the sky retreated, and she was back in her bed.

Innocenta awoke refreshed. She still believed in love and discovered that she also believed in salvations of other kinds. It was going to be a good day. Without warning, Raul Theodore's voice boomed a long string of numbers from his bedroom. What else could Innocenta do but smile?

Innocenta found the kitchen to be a hive of activity; today was the solstice and its celebration.

"Do you need any help before I whisk Raul Theodore to his final tests?"

"No, we've done so much ahead of time that we just have last minute stuff, and Barrington will barbeque the game hens when the guests start to arrive."

Consuelo poured coffee, and Innocenta took a chair.

"You know, Mother, I was very upset last night with Diego. I wanted those two men to get together. Frankly, I didn't fully comprehend what you and Consuelo were telling me in your roundabout ways. But last night, I had such a peaceful vision that I realized that my own strong view blocked out everything else. I need to learn to relax, the way you do, and let my intuition speak to me instead of drowning it before it has a voice. I think Diego and the archbishop devised an elegant solution to a quandary even if it's not the solution I wanted for Diego and the monsignor."

Theodora Mercedes glowed from within. Innocenta had learned that she should master herself before she could master the gift.

"I'm embarrassed that it took me so long to figure this out, I feel like a fool."

"Now wait a minute, Innocenta, last night you accused me of being cleverer and wiser than you could ever be. I told you not to be so sure of your conclusion. Do you know why I said that? I was about your age when I learned that lesson. Don't you think that a headstrong woman who quit her church at ten, and ran off to live with her lover when that wasn't done, would have the same problem?"

"Mother, really, I had no idea?"

"Yes, and do you know who taught me that lesson? Your grandmother, Genoveva."

Innocenta and Consuelo gasped. "Genoveva, how?"

"I was so determined that she should like me and I should like her that I blocked out all her devious and nasty machinations because I would see what I wanted to see. I gave her a dozen second chances because of my own blindness and idealism. It was when your father died that I really saw Genoveva for what she is. She ignored my grief and behaved as if she were the widow and most injured. She attracted so much attention to herself at your father's funeral that I felt invisible and hurt. Then it hit me; Genoveva is and always was a person of bad character. It took her behavior when, I assume, we were both at our low points for me to see it. So, I'm not so wise and clever, Innocenta; I'm just older and more experienced."

No one spoke for several sips of coffee while Innocenta and Consuelo savored this new insight.

Finally, Innocenta muttered, mostly to herself, "Everything in its time, everything in its time."

Innocenta rose and kissed her mother on the mouth and started out of the kitchen.

Through her smile and delight, Theodora Mercedes cried out, "It's going to be a fabulous day, Innocenta. Will you be home for the celebration?"

"Oh yes, Raul Theodore should be finished by two this afternoon. We'll be back no later than three."

Innocenta went to check on the children. She and Raul Theodore were gone by nine-fifteen. It would be the last time Theodora Mercedes or anyone in the household would see them today. Even the skies would be darker and retreating tonight.

CHAPTER FIFTEEN
Consuelo Margarita de Maria Pépin

Consuelo Margarita de Maria Pépin had had doubts about her beliefs for at least ten years prior to Innocenta's and Raul Theodore's disappearance on the summer solstice. Moreover, she had been in crises of both religion and faith ever since her whimsical decision to attend the Social Liberal Church with Doña Theodora. In only three days, she had felt or displayed emotions that were rare and unaccustomed to both her and her adopted family.

The reserved Consuelo had always been a devout Roman Catholic and had briefly considered entering the convent when her unrequited love, Oscar Padilla de la Mancha, married Consuelo's outgoing sister. The idea was short-lived. Consuelo was too smart, too interested in life, and more resilient than even she suspected. She went to work instead, maintained her devotion, and met Theodora Mercedes.

On Saturday, Consuelo had attended her first Roman Catholic ordination rites. Consuelo was not prepared for this experience. She struggled against her amusement with the pomp, the cacophonous music, and the ecclesiastical drag; she still coveted those brocades. Perhaps, she was seeing everything through Theodora Mercedes' eyes. She had referred to the event as "theater." But her amusement vanished when she witnessed the humiliation of the ordinates when they lay face down, stretched out like lambs on spits, and declared themselves to be instruments of the church. Consuelo felt transported to an earlier, meaner time while maintaining her twenty-first century sensibilities. Moreover, Consuelo was a highly intelligent woman, and the rites strained credulity; she was horrified. The day had been saved by an unforgettable reception that smoothed her frayed nerves like electrical tape applied to a short circuit. Regardless, her taste for church ritual had soured and the aftertaste would linger for days—critical days that would result in noticeable behavior changes.

Sunday morning had been a joyous awakening after a great deal of fun and overindulgence at the reception. The entire family was gathered in the house, and everyone was jubilant about the Social Liberal Church and its services. After Saturday's demeaning scenes at the cathedral, the anticipation of a simple Social Liberal service would be a ritual cleansing. Caught up in the revelry, Consuelo, surprised by Theodora Mercedes' invitation, willingly had accompanied her mentor to her church. Her exuberance momentarily cancelled out the risks. Nevertheless, she was dismayed, even frightened, that she had enjoyed a non-Christian service that had touched her deeply, spiritually, and emotionally. The dismay was due to a lack of any Christian references in the entire one-hour service. No mention of God, Jesus, salvation, or saints had any place in the sermon. Yet, the service was filled with grace. Consuelo already half-believed that she was destined for hell simply for attending a non-Roman Catholic service. By enjoying the service, even being touched spiritually, Consuelo would have to confess to these grievous sins—attending and enjoying. Nevertheless, Consuelo's subconscious was collecting evidence of God's inhumanity, but, for now, she was angry; angry at her own folly.

Her anger became directed at Theodora Mercedes and her pagan family. Consuelo had endured, even thrived, under the roof of these star-gazing, summer solstice celebrating heathens. Theodora Mercedes was her best friend and confidante; no blood-relative could compare. She was closer to her than to anyone on Earth, and she idolized her despite Theodora Mercedes' being her employer. How could she lash out at her beloved Doña Theodora? One did not do that to one's employer; moreover, the idea of hurting the one closest to her heart was out of the question. Yet, Consuelo's anger required an outlet just as electricity requires a circuit to shock the careless. Consuelo could find no suitable electrical tape to stop the flow of her vexed volts. For three painful days, Consuelo had nearly lashed out at Innocenta, the children, and Father Diego—nearly, but Consuelo found she hadn't the strength to follow through. Now, the dismay and anger morphed into an escalating frustration.

Consuelo slammed innocent pots and pans in the sink. She dusted with the energy of a cyclone punishing defenseless furniture. She shook the sand off The Unremarkables' dresses with a vengeance that even the usually dull Unremarkables noticed. They looked to her, trying to understand what they had done to merit the tight grips and the slaps in their laps to shake out the last grains of sand. Consuelo's frustrated actions had caused The Unremarkables to avoid her since Sunday afternoon.

If the throes of her complex emotions and deadly sins were not enough, a priest who questioned his calling was now living in the same house. Surely, a priest with a questioned vocation was bad enough, but Doña Theodora and Innocenta were counseling him to question more deeply. Doña Theodora had actually compounded the questioning priest's problem by inserting herself into his debate. First, she went to see the monsignor, and then she counseled Diego to follow his doubts to a conclusion. Doña Theodora had housed him in Barrington's bedroom with its nearly pornographic poster of a desirable man. Consuelo had made an early decision; she would monitor this dire situation. She eavesdropped, missing no opportunities to record, in her mind, every conversation. By Tuesday evening, Consuelo was dining with Diego. By Wednesday morning, she was having coffee with him. She would take no chances that Diego would be alone with either Doña Theodora or Innocenta.

Consuelo had no way of predicting how complex these days would become. Her best friend and employer was feeling tired and, in Theodora Mercedes' own words, "depleted." She even admitted to manipulating Diego because of her weakness. Consuelo was worried; Doña Theodora had rarely been ill and normally had the energy of a forty year old. What was wrong? She claimed only to be tired, but her eyes and face betrayed something more; something deeper. Consuelo knew that if she asked Doña Theodora if she were ill, she would get a terse response. The woman's pride in her strength and physical youthfulness made her defensive; the defensiveness emerged as anger if questioned. Consuelo would have to watch her closely.

Another complexity was Father Diego, the man, charming and intelligent. Worse yet, his sincerity made it impossible for Consuelo to maintain her contempt for him. Although she deplored a priest's questioning his vocation, she liked Diego. Consuelo's disapproval of Diego was increasingly tempered by his fine attributes. On Tuesday morning, Diego came downstairs looking like any woman's dream. His hair begged for a woman's fingers; his perfect manly face, with enormous brown eyes and full masculine lips that needed passionately to be kissed; Consuelo was first smitten by him and then by memories of her nearly forgotten Oscar. Making matters worse, Genoveva, that awful, controlling, plotting, harridan, had provided Diego with plausible reasons for escaping his vows. Consuelo believed that only a woman of Genoveva's base character could have stirred the cauldron that had created Diego's bitter soup. This was like a final blow. Despite her faith, she now empathized with him.

Why had her God chosen all of these circumstances to strike her at once? In a universe of perfect storms, Consuelo's God had provided one just for her. All that was missing was the Sphinx asking her riddles whose answers were matters of life and death. Life and death, these were the twin foundations of her Roman Catholic religion. Live a decent life, put your faith in Jesus Christ as your savior, stay a Roman Catholic in good stead, and die in the state of grace; your ticket to Heaven is assured. If any one of these tick marks were in the wrong column, then it was to hell with you. Despite attending Holy Mass two or three times per week, Consuelo had begun to have doubts even prior to this weekend.

How could a woman as decent and spiritual as Theodora Mercedes be condemned to hell? She thought Jesus had been a worthy prophet, but not necessarily the only one and not a god. She was not a Roman Catholic, yet was a regular worshiper in her church. Surely, the formulas for getting into heaven, if it even existed, were not so hermetically sealed that the fresh air of Theodora Mercedes and her entire family, for that matter, would not be allowed to be breathed in heaven's atmosphere. Surely, there was a state of grace for Diego that did not require priesthood. Consuelo was consumed by doubt, and doubt was the opposite of faith, surely a mortal sin. No amount of holy handwringing could peel away the doubt, the damned doubt.

Tuesday night, Consuelo went to bed physically and spiritually exhausted. She felt that every last drop of precious blood had been drained from her. The food for the summer solstice celebration was finished and only would require setting-out in the early afternoon. Her spiritual exhaustion was like a balloon that lacked the proper heat to stay aloft. She lay on her side processing her doubts, feeling her sins, and letting a few tears run down to her pillow. At long last, Consuelo fell asleep.

In her dream, Consuelo was lofted into a hole in the sky. She was surrounded by stars, constellations, and a hundred comets. There was a rip, a hole, in the sky, and the hole seemed to be there for her. It was empty and black as soot. Consuelo looked down; the Earth appeared small. She scanned the universe. Only the stars provided any meaningful scale, however paltry, but she could *feel* the immensity of the cosmos. Diego appeared before her like a hologram coming slowly into focus. He did not speak, but she understood that he was asking her for her counsel. Consuelo was horrified. Diego wordlessly repeated his demand. She understood that she was not being given a choice; she must answer. Consuelo felt like God's unworthy proxy. Now, her truth came out; whatever Diego decided to do, in good conscience, was the right thing to do. God surely was aligned with his right to do the right thing. Diego smiled with relief and drifted away.

Theodora Mercedes appeared, again, like a hologram coming into focus.

However, she spoke: "Consuelo, do you condemn me to hell for eternity?"

Consuelo was horrified a thousandfold. How could she answer?

The only possible way was to tell the truth again. "No, I do not. You are a good woman."

"But you have condemned me in your mind for thirty years, why do you save me now?"

"I do not save you, Theodora Mercedes; we are all saved by the simple virtue of being human. You are saved. We are saved."

Consuelo reached out to Theodora Mercedes, but Theodora Mercedes drifted away as well.

Consuelo fell to Earth and landed in her bed with a thump. She awoke immediately with a lighter heart and buoyant spirit. Realizing that she would have to process this dream to understand it fully, Consuelo turned on her side again. She did not linger; physical exhaustion commanded her to rest.

"Doña Theodora, may I speak with you?"

Consuelo had knocked on her bedroom door and entered.

"Yes, Consuelo. What's wrong?"

"Well, nothing's wrong; that may be the problem."

Theodora Mercedes looked puzzled but patted her bedside, indicting that Consuelo should sit.

"I have been a devout Roman Catholic my entire life."

"Yes?"

"Please don't interrupt; I have to get all of my thoughts out at once."

Theodora Mercedes nodded.

"For thirty years, I have believed that you are going to hell. You are a pagan and have an inexplicable 'gift' of questionable origin. But, I have been plagued by doubts for years. Since Saturday, all my doubts have occupied my soul day and night. I have been upset and have behaved uncivilly to everyone in the house. For me, doubt is the opposite of faith, and a lack of faith is a mortal sin."

Theodora Mercedes was fascinated by this confession of the soul.

"I have been upset by Father Diego; his homosexuality, his doubts, your counsel to him. But I have changed my mind. I see things more clearly and without the burden of Roman Catholic dogma and the—dare I say it—caprices of a tin god."

Theodora Mercedes was not expecting this last phrase and her face reflected that. Quiet tears began to roll down Consuelo's face.

"I believe that we are all saved, that Diego will make a good decision, and that it will be the right decision. Moreover, I don't believe that my doubt is a sin. Doubt has been like a tool that has allowed me to think through the inconsistencies of my beliefs; call it a 'spiritual technology.' Yet, Doña Theodora, I have lost my faith. I am a jet plane in an indeterminate holding pattern. I don't know if I can continue being a Roman Catholic. I don't know where my faith belongs, what's left of it, anyway. If I continue to seem unsettled, then it's because this is where my mental energies will be; where do I belong? Please try to understand that this has not been an overnight transition. I have been hiding my struggles for years and years; and how I have struggled. The events of the last few days have forced me to see what has been there for a long time. They say that alcoholics have to hit rock bottom to become sober. In my own way, that's how I feel. Since Saturday, I have bounced off rock bottom repeatedly. My spiritual technology made sense of my experiences and beliefs, at last. But now I lack a sense of spiritual direction. That's why I'm crying. That's all, Doña Theodora; I just thought that you should know."

"Thank you, Consuelo. Your candor kept me spellbound. I believe that I understand. If you would ever care to have a discussion about this matter, you know I am here for you."

"Yes, I know."

Consuelo wiped away the tears and began to stand, but Theodora Mercedes grabbed her before she could get away and gave her a bearhug.

"Now, I must get today's celebration ready. I think it will be our best one ever!"

Consuelo stood, turned, and exited without looking back. Theodora Mercedes fell back onto her pillow. She had had the same dream last night, Consuelo's dream. Now, she realized what the third rip in the sky symbolized and why it was the only one unmended. However, Theodora Mercedes had confidence that the amazing Consuelo would arrive at some new theological verities. Neither she nor Consuelo knew that, with one exception, it would be an entire year before Consuelo would attend church services again—about the time it would take for the sky to heal.

Setting up the celebration was routine for Consuelo. She had Innocenta, Bart, Barrington, and James to order around. Diego helped, but Consuelo declined to treat him like the others. They all bowed to her commands as she was immaculately organized, experienced, and brooked no discussion. The men did all the heavy lifting; tables, chairs, punch bowls all needed to be put out. The women decorated the plates and carried them out. Barrington and James decorated the tables and gardens while Bart watched them in wonder. Consuelo frequently smiled at Diego with genuine affection, but offered only mundane pleasantries; she neither wanted to pry nor congratulate him. Diego, whose experience of Consuelo had consisted of odd looks and mostly silence, was confused. At least, she was now being consistently cordial to him.

Innocenta disappeared with Raul Theodore at nine-thirty for his last round of tests. They would be back no later than three. The guests began arriving at two o'clock sharp. Some entered through the garden gate; others knocked on the front door.

Once the celebration was underway, Consuelo was as free as anyone else in the household to enjoy herself. The family shared the hosting duties of filling drinks, fetching more napkins, and greeting everyone. Barrington would man the grill after the ceremony.

At three, someone knocked at the front door. A tidy man wearing a splendid Panama hat, dark glasses, a long-sleeved, white *guayabera* shirt, and tan linen slacks stood at the door.

Consuelo did not recognize him, "Yes?"

"Hello, I am here at Mrs. Vigil's invitation."

Consuelo thought that the small, but attractive, man looked nervous. "Please come in, I will bring her."

She was exiting the kitchen door before she realized that she didn't ask the man's name.

"Ivan, you came. What a wonderful surprise; I was so hoping that you would. Let me get you a drink, and then I want you all to myself for a few minutes."

Ivan asked for a beer. Consuelo brought one to him, and Theodora Mercedes took Ivan upstairs to her study. Consuelo watched the door close, and joined the celebrants in the backyard without ever realizing who the man was. When they joined the entire group, Consuelo could hear Ivan marveling at the size and scope of Theodora Mercedes' collection of liturgical music.

Theodora Mercedes grinned. "Is it irony, paradox, or just the eccentricity of an apostate?"

Ivan did nothing to stifle his laughter. Consuelo found that she liked him, whoever he was.

At four, the entire group of summer solstice celebrants, including Ivan, gathered in a circle holding hands. In the center of the circle, Barrington had placed a painted, ceramic birdbath; an ersatz altar, empty of water.

Theodora Mercedes began. "Today, we celebrate the summer solstice, its beauty, and the harmony of the universe. It is our privilege to stand at the center of sacred geometry. Whatever god or gods you pray to, or none at all, we all feel the awe, the majesty, and the magic that brings us this perfect day. Today, the sun, the Father of Life, shines its longest hours on Earth, our Mother of Life. Everything is in a balance that satisfies our reason and delights our spirits. Science and mystery are hand-in-hand, and we are humbled by their gifts. We offer the universe and the higher power of your understanding our humble gifts of thanks; the gift of beer—grain, water, and nature's alchemy; fruits and corn pollen, the gifts of plants; pure water, the purest gift of the Earth; and a lamb bone, the ultimate gift of nourishment and a reminder of life and death."

James had provided the corn pollen as a gift from a representative, himself, of the Diné people. Barrington and James solemnly placed each offering in the birdbath as they were named, bowed their heads, and then rejoined the circle.

"We offer these gifts to remind us of our bounty, our duty to the Earth, and our humility in the face of the ineffable. Let us have a moment of silence." The entire ceremony took an unhurried twenty minutes. The celebrants then broke the circle to partake of the food and drink.

Theodora Mercedes had barely begun the ceremony when Consuelo heard a noise. She quickly backed away from the circle with as little disruption as she could manage. Consuelo opened the front door. Sitting below the bottom step was Genoveva and two retainers. The ancient, creaky Chrysler Imperial limousine was the noise that had alerted Consuelo. Genoveva was wedged into her father's wheelchair, looking like a mobile snow drift covered in soot. Her red wig, resplendent in its unnatural hue, was off-center and appeared to be nodding a hello to the neighbors. The neighbors, however, were all in Theodora Mercedes' backyard and missed the frightening salute.

Consuelo knew that Doña Theodora was just beginning her summer solstice ceremony and could not be interrupted. She knew that Genoveva would insist and, equally, that she would refuse to interrupt her. As the only member of the family who was available, Consuelo had to decide what to do. It did not take her long to arrive at a suitable conclusion: do what Theodora Mercedes would do; get rid of Genoveva.

"Yes?"

"Theodora Mercedes, come out here! I demand to talk to you!"

Consuelo, in addition to her decisive course of action, was not in the frame of mind to tolerate Genoveva's intrusion any more than she would have welcomed an unchained pit bull. Moreover, something aroused in her like a tsunami kicked into motion by an earthquake.

"Doña Theodora is busy, too busy for you to disturb."

"Who are you to tell me that? Aren't you just the servant girl? Go get her!"

"I may be a servant girl to you, but I am a part of this family, and you will not disturb us today."

"I demand that you get her. I know that she is responsible for Diego's leaving the country. I know it!"

Consuelo looked at Genoveva skeptically. "How do you know this?"

"How dare you question me? Diego came to tell me on Tuesday afternoon after his interview with the archbishop. He would not even come into my house. He just made his announcement from my front porch and then left as if he were being chased by a dog. That's how I know!"

Consuelo noted that Diego had never mentioned having done this, at least not within the bounds of her eavesdropping.

Calmly, quietly, and slowly, Consuelo responded, "Perhaps, Diego felt, rightly so, that he *was* being chased by a dog: a cur."

Genoveva, unused to being spoken to like this, inhaled the local air to the end of the block.

Before Genoveva could speak, Consuelo fired another riposte. "Diego has said all that he intends to say. As for Doña Theodora, she has nothing to say to you on this subject or any other. Now, leave this property, or I will call the police and have you forcibly removed."

Consuelo turned and returned with the cordless house phone. Genoveva was sputtering. Consuelo wondered whether she was acting, having apoplexy, or a heart attack. It didn't matter; Consuelo could just as easily call 911.

"Old woman, you are a hound from hell. Go straight to church, confess your sins, and then go home; go home and don't bother Diego again. Your confession should take hours anyway."

Genoveva said nothing, but her retainers quickly turned her chair and trotted to get her back to the ratty Imperial. Consuelo stood her ground with her index finger in the phone dialing position. Genoveva uttered an oath as her retainers struggled to reload her into the limo. Finally, they drove away sputtering oil and hellfire fumes, and creaking like condemned bones until they turned the corner out of earshot.

Consuelo paused in the parlor and decided to sit down. She hadn't had this much adrenaline in her arteries in recent memory. Consuelo sat up straight and took ten deep breaths. Several minutes later, Consuelo was grinning with satisfaction. She had saved Theodora Mercedes and Diego from a needless and useless confrontation with a woman who only merited the worst kind of pity.

Just then, Theodora Mercedes walked into the parlor.

"Consuelo, I saw you slip out, and you missed the entire ritual. At first, I thought it was because you joined hands between Ivan and Diego and had recognized Ivan. Then, I heard shouting in the distance and realized that you left us for another reason. Is everything all right?"

"No, I didn't recognize him. Should I have? Well, never mind that now, Doña Theodora. Sit down; I have a story to tell you."

Five minutes later, the two women were laughing heartily and speculating about what Genoveva might be doing as they spoke. Their laughter subsided.

"Still, Doña Theodora, I feel sorry for her. She is a miserable creature who has wasted her life."

"You have a great heart, Consuelo. Still, no other family member could have handled that woman as well as you did. As far as I'm concerned, we share the same blood, and I'm so proud to have you here."

Theodora Mercedes leaned in and gave Consuelo her second bear hug of the day.

"So, who is Ivan?"

"I promised him anonymity, but I will tell you this if you promise never to repeat it."

Consuelo nodded solemnly.

"Ivan is the given name of Monsignor Szabo."

Consuelo gasped and threw her hand over her mouth as she grasped her error when she answered the front door much earlier in the day.

"I thought he behaved strangely, but he looked very nice. I promise to keep his secret. Damn, he had some nice brocade too."

They laughed again.

It was now four forty-five. "I wonder where Innocenta and Raul Theodore are."

The phone rang in Consuelo's hand. "Yes?"

Theodora Mercedes could hear a loud, excited voice and watched as Consuelo's face lost its color.

"Yes, I'll tell her. Please call back as soon as you can, Innocenta."

Consuelo pressed the Off button and looked at Theodora Mercedes. "My God, Raul Theodore is missing."

Theodora Mercedes looked faint but only slumped on the sofa. Consuelo burst into tears of terror.

CHAPTER SIXTEEN
Raul Theodore Vigil Silert

Raul Theodore Vigil Silert awoke with a throbbing headache, nausea, and disorientation. These were the immediate effects of unconsciousness caused by a chemically soaked handkerchief, abruptly, brutally slammed upon his nose. Had Raul Theodore seen Dr. Vanitia Fellini creeping up like a malevolent waitress, he would have screamed, kicked furiously, and cried out for his mother. However, Dr. Fellini, dressed as a bistro server, calmly walked up behind Raul Theodore, ostensibly to deliver his juice, and took him without a struggle or a witness. The two student proctors were in another room texting their friends, as do all young adults in that age group. Innocenta was in the lobby actually talking with Bart on her phone. This was typical of her age group. As a result, neither the three, nor anyone else, saw Raul Theodore vanish.

Raul Theodore lay on his cot trying to keep panic at bay while getting some, any, orientation to his surroundings. Ordinarily, the brilliant boy would have noticed the overhead industrial lighting, the hum of computer cooling fans, the extraordinary number of pipes crossing the ceiling, and the total absence of outside noise—no cars, trucks, sirens, nothing at all, not even a reassuring bird call. The throbbing in his head and haze in his eyes compelled Raul Theodore to shut them again. His nausea abated somewhat but not his tendency toward panic. Where was he? Where was his mother? Was he still at the school?

Someone was speaking his name, but Raul Theodore decided to feign sleep as a way to avoid being more frightened. Besides, the woman's voice sounded like it was being projected from a tin can. He fell asleep.

Outside of Raul Theodore's current environment, the Santa Fe police, campus Police, New Mexico State Police, and the FBI were all attempting to ascertain his whereabouts. His family alternated between hysterical tears and maddening helplessness. Angelica Gertrudis took to her bedroom and would not come out. Her sister could hear her wailing that night; she was sleepless again. Barrington's inherent weaknesses, like cracks in fine marble, separated, surfaced, and became weaker. He had no sooner come to terms with the virus in his body, with tremendous support from James, when Raul Theodore was kidnapped. Barrington was falling into the abyss of despair; James' hands were overflowing caring for his partner and he was concerned that Barrington might fall back into substance abuse. Consuelo, the nearest person to being a nanny in the Silverton-de Baca household, was next on the rung of most distraught. Consuelo held herself outwardly strong but often burst into tears when she was alone. Bart took the rest of the week off to attend to Innocenta but was numb. Innocenta tended to Bart more often than the reverse. Diego had to leave, on schedule, Thursday morning. James promised him updates on Raul Theodore. Innocenta and Theodora Mercedes strengthened each other like pillars on a bridge. Their immediate tears, panic, and despair had quickly surrendered to the work of cooperating with the authorities and finding Raul Theodore. Nevertheless, the panic was just enough to keep Innocenta's gift at bay.

Raul Theodore came out of his drug-induced stupor exactly twenty-four hours following the attack. The chemicals were an overdose for a seventy-two pound boy.

"Would you like some water?"

"Yes."

His voice cracked with dryness.

After drinking a few sips, he demanded, "Where am I? What did you do to me, and where's my mother?"

She smiled,."I am Dr. Fellini, your waitress. I think you need food. Do you like yogurt?"

"Yuk. Don't you have any cheese and crackers?"

Dr. Fellini turned, walked around a table filled with equipment, and disappeared. Raul Theodore sat up. Now, he properly noticed all the attributes of the room that appeared so nebulous hours ago. He could also see the computers, windowless concrete walls, white boards with calculations scribbled over each other, and a panel that appeared to be devoted to security.

"Here are your cheese and crackers, Raul."

"My name is Raul Theodore," he replied with utmost seriousness.

"I'm so sorry, Raul Theodore. May I call you RT?"

RT did not answer for a while. He stared at Dr. Fellini with contempt, narrowed eyes, flaring nostrils, and a red face. The fluorescent lighting heightened the effect of his anger.

"Now, RT, we are going to be great friends if you will just give me a chance. And, I am here to wait on your every need."

"What am I doing here? Wait, where am I?"

"We are in a secret place where we can work with no interruptions, RT."

Raul Theodore did not touch his cheese and crackers; he was suspicious of them.

Dr. Vanitia Fellini had been employed by the Pajarito National Lab for ten years. Initially, she was regarded as one of the most promising young physicists to join the organization. Her results and attention to detail were exemplary. Dr. Fellini's personality was outgoing in a warren of glum, serious, nose-to-the-computer-screen scientists. She was popular with everyone except the most humorless, to whom she was a distraction. That would put her ratio at fifty percent popular to fifty percent intolerable. Dr. Fellini began to fall out of favor with everyone when her project proposals began to exhibit far-fetched qualities. She grumbled when her projects were unapproved and did most of her work on others' projects grudgingly. Her last project proposal, a hyperspace drive that was deemed impossible, put her "over the top." Although everyone at the lab knew that huge federal budget cuts were coming at the end of the year, management took the opportunity to terminate Dr. Fellini's employment months early.

Her passes and security clearances were stripped, but Dr. Fellini was too clever for them. She had seen her dismissal coming and taken the opportunity to murder a colleague, Dr. Connie Costanza. Dr. Costanza was murdered, her body hidden in an unused laboratory bunker, and her passes appropriated by Dr. Fellini. It was all done with utmost care, planning, and execution. The passes didn't even require altering; the doctors could have been sisters. In fact, they were, identical twins. Well, nearly identical. Dr. Costanza was highly regarded but dead, with no one having noticed her missing. Officially, she was at a conference in Bern, Switzerland, for five days followed by a week of vacation. The great flaw in the security system was that it didn't notice that Dr. Costanza should have been out of town.

"I think that you are a genius, RT."

Raul Theodore was just child enough that he was seduced by his new nickname and the compliment. Wasn't it true that only the very coolest kids had nicknames like "RT?"

"What do you mean?"

"You are more facile with quantum mechanics, general physics, and anything to do with calculations than anyone who has ever been tested by the UNM extension. I know; I checked. We are going to work together on a fun project. How does that sound?"

Raul Theodore was too intrigued and dropped his resistance momentarily.

"What project?"

"Oh, excellent, you are interested. But first, let me make you some peppermint tea."

The waitress disappeared around the corner again.

Raul Theodore ran to the nearest door. He bounced off it. The door was blast-proof and locked. He looked for other doors. They were all the same.

Raul Theodore was about to try his third door when Dr. Fellini came around the corner with his tea. "Don't touch that!"

Raul Theodore, caught by surprise and her loud voice, halted in mid-stride. He turned around.

Dr. Fellini's face had flared warning-light red. "Don't ever get near that door again. Do you understand me?"

Her face was now plum purple in the neon glare. Raul Theodore was genuinely frightened for the first time; he had never seen a face like Dr. Fellini's. He ran like a rabbit to the safety of his cot.

Had Raul Theodore known what was behind door number three, he would have stopped voluntarily. The door opened into a large locker, built into the native rock, the Bandelier tuff, and contained several bags within bags. He was too young to meet Dr. Costanza in her tawdry condition; the rope was still securely bound around her lovely, dead neck.

"Drink your tea. If you disobey me, I will tie you to this cot. You will have no cheese and crackers and no more tea."

As quickly as Dr. Fellini angered, she returned to the calm demeanor of a terrier that has shaken its prey to death. Raul Theodore's eyes could not have been opened wider.

"I want my mother."

"Your mother is not here, RT, and she is never coming here. Now, let's talk about our project."

"Innocenta, now is your time. Raul Theodore needs you. I can feel that he is in serious trouble but not in any immediate danger. The gift is passing itself to you from me. You must clear your head and heart, or you will block it. Can you feel Raul Theodore, Innocenta?"

"Yes, Mother, I can. He's scared, but safe for now. I think he's calling out to me."

"You need to find him, Innocenta."

"But the police, the FBI, surely they will find him first. What can I do?"

"You can help lead them to Raul Theodore."

"I think I'll go to police headquarters right now. I can feel Raul Theodore. He's not close by, but not far either. Goodbye, Mother, I'll call you."

Innocenta grabbed her bag and keys and then headed to her car. She hadn't even bothered to put on make-up.

"Have you ever heard of the Infinite Improbability Drive, RT?"

Raul Theodore was silent as he played back this term. He could feel it buried in his head, like when someone meets an acquaintance on the street. He or she is unexpected, and it takes the brain a few electrical cycles to locate the name and proper context. In the brain-flash that located the Infinite Improbability Drive, Raul Theodore made a discovery that required a leap of logic. He decided to test a theory.

"You should meet Consuelo."

"Is she a physicist?"

Dr. Fellini's eyes looked at Raul Theodore with feral enthusiasm. He forced himself to remain calm.

"No, but she is Hooloovoo."

Dr. Fellini gasped with surprise and awe, "Oh my, Hooloovoo, the super-intelligent shade of blue. Perhaps I should have brought her here too."

Raul Theodore confirmed his hypothesis but squirmed when he heard this last statement; Dr. Fellini was operating with the novels of Douglas Adams as her texts and was, in Raul Theodore's word, "loony." He would have to do some planning to escape this crazy woman and go home to his mother.

"I'm tired; can I take my nap?"

"Yes, of course, but don't sleep too long; we need to get started. They may be coming."

Whoever "they" were, Raul Theodore hoped their arrival was not delayed. Now, he had time to think.

"I . . . am. . . telling . . . you . . . that . . . he . . . is . . . not . . . far!" Innocenta, shouting, was frustrated by the condescending looks, words, and officers who simply left the room. "You have no other leads, but you won't listen to me either. Find . . . my . . . son!"

The FBI forensic psychologist arrived. The relieved looks on the officers' faces informed Innocenta of her identity. She was about Innocenta's age, alarmingly thin, and had female baldness. Innocenta had to actively refrain from leaping to conclusions about her based on appearance. This group thought Innocenta was mad; she did not need to alienate the one person who could be the most helpful.

"Hello, I'm Dr. Grisalva. I'm happy to meet you, Mrs. Silert."

Innocenta refused to reply because she feared saying something wrong early in this acquaintance. She simply breathed deeply and slowly.

"I see that you're upset, Mrs. Silert, but who wouldn't be? Perhaps, we can get some coffee and talk in private."

Innocenta turned and glared at the condescending group. "Yes, thank you. It would be a great improvement to being in this room."

Many of the officers stared at their shoes when they heard Innocenta's words and, more importantly, her corrosive tone. She followed Dr. Grisalva out.

Innocenta's fears for Raul Theodore overrode any fear of embarrassment; before the office door closed, she was explaining the gift to Dr. Grisalva. The psychologist, initially surprised at Innocenta's opening-up with no prompting, listened, rapt with the unusual and detailed description. They would speak for several hours.

Raul Theodore was curious and clever, "Where is the reaction chamber?"

"So, you are ready to help me."

"Is it far?"

"It's located down a corridor behind this blast-proof door." Dr. Fellini indicated the door at the farthest end of the room. "You cannot go down there. It's too dangerous. I will handle any adjustments and observations.

If there should be an accident . . . "

"Can you show me your calculations?"

Thus, this unlikeliest of teams began their work. Dr. Fellini, seemingly permanently dressed as a waitress, showed Raul Theodore the basic principles of the drive on the white board. It made little sense to Raul Theodore, but he knew just to keep nodding his understanding. This waitress was truly loony, he thought.

"Do you have any questions about the basic concepts, RT?"

"No."

Dr. Fellini looked flummoxed, "Are you sure?"

"Yes."

She stared at Raul Theodore for an amount of time that he would have measured in increments of Universal Coordinated Time based on the vibrations of cesium-133 atoms in the U.S. Atomic Clock.

"Well, then," she was hedging, "let's continue on the computer."

Like any good waitress, Dr. Fellini led Raul Theodore to be seated at a computer station connected to routers that lined the nearest wall.

Raul Theodore studied equations for hours while Dr. Fellini prattled about their every detail. She was unaware that Raul Theodore had not actively listened to a word. Hours later, Raul Theodore turned to Dr. Fellini. She was gone. He arose, scanned the room, and listened. There was a faint murmur mixed in with the humming of cooling fans. Following the murmur, Raul Theodore found Dr. Fellini sitting at a table muttering to a person or persons that he could not see. The table had a two-burner hot plate with a tea kettle on it. Below sat a mini-refrigerator humming along with the cooling fans. The sounds were syncopated, punctuated with occasional upticks in volume coming from Dr. Fellini.

"Dr. Fellini?"

There was neither a response nor any physical hint that she had heard him.

Raul Theodore, known for his booming, numerical pronouncements, raised his voice. "Dr. Fellini?"

Dr. Fellini arose from her chair screaming, turned her florid face towards Raul Theodore, and then grabbed his throat. Her screaming was incomprehensible, but her face was inches from his as she choked him. When Raul Theodore was moments from passing out, Dr. Fellini appeared to realize who she had in her talonlike hands. A horrified look was quickly followed by her releasing him.

"I'm sorry, I'm sorry. Are you all right, I'm sorry, I'm sorry?"

Before Raul Theodore could catch enough breath to reply, she burst into tears and slumped to the floor like a dirty restaurant towel. Dr. Fellini was unconscious.

"Mrs. Silert, that's a very interesting story."

"Don't patronize me! Every word is true. My son is alone with his kidnapper and is scared to death. I need action, not your cheap words. What are you going to do about him?"

"Mrs. Silert, I did not mean to sound patronizing. It was my poor attempt at sounding objective. Frankly, there is so much we simply don't understand. There seem to be patterns to the universe about which most humans can only guess. Some people see spirits. Some have visions of future events or the present. We, in our forced objectivity, pooh-pooh them, but the real truth is that we dismiss anything we can't explain with science. That doesn't mean they don't exist."

Dr. Grisalva paused and looked into a landscape only she could see.

"Someday, I would love to visit India. It seems to me that Eastern people observe things more finely than we do in the West. Did you know that Buddhists throughout Asia believe that the spirits of the dead remain on earth for sixty to seventy days before the spirit is elevated or reborn? They believe in reincarnation, as do I. Every atom of our bodies is reborn in a sense; as a flower, a creature, a dust mote, another person, or all of them. In my thinking, how can I not believe that our spirits are reincarnated at some point?"

"Why are you telling me this?"

"Because I want you to know that I believe you. In fact, I'm a little jealous of your gift."

Innocenta evaluated this woman as she spoke. Was she humoring her, or were her explanations rooted in her reality? The gift was not speaking; it was blocked. Innocenta felt that she had little choice but to trust Dr. Grisalva.

"Dr. Grisalva, I have to find my son."

Without any warning whatsoever, Innocenta lost her breath. She clutched her throat and began turning blue as Dr. Grisalva eased her down to the floor. As suddenly as her breath had left her, it also returned.

"Someone just choked my son."

Raul Theodore's connection to his mother overrode Innocenta's blocking of the gift. Her eyes were bloodshot and filled with terror, Raul Theodore's terror.

"Are you sure? Did you see it?"

"He's OK now; she let go."

"She, who is this 'she'?"

"I don't know, but she released him. She choked him and then released him."

"Mrs. Silert, I am going to get you some water. I want you to lie calmly on the floor and regain your breath."

Innocenta had no objection to staying where she was. She had been terrified by what she had felt and sensed without actually "seeing" it. What could Raul Theodore be feeling?

Dr. Grisalva returned with a glass of water, the senior FBI agent, Agent McPhee, and the Santa Fe chief of police. Innocenta agreed to be hypnotized. At first, Innocenta's adrenaline level and her immediate concern for Raul Theodore prevented her from going under. Dr. Grisalva persisted, and Innocenta relaxed.

"What does Dr. Fellini look like?"

"Dr. Fellini, Innocenta. Who is Dr. Fellini?"

"She is with Raul Theodore. She was crying; now, she's unconscious."

"Can you tell me what she looks like?"

The other three people in the room searched each other's faces for any crumb of helpful information.

"Innocenta, was she at the college for Raul Theodore's testing?"

"No, I never saw her."

"How do you know her?"

"She called on Sunday to remind me of his testing to begin on Monday. Her voice was odd."

"She called you on a Sunday, and her voice was odd? How was it odd, Innocenta?"

"I don't know; it was just odd, like she was nervous or something."

The three scrambled out of the room. The officers found the phone numbers of the two test proctors. Neither was a suspect or even a person of interest. They had been interrogated on Wednesday, but the name Dr. Fellini was never mentioned by either of them.

"I got ahold of Miss Turner. She said that Dr. Fellini was one of the adjunct faculty members from Pajarito Labs who monitored Raul Theodore's progress on his UNM-provided computer. However, she was fired two months ago."

"Fired for what?"

"Miss Turner didn't know, but she did say that Dr. Fellini was developing a reputation for being unpredictable and had some unorthodox ideas about physics. No one knows where she is."

Thus began a frantic search for Dr. Fellini, her car, her last known address, and the questioning of fellow physicists and neighbors.

"What are you doing, RT?"

"Working on your equations."

"Oh, good."

Dr. Fellini was pallid and roaming through the dark caverns of her psychotic mind. Her bony hands and forearms were in constant, agitated motion. She was afraid of RT; afraid of his superior intellect; afraid that she had maximized her own potential to solve the problem of the Infinite Improbability Drive. She wandered off with no explanation.

While Dr. Fellini had been on the floor in a faint, Raul Theodore took the time to study the security control panel. First, he had to find a key for the lock. Above the workstation that appeared to be reserved for one in-charge, he found an unlocked key box. All the keys were labeled properly. Raul Theodore opened the security panel, found the emergency escape switch, and shut the panel door. He did not lock it and returned the key. By the time Dr. Fellini revived, Raul Theodore was sitting at his work station entertaining his mind by fixing Dr. Fellini's fanciful calculations. He knew that nothing he did could create the fictitious drive that she coveted. However, at the moment, he was enjoying making corrections.

"How is it going, RT?"

"I think we have a lot more work to do before we can create the Infinite Improbability Drive. These calculations seem to point to creating cold fusion. Do you think the drive works that way?"

An overdose of grandiosity overtook Dr. Fellini. "Of course it's based on cold fusion. Don't you think it's obvious? Maybe you're not as smart as you think."

Her tone was menacing, but she kept her shaky hands off Raul

Theodore.

"OK, I'll keep working on these. Can I have some tea?"

"No, you'll get more tea when I see some progress."

Raul Theodore did not flinch or turn around. He kept working on her absurd calculations. Dr. Fellini's demeanor could swing from solicitous to threatening and back with no warning. He would have to be coy about his plan to escape.

"Mother, come with me."

"No, I can't; I'm too tired. You will have to go alone or take Bart with you."

"Mother, what's wrong? You haven't been well in weeks."

"Nonsense, have you seen me even suffer even a cold or allergies?"

"No, but you seem to have so little energy."

"Innocenta, yesterday we had an afternoon summer solstice celebration, followed by your son's disappearance. We have been up all night. What kind of energy do you think I can muster right now?"

"I'm sorry, yes, you're right; we are all worn-out."

Theodora Mercedes examined her daughter in the pause. Innocenta looked gauzy and pale.

"Nevertheless, Innocenta, this is no time for weakness on your part. You must do whatever it takes to get Raul Theodore back."

Innocenta stopped, turned to her mother, and then sat next to her on the sofa.

"Mother, there's something else. When the detectives left after hearing the name 'Dr. Fellini,' I began having sight into Raul Theodore's plight. Even Dr. Grisalva had left the room. Mother, he's in a lab with this woman. She's making him help her with something by threatening him. I can feel where he is; it's in that direction."

Innocenta was pointing west by northwest.

"Do the police know about this?"

"I can only suppose so."

"Pajarito Labs is in that direction, Innocenta; it's not far as the crow flies. Is he that close to us?"

"Yes, Mother, he is. He's that close to us and in that direction. I'm going to go find him."

Innocenta kissed and hugged her mother as if it were the last time, grabbed her bag and keys, and then left by the back door.

The various policing agencies were busy interviewing physicists, Pajarito Labs Security, Dr. Fellini's neighbors, and following every lead. They could identify no known motive for Dr. Fellini's kidnapping a child, even a brilliant one, like Raul Theodore. There were no useful leads. Dr. Fellini had vanished so effectively that she never might have existed. Even the FBI agents were at wit's end.

Raul Theodore's plan was almost ready. He repeatedly encountered delays because he could not stop thinking about his mother. If Raul Theodore had realized that by doing this he had become a homing beacon for his mother, then he would have ceased calculating and devoted his thoughts to Mom. His mind was only on those two subjects, Mom and calculations, punctuated by visits from Dr. Fellini that were becoming more like flybys.

Dr. Fellini was spending much time at her desk, drinking tea, and talking to people who weren't there. Occasionally, she would turn towards Raul Theodore, behind the partitions that defined his workspace. Less often, she would check on him. She was identifying Raul Theodore more and more as one of "them." They might be coming. They are trying to stop me. They have never appreciated my genius. Perhaps Raul Theodore had been a plant. Dr. Fellini, waitress on her own space ship, was now nearly certain that he was planted by "them." Fine, she would wait. He could prove himself by finishing her own brilliant calculations, or she would have to kill him. It wouldn't be hard. After killing her twin, this murder would be easy. Yes, she would wait. Raul Theodore would make the decision for her.

Dr. Grisalva had been working with the police agents, particularly the FBI, attempting to profile Dr. Fellini. She had located Dr. Fellini's general physician who graciously allowed himself to be interviewed at nine in the evening. He had confirmed that Dr. Fellini was erratic, perhaps paranoid and he suspected that she was drifting towards mental illness. However, he had not seen her for at least ten months. Dr. Grisalva returned to her office by ten-thirty Thursday night. She sat at her desk reviewing every detail of the last twenty-four hours. Surely, there was something she had missed. Her elbows were on her desk, and her face was in her hands, and then she saw it staring right at her—the video camera.

When Dr. Fellini was named by Innocenta, everyone rushed out of the room. However, Innocenta was still under hypnosis and being video-recorded. Dr. Grisalva had returned to her office and brought Innocenta out of hypnosis. Perhaps, Dr. Grisalva had missed something. When she started the playback, Innocenta was describing a lab and a direction. Innocenta could feel Raul Theodore in the direction of west by northwest. Pajarito Labs was in that direction. Dr. Grisalva called out for Agent McPhee. Within minutes, she, McPhee, and a dozen other law enforcement officers were headed west by northwest.

Innocenta turned left onto State Highway 4. The main section of the Pajarito Labs was straight ahead, but she could feel Raul Theodore to her left. Innocenta let insight and intuition guide her. If the gift were willing, then it would do the rest. She drove into the bedroom community of White Rock. Innocenta could feel her son getting closer. Innocenta drove through town and out the west side.

Raul Theodore had become distracted by his fear of Dr. Fellini. On her last fly-by, her eyes were beyond feral; they were maniacal in their intensity. Raul Theodore thought she looked like someone who had not slept in days. He was right. Moreover, the lack of sleep was intensifying Dr. Fellini's psychosis. She was now arguing with "Connie," although no one else was in the room. Raul Theodore's mind kept wandering to his mother. He wanted to cry but was too frightened. He kept calculating despite his wandering mind and fears. Raul Theodore had strengths within himself that no one ever suspected. During Dr. Fellini's last unconscious phase, there had been several of these; Raul Theodore had opened the forbidden door to the reaction chamber. He understood enough about electricity to follow the wiring. While there was no voltage flowing, he crossed two circuits that were marked: "Danger, High Voltage." They were behind the reaction chamber and not likely to be seen. Raul Theodore had no idea what would happen when the electricity was allowed to flow. His guess was that it would be like Fourth of July fireworks, but he did not intend harm to Dr. Fellini. Raul Theodore was both afraid of and sorry for her. He guessed that she was lonely and miserable, two subjects close to him as well.

"I'm almost ready to run the first experiment."

"What first experiment, you little spy?"

Raul Theodore turned, alarmed, feeling like something dreadful was about to happen to him.

"We need to create an event horizon as the first step before we can proceed to the next steps."

He was improvising at a rapid rate even for his intellect.

Dr. Fellini's face softened. "Yes, yes, of course. You have calculated the parameters for the event horizon?"

"Yes, we only need a small, brief one to prove that we can do it. I'm ready if you are. I've programmed the reaction chamber. If you power it up, then I only have the initiate command."

Dr. Fellini was dancing in circles and giggling maniacally. She stopped as suddenly as she had begun, like a wind-up nun with a ruler that had run out of spring drive.

"Are you sure?"

"Yes, your calculations were accurate. They only needed a few adjustments; you were missing a minus sign in a key place."

"A minus sign—minus signs always trip me up. Let's do it."

Raul Theodore asked a question to verify his newest hypothesis. "Can I go with you into the reaction area?"

"No, I told you; it's too dangerous for you. If this doesn't work, then I'll need you to try a second time. You can't get hurt. I'll go in myself and shut the blast door. You can monitor the reaction from your work station."

It worked; he had bought her trust and verified that she would lock herself in the danger area.

Innocenta had parked her car. It was a dense black night on the Pajarito Plateau, and she passed over locked driveway gates by feeling her way. Innocenta had set off alarms at central security but had no idea that she had done so. Infrared cameras were following her stealthy movements. She continued up the drive towards a fenced-in area. The gate was unlocked.

Raul Theodore finished "instructing" the reaction chamber. In fact, he was pretending to do so. Dr. Fellini did not check on him. She danced while he typed.

"We're ready."

"How wonderful! As soon as I've secured the blast door, initiate the command, and I'll switch on the power."

"OK, Dr. Fellini."

She tidied up her waitress uniform, gave RT a big kiss on the top of his head, and disappeared.

"All right, I'm closing and securing the blast door. Send your command."

Raul Theodore heard the door close and bolt and then silence. He ran to the security panel, threw the switches that unlocked the exterior doors, and bolted the reaction chamber blast door from the outside. Just as he was exiting, he heard and felt a tremendous blast shake the earth beneath his feet. Terrified, he was thrown straight into his mother.

Pajarito Labs Security, Dr. Grisalva, Agent McPhee, and a host of other law enforcement personnel came running up behind Innocenta. They were still one hundred yards from her when the blast knocked them off their feet.

"Mom, you're squeezing me too hard."

The carbon black night suddenly was illuminated by high-powered lights coming from the east. Innocenta was still holding Raul Theodore when she was surrounded by agents who assumed that she was either a spy or Dr. Fellini. They were positively identified and then debriefed all night. Raul Theodore was given first aid for the bruises on his neck. Innocenta minimized the role of the gift in finding Raul Theodore. Dr. Grisalva did not add any unnecessary information. As far as the authorities were concerned, this was one of those inexplicable connections between a mother and child. Some things that cannot be explained scientifically are dismissed. Silverton-de Baca House had erupted in cheers, laughter, hugs, and tears of relief when Innocenta had been allowed to call. However, Innocenta and Raul Theodore would not be home until eight o'clock Friday morning.

Dr. Grisalva drove Innocenta's car, taking Innocenta and Raul Theodore home, and immediately was picked up by Agent McPhee. Innocenta and her son walked hand-in-hand through the back door to jubilant mayhem upon their arrival. Forty-five minutes later, with countless stories and details still untold, everyone agreed to go to bed. Barrington lingered in the parlor and began laughing hysterically. Five uncontrolled minutes later, while James held him, Consuelo delivered a tremendous slap across Barrington's face. The hysteria ceased before the sound of the impact could stop echoing in the room. Consuelo appeared to be just as positively affected by the action as Barrington. She clearly showed shock in her beautiful face at what she had done and then sank into the sofa next to Barrington. Consuelo slowly embraced him and all sounds and action stopped.

The only other witness was Angelica Gertrudis, who remarked, "Wow, I thought I hit him hard; good thing he doesn't wear dentures."

They lingered another five minutes to ensure that the episode had passed, and then all four went to their beds. It would be known in the house as "Lost Friday," the day everyone slept through an entire day.

Innocenta would not allow Raul Theodore to sleep in his own bed. She, Bart, and her son curled up like spoons on Innocenta's bed and slept like the dead. The first night was quiet. The succeeding three nights were disrupted by Raul Theodore's nightmares. By the fourth night, all three slept soundly, and Raul Theodore appeared to have recovered completely. Dr. Grisalva phoned on Monday to recommend counseling for Raul Theodore and Innocenta. Innocenta had read that unless children did not overcome trauma on their own, counseling could actually extend the recovery time. She politely declined the suggestions and promised to watch Raul Theodore carefully. However, by Tuesday morning, Raul Theodore was back to his usual self, calculating away, content, and, seemingly, had put the entire episode behind him. Not a soul ever told Raul Theodore what was in the locker or what had ultimately happened to Dr. Fellini. The authorities could see no reason to burden him with the knowledge that he accidently had incinerated his captor. Innocenta would ensure that he stayed innocent.

When the various authorities sorted out who had jurisdiction over the crime scene, it was the Feds; they, nevertheless, all went into the bunker together. Such is how authoritarian minds operate. The search of the outer bunker revealed Dr. Costanza's body, immediately misidentified as Dr. Fellini. Horror ensued when they thought that little Raul Theodore had perpetrated her murder and multiple entombments. However, there also was general relief to find mad Dr. Fellini deceased until they opened the ruin that had been the reaction chamber and found another body, this time charred and partially dismembered. Now, everyone was confused. Later, dental records would sort out who was who. On the spot, the Feds decided that there existed far too many security issues with a series of crimes that occurred on highly secret property. They classified and censored the case. The official story of what occurred on Lab property was a "minor accident with two fatalities; no radiation released"—no names, no more, no less. Drs. Fellini and Costanza disappeared from history. Two sisters, twins, physicists, and victims disappeared identically, presumably forgotten by the world.

The various jurisdictions agreed that Raul Theodore had been found wandering down a road late at night and had been picked up in Santa Fe County by the Santa Fe chief of police. Innocenta was excluded from the story of Raul Theodore's retrieval. The chief had the good sense, frankly at the insistence of the FBI, to station an officer in front of Silverton-de Baca House to ward off the press. On Monday, Innocenta agreed to pose for photographers with Raul Theodore on the front porch. She issued a press release provided by the FBI and didn't reappear or leave the house for another week. By then, the press had moved on to other issues; a deputy in the Mayor's Office had been embezzling city funds while operating a prostitution ring. Records had been found, important names had been entered, and the scandal would be colossal. Nothing relieves the annoying presence of the press like a fresher story more sensational than your own. Angelica Gertrudis had disdainfully referred to the reporters as "corpse flies." She would know.

Silverton-de Baca House had no group meals until dinner on Tuesday night. All meals since Innocenta's and Raul Theodore's triumphant returns had consisted of raiding the refrigerator. But Tuesday night, Theodora Mercedes, Innocenta, and Consuelo prepared a large, formal meal; it was time to celebrate. Bart offered a toast, Barrington offered another, and everyone ate like a famished pride of lions. Only Theodora Mercedes silently observed a change in the dinner table dynamics. Whereas she had always commanded the table, even if by her silent presence alone, all the eyes and attention now were focused on Innocenta. Innocenta did nothing to encourage or actively cause this sea change; she simply enjoyed the evening. Theodora Mercedes noted that the gift, its subtle powers, and the charisma it brought to the vessel had shifted. Her time had passed.

Innocenta emerged triumphant. The kidnapping had tested her command over herself. Now, she was in command over the gift and stronger emotionally and in all ways. Innocenta noticed the changes in herself without realizing the accompanying changes in her mother. It would be several weeks before Innocenta would have this awareness thrust upon her. Meanwhile, she fawned over her children, Bart, and the rest of her family. On Wednesday, in a moment of irony perhaps showing how he had recovered, Raul Theodore asked that everyone call him RT. Out of range of his hearing, this caused stirs of laughter, but everyone honored his request except Theodora Mercedes.

CHAPTER SEVENTEEN

Theodora Mercedes Silverton Vigil

Theodora Mercedes Silverton Vigil lay in bed reflecting like a deep pool. The inhabitants of Silverton-de Baca House had persevered over a tumultuous week. There had been the summer solstice celebration, Genoveva's visit truncated by none other than Consuelo, and the incognito visit by the monsignor. Those were minor events, like getting the hiccups, although Genoveva could have been a bad rash. Moreover, Raul Theodore had been kidnapped and found, Diego had opened the door to personal insight and then left for Minnesota, the press had been mollified following Raul Theodore's retrieval, and the inhabitants at the house were emotionally recovering at their individual rates. These were events that left everyone mentally scratching as if the entire household had gotten shingles on the brain, heart, or soul. The most important event, and the least noticed, was the passing of power from Theodora Mercedes to Innocenta. Only Theodora Mercedes had noticed. Its importance did not escape her; she felt as if she was examining her own reflection in a pond with the reflection assuming primacy over her. This made Theodora Mercedes feel odd, but she accepted the inevability of fate.

On the Tuesday following Raul Theodore's return, the family had gathered for its first group dinner. Afterwards, everyone, even the children who could not be out of Innocenta's sight, retired to the backyard to admire the stars. It was the first time every person in this house relaxed and breathed normally. They held hands, they laughed, they pointed at stars, and some cried noiselessly in the calm following averted calamities. No one would get up and go to bed; the spell could not be broken. Finally, Innocenta announced that she was going to bed. Reluctantly, everyone followed her example, and the first near-normal evening ended. The stars ensured everyone's safety that night.

As the week took on the mantle of mundane normalcy, Theodora Mercedes ran a series of errands. Actually, she had been in and out of offices: her general practitioner, her gynecologist, radiologists, and oncologists. Her interminable fatigue was caused by stage four ovarian cancer. Theodora Mercedes had accepted the news stoically. The oncologists had suggested chemotherapy to slow the progression of this all-consuming insult of a disease. They admitted that the therapy would buy only a few weeks of life and those weeks would be rendered miserable. The misery would spread from Theodora Mercedes to the entire household. She politely declined the offer. Any immediate misery would be hers alone for the time being.

Theodora Mercedes dropped in on her general practitioner for the last time. "I have been having trouble sleeping."

"Is this new? You've never mentioned it?"

"Yes, quite new. I need something effective."

A dialogue in code progressed to its merciful conclusion; Theodora Mercedes got a prescription for long-acting oxycodone in its highest concentration.

"Thank you so much, Dr. Reveles."

He was silent, sad without showing a scintilla of his feelings, and gave Theodora Mercedes a last embrace. Dr. Reveles' stoicism evaporated like a rain puddle in August the second she left him. He sat in his chair and shook, but he was too old and too experienced to cry. For thirty years, Dr. Reveles had administered his care to a woman who never had anything worse than allergic sinusitis. Now, he would lose her in a comparative instant. Theodora Mercedes had been close to Dr. Reveles for thirty years. Now, she had hugged him for the last time. She refused to weep and walked into the pharmacy to fill the prescription.

Neither Theodora Mercedes nor Dr. Reveles knew that they shared a loose tie to Consuelo. The current Dr. Reveles was a descendent of the Dr. Reveles who had treated Father Jones, the rapist with only one remaining testicle. This was typical of the common, if unknown, ties between old Santa Fe families. Perhaps, this keeps them close-knit without their knowledge, but with ties that run deep, invisibly, and spring from the very rocks and earth beneath their lives.

"Innocenta, have you ever thought of getting married sooner instead of later?"

"Mother, the gift amazes me; how did you know I'm pregnant?"

The still naïve Innocenta had attributed her mother's question to forces that had already diminished. The reflection still deferred to she who was already fading in the light.

Theodora Mercedes did not educate her daughter and simply smiled, "I'm so happy for you, Innocenta. It's your third daughter."

"Yes, I think so. It's too early for an ultrasound, but I can feel her. This house will have three third daughters in residence."

Theodora Mercedes had no intention of telling Innocenta of her medical diagnosis now or soon after this conversation. "I hate to sound old fashioned, but maybe you should move up your wedding."

"I have already spoken to the minister by phone. She can marry us this Saturday."

"This Saturday, Innocenta? That leaves no time for planning anything."

"Mother, I have had a big wedding; I don't need another. Besides, Bart likes the idea of a quick, low-key wedding. That's so like a man, don't you think?"

"I think Bart is anything but a stereotype, Innocenta. He's an introvert; let's leave it at that. You fell in love with a wonderful man, Innocenta."

Innocenta grinned with agreement.

"All right, Saturday it is. Shall I assume that I need only to show up?"

"Yes, but you, I, and the children will ride together to the church."

The embrace that followed was unusually tight.

Theodora Mercedes went to see her lawyer. She insisted on waiting for the codicils to be typed, proofed, signed, witnessed, and copied before she left the office. Everything that needed to be done was done.

During the weeks that followed, Theodora Mercedes spent as much time as she could with each family member. She never allowed a hint to escape regarding her condition. Meanwhile, she was calculating when her rate of decline and the need to tell her family that she was terminal would intersect. Hoping for four weeks, Theodora Mercedes lit a single candle to All the Gods of the Americas.

The wedding was as brief as it was rapid in its arrival. The de la Madrids attended, as did James. The reception was held in the small narthex outside the sanctuary. Innocenta was radiating good health and extreme happiness with no tell-tale baby bump. Bart was equally radiant until he walked his wife down the aisle. He wept tears of joy and could not stop smiling.

"Now, Bart, you are going to ruin the wedding pictures if you keep doing that. Come with me a minute."

Theodora Mercedes walked off with Bart and took him into the empty ladies' room. She kissed Bart on the lips, grabbed a tissue, and lovingly mopped up his tears of joy.

"You look so handsome, Bart. More importantly, you make my Innocenta so happy. As for me, you have created a selfish interest in this marriage, the missing third daughter in a line of third daughters."

For the second time since Bart had known Theodora Mercedes, he fainted.

"Well, how did I know you hadn't told him? Why did he think the marriage was being so rushed?"

"I didn't have time to tell him. Besides," she paused, "I didn't want him to marry me for the wrong reason."

"Innocenta, that's silly. The man adores you. How could you not tell him?"

Innocenta felt silly. Her husband of ten minutes was lying on the ladies' room floor, out cold. Now, Innocenta burst into tears.

"Oh, for god's sake, now I'll have to get the boys in here," and Theodora Mercedes left to fetch them.

Fifteen minutes later, Theodora Mercedes approached Barrington and James. "I want you two to promise me something; some time, I hope it's soon, you will make the final commitment and get legally married. It may not be in New Mexico, but I want you to do this. It's important; I don't want my two sons to be any lesser citizens than Innocenta and Bart. Promise me, please, that if your hearts tell you that you will always be together, that you will do this."

James was still processing the phrase "my two sons" and did not respond. Barrington examined his mother carefully before he answered; there was more to this demand than met the ear. There was more than just the opportunity of broaching the subject, conveniently, at his sister's wedding.

Barrington's intuition would not take him farther than this simple suspicion. "I promise, Mother, but I can't speak for James."

James, hearing his name, returned to the present. "I'm sorry, what was the question?"

"James, if I ever had another son, I would want him to be you. Will you legally marry Barrington if that commitment is in your heart?"

James was bursting with pride. "Yes, Theodora Mercedes, I promise. I would do it tomorrow if I could."

"There's no hurry James, but I am delighted to know it."

In fact, they would legally marry four years later in New York City. They would choose New Year's Eve day and wait in line four hours. It was a day to be remembered and a night of dreams in neon, glitter, and bliss.

Three and one-half weeks after leaving Dr. Réveles' office, Theodora Mercedes felt the urgency to tell her family about her cancer and its outcome. She decided to follow a pattern to the discussion; no word would be said about the decisive, terminal pills. Theodora Mercedes would prepare each for bad news, deliver the news, let each cry and ask questions, and then, finally, forbid each from crying in her presence again. That could be done in private or at her memorial service. She would forbid telling the children. Theodora Mercedes did not need her family making her depressed. She would deal with death and dying in her own proud, equable, manner. She would shower each day, dress in her usual clothing, do whatever the day demanded, and then dress for dinner.

Theodora Mercedes started with her third daughter.

The diagnosis had answered many of Theodora Mercedes' questions; "Innocenta, do you remember how uncharacteristically furious I was with your cousin, Alfonso?"

"Yes, Mother, I do. I had never seen you behave that way toward anyone."

"Yes, I was terrible, wasn't I? Do you recall how vivid your dreams of death were, the dream with the green eyes and chanting?"

"Oh yes, I was so frightened."

"Innocenta, did you ever wonder if there were a reason for my behavior with Alfonso and why I could not see enough to save Alfonso?"

"Yes, especially about saving Alfonso: the gift always provided enough insight that I thought you should have saved him."

"I would have saved him if I could. The gift didn't provide its usual line of sight. My sight was blurred and hazy. It has continued to decline in me. Innocenta, the gift has been moving itself from me to you. Don't you feel it getting stronger within you?"

"Yes, when Raul Theodore was kidnapped, I wondered why I could sense him so keenly and you could not. At the time, I thought it was just a mother's unseen tie to her son. But now I see. Mother, what are you leading up to?"

Theodora Mercedes delivered the news in straight-forward fashion.

The tears and questions flowed like Sangre De Cristo mountain streams: "Are they sure? Are they absolutely sure? Are you sure that the chemotherapy won't cure you?"

Theodora Mercedes reassured Innocenta that she knew whereof she spoke. At last, when Innocenta was convinced that all her questions, for now, had been asked and answered, she started down the four-wheel-drive road to grief. She would bounce around through shock, anger, denial, and acceptance as if she were lost on a strange highway. It *was* a strange highway; the exit she sought did not exist. Theodora Mercedes secured Innocenta's promise that only she, Theodora Mercedes, would tell everyone in the household of her fate. Innocenta was allowed to tell Bart herself. When she told him, he was withdrawn for days. On the third day, after they were in bed and had turned out the lights, Bart wept quietly and at length.

Barrington surprised his mother; he took the news with uncharacteristic strength. In reality, he immediately had slipped into a numbing denial. He would suffer the shock the following day. With Theodora Mercedes' permission, Barrington told James. He wept openly in front of Barrington and maintained his self-control in Theodora Mercedes' presence. Only once did she catch him looking at her at dinner with a trace of despair. James looked away quickly and admonished himself for wearing his heart on his face and in his normally joyful eyes.

Angelica Gertrudis collapsed. In only three months, she would lose the three souls closest to her own: Reigh, Alfonso, and, now, her younger sister. Their losses represented more than she could bear. The emotionally battered Angelica Gertrudis took to her bed for four days, neither eating nor sleeping. Innocenta wisely decided that this seemed a resurgence of chronic melancholy, only recently tamed. "Who can blame her?" she thought to herself.

On the fifth day, Innocenta and Consuelo took Angelica Gertrudis to Dr. Reveles' office but only after Theodora Mercedes had entered her room and persuaded her that she required help. The medicines for depression and anxiety took several days to express themselves. Incrementally, Angelica Gertrudis found that she could function throughout the day, but she could find no joy in anything. Only her time with Raul Theodore seemed to help her. He would save her twice in three months.

"Consuelo, have you ever thought that we were fated to meet? Have you ever thought that we have known each other in prior lives?"

"I'm not sure that I believe in either fate or reincarnation, Doña Theodora."

"However, you have had these ideas cross your mind, correct?"

"Yes, they have."

"Do you think it was merely a coincidence that I walked into your flower shop? Perhaps, I was looking for you; perhaps, you were waiting for me?"

"OK, yes, I do believe that it is possible. At first, I thought that God had sent you to rescue me from something, depression, maybe. But, I haven't believed in a personal god for some time now. I believe in something bigger than even gods, Doña Theodora. I do think that I am supposed to be here, with you, in this house. But, still, I don't know if I would call that fate."

"Oh, I'm happy that you think we are supposed to be together. But, do you believe that we have known each other before?"

Consuelo shifted a little in her chair. She thought the study was a little stuffy and opened the window. Theodora Mercedes was slightly amused by Consuelo's telling actions; she was wondering how much to admit. Consuelo sat again. Theodora Mercedes looked toward Consuelo but not at her.

"Reincarnation is a difficult topic, isn't it?"

Consuelo did not reply, so Theodora Mercedes waited.

At last: "Let me say this, I believe that you are a very old spirit. The closeness I feel with you could be interpreted as you say, but I don't know."

"Consuelo, I think that in previous lives we had other bodies, perhaps male and female. I believe that we were lovers. I believe that I was your man and you were my woman. We were very much in love, Consuelo."

Consuelo could not reply. This conversation was like riding a rocket; too fast and not under her control.

"Consuelo, I must leave you again."

Theodora Mercedes followed her patterned speech until the climax. Consuelo threw herself on Theodora Mercedes and cried with all her being. Theodora Mercedes held Consuelo's head to her own chest and let her weep.

"We will meet again, Consuelo, I promise you; we will meet again."

"Innocenta, will you do me a favor?"

Innocenta was happy to do her dying mother a favor, any favor. She walked to the cathedral on the chance that Monsignor Szabo would be there. Had he not been there, the walk would have been therapeutic and necessary, even if Innocenta did not realize it. He was in, and she invited him to visit Theodora Mercedes, who was feeling "a little under the weather." He would walk to the house later that afternoon under skies that were about to open up with heavy monsoon rains. By the time he arrived at Silverton-de Baca House, his dishwater blond hair was stuck to his scalp.

Theodora Mercedes opened the front door, quickly ushered in the monsignor, and ran to get him a towel. He noted that she had trouble catching her breath. They ascended to Theodora Mercedes' study and, shortly afterwards, Consuelo brought up tea. Ivan was unprepared for the music which Theodora Mercedes immediately turned down to background music.

"What is that?"

"The music? It's Ali Akbar Khan's *Morning and Evening Ragas*. Do you like it?"

"It's . . . interesting."

"Ivan, I know what that phrase means. It means that you don't like it and don't wish to be rude."

Ivan smiled and blushed as she stopped the music.

Theodora Mercedes made friendly conversation for about twenty minutes before she broached the subject. Ivan, who as a priest was used to hearing this type of news and administering to the dying, expressed little emotion. He was professional. However, inside, he was asking himself why this woman, the closest friend he had made since his mother died, should be taken from him so quickly. Was his god reminding him of his vows? Before Ivan left, Theodora Mercedes extracted a promise; Ivan would attend her memorial at the Social Liberal Church and read Tennessee Williams' wonderful poem from *The Night of the Iguana*. Ivan knew neither the play nor the poem but promised that he would remedy his ignorance as soon as he could. Ivan left knowing that he would never see his new friend, Theodora Mercedes, alive again. He thought of his dead mother on the walk home and cried with the same profusion as the pouring rain. It was a good disguise.

"I have been wondering when you would come in to talk. I know that you're terribly upset about this, but sit here on the bed and let's discuss your grief."

Barrington was not surprised that his mother knew he would come and his purpose.

"Oh, Mother, I love you so much. I don't know how I will be able to live without you."

Theodora Mercedes reached for his hand and squeezed while Barrington welled up.

"Son, you will be able to live without me. Thousands of generations of sons have done this before you. You will be extremely sad for a while, but James will be there for you. Little by little it will get better. Barrington, you won't ever get over my death, but you will learn to live without my physical presence. That's how we deal with the death of loved ones and we go on."

"But, Mother, you've always been there for me and I've needed you so much and so many times."

Barrington's tears now freely flowed.

"Son, you have been through many trials. I honestly believe that the worst will be behind you. The abscesses in your heart are gone; don't dwell on the scar tissue. When you need me, look inside. It's a cliché, but our loved ones do live in our hearts. Maybe that's the source of our immortality. When trouble rears its ugly head, just think of all you have endured already. If you don't know what to do, then just seek inside. Barrington, you're stronger and wiser now. You're wise enough to confide in James. You're strong enough to confide in your aunt, Consuelo, and, especially, Innocenta. Between your strength and wisdom and theirs, there is nothing that can harm you. But, you have to learn to believe in yourself. Everyone else believes in you. I believe in you, Barrington. I can die in peace knowing that you will be fine."

Barrington was pensive; Theodora Mercedes knew that he was weighing the truth of her words. He was taking measure of his belief in himself.

"I understand you, Mother, but it will take me some time to connect with believing in myself. Right now, all I can do is cry and grieve."

"I understand, Barrington. Your fears and despair are natural. You were once my little boy. Now you are a grown man with a full life. Your fears are stemming from the little boy still inside you, Barrington. Most of being a true adult is leaving childhood fears and resentments behind and living as the adult you wish to be. You have just a few steps left to go. I certainly don't want to die, but I'm not afraid either. Barrington, my death may be the next big hurdle for you. Seen that way, my death will be good for you."

Barrington was horrified, "Mother, how can you say that?"

"I can say that because it's true. Barrington, look at me. You know and I know that what I just said may be unpleasant to hear, but it's the truth. The strong, wise man is ready to emerge into his full power; let it, become the man you wish to be. Grieve, then stand on your own, Son."

"Oh, Mother," and Barrington buried his face on Theodora Mercedes' chest.

When he had cried sufficiently, Theodora Mercedes made him sit up.

"You will be sad for some time. Then, you'll get better; you will go on with your beautiful life. Eventually, you will smile when you think of me. You may still cry a little afterwards, but when you smile first, that's when you know the peace that comes with living with my absence. Promise me that you will remember this conversation and live through to the other side of grief; promise me, Barrington."

"Yes, yes, I promise. I'll do my best, Mother. I love you so much."

"And I will always love you, Barrington, even on the other side."

Theodora Mercedes smiled at her youngest, most vulnerable child knowing that he would endure and flourish. Barrington read the smile for what it was and began to feel a tiny bit of peace.

Theodora Mercedes slept fitfully after Barrington left her. The pains and internal imbalances were making each day increasingly uncomfortable. She awoke the next morning and saw Innocenta hovering over her with a tray of hot tea. She could smell the peppermint. Innocenta put down the tray, propped her mother up with pillows, and poured her a cup.

As she handed Theodora Mercedes the cup and saucer, her mother asked, "Innocenta, will you hear my confession?"

Innocenta thought her mother had lost her mind. Had the cancer invaded her brain?

"What?"

"I have a confession to make."

Innocenta had no idea how to respond.

"I have only hated one person in my entire life, your grandmother, Genoveva. I know that you may have thought, at least at times, that I also hated Alfonso, but I didn't. Alfonso merely annoyed me. But that woman, Genoveva, I truly do hate. She is the embodiment of everything I despise in another human being. I won't list them; I'm sure that I'll forget a few dozen qualities."

Innocenta still had no idea how to respond.

"There, I have confessed it. I feel so much better not taking this to my grave."

"Mother, you continue to astonish me, even now."

"Thank you, Innocenta; I count astonishment as one of my primary charms."

What could Innocenta do except chuckle?

Theodora Mercedes changed the subject. "Well, Innocenta, have you come to terms with my leaving you so suddenly?"

"Oh, Mother, you know I haven't."

Theodora Mercedes smiled and gave Innocenta her most mischievous look. "I think you have, or at least started to, Innocenta."

A look of unwelcomed dread crossed Innocenta's face and she sat on the side of the bed.

"All right, I have in some ways. I keep thinking about how I will step into your shoes. I keep thinking that it's not fair; I am not you. I keep thinking about how everyone in the house will look to me instead of you. I keep thinking about your amazing facility with the gift. I think; I think; I think!"

She burst into sobs and shrank toward her waiting mother.

"Innocenta, stop thinking for a while. Let me tell you something; you are the most extraordinary woman I know. You are not me; you will be more than me."

"Oh, Mother, stop it! You're a one of a kind."

"Yes, I am, but so are you. Innocenta, you are wise beyond your years and as strong as Tesuque Peak. Don't you know that without you, I don't know how I would have coped with all the problems we've endured. You think I'm so strong, but the truth is, you were beside me making me stronger through every crisis. Your father's sudden death almost broke me in two, but my mature, little Innocenta was there by my side. It's been that way ever since, through every crisis. I tried to shield you from that fact because you still deserved to be young and carefree, to have a childhood. Imagine what kind of mother I would be if I had thrown my weight and worries on you the way Genoveva has done to Diego. That poor man had no childhood. Now, you will be head of this household because I will not be here, Innocenta. You take over, be strong, have some doubts, but persevere just as all our third daughter forebears have done."

Innocenta looked into her mother's face and recognized that Theodora Mercedes was telling her truth. Still, she looked up and out the window in despair.

"Innocenta, I am not saying that you won't grieve, cry, and miss me. Honey, I'm going to miss you! But, you will endure and be the best head of household yet. I know it. Have you ever known me to be wrong?"

Innocenta paused before answering. "Well, you did let me marry George."

They looked at each other and laughed lightly.

"What can I say, Innocenta? You were in love and, at the time, he looked all right to me. We both learned something about the facades of men thanks to George. Now, look at Bart. I'll bet everything that neither of us is wrong about Bart."

Innocenta rewarded her mother with a broad, genuine smile.

"Innocenta, let's not make light of the issues. Barrington will depend on you as much as he depends on James. Your brother still has some growing to do. Angelica Gertrudis will grieve, but she is also a strong woman. The most disconcerting person may be Consuelo. I don't believe that she will see you as attempting to fill my shoes. She's an old soul. She knows that you are a woman of deep roots and strengths. She respects you. You will replace my role, but not replace me. Consuelo knows that. She will be a great help to you emotionally and physically. I hope that, in time, you come to see Consuelo as the extraordinary woman she is."

"Actually, Mother, I see that already. Consuelo has changed over the last few years from a shy person keeping to the background to a confident woman. Sometimes she still has issues with the gift, but she also works to overcome those. She tries to understand and accept it. Consuelo showed her stuff when Genoveva came by and she was a great help when Raul Theodore disappeared. You were already ill and she stepped in to help."

Theodora Mercedes nodded gently, sporting a large grin; her daughter was halfway there already.

"And," a dramatic pause, "then there's Bart. That's the kind of man I would want at my side; what a treasure he is."

Innocenta was introspective for a few minutes. Theodora Mercedes watched her eyes.

"Mother, what about the gift?"

"Innocenta, it's yours, one hundred percent, at least until your daughter is old enough to share it with you."

"But, do you have any advice is what I'm asking."

"Advice on the gift, none. You know how it works and you know what blocks it. Use it well."

"But, Mother, surely there is more you can tell me."

"Innocenta, only this; the gift is a rare treasure. It uses you for good if you are open to it. You want me to tell you what to do. Keep your mind and emotions open. That's the only way to make the most of the gift. Don't let it frighten you, Innocenta. In the past, you have let the gift scare you into a tizzy. Stay calm and pay it the attention it's due."

Innocenta was intimidated by the gift but thought that had been her secret. Her mother's painfully extracted advice made sense.

"Mother, I am not happy about this. I will cry and miss you terribly. But, I understand and believe you. In fact, I believe in myself. I just have to remind myself of that fact while battling through the grief. Mother, do have any idea how lucky I have been to have you for my mother?"

"Innocenta . . . "

"No, no, don't say a word. I am talking now. I feel like the luckiest daughter in the world. I will do everything to live up to your model of womanhood." Innocenta smiled at her mother from her heart. "I love you, Mother."

That evening, Theodora Mercedes asked to be taken to the backyard. She wished to enjoy the stars one last time. Innocenta, Angelica Gertrudis, and Consuelo kept her company. They even shared a last bottle of wine. Without verbalizing it, everyone present knew that this was the last star gazing evening with Theodora Mercedes. Only when Theodora Mercedes nodded off did they carry her back to bed and say "good night." Afterwards, each woman in her own room, the silence overpowered them and tissues were used to dab wet cheeks. Consuelo cried herself to sleep.

Theodora Mercedes' last days were spent in bed. She was getting too weak to move under her own power and was in pain. Innocenta was not allowed to call Dr. Reveles or any other physician. Theodora Mercedes would tough it out until her last breath. The household entered individually every day to say good morning or good night. The adults would linger and pretend to converse while pretending that little or nothing was wrong. This is the burden of those who will be left behind—to carry the weight of impending death and grief on a stiff upper lip.

"My mother and grandmother came to see me last night. They are waiting for me on the other side."

Innocenta said nothing despite her mother's providing a clue.

"Innocenta, will you put on my music?"

"Of course, Mother. What would you like, Pergolesi?"

"Oh no, I want *Southern Cross*."

Innocenta turned around. "*Southern Cross*, by Crosby, Stills, and Nash?"

"Yes, not the CD; I want the vinyl."

Innocenta found it on the turntable, ready to go. Theodora Mercedes had taken her determinate pills, the entire bottle, twenty minutes earlier.

As the song started, Theodora Mercedes asked, "Do you think that there might actually be a heaven?"

"No, Mother, and neither do you."

"I know. I was just hoping that if heaven exists that Crosby, Stills, and Nash did the sound track."

Horrified, Innocenta realized that her mother had chosen this afternoon to pass. Theodora Mercedes stretched awkwardly from head to toe and then relaxed in the same sequence. When Crosby, Stills, and Nash reached the line, "Spirits are using me, larger voices callin'," in their dulcet, angelic harmonies, and hard-won wisdom that leaves one injured but living to sing the tale, Theodora Mercedes exhaled her last breath and passed to a parallel universe beyond any sight the living have acquired.

Innocenta realized at once what had occurred. She held her mother's right hand in hers, kissed the hand while moistening it with a few tears, and looked at Theodora Mercedes' face. It was inanimate but smiling, slightly.

"Oh, Mother, how could you leave so early? Your mother lived to ninety. Her mother lived to ninety-four. Why have you left me?"

She knew that her mother would not answer, just as she already knew the answer: "That's the way it is, don't expect to understand, but you must accept it."

Innocenta touched her forehead to her mother's. What passed between them, forehead to forehead, will stay between them. Innocenta didn't move until Consuelo came in later and stopped in her tracks.

CHAPTER EIGHTEEN
Silverton-de Baca House

O n a day as bright and beautiful as Consuelo's eyes, Theodo-ra Mercedes' memorial service was held one week following her death. The doors and windows of the small Social Liberal Church were open to the fresh air. Theodora Mercedes' ashes were in a brass vessel next to the painting of her that had been completed when she was in her fifties. Later, the painting of Theodora Mercedes' mother, hanging in the study, would be moved to the top of the first staircase. Innocenta would take over the study and hang her mother's portrait where her grandmother's had hung. Curiously, all the third daughters had been painted, framed, and hung in the house during their lifetimes; the men of the house never showed any interest. Consequently, the men were represented by photographs along the walls.

Bravely, Barrington spoke of his mother, her love, her devotion to her family, and her rescuing him when he needed her. He had never burdened her with knowledge of his health status. This was a measure of the strength he possessed inside, one he did not yet appreciate—keeping such an enormous secret from someone as gifted as his mother. Theodora Mercedes would have been proud of Barrington. Several church friends spoke, as did the minister, and Angelica Gertrudis. During the week between Theodora Mercedes' death and her memorial, Innocenta had asked Consuelo to speak at the memorial several times, but she could only respond with tears. Then, abruptly, as the service was nearing its midpoint, Consuelo arose and went to the podium.

"Theodora Mercedes was unlike any woman I have ever known. She was my employer, but she was also my best friend and big sister. There is a hole in my soul right now. I love you Doña Theodora."

The next speaker was Ivan, incognito again, dressed in street clothes and dark glasses, who introduced himself as "Ivan, a friend of Theodora Mercedes."

Ivan then introduced the poem. "When Theodora Mercedes asked me to read this poem at her memorial ma—uh, service, I was unfamiliar with the play, The Night of the Iguana, and with the poem imbedded in the play. She told me that it was her favorite play of all time. When I read the play and the poem, they both challenged my beliefs, but I also could see why Theodora Mercedes would love them. Tennessee Williams is challenging God, seen as heartless in the play, through an Episcopalian minister who is all too human. The poem, composed and recited by the world's oldest practicing poet, is beseeching his god to grant him the courage to die with grace. This struck me as odd. Certainly, Theodora Mercedes challenged beliefs as forcefully and intelligently as anyone I've ever encountered. I didn't necessarily agree with her, but, alas, she never asked for my permission or approval either. Theodora Mercedes faced death as courageously and gracefully as anyone I've ever known. And then, it struck me like a bolt from heaven, the poem is not for her, but for us, for her family, and for everyone assembled here today. Theodora Mercedes is asking each of us to accept her death with courage and grace."

Ivan took a breath, and with a voice that broke only once, read the Williams poem.

As he read the final line, Ivan looked up and said, "I, too, will miss you, my friend. Know that you are loved and will always be loved."

While Ivan was stepping down, the breezes announced a new party to the proceedings. Tabu registered its distinctive presence and the Silverton-de Baca family knew that Genoveva and her entire household had arrived. They were late, very late. Someone had the discretion to not attempt moving the old woman into a pew. They parked her in her wheelchair in the main aisle, and then seated themselves. Norma, Genoveva's daughter, sat behind Genoveva, alternately fanning herself, and then fanning the vapors emanating from the back of the wheelchair. Whenever she heard the sound of Velcro, Norma cleared her throat and fanned lower. Consuelo expected Genoveva to put on a great show of grief and theatrical thrashing about. Instead, she was quiet but gaseous, shed a few silent tears, and stared at her lapdog. Perhaps, Genoveva did have a place in her heart for Theodora Mercedes. If so, it was too late. The service resumed.

Innocenta's eulogy, the last item on the program, was the most telling. "All children believe their mother is extraordinary. My mother was beyond that. If you knew her, then you know that I am not exaggerating. She told me a story when I was mature enough to understand it. I had asked her why we weren't Catholics like so many of my friends. Mother attended Mass one day. Already, she had been troubled by many aspects of the religion into which she had been born. The reading that day was from Exodus at the end of chapter 17, "A Battle Against the Amalekites." I won't read it here today for reasons that will become obvious. In that story, the Israelites engage the Amalekites in battle. While Moses has his hands up to the god, the Israelites are winning the battle. When he tires and his arms begin to come down, the Amalekites begin winning the battle. So, Moses' arms are propped up so that they may not come down and the Amalekites are slaughtered down to the last woman and last child.

Mother was horrified and then it got worse. The god then commanded that the battle be recorded for all time and that the name of the Amalekites should be forever forgotten. The irony of this last part was not lost on Mother. The sermon that day, based on the reading, was the lesson that we must be in constant prayer with the god. She was now doubly horrified. Mother was outraged by this petty, cruel god of the Middle East, and she was outraged that the Abrahamic religions would still worship a god that she considered a monster. She walked out of her church, abandoned her religion, and searched for a new faith when she was just ten years old. Eventually, she settled here.

"In her teens, she ran off with her lover. Although she loved my Dad, her second cousin, she told me recently how happy she was that I married someone with no blood relationship. For generations, Vigils married de Bacas and vice versa. Only a few other names appear in our genealogy. This was to keep the Spanish blood as pure as possible. When she realized that she had inadvertently helped to perpetuate this racist custom, she was disappointed in herself. She never loved my father any less. But, she was delighted that I married Bart Alexander Rael de la Madrid and that my brother, Barrington, will marry James Wheeler Many Ranches, a Diné of the Butterfly and Piñon Jay Clans, sometime in the future. What I'm trying to say is that she broke most molds and traditions, sooner or later. Theodora Mercedes never simply accepted what was deemed normal, moral, or expected; she charted her unique way and sailed with enthusiasm.

"Mother's religion was the culmination of a lifetime of searching. I have never known anyone who read as many scholarly books on any and all religions. When she died, she had just finished a book about the political construction of the New Testament. She probably knew more about Catholicism and Christianity, the religions she rejected, than anyone in this room, perhaps with a couple of exceptions. My mother chose nature as her god. There was no old, bearded man in the sky for her. She believed that the entire universe, including every person, plant, and animal on the planet, to be a part of god. Theodora Mercedes was a Panentheist but had a special relationship with the gentlest gods of the Americas, especially the Mother Gods. Indeed, if you spent any amount of time around Mother, then you know that her trademark exclamation was, 'By All the Gods of the Americas!' To her, every day presented a new lesson for living and consciously appreciating the ineffable of which we are all a part.

"My mother centered her life around her family. With traditions, religion, and social attitudes in constant flux, my mother concentrated on the one thing she could count on, her family. She nurtured us, never judged, picked us up when we were down and out, pushed us to become the adults we were meant to be, and always loved us unconditionally. No one knows this more than my brother. We almost lost him, but she would not give up or let him go. She was proud of her children, her grandchildren, and her extended family. My mother took our sister, Consuelo, who is not a blood relation, and treated her like family. In time, Consuelo became family, and, as far as my mother was concerned, she became a blood relative. The rest of us embrace Consuelo the same way and with all our hearts. Lately, the family has included Bart and James, whom she loved as if they were her own children. Frankly, my mother was keenly aware of her central role in the family; she loved the job.

"Theodora Mercedes also thought of family as a concept. She was tireless in helping the homeless and always participated with this church in feeding the homeless at the shelter. We spent many Thanksgiving and Christmas Days working at the Salvation Army. All she ever said was, 'Children, these people need us. We do not turn our backs to the needy.' We never argued and she helped to build our characters by taking action and not just by offering words alone. Theodora Mercedes extended her hand in all directions, the hand of love and friendship. Sometimes, (here Innocenta winked at Ivan), her friendships even surprised those she befriended. My mother was an amazing, openhearted person. This is how I will remember her most—family oriented and openhearted.

"Finally, let me offer this prayer." Innocenta finally began crying. Bart walked to the podium and put his arm around Innocenta.

She recovered, Bart stayed there holding her, and she continued. "God of Many Names and Mysteries Beyond Our Naming, we have run the course with Theodora Mercedes Silverton Vigil. We reluctantly, but inevitably, let her go. It is our final act of grace for her. She takes our love and respect with her on her journey. She gave more than she could ever receive from us who remain behind. Take her gently to the next level of existence; we leave her in your invisible hands. May she sleep in Wisdom's Dreams, Amen. Goodbye, Mother, I will always love you."

The joyous memorial turned tear-filled. As the music system began to play Ludwig von Beethoven's first movement from his *Symphony No. 6, Pastoral*, the attendees sat in their pews for a minute, listening to not sad, but joyous, music, before one got up and kissed the brass urn. The service was over.

In her will, Theodora Mercedes followed the multigenerational practice of leaving the bulk of the estate to Innocenta; third daughter to third daughter. The children, soon to be four of them, had trust funds. One recent codicil established the trust for Innocenta's fourth child. Barrington was given a one-time cash inheritance. Theodora Mercedes owned a rental house that happened to be next door to Consuelo's niece. Consuelo now owned the house with the proviso that she could continue in her position for as long as she wished and could move to her own house whenever she wished. Consuelo now had two incomes. Consuelo would continue working for ten more years. She wanted to help raise the third daughter. Consuelo, now a surrogate, would help to pass on Theodora Mercedes' values.

Now, one week after the memorial service, August the fourth, a break in the monsoon rains allowed a window for Barrington, Bart, and James to take Theodora Mercedes' ashes to the top of Tesuque Peak. They could have driven to the ski lifts and easily ascended, but they parked at Aspen Vista and hiked the six miles to the top, passing through the aspen grove that leaned towards them with anticipation, limber pines that lost their indifference, dwarf firs, and spruces that lifted their limbs to embrace them, to the attentive tundra, finally, at the top. The mountain had been waiting with an unequaled patience. The winds, as usual, were blowing from the southwest, and it was cool at over twelve-thousand feet. The three men joined hands in silent prayer and meditation. When Barrington broke the circle, he pried the lid off the urn, lifted it to the heavens, and started to pour into the southwest wind. Theodora Mercedes' ashes would blow into the Sangre de Cristo mountains, down the lush eastern slope, and then down to Santa Fe Lake. Without warning, the wind shifted with firm conviction toward the southwest, and Theodora Mercedes sparkled with sunlight on her way down into the expectant aspen grove on the west side. Barrington looked at Bart and James with questioning eyes. Not a word was spoken for minutes.

James finally announced, "The spirits have committed Theodora Mercedes to the aspens. This is a good sign."

On the descent, Barrington felt free to actually observe his surroundings. The ascent had been accomplished with unseeing eyes and only the inner mind. Now, Barrington noticed the colors, finding himself focused on the fir trees.

"James, what color are these trees?"

James halted, took a few steps back toward Barrington, and then followed Barrington's line of sight. "They're blue spruces."

"I know that, but what color are they?"

James was confused as the name of the tree was self-explanatory.

Then Barrington spoke again. "I wish Mother were here."

In the following silence, James examined the spruces again. Barrington was right; the trees named "blue spruce" were hardly just blue. They were also green, opaque, sharp-needled, brushy, and powdery-looking, and, yes, blues of many hues.

"We take so much as merely given. Blue spruces are blue. But, actually, they're a complex symphony of colors and textures. They remind me of Mother. I wish she were here; she would know how to describe those colors."

Barrington let out a sigh; James, realizing that Barrington was getting accustomed to living without Theodora Mercedes, put his arm around Barrington's shoulder, and they continued down to catch up with Bart.

It was six in the evening when the three returned to the house. They had climbed nearly three thousand feet on foot and had returned the same way, twelve miles. Everyone had been sitting in the backyard all day, and they were still there.

"I could see her ashes from here, Barrington; I was expecting it."

"What do you mean, Consuelo?"

All eyes turned to her.

"One of our last conversations was about reincarnation. She said that she believed that her soul needed a break. The deaths of Alfonso, Reigh, and Mr. de la Madrid broke her heart, and the kidnapping sapped her last strength. She believed that even a strong person like her had limits. Theodora Mercedes told me that she wanted to spend some time as part of an aspen grove before she came back again as a person. So, she is up there, just as she wished. Tomorrow a small sapling will emerge from the earth. It will contain her spirit. I believe that she is content. And, at least I know where I can go to speak with her."

Consuelo smiled up at the mountain with its luxuriant carpet of bright green aspen trees. Everyone else followed her eyes up to the same spot.

When Barrington learned that Innocenta was expecting her third daughter, he decided that she needed another bedroom. He moved out permanently and moved in with James. He and James agreed to take Barrington's cash and James' equity and build a place to live that was theirs, not James' alone or James' with Barrington in residence. They wanted a place that belonged in name and spirit to them equally. The house would have to wait two years; James still had to complete the colossal and complex statue of Popé.

When school started again in late August, Raul Theodore was a celebrity. He had been kidnapped and was missing for two days, and then escaped his kidnapper. Moreover, he had gotten a ride in a police car. Raul Theodore was a reluctant star. He had pushed the events into lock-boxes within his complex head and had no wish to unlock them. Raul Theodore was so unresponsive after the first day of adulation that even the girls, fawning over him continuously, gave up and went about their normal business. The Unremarkables, touched by the caché of being related to Raul Theodore, were also momentary celebrities. Because they were so distant, their newly earned attractiveness died a quick and merciful death. By Wednesday of the first week of school, everything had returned to normal.

In May, James' sculpture was unveiled. The local and national press covered the story. The artistic press was represented by New Mexico, Southwest, and international art magazines. Even James' mother was there. James had called and wanted Barrington to drive to Window Rock to pick up his mother. Mrs. Many Farms would not hear of it. She said that she would be there. Evidently, she had browbeaten her two wayward, homophobic sons, Sam and Phil, into driving her to the upper Rio Grande Valley and the casino/hotel. Sam still sported a limp in his left leg, but Phil had a black eye-patch where his right eye used to reside. James and Barrington were alarmed to see them; the memory of that fight was rekindled on sight. However, Mrs. Many Farms had extracted solemn promises from Sam and Phil that they would be perfect gentlemen and not ruin James' day. When the sculpture was finally unveiled after the interminable speeches and a minority of jeering from Puebloans who did not appreciate a Diné sculpting an *Ohkay Owingeh* hero, the crowd gasped with appreciation. Popé was heroic in countenance and size. Unlike many Native American sculptures with their stylized, abstract faces and forms, this Popé was a real man, a leader, resolute, and triumphant. The remaining figures in the sculpture, representing the various Pueblo chiefs who participated in the revolt, were distinctive and individualized. Each wore the trappings of his respective Pueblo and carried himself with pride and vision in his eyes. The crowd, silent after the initial gasp, then broke out in cheers and enthusiastic clapping. Sam and Phil put their fingers to their mouths and let out sharp, loud whistles of approval. They were proud of this gay sculptor brother that they had only known by their stereotypes and one great all-out fight. James' joy could only have been bettered if Theodora Mercedes had lived to see this. Alas, she had been an aspen tree for nine months now. Perhaps, she could see this. James was hopeful that she could.

CHAPTER NINETEEN

Sarah Theodora Vigil Israel de la Madrid

S arah Theodora Vigil Israel de la Madrid had been born on April
fourth. She had wisdom in her eyes, which were newborn blue.
Everyone was divided about what their final color would be. Theodora Mercedes had told Innocenta that her own mother had speculated
that children are born with the memories and wisdom of their past lives,
but by the time they learn to speak, the gods seal away their knowledge.
She related the Hebrew myth of the angel at the last step of the birthing
process who pushes her finger into the child's lips to seal in the secrets of
the ages. Thus, we are all born with an indentation above our upper lips
to show that we have been passed by the Silencing Angel.

Innocenta looked at Sarah and chose to believe that the child's
grandmother was right and that the Hebrew myth expressed great wisdom.
But Innocenta failed to notice something of great importance.

In any case, Sarah would carry on the line of extraordinary third
daughters of third daughters. Innocenta knew that her mother was pleased.

Edward F. Mendez is an ordinary tree, of no specific species,
growing in an ordinary copse.
He has been diligent about growing down
to reach his full spiritual potential.
Ed describes himself as a mystic, humanist,
Panentheist with pagan leanings,
and a proud Social Liberal,
although not a very good one.
Few consider him brilliant or worth knowing.
Many consider him to be a fool.
Let it be for the reader to decide
one way, or the other,
or to put him in a different category altogether.
In any case, his spouse, Raymond J. McQueen,
thinks him of marriageable quality.
They live outside of Santa Fe with Oscar the rescued pup.

Recent Releases by Casa de Snapdragon LLC

Over Exposed
Terri Muuss
ISBN: 978-1-937240-23-3
Genre: Poetry

Muuss brings us close to what we might describe as the secret war, the intimate war, which resides in closed rooms, in seemingly ordinary homes. Yet these poems are written, reader, with such delicacy, such concern for image, for pause, and purpose-for, in fact, beauty. Yes, these poems and prose pieces turn on the beauty of poetry, of what art can accomplish. I bid you open the book.

Echoes of My Soul
Lisa Arnold
ISBN: 978-1-937240-17-2
Genre: Poetry

Echoes of My Soul is a collection of poems from poet Lisa Arnold. Lisa's poems explore faith, spirituality, fear, death, hope and redemption and are heart-wrenching and spiritually uplifting. Lisa touches on various dark themes as well such as isolation, insanity, rage, loss of faith, longing, homelessness and death. *Echoes of My Soul* is a striking debut from a gifted and prolific poet that takes readers on a journey and allows readers to peek inside one woman's heart and soul.

6927036R00170

Made in the USA
San Bernardino, CA
19 December 2013